LION OF THUNDER

A MEDIEVAL ROMANCE
SONS OF CHRISTOPHER DE LOHR
PART OF THE DE LOHR DYNASTY

BY KATHRYN LE VEQUE

Westley de Lohr has lived a charmed life as the youngest son in an enormous family. Always viewed as the "little brother," he's eager to make his mark in a family full of brothers who have already made theirs.

Christopher de Lohr's (*Rise of the Defender*) youngest son takes front and center in this epic Medieval Romance. Sins, sacrifice, and secrets are the order of the day in LION OF THUNDER!

Strong women, enemies to lovers, and a little grumpy sunshine prevail!

Westley de Lohr has a secret—he's been betrothed to the young girl whom he couldn't stand as a child. Her father was a powerful neighbor, and Westley's father, seeing an opportunity, brokered a betrothal for his youngest son. As her father's only daughter, she would inherit a strong fiefdom, and Christopher wanted that for his son.

But things have changed.

Elysande du Nor used to pull Westley's hair and make his life miserable, but somehow in that childhood fighting, two fathers saw the opportunity for a betrothal. The truth was that Elysande grew up, fostered as a proper young woman, but never lost that tomboyish nature. When Westley finally shows up at her family home to claim his betrothed, Elysande realizes the boy she used to taunt has, indeed, become a man.

And a very handsome one.

After a few initial fireworks, and not good ones, Westley and Elysande come to know one another as adults. But trouble is brewing. A knight who is fond of Elysande betrays Westley to a mortal enemy. While Christopher and the rest of the de Lohr war machine try to figure out how to reclaim their son, Elysande goes straight to Westley's captor with a proposal.

And it's not what anyone expected.

Join Westley and Elysande as two childhood enemies grow to love one another as adults, where passion and loyalty grows into something stronger than life itself. Courage is something that stirs the soul, and Westley and Elysande must show their mettle in a situation that becomes more dire than either could imagine, but when death comes for a loved one, the entire House of de Lohr must pull together one last time.

Bring the tissues for this impactful, poignant romance.

HOUSE OF DE LOHR MOTTO

Deus et Honora
God and Honor

AUTHOR'S NOTE

When discussing the de Lohr brothers, Peter summed it up best:

Curtis is the strong one, Roi is the smart one, Myles is the fearless one, Douglas is the wise one, and Westley is the lively one.

And now, we've reached Westley's story. The last Sons of de Lohr tale. You'd better believe we're going to go out with a bang.

So let's talk about Christopher's age in this one. We are at the last book and it is set in the year Christopher dies. I'll say that up front. But keep in mind that Christopher died at ninety-two years of age. David lived to one hundred. There is great longevity in the de Lohr family, but also, the fact is that Christopher was nearly sixty when Westley, our hero, was born. Dustin, being a good sixteen years younger than her husband, was still in her childbearing years at that time. Fun fact: Christopher and I share the same birthday!

I'm actually rather sad that this is the last Sons of de Lohr story to write about. But, much like other series, there were only so many sons, so it has to end at some point. Westley, as we discover, isn't like the usual heroes. He's not really like his brothers. He's extremely smart but still has that "youngest brother" mentality, which Elysande, our heroine, must help him grow out of. If you've read the de Wolfe Pack series, "Storm-wolfe" is the tale of the youngest de Wolfe brother, and, much like Westley, Thomas had some trouble in the shadow of his great older brothers.

Speaking of siblings, let's discuss the de Lohr sisters—there are four of them. Christin, Brielle, Rebecca, and Olivia Charlotte. Christin and Brielle play a role in this story and, honestly, I love those two. Christin had her story told in "A Time of End" and we found out she's an Executioner Knight agent. Brielle's story was told in "The Dark Conqueror" and we discovered that she and Ajax de Velt's youngest son, Cassian, had loved one another since childhood. Olivia Charlotte, or Honey as she's known, appeared in "The Thunder Lord" because she married the Earl of Coventry and gave birth to the Lords of Thunder— Gallus, Maximus, and Tiberius. I love those three, and the fact that they are Christopher de Lohr's grandsons makes that series a personal favorite. The only sister we really haven't seen much of is Rebecca. We know she has red hair and we know she married (that was mentioned in brother Roi's tale), but other than that, we just don't see much of her. But we will—maybe not in this book, but we'll see her at some point. I will say that she has a birth defect, so that's probably why we don't see her too much. But that will be explained later.

Let's review the sons (and daughters) of Christopher and Dustin to date. The title of their novel is in parentheses.

- Peter (*The Splendid Hour*) Lord Pembridge, eventually Earl of Farringdon. Garrison commander Ludlow Castle
- Christin (*A Time of End*) Married to Alexander de Sherrington, Garrison commander of Wigmore Castle
- Brielle (*The Dark Conqueror*) Wife of Jax de Velt's youngest son
- Curtis (*Lion of War*) Earl of Leominster (heir apparent to the larger Earldom of Hereford and Worcester), Baron Ivington

- Richard "Roi" (*Lion of Twilight*) Earl of Cheltenham
- Myles (*Lion of Hearts*) Lord Monnington of Monnington Castle, a Marcher lordship—Lordship of Doré
- Rebecca
- Douglas (*Lion of Steel*) Earl of Axminster
- Westley (whose middle name is Henry and he was sometimes referred to as "Henry" when he was young) (*Lion of Thunder*) Lord Ledbury and Staunton
- Olivia Charlotte (the future Honey de Shera from the Lords of Thunder series—*The Thunder Lord*) Countess of Coventry

What else can I tell you about this book? I've hinted at it in the past, so I'll come out with it here. If you have a problem with the death of a major character, then be advised. It's very difficult for me to write the death of a beloved character, but I believe that these people deserve a good death. They deserve to be loved and mourned just like anyone else. We cheer them in their prime, we fall in love with them, and life continues on until they pass away. If you're a man like Christopher de Lohr, then you've been in nearly twenty of my novels and probably more, so we see Christopher all the time, more than any other hero I've ever written about. Even if he's gone in one book, he may be alive in the next one you read, so these characters we love never really die. But when they do, they deserve to be mourned. They've earned it, haven't they? What a privilege it is to be with them on the journey of their life—and death.

But, honestly, they never really die. Whenever I write these books that include characters I've written about many times over—like Christopher—they sit with me as I write. I can see his face plainly. I can see him in his prime, with his thick blond hair combed back on his head, his neat beard that's slightly darker than his hair, his sky-blue eyes that are a little almond-shaped. He has a strong nose, eyebrows that don't really arch but rather tilt up at the ends, and he's got a square, solid jaw under that beard. When he smiles, he's nothing but teeth. Big, straight teeth. It's a heart-melting smile. If you could see him like I see him, you'd think he was really hot. Because he is! Even now, as I type, he's sitting in the chair in my office, looking at me. Sounds weird? Not really. The spirits of these characters are always with me, more prominently when I write about them. Like any mother, I've essentially given birth to them, so they are real to me in a sense. I hope they're real to you, also.

But I digress.

And now, the usual pronunciation guide:

Elysande—basically Ella-sond

Arius—AIR-ee-us

And with that, I think you're all up to date. This one really is an epic, so sit down, buckle up, and enjoy the ride. I think—I hope—you're going to love it. It was truly a labor of love. Lastly, I will also tell you that the Prologue is actually the Epilogue, so you'll see the end and then see the journey to get there. When you read the entire story, you'll understand why.

Get ready for an old-style Le Veque romance!

Hugs,

Kathryn

PROLOGUE

Year of Our Lord 1251
Massington Castle, Herefordshire
Demesne of Westley de Lohr, Lord Ledbury and Staunton, Duc
de Nevele

"NEVER… *AGAIN!*" THE woman seated upon the birthing chair, deep in the throes of labor, had been cursing her situation for the past two hours. "I will *never* do this again. Do you hear me?"

The women attending her birth were trying not to grin. Dustin, Countess of Hereford and Worcester, was holding the right hand of the woman while a midwife nestled between her legs, monitoring a little head that was trying to push its way into the world.

"Of course, Ella," Dustin said, squeezing her hand and kissing her temple. "Never again."

A contraction rolled over the woman in the chair and she grunted loudly, trying to push forth a very big baby that had been almost a full day in coming.

"If he so much as looks at me again, I shall gouge his eyes out," she said, gripping Dustin's hand to the point of breaking bones. "If he says to me that he wants more children, I will chop him into tiny pieces and send him back to you. And you will not bury him!"

Dustin couldn't help the giggles now. She looked at the woman's own mother on the opposite side of her, holding her left hand, and the two of them were in stitches with the sheer rage coming from the woman in childbirth.

She was positively hilarious.

"I am not to bury him?" Dustin said. "What do I do with his pieces, my darling?"

"Leave him for the birds," the woman growled. "Let them pick his bones clean. That is what he deserves for doing this to me!"

Another big contraction rolled over her and she cried out as she bore down, encouraged by the women around her.

"The head is birthed, Lady Ledbury," the midwife said happily. "Small breaths, my lady. Pant shortly. That's right, lass. You're doing splendidly."

"I hate you," Lady Ledbury spat. Then she looked at her mother. "And you. I hate you, too. I hate everyone. I especially hate my husband."

Dustin burst out in a fresh round of giggles. "Should I tell him to flee?"

Lady Ledbury turned to her mother-in-law. "Would you, please?" she said seriously. "Tell him to start now. He will need time to get away from me because at this moment, I could leap out of this chair and—"

Another wave of contractions hit her and she bore down again, but the midwife quickly put a stop to it. "Nay, lady, do not push," she said, clearly trying to do something with the child. "Not yet. His shoulders are not turning yet."

That brought a groan of pain from the laboring woman. At that moment, the chamber door opened and a dark-haired woman entered, bearing hot water and towels. Dustin motioned for her daughter to set the things down.

"On the table," she told them. "Chrissy, come here. Hold Ella's hand before she breaks mine."

Christin de Lohr de Sherrington, who had birthed seven children herself, quickly took her mother's position and put her free arm around Lady Ledbury's shoulders, hugging her.

"I know this is awful," she said. "But it will be over soon, I swear it. You will soon be holding your handsome son in your arms."

Lady Ledbury liked Christin a great deal. She leaned into her, accepting the comfort, as Dustin got down on her knees next to the midwife. Dustin had birthed ten children herself, so she'd been through this a few times. She knew how it worked. The baby's shoulders were wide and the midwife was trying to move them into the proper position. Between the midwife and Dustin, they were able to move the baby slightly, and with the next big contraction, Lady Ledbury bore down and the baby slipped right into her grandmother's hands.

"He's here, Ella," Dustin said happily. "You have a son. A very big son!"

Lady Ledbury was leaning against Christin as her own mother let go of her left hand to see to her very first grandchild.

"Is he well?" Lady Ledbury asked, breathing heavily from the exertion. "Does he have ten fingers and ten toes?"

At that moment, the baby let out a wail and the women in the room collectively gasped with joy. They began laughing and weeping at the same time as Dustin cleaned off the baby and the midwife dealt with the afterbirth.

"Let me see him," Lady Ledbury begged. "Oh, please let me see him."

Dustin was cleaning the blood away before tightly swaddling the baby in a towel. Lifting him up, she handed the child to Christin, who in turn put him in his mother's arms.

"He looks just like Westley," Dustin said, smiling broadly. "From that cry, he sounds like him, too."

Lady Ledbury laughed through her tears. She was no longer cursing her husband now that the joy of her newborn was filling her heart and mind. She had a big, fat baby in her arms with her husband's blond hair and big mouth, and she inspected his fingers and his feet and toes as the child wailed and squirmed.

It was the most magical moment of her life.

"Mother?" she said to her own mother. "Did you see him?"

Lady Ledbury's mother came near, gazing at her new grandson with the greatest of delight. "He looks a little like your brother, I think," she said, misty-eyed. "Emory had that same turn of the nose."

Lady Ledbury laughed. "Do not tell my husband that," she said. "But... I wish I could tell Father he has a grandson. I do believe he would be happy about it."

Lady Ledbury's mother put her hand on the baby's head, gently. "Mayhap," she said softly. "But Marius chose to remain locked in grief since the day your brother died, and it was the grief that killed him. And the drink."

Lady Ledbury felt a stab of sadness for the death of her father just a few months earlier. She agreed with her mother that alcohol killed him because he'd drowned himself in it for years. It was the only thing that eased his agony after his only son's death, and it wasn't anything he ever wanted to recover from. His death had been from a drunken fall, and Lady

Ledbury knew that the constant intoxication had caused it. She could only hope her father was happy now, happy in eternity with his only son.

At the moment, Lady Ledbury was quite happy on the mortal plane with hers.

"I wish Freddie were here, at least," she said, gazing lovingly at the infant. "My dearest cousin. She would be so thrilled for me."

Her mother gently touched her cheek. "Freddie is with her de Sherrington husband in London," she said. "You know that she could not come, but I will send her a missive announcing the babe. She'll be having her own in a few months."

"I know," Lady Ledbury said. "I think it's wonderful that our children will be able to grow up together."

"*Mama!*"

Someone was calling up to the keep from the bailey outside, causing everyone to turn in the direction of the windows that overlooked the main bailey of the castle. With a grin, Christin went over to the window and peered out of it to see her brothers—all of them—out in the bailey along with several grown nephews. As was usual when children were born, the men retired to wait as the women did the work, but in this case, they'd been in the great hall of Massington and they were all fairly drunk. When Westley saw his sister, he extended his arms beseechingly to her.

"Chrissy!" he called. "I heard a baby cry. Is my son here? Finally here?"

Christin turned to Lady Ledbury, with the baby in her arms as her mother was inspecting the child.

"Well?" she said. "What do you want me to tell him?"

Lady Ledbury smiled, tears in her eyes. "Tell him that he

has a fine son," she said. "And tell him that I love him very much."

Christin turned back to the crowd below. "You have a son, Westley," she called down to them. "Congratulations. And your wife says that she loves you very much."

A collective roar went up from the men in the bailey, all of them hugging Westley and raising their cups. Westley was so happy that he spun around in circles before coming to a halt, laughing. Then he bolted for the keep.

"I'm coming up!" he shouted. "I must see my wife and child!"

As the crowd of men retreated back to the great hall, Westley ran up the stairs until he came to the chamber he and his wife shared. But when he tried the door, he found it bolted. Sadly, he rattled the latch.

"May I come in, please?" he said. "Please, my love?"

Inside the chamber, the midwife was having some difficulty with the afterbirth and Lady Ledbury was back to being in pain. She handed the baby over to her mother so she could concentrate on finishing the birthing process.

"Not now," she said, grunting. "Wait a moment, please."

"But I want to see you!"

"Westley, please wait until I am presentable," she said irritably. "I am not finished with this yet."

Westley's joy was diminishing as he heard her grunt and groan. "Is something wrong?" he said, feeling some panic. "Please, Ella... is something wrong?"

"Nothing is wrong," Dustin called to him, watching the midwife work. "Birth is a long process, West. Be patient, please. You will see your wife and son soon enough."

Outside on the landing, Westley was feeling some sadness.

He could hear the baby crying and his wife grunting, and it made him feel so incredibly helpless. He'd purposely stayed away from the keep since his wife's labor started simply so he wouldn't have to hear her cries of pain. He couldn't stand it. Sliding down the wall next to the door, he ended up on his buttocks, listening to the distressing sounds in the chamber.

"I cannot wait to see Arius," he called through the door, trying to focus on the positive. "That is the name we decided on, is it not? Arius de Lohr. He will be the most powerful knight on the marches. Far more powerful than any nephews I have. Arius Christopher de Lohr!"

The groaning inside the chamber had died down a little and Westley lifted a hand, putting it against the door as if to feel his little family inside. He was drunk, that was true, and it made him more emotional than usual. All he could see was his wife in the midst of labor, blood flying everywhere, and at the end of it came a son that was the size of a…

"Oh, God," he muttered. Then he called out to his wife. "My dearest? Is our son so large that he is making you weep? Did you give birth to a baby the size of a newborn calf?"

Inside the chamber, Lady Ledbury heard him. "A *what*?" she nearly shrieked. "Of course not, West. He's a perfect size."

Westley pounded on the door softly. "I do not believe you," he said. "You have given birth to a giant child and you are afraid to tell me. Mama, does he have a head the size of a pumpkin?"

Dustin started laughing at her ridiculous son. "Westley, do shut up," she said. "He has a perfectly sized head."

Westley could hear her laughing. That gave him some hope that the situation wasn't so dire, and he slumped against the wall as he thought of his firstborn.

A son.

"I am a father," he muttered to himself, smiling. Then his smile vanished. "Mama? Arius is the first grandson born since Papa…"

He couldn't finish the sentence, but they all knew what he meant. Since the passing of his beloved father last year. Inside the chamber, Dustin's smile faded as well.

"I'd not thought of that," she said to her son. "But it is true. That shall always make Arius special to us, don't you think?"

Westley thought on the faceless son he would soon be holding, the one his father would never see. Emotions were bubbling up in his chest so that it was difficult to contain them. It was such a joyful moment, but it was also a bittersweet one. Some people died, others were both, and life just kept moving on whether or not one was ready for it.

"I shall sing a song to my son," he said after a moment. "A song meant just for him so he will hear my voice and know me."

Exhausted after the passing of the afterbirth, Lady Ledbury seemed to come alive at the mere mention of one of her husband's songs. She'd spent their marriage, and even before, listening to the songs Westley created off the cuff, sometimes wild and senseless songs, but always incredibly entertaining. She knew that this birth had his emotions surging because of his father's absence, and she was genuinely sympathetic, but not sympathetic enough to sit through one of those silly tunes.

Maybe later, but not now.

She needed help.

"Nay, Mama," she said to Dustin. "I am not in the mood for one of his songs. He'll sing about pumpkin-headed babies coming out of my privates or he'll sing about my giving birth to a calf. Please do not let him do it."

Dustin understood. "Westley?" she said, calling to the door. "If you sing one of those songs, I'll not let you—"

It was too late. Westley began to sing through the seam in the door.

My son, my son!
I bear advice for you.
When I was a child, I met a wandering man.
"How can you wander?" asked I.
And he gave me his wise reply.

Do not live your life like a stupid fool, my son.
Today might feel like a day to be stupid,
But that is no way to exist.

The next day, I thought my eyes had broken as I gazed upon
*   my son.*
We will cry so well together, lad.
We will smile together, all around England.
We will kill happily.
We will...

"Westley, no more!" Dustin yanked the door open. "Stop singing that ridiculous song and come in and see your son before I have to cut my ears off to stop myself from hearing your singing."

With a grin, Westley lurched to his feet, feeling a little woozy from the drink, but it didn't stop him from coming into the chamber. Yet his grins were met with a pale wife and blood on the floor, on her legs, and the hem of her shift. The smile vanished from his face as he went to her, appalled at the sight of so much blood.

"Are you well?" he asked with horror, reaching out to take her hand. "Oh, God, Ella. Do not die!"

He wrapped her head and shoulders up in his big arms, hugging her tightly as she comforted him. "I am not going to die," she assured him softly. "It is the fact of childbirth. I told you not to come in until it was over."

He bent over, kissing her head gently. "I could not stay away any longer," he whispered, his lips against her forehead. "I had to see you."

"West?" Dustin said softly. "Do you wish to meet your son?"

Westley was still holding on to his wife as he turned to see his mother holding a little bundle. Awed, and perhaps even a little afraid, he peeled back the swaddling from the child's face and was met with perfect features and tufts of blond hair.

"Oh… God," he breathed. "Look at him. He is magnificent!"

Smiling, Dustin moved to place the baby in Lady Ledbury's arms. As she stepped back to stand with Christin and Lady Ledbury's mother, all of them smiling at the new family, the new parents took a good look at their son.

"He has fingers," Westley announced as if thrilled and surprised. "Mama, did you see? He has all of his fingers!"

Dustin chuckled, as did Lady Ledbury's mother and Christin. "Aye, I saw," Dustin said. "He has all of his fingers and toes."

Westley had the swaddling pulled open so he could look at his son's legs and feet. Even his belly. It was round and he rubbed it gently, grinning at the fussy baby. But all the while,

Lady Ledbury was watching her husband and the absolutely unrestrained joy over what he was seeing. It was enough to bring tears to her eyes.

"Arius Christopher," she murmured. "He looks just like you."

Westley couldn't take his eyes off the baby but managed to kiss his wife, sweetly, on the lips. "He looks like a de Lohr," he said. "I think he's going to be blond."

"Of course he is," Lady Ledbury said. "He'll make you proud, my love."

Westley looked at her then. "He already has," he said. "And so have you. This is a moment I never thought I would experience, not ever."

"Having a son?"

He shrugged, looking back at the baby. "Having a son with someone I love more with each breath I take," he said. "I could sing a song about it, but I do not think you want me to."

Lady Ledbury snorted, putting her hand on her husband's cheek. "You have sung plenty of songs about it," she said. "But I like it much better when you simply tell me."

He kissed her palm. "I love you very much."

"And I love you very much," she said. "Did you stop to realize what day this is?"

He nodded, pushing his big finger into the baby's hand and being rewarded with a strong grip. "Aye," he said. "It is my son's birthday."

"It is your father's birthday."

Westley's eyes widened and he looked at her. "My God," he said in shock. "I do not know why I did not remember that."

"I thought you did, West," Dustin said from her position over near the wall. "What a wonderful way to honor your father, with a grandson born on his birthday. He would have been delighted."

Westley turned his attention back to his son. "Arius Christopher," he murmured. "You shall bear his name and his birthday. But you do not know how close you came to not being born, lad. I'll have to tell you how your mother and I met someday. You'll never believe it."

That had Lady Ledbury laughing softly. "Sometimes I still do not believe it either," she said. "If my mother had not been so stubborn…"

"And if my father had not been so stubborn…"

"We have them to thank for our happiness, West."

Westley nodded, still fixated on his son. "And I do, every day," he said. "But those first few days were certainly days of chaos and rapture."

"It will make quite a story when our children are old enough."

Lady Ledbury was absolutely right.

The tale of Westley de Lohr and Elysande du Nor made quite a story, indeed.

CHAPTER ONE

Two Years Earlier
Year of Our Lord 1249
Lioncross Abbey Castle

THE BLOW CAUGHT him off guard.

Curtis ended up flat on his back, looking up at the ceiling and laughing so hard that he couldn't catch his breath. In fact, he was starting to see stars because of it. He heard a crash beside him and saw Roi go headfirst into a wall in a blow that nearly knocked the man silly. But Roi was grinning. Curtis had seen that much. As Roi stumbled over and reached down to pull Curtis off the floor, they were both laughing so deeply that Roi ended up stumbling to his knees as Curtis sat up.

The entire situation was hilarious.

At least, for them.

Over near the door, their younger brothers, Myles and Douglas, were wrestling with the source of their amusement. Their father, Christopher, had dictated that Westley should clean up because the entire family was departing for Massington Castle, but Westley would rather run away than do what he was told. He was *not* going to depart for Massington, he'd said, and he didn't want anything to do with a betrothal that had been agreed upon when he was eighteen years of age. A betrothal to a young woman with a family fortune and a pedigree that went back centuries, but she had been the bane of his existence when they'd been younger and he wanted nothing to do with her.

Nothing!

He'd emphasized that point by trying to storm out of his father's great solar, and his father, annoyed with his youngest son's tantrum, had ordered the brothers to restrain him. Even now, Christopher was seated over near his enormous oak table, the one with the legs carved into proud lions, and watched with displeasure as his youngest son nearly flattened both Curtis and Roi when they moved to capture him. But Douglas and Myles weren't going down so easily.

They thought it all great fun.

Four laughing men and one snarling one.

It was ridiculous.

"West," Christopher said patiently, wincing when Westley's big foot caught a chair and smashed it to kindling. "Westley, stop your foolishness. It will do you no good."

Curtis and Roi were up now. Douglas and Myles had Westley mostly restrained, so Curtis got in behind him and grabbed him by the back of his head, all of that long blond hair wrapped up in Curtis' big hand in a most effective way. But Westley resisted, refusing to shout in pain, refusing to acknowledge he was quite possibly already defeated in his quest to leave the solar.

But there was no possibility that he was going to surrender.

"Papa, I told you that I am *not* going to marry her," he said through clenched teeth. "It is out of the question."

Christopher gazed at him steadily. "I never asked you a question," he said flatly. "I *told* you what you would do. Now you shame me by this display of idiocy?"

"I have a right to marry whom I want to marry."

"Whom do you want to marry?"

"*Not* Elysande du Nor!"

Christopher sighed heavily, eyeing the four brothers who now had their youngest sibling gleefully restrained. It was a stalemate at that point, and Christopher thought that maybe the older brothers were having too much fun at Westley's expense. He had historically been such a pain in their backsides that any chance to teach him a lesson was happily taken.

Too happily.

As Christopher watched, Myles slapped Westley on the cheek, perhaps a bit too hard, so Christopher knew he had to call an end to the brotherly vise before a real fight broke out. He finally nodded to Curtis, a silent command, and the eldest brother immediately released Westley, followed quickly by the others. Westley pulled away from the group, indignant, and shoved Douglas back by the chest when the man could not control his grinning. As he angrily eyed his brothers, fists balled, Christopher caught his attention.

"West," he said, "what is the source of this reluctance?"

Westley rubbed the back of his head where Curtis had yanked on his hair. "What do you mean?"

"Precisely that. Why do you not wish to marry her?"

Westley frowned. "Do I truly have to explain this again?"

"I am afraid you must."

Westley sighed sharply. "I've told you all of this before," he said. "She made my life miserable when we were young. Do you not recall this? We fostered together at Warwick Castle when I was young, and for two years she made my life miserable. She would pull my hair, steal my shoes, and a host of other things. The girl is a demon!"

Christopher tried not to grin, fighting the urge because Westley was being so dramatic. "You had seen sixteen years and she had seen merely eight. How much lasting damage can such a young girl do?"

Westley rolled his eyes. His history at Warwick Castle was well known. All of the de Lohr brothers had begun their training at smaller castles, but the tradition was to graduate them to Kenilworth when they reached puberty. However, instead of Kenilworth, Westley had gone to the equally imposing and politically strategic Warwick Castle because Christopher, a man who had guided the path of England since the reign of King Richard, wanted Westley to have a different experience than the rest of the family. Christopher was afraid that if Westley had followed the pack to Kenilworth, as the youngest de Lohr he would never be able to stand on his own. He would forever be the youngest brother of Myles and Douglas and Roi and Curtis, always existing in his older brothers' shadows.

Always trying to match their accomplishments.

Therefore, Christopher had wanted him to have something all his own when it came to his training because he needed the confidence of not having brothers to live up to. Westley was the emotional sort, a man of great charisma and humor, but he could also be explosive, as was being demonstrated at this moment. Little Westley was still under the shadow of his oldest brothers as they hovered around him, waiting for him to try to run again. With a wave of his hand, Christopher sent them out of the solar, leaving him alone with Westley.

He eyed his most resistant son.

"What is the issue, West?" he asked seriously. "You have known about this betrothal for years. You have had plenty of time to accept the situation. Why are you so opposed to it?"

Westley sighed sharply. "I suppose I thought it would be dissolved," he said. "Long betrothals often are. I've seen it happen before."

Christopher shook his head. "Not this one," he said. "You do realize that Elysande's father, Marius du Nor, is Lord Ledbury and Staunton? It is a powerful fiefdom."

"I know."

"He is also the Duc de Nevele," Christopher said. "A *duc*, lad. Our original contract called for you to inherit the Staunton landed title, but after the death of his heir a couple of years ago, everything will go to you when you are married to his daughter. It is a title that is greater than my own."

Westley knew that. It wasn't as if the du Nor family was impoverished or without substance. He could hear the hope and pride in his father's voice as he spoke of his youngest son inheriting a duchy, something that would outshine every male in the de Lohr family. Not that it wasn't attractive, but in order to gain it, Westley had to sell his soul to the devil.

A devil named Elysande.

"Where is that duchy, anyway?" he asked, sounding as if he really didn't care.

But Christopher knew there was a seed of interest or his son wouldn't have asked. "Flanders," he said. "It is quite large, from what du Nor has told me, and quite rich. Their primary industry is horses."

"Horses?"

"Muscular, beautiful Flemish warmbloods," Christopher

said. "Selling those big black steeds to warlords has made Marius richer than God."

Horses, Westley thought. He remembered hearing that, long ago, but the truth was that he'd purged any knowledge he'd ever had about the du Nor family, including the betrothal. Out of sight, out of mind, and he really had hoped his father would find him a better match at some point. But that hadn't happened. Still, he had a great love for horses and a better eye for horseflesh than most, so he'd be lying if he declared he had no interest in that particular industry now that his memory had been refreshed. He probably had more interest than he should.

But he was still hesitant.

Christopher's expression suggested that he sensed something more to the situation than met the eye. The Westley he knew was obedient to a fault, so the man's abject resistance told him that there was something more to it.

Perhaps something more… *sensitive.*

"Is there another woman?" he asked quietly. "West, I know you have a love of women, so it would come as no surprise if there were someone else you wanted to marry, but if there is, I am not aware of her."

Westley was shaking his head even before his father finished speaking. "Nay, it's not that," he said. Then he cocked his head. "Well… mayhap not entirely that. But there *is* Cedrica."

"De Stefan?"

Westley nodded and averted his gaze. Suddenly, he was much calmer than he had been since entering the chamber. The mood had cooled, his brothers weren't waiting to pounce on him, and it was just him and his father.

The man he loved most in the world.

The man he could always talk to, no matter what.

"I did not know you were serious about Daventry's daughter," Christopher said, sitting back in his chair and eyeing his son. "You never seemed to be."

By this time, Westley was facing the lancet windows that overlooked the enormous bailey of Lioncross Abbey Castle. He'd been born here, as had all of his siblings save Peter, the eldest son. Peter had been the result of a relationship between his father and another woman long before Christopher had met Dustin, his wife. The love of his life. Westley loved his parents deeply and never wanted to hurt or shame them.

But there was a time for everything.

Even a moment Westley had hoped would never come.

"Papa," he said, sighing heavily, "there is something you should know."

"What is it?"

Westley closed his eyes, briefly, in a moment of pain. When he opened them again, there was pain there. "Cedrica and I have been keeping company for the past few months," he said. "She is pretty and kind. Mayhap a little dimwitted at times, but she is submissive and obedient. A good lass."

"And?"

Westley grunted softly. "And you should know that I have bedded her," he said reluctantly. "Daventry does not know this, of course, and Cedrica and I were just having a good time, but… but she thinks she might be with child."

Christopher's eyes closed for a brief moment also as he struggled against rage that threatened to bubble up out of his chest and blow off the top of his head. He ended up putting his fingers against his forehead, trying to rub away the pain that was already starting to throb. Westley always gave him a headache. But this was more than an aching head.

It was a stab of fury.

"You bedded the Earl of Daventry's daughter and now she may be carrying your child?" he managed to spit out.

Westley turned to look at him. "Aye," he said. "Papa, I am sorry. I am so very sorry. But you should also know that Cedrica has taken others to her bed. I am not the only one."

His tone was half pleading, half defiant. Christopher had to put both hands on his face to keep the shout of disbelief in his mouth where it belonged. He just sat there, hands on his face until he was sure he wasn't going to spew a stream of curses in Westley's direction, before finally lowering his arms.

"And that is your defense?" he said. "When Daventry comes to cut your bollocks from your body, you will tell the man that his daughter spread her legs for others, so you should not be punished? Is that it?"

Westley shook his head. "I do not know what I should do," he said honestly. "I only found out two days ago when I went to visit her."

"You said you were going to Coventry to see a particular horse seller."

"I lied. For that, I *am* sorry."

"So am I."

"I wanted to seek your counsel about this before you told me about Massington."

"And that is why you contest this marriage?"

"Aye."

A heavy silence settled as the truth behind Westley's resistance was revealed. Like a naughty secret, it had been brought into the light and the reality of it was not pleasant. Westley watched his father as the man sat at his table, lost in thought, clearly trying to decide the worst of all punishments for his fool of a son.

Not that Westley blamed him.

The situation with Cedrica was a dark secret he'd hoped he would never have to tell his father because he was hoping she was wrong. Or if she wasn't wrong, perhaps she would confess that Westley wasn't the father at all. All Westley knew was that he seemed to be perpetually disappointing his father, something he didn't want to do but seemed to have a talent for.

Once again, he felt like a failure.

Westley found himself studying the man he most wanted to emulate. Christopher was quite elderly, and, being that he was the youngest son, Westley had been born when his father had seen more than fifty years. Both Westley and the youngest daughter, Olivia Charlotte, had been born when their father was considered elderly. That meant that these days, Christopher was extremely old even by the day's standards, a Methuselah who had lived through four kings and hundreds of battles. His mane of golden blond hair had turned white years ago, as had the trim beard that he'd always had. No one seemed to remember him without it, not even his wife. The man before Westley was the greatest knight of his generation, a man who was a living legend.

A living legend that Westley had disappointed.

"Papa, I do not know what to say," he finally muttered. "I do not make excuses. I am willing to face the consequences. But please… please do not hate me for this. I could not bear it."

Christopher glanced over at him. "West, there is no hate in my heart for you," he said. "You know that. It is not as if you have not done what every man I know has done."

"Impregnated a woman?"

Christopher snorted. "Nay, you idiot," he said, a grin flickering on his lips. "Bedded a woman you were not married to. You are young and virile. I understand that. But we are in a bit of a quandary if Daventry's daughter is, indeed, with child and the child is yours."

"I have thought on this," Westley said, wanting to contribute a solution to the situation he'd created. "I have money and I could offer to send Cedrica to France, where she could have the child and leave it there. No one need know."

Christopher eyed him. "I do not want a de Lohr grandchild in the care of someone I do not know or trust, or worse, placed with peasants who cannot feed it," he said. "Although I understand what you are saying, I will not lose control of a child if he, or she, bears my blood. We will bring the child back and say it is a foundling or something. And Daventry will undoubtedly want compensation."

Westley knew what he meant. "I do have money, but not great wealth," he said. "I can offer him what I can bear to part with."

Christopher shook his head. "I will pay him," he said. "You needn't worry about that. He would not be the first father who had to be paid off because of a compromised daughter and he will not be the last. But he will probably want something more."

"Like what?"

"My sworn allegiance," he said. Then he grunted. "And I cannot stand the man, so if you had to fornicate with someone's daughter, why not do it with someone I at least like?"

Westley sensed some humor in that question. "Mayhap next time."

That wiped any hint of peace off Christopher's face as he jabbed a finger at his son. "There will not *be* a next time," he said. "You are going with me to Massington and you will marry

Elysande du Nor, as we have agreed to."

Westley could see that his father's anger was back again. "But—!"

Christopher cut him off sharply. "There will be no questions or resistance from you," he said. "You are contractually obligated to marry Elysande and I do not care if she vexed you as a child. That does not matter. She is a woman grown now and you will learn to tolerate her. Do you understand me?"

Westley was starting to turn red in the face. "I understand you," he said through clenched teeth. "But I—"

Christopher interrupted him again. "Resist me and I will take you over to Daventry myself this very day and tell him what you have done," he growled. "You can marry Cedrica and spend the rest of your life with a woman who more than likely will not be a good wife to you. If she does what you say she does, then you will spend your life wondering if your sons are your own and not a stable servant's. Is that the life you wish?"

Westley's jaw was grinding. His father had him cornered and they both knew it. "Nay," he said slowly. "It is not."

"Then shut your lips and obey me," Christopher said, standing up. When he rose to his full height, he was an incredibly imposing man with an air of authority unmatched anywhere in the known world. "We leave for Massington today, so prepare for the journey. Your mother is coming with us and she will not be disappointed."

Westley was down but he wasn't out. He had a temper, something he had difficulty controlling at times. "You can threaten me with Daventry," he said. "You can threaten me with whatever you like, but that does not mean I will go willingly. It means you are forcing me to do something I do not wish to do."

"Of course I am," Christopher said. "And you will do it."

Stubborn Westley made an appearance. "And if I do not?"

Christopher came around the table, eye to eye with the son who had not inherited his height. At six feet and a few inches, he was not the tallest of the de Lohr brothers, but he was built like a bull and had enormous shoulders. Those attributes made Westley as formidable as his father by sheer breadth and size.

But not this time.

"If you do not," Christopher said, eyes narrowed, "then I shall tell your mother what you did to Cedrica. You may be able to survive me, lad. But you will not survive her."

Westley eyed his father hatefully. Nothing the man threatened was untrue. Westley's mother was a cyclone of immense power and ruled Lioncross with an iron fist. It had always been thus. Before he could open his mouth, however, the solar door swung back on its hinges and two women entered.

Westley found himself facing off against his older sisters, Christin and Brielle.

At first glance, any normal man wouldn't have thought that an issue of any kind, but Westley knew different. Christin, years ago, had been a trained spy and assassin, a rare female operative in a secret guild known as the Executioner Knights. It was how she'd met her husband, in fact, another agent with the Executioner Knights and perhaps the world's greatest assassin himself.

Alexander de Sherrington, known as Sherry to his friends, was nothing to be trifled with.

Nor was his wife.

Therefore, Christin was formidable in any given situation, but this particular situation was made worse by the fact that Brielle, a mere eighteen months younger than Christin, was also a trained warrior. All of the de Lohr daughters—four of them—had been trained to fight, only Brielle had taken it a step further. She could fight and joust and do anything else she put her mind to, so the sisters were now evidently united against their youngest brother, so much so that Christopher was on his feet.

He didn't like the mood of the chamber.

"You were not sent for," he said to his daughters. "Why are you here?"

Like good hunters, neither Christin nor Brielle would take their eyes off Westley. "Curtis told Mama what Westley has done," Christin said. "She thought he might be fighting with you, so we came to lend a hand."

Meaning they had come to defend their elderly father, which had Westley on edge. He didn't trust his sisters not to try to jump him, so he backed up, fists curling into balls, waiting for the attack. Christin and Brielle may have been women, but they were de Lohr women. That made them different, like Valkyries. But Christopher put himself between his children, effectively stifling any potential violence.

"We are not fighting," he told his daughters. Then he pointed to the door. "Get out. I appreciate that your mother sent you here to save me, but please get out."

Christin's line of sight with Westley was broken when Christopher intervened and she found herself looking at her father. "Papa, I do not mean to argue with you, but you know what the physic said," she said. "You must not exert yourself, and if Westley is causing you unnecessary worry, then he must be removed."

She meant every word of it and was prepared to carry it out. Christopher looked at his daughters, two of the strongest women he knew. They had their mother's fire and his strength. Christin had inherited Dustin's short stature, however, while Brielle had inherited his height. She was tall and long-legged and strong.

Christopher put up his hands to calm them.

"We were not fighting or arguing," he assured them. "I am not under any undue strain."

Brielle, who was armed, lowered her sword and frowned. "Papa, I came all the way from Pelinom when Mama wrote me and told me about your health," she said. "I have watched you play with my younger children most happily since I have been home and you have seemed to be doing so well."

"I am," Christopher insisted. "I am quite well."

"But you had a sinking episode two months ago that caused your hands to be weak and your head to ache," she said. "Mama was certain you were dying."

"Your point?"

She lifted her hands, frustrated. "I do not want to see you die!" she said. Then she moved around him, motioning to Westley. "West, get out of here. Stop harassing Papa. And whatever he has told you to do, you will do. Do not cause him any trouble."

Westley stayed well away from his armed sister even though he was more than a head taller and a hundred pounds heavier. "I have not harassed him," he said, though he was doing what he was told. "We were having a serious conversation, one that you have interrupted."

"Do it later," Brielle said, waving her hands at him as if to sweep him out of the chamber. "Get out of here and let Papa rest."

Westley did as he was told, but he came to a halt just shy of the door because he realized he didn't want to leave. He was so used to being the little brother taking orders from his big sister that he'd moved automatically.

But he stopped himself.

He wasn't going to listen to her this time.

"As shocking as it must seem to you, I happen to have serious matters also," he said. "This is a private matter between Papa and me, and I do not appreciate your barging in and ordering me about."

Brielle sighed sharply. "What matter?" she said. "That you do not wish to marry Elysande du Nor?"

Westley frowned. "What do you know about it?"

Brielle shrugged. "What do you think our brothers are talking about out there in the entry?" she said. "You are betrothed to Elysande and you do not want to marry her. Why not?"

Westley didn't like being questioned. "If you knew anything about her, you would not be asking me that question."

"*I* know something about her," Christin chimed in. "I know that she is a remarkable woman. My sons think so, in fact."

Westley thought that was a ridiculous statement. "Which ones?"

"Andrew and Adam."

Westley rolled his eyes. "They are married, Christin," he said. "Why are they even looking at another woman?"

"They knew her before they were married," Christin said. "West, her family is a patron of St. Peter's Church in Leominster. Curtis knows the family well, since that is his demesne. Do you not even know this?"

Westley shook his head and moved away from the door. "I do not know and I do not care," he said. "This is between me and Papa."

"And me."

The voice came from the door, and they turned to see Dustin standing there. Lady Hereford, Dustin Barringdon de Lohr, was gazing steadily at Westley. She and her son shared similar facial features and eye color, though Westley's leaned toward blue while Dustin's were a pale shade of gray. It was really blue, but it looked gray in most light. Her hair, with streaks of silver in it, was braided and wound around her head. The woman was ageless and beautiful, small and full-breasted, but she projected nothing but strength and determination. Attention on her son and husband, she stepped into the chamber.

"Brie," she said quietly, "Chrissy, you may leave. Thank you for your assistance."

Dustin's soft command was the only thing that was going to remove Christin and Brielle from the chamber. Brielle backed out, unwilling to turn her back to her volatile brother, while Christin jabbed a finger at him, silently commanding him to behave himself, before slipping from the room. Once they were gone, Dustin closed the door quietly.

"You did not have to send them after me," Westley said. "Papa and I were having a private conversation."

Dustin eyed him. "Curtis is out there with a lump on the back of his head and Roi has a knot on his forehead where he hit a wall, I am told," she said. When Westley opened his mouth to defend himself, she lifted a sharp hand. "Silence. You will not speak. You have done too much speaking and now it is time for you to listen. Are you listening, Westley?"

When she used that tone, Westley knew he was sunk. He glanced at his father, whose expression suggested that Westley deserved everything he was about to get. In fact, he turned away and headed back to his table as Dustin faced off against her enormous, and stubborn, son.

"Now," she said quietly. "Westley, I will come to the point. There is a time in our lives when we must all do what we are told. Your time has come. You will marry Elysande du Nor, as you have known for years, and there will be no more said about it. Resist or continue this foolishness and your father will send you far to the north, where you can fight the Scots on a daily basis and wish you were back on the marches with your family. You will be miserable and exiled and I will not regret that your father has sent you there because, as it is, you are showing the man incredible disrespect. Is that what you intended?"

Westley had to think carefully on his answer. "Of course not," he said. "But this is not a marriage I want."

"Why not?"

Westley was hesitating, wondering if he should tell her about Cedrica, when Christopher spoke up. "Because there is a concern," he said. "He may have impregnated Cedrica de Steffen."

Dustin looked at her husband sharply. "Lord Daventry's trollop of a daughter?"

Christopher nodded, extending a hand in Westley's direction to convey that their son knew about the trollop part firsthand. Dustin's eyes widened as she returned her attention to Westley.

"Is this *true*?" she hissed.

Westley had never felt more remorse in his life than he did when he nodded to his mother's question. He could just hear her shock and disappointment in her tone. "Aye," he said after a moment. "That is what Cedrica has told me."

Dustin's jaw began to flex. "And there is every possibility

that she is telling the truth?"

Westley nodded his head and hung it. He couldn't look at his mother any longer. Dustin, however, was looking over her big, handsome, positively stupid son as the wheels of thought churned in her brain. The reality of the situation was weighing more heavily upon her by the second, the ridiculousness of it, the scandalous nature of it, and most of all, the truthfulness of it—there was every possibility that Cedrica de Steffan was lying to capture a de Lohr husband.

That was the first thing that came to mind.

In fact, she could see this situation for what it was already.

"You played into her hands, West," she finally muttered. "Cedrica de Steffan's father cannot find a decent husband for her because of her reputation, and you played right into her hands when you bedded her. I am certain she was not a difficult conquest, was she?"

Westley could hear the contempt in his mother's tone and shook his head, still unable to look at her. "Nay," he said, barely above a whisper. "She was not."

Dustin sighed heavily and turned away, contemplating the situation. She was cunning and political and she knew how to take care of any given situation. Even one involving a son who thought more with his cock than with his brain. Westley had matured into a fine man, but he was making a few serious mistakes along the way. A mistake that Dustin was going to have to correct if there was any hope of salvaging his life and reputation. Forget the fact that he was a grown man who had made his own decisions. In this case, she was going to have to make a decision for him.

If what he said was true, he'd gotten himself into a hell of a mess.

"And you are certain she is even pregnant?" she said, turning to him. "Has she given you any proof?"

Westley shook his head. "Nothing but her word."

"She does not have a rounded belly?"

"Nay."

"Does her father know any of this?"

Westley shrugged weakly. "I do not know," he said. "If he does, he's not said anything to me about it."

"Only she has spoken of it."

"Aye."

Dustin deliberated on that a moment longer before speaking. "Then I will deal with Cedrica de Steffan," she said. "But you *will* marry Elysande du Nor and we will never speak of this situation again. Do you understand me?"

Westley did look at her then. "What do you mean, you will deal with her?"

Dustin waved him off. "Never you mind," she said, looking to her husband. "Take him to Massington and have the wedding mass the very day he arrives. Do not wait for me. I have business to attend to."

Christopher was looking at her with some surprise. "What are you going to do?"

Dustin didn't answer him. She moved to the solar door and opened it, only to see her children still gathered in the entryway. Her gaze sought out her daughters.

"Brie?" she said. "Chrissy? We are going to Daventry. There is a woman we must see."

That command had Christopher on his feet. "*What* are you going to do?" he asked again. "Why are you taking the warriors with you?"

Dustin looked at him then. "I am going to throw out the

rubbish," she said. When he lifted his eyebrows, she simply waved a hand at him. "A figure of speech. I will inform Cedrica de Steffan and her father that they'll have no de Lohr husband because I will find every man that Cedrica has ever bedded. Chrissy and Brie are going to help me and I will bring them right to Daventry's doorstep. I'll also bring the priests from St. Peter's Church in on the situation, something I'm sure Daventry does not want. I'll get Westley out of this predicament if I have to shame that family all over England, but one thing is for certain—if Westley does not marry Elysande and do it immediately, then he will have to face my wrath when I return. If he thinks he is man enough to do that, then I invite him to try."

Christopher looked at Westley, who was looking at his father as if the man could save him. "Nay, sweetheart," he said after a moment, his attention returning to his wife. "That will not be necessary, I am certain. He'll do as he is told."

Dustin's eyes were like cold steel as she looked at her youngest son. "After what I must do for him, he'd better."

Westley required no further convincing after that.

They were on the road to Massington within the hour.

CHAPTER TWO

Massington Castle

T HE SUN WAS bright this day, deceptive in its splendor because the day was so cool. It was autumn, typically wet and cold for the most part, but this season had been unusually dry. It was the cold without the wet, though if one stood in the sun long enough, there was some warmth to it.

In short, it was a glorious day.

But not for one of the heavily armed combatants in a corner of Massington's bailey. There was one who was winning and one who was losing, and a crowd of bored soldiers had gathered to watch. The two were circling one another while a very large man with skin the color of leather and bright blue eyes watched from a flight of steps that led into a nearby tower.

He shouted to the one who was winning.

"He's trying to get in behind you," he said in a heavy Teutonic accent. "You must prevent him from doing so or he will defeat you."

The combatant he was yelling at seemed to take the suggestion to heart because the figure suddenly charged the foe, head-on, hitting low and trying to knock the opponent off his feet.

Then the figure jumped on top of his chest, pinning his arms, and began taking swings at his head. With arms restrained, the opponent was helpless.

The man on the stairs came flying off.

"No more," he said, grabbing the attacker from behind and pulling them off the man on the ground. "Enough, Ella. You've made your point."

Lady Elysande du Nor ripped herself from the man's embrace, yanking her helm off and tossing it to the ground. With rage, she faced the man with the bright blue eyes.

"You told me that he was going to try to come in behind me," she said. "In a real battle, I would have to disable him. *That* is what I was trying to do. That is what you have taught me to do, Harker."

Harker of Kent merely smiled at his protégée, something that bordered on pride, though he wouldn't give her the satisfaction of knowing he was pleased with her. To do so would be to encourage the lass' already sizeable ego. But the man on the ground propped himself up on his elbows, pulling the helm off his shaggy blond head.

"You were trying to kill me," the young knight said, climbing slowly to his feet. "You get so bloody angry sometimes."

Elysande stood her ground. "You provoke me to it," she said. "You try to be intentionally tricky, Olan. I do not like it."

Olan de Bisby's eyebrows lifted. "And you think an opponent in battle is going to play fair?" he said. He looked at the man with the bright blue eyes. "I told you it was a mistake to teach her how to fight, Harker. She puts too much emotion into it."

Harker fought off a smile. There was emotion around here, but it wasn't coming from Elysande. It was coming from a young and talented knight who happened to be quite fond of Lady Elysande, feelings that weren't reciprocated. Sort of. Maybe they were just a little, but not nearly so much as what Olan felt.

That made the days at Massington Castle and these moments of combat… interesting.

They were also days of chaos.

Harker had been a knight a very long time. He'd been a young man back in the days of King Richard and then King John, a newly minted knight from Saxony who found warfare in England more interesting. His real name was Harker Saxe von Lauenburg, but he'd sworn fealty to a lord in Kent when he first came to England and preferred to stay with that identification. He'd fought with de Lohr and then the House of de Nerra, the Lords of Selbourne to the south, before ending up with Marius du Nor and his small but well-trained army. He was the commander of the army here, where in other, larger armies, he was simply one of the knights. He'd rather be in command, but because he had no real noble background, having been knighted by a knight he'd been a servant for long ago, he didn't have the pedigree required. But he had the skill.

And the love of a fight.

The current fight before him was in the form of Lady Elysande. Since losing her older brother two years ago in a horse-riding accident, she had asked Harker to train her in the hopes of pleasing her grieving father. The only problem was that Marius found his pleasure at the bottom of a wine bottle these days and not in a daughter who was desperately trying to make up for the son he'd lost. It was a complicated situation, to be sure, but Harker was doing his best to train the fiery, strong, and sometimes overbearing Elysande.

Who also happened to be a woman of extraordinary beauty.

That was where Olan came in. He'd spend days and months and years being in the orbit of a woman who was more beautiful than nearly anyone in England. She had long auburn hair that fell in ringlets with a hint of gold to them and eyes of a pale hazel. But her face was where the true physical beauty was, with a pert nose and wide-set eyes, and a smile that could set a man's heart to racing. The truth was that Elysande wasn't really aware of the effect she had on men, which was tragic in Olan's case. The man practically followed her around on his knees, and although she was fond of him, she'd never quite given him the response he needed.

Not yet, anyway.

The problem was that the woman was headstrong and aggressive. She wasn't the shy and retiring type. Therefore, the situation wasn't going to get any better with the battle going on between them. He was humiliated and she was angry, so Harker motioned for her to follow him as he began to wander away from the area where the army usually trained.

Reluctantly, Elysande followed.

"What is it?" she demanded, annoyed. "Are you going to lecture me? Save your breath. I did everything you told me to do."

Harker nodded patiently. "You did," he said. "But Olan is correct. You are going to get yourself killed if you do not take the emotion out of the equation. I have told you this from the start."

Elysande frowned. "Emotion is what motivates me."

Harker shook his head firmly. "Remember something," he said. "Battle is not personal. Battle is simply the state in which a man, or a woman, either survives or dies. Battle is nothing more than survival of the strongest and that is how you should look at it. If you become emotional about it, then that weakens your foundation. You start to worry about everything other than survival. You start to worry about your opponent and what he is thinking. Mayhap you worry about you and your own mortality. Worry will kill you, my lady. You must erase it from your mind in battle."

He made sense, though Elysande was loath to admit it. She didn't like it when Harker was right.

Which was frequently.

"And if I do not remove it?" she asked.

He lifted a dark blond eyebrow. "Then you are already dead."

He said it with such finality. Feeling rebuked, she simply shrugged and handed him the sword that was still in her hand. Harker's eyes were glimmering with some amusement at his extremely stubborn student, but he knew Elysande. God love the lass, she always wanted to be the best in everything she did. She wanted to be right in every opinion, every bit of knowledge. She had the heart of a warrior and the soul of a tyrant, which greatly amused him. If he'd had a daughter, he would have wanted her to be exactly like Lady Elysande du Nor.

There was no one finer.

"Ella!"

A shout came from the direction of the keep, and they turned to see a woman in fine silks coming in their direction, waving at them. She was short, a little round, and had Elysande's lovely hair, only it was piled atop her head and tucked deep under a pale wimple.

Lady Esther du Nor waved again at her daughter.

"Ella!" she said, coming closer. "Ella, you must come with

me immediately. You were supposed to come inside an hour ago."

Elysande immediately dropped her shoulders and her head. She looked like a child who had just been caught doing something naughty and now must face the punishment. As Harker made himself scarce, Esther ran right up to her daughter, grabbed her by the wrist, and began to drag her toward Massington's enormous, square keep.

"Come along," she said. "Your betrothed will be here soon and we must prepare. You cannot go to the man smelling like… well, a *man*."

That was it for Elysande. She plopped right down in the dirt as her mother held her wrist.

"Mama, must I?" she said. "We have already had this conversation, too many times."

Esther's eyes narrowed at her petulant daughter. "Aye, we have," she said. "But that does not change the situation."

"I told you that I do not wish to marry Westley de Lohr!"

Esther wouldn't hear the same argument yet again. "Get up," she said. "You are not a five-year-old child. Well-bred young ladies do not sit in the dirt."

"They do if they are unhappy," Elysande said emphatically. Then she lay down, spread her arms and legs out like a starfish, and stared at the sky. "Mama, *please*. I have told you and Papa time and time again that Westley and I are ill matched."

Esther put her hands on her hips and frowned. She didn't like her daughter's display of temper and looked around to see who else was watching, only to see Harker standing several feet away, where he'd come to a halt. He was grinning. But he caught Lady Ledbury's eye and quickly wiped the smile off his face, rushing off for good this time. Somewhere over by the wall, Olan was doing the same. He, too, was disinclined to invite Lady Ledbury's wrath, so he hastened up to the wall walk where she couldn't yell at him.

But Elysande didn't care about her mother's wrath.

She continued to lie in the dirt.

"Mama," she said with frustration, "I told you and Papa when you first brought about this betrothal that it would not work. I told you that years ago."

Esther simply motioned to her. "Get up, Ella."

Elysande refused. "You are not listening," she said. "You never listen to me and the only way I can *force* you to listen is if I do things like this. If I lie in the dirt. Mama, I swear to you that if you do not listen to me this time, I will remain here until you do."

Esther didn't like being embarrassed. She didn't like it when her daughter did things she wasn't supposed to be doing. She was fully willing to ignore her daughter, as she did most of the time, but in this case, she was being humiliated and that made her unhappy. But she also knew her daughter was stubborn enough to do what she said.

She *would* remain there until her mother heard her out.

"What, then?" Esther said impatiently. "And I do not want to hear what an unsuitable match Westley is because that is not true. He's more than suitable. He's a de Lohr."

Elysande sighed heavily. "He smells."

Her mother peered at her. "He does *what*?"

"Smells," Elysande said, louder. "Mama, you have no idea what it was like fostering with him. I was young, but I remember."

"You remember that he smells?"

"Like a compost heap," she insisted. "He was big and

smelly, a complete bully to everyone around him, and kept throwing around his family name. He was a boor!"

Esther was trying not to smile at her dramatic daughter. "And how old were you when you first met him?"

"Eight years of age," Elysande said. "He was sixteen years, I think. I knew him for three years and in all that time, he never smelled better and he never became less of a bully. Why should you want me to marry someone like that?"

Esther could hear the fear in her daughter's voice. Not much, because Elysande didn't like to show fear, but it was there. The fear of a young woman facing an unknown future. She was trying to find excuses about her betrothed, something she'd known about for years. Ever since Marius had summoned the courage to approach the mighty Earl of Hereford and Worcester about a betrothal between his youngest son and Marius' only daughter. It had been a bold proposition, but the earl had several sons and not all of them were going to end up with heiresses. But Marius offered Westley a landed title, nothing of real political value, but it came with a couple of villages and herds of sheep. The income from it was good.

To his surprise, Christopher took it.

"You ask why I should want you to marry someone like that?" Esther repeated after a moment. "Because your husband is from the House of de Lohr, the grandest house on the marches. Christopher de Lohr is a living legend in England and your children will bear the name. They will have the finest opportunities. Mayhap that does not mean anything to you now, but as a mother, it will. I should want you to marry someone like Westley de Lohr for the opportunities it will give you."

Elysande wasn't convinced. "There are other opportunities," she said. "Not just Westley."

"What opportunities?"

Elysande sat up, shaking the dirt out of her hair. "Olan," she said. "He is from a good family."

"You want to marry him?"

She immediately shook her head. "Nay," she said, but realized she shouldn't have discounted him so easily if she was trying to get out of a betrothal. "What I mean to say is, not at the moment. But mayhap I will, in time."

"How *much* more time?" Esther asked. "You have already seen twenty years and eight. You are far past marriageable age, Ella. You should have been married ten years ago."

Her advanced age was a sore subject. Elysande averted her gaze, feeling much like lying back on the dirt and having a tantrum again. "Thank God I was not," she said. "Married to Westley with a gaggle of smelly children just like their smelly father."

"That is your future, so you had better become accustomed to it."

Elysande grunted unhappily and shook her head. "We have been betrothed for years," she said. "Eighteen, to be exact."

"That is a ridiculously long betrothal."

"It's not long enough."

Esther frowned. "The only reason it was so long is because every time your father brought it up to Hereford, he would make excuses about his son being unwell or unready or un… something," she said. "My suspicion is that Westley is as reluctant to marry you as you are to marry him, but that is of little matter. You will both do as you are told."

She sounded final and Elysande knew that she meant it. They'd done nothing but argue for days about this, ever since

Hereford sent a missive declaring that it was finally time for the betrothal to come due. That had come like a punch to the belly for Elysande, who was hoping Westley and Hereford would just forget about her and move on. But that was not to be the case. With a grunt, Elysande stood up from the dirt, brushing herself off and creating a dust cloud around her.

"I suppose if I have no choice, I'll take the one with money and a legacy," she said, sounding resigned. "Olan is nice, and he can be sweet, but I do not want to spend my life ordering my husband about, and that is exactly what I would be doing with Olan. He is so subservient that it is sickening."

A smile tugged at Esther's lips. "There is always Harker."

Elysande looked at her in horror. "He is an old man!"

Esther chuckled, taking her daughter's hand as she began to head toward the keep. "There is also Samson Fitz Walter," she said. "He has been at your father to break the de Lohr betrothal. He is quite interested in you."

Elysande shook her head. "He is only interested in our lands," she said. "They border his. If he marries me, he more than doubles his lands."

Esther thought on the neighboring warlord who was rather mysterious, a man with rough edges, though he seemed to be polite enough. "Possibly," she said. "Your father said he is from a family that used to serve King John, long ago, but beyond that, I do not know of his pedigree."

Elysande didn't either, and she didn't care. "There is something about him that makes me uneasy," she said. "I am not sure what it is, but there is something in his eyes that is… oh, I do not know… possibly disturbing."

"How do you mean?"

Elysande shrugged. "As I said, I do not know," she said.

"Mayhap it is the way he looks at me. Like he is looking into my soul and he wants it. Papa said that when he refused the man's offer to break the betrothal with Westley, Samson evidently showed some temper."

"Is that so?"

"Declared his undying hatred for Hereford. Papa said the man had quite a fit about it."

"Then mayhap it is best that we not break a de Lohr betrothal for a man who has fits."

Elysande pondered that for a moment. "Speaking of fits," she said quietly, "do you think Papa will be up to Westley's visit? How is he feeling today?"

Esther knew what she meant. Marius indulged in a bottle daily no matter how much she tried to keep it away from him, and today had been no exception. That left Esther and Elysande covering up for Marius whenever visitors were around—and, of course, that meant relaying commands directly to Harker and saying it was on Marius' behalf.

But Harker knew the truth.

Given that he was bedding his lord's wife, he knew everything.

They were nearly to the keep now. The conversation died as they headed up the wooden stairs to the entry and the two-storied foyer beyond. Mural stairs, with painted scenes on the walls, beckoned them to the upper floors where maids were waiting with a bath and a change of clothes. They had received word from Hereford that he and Westley were on their way, but there was no telling when, exactly, they would arrive. The usual journey from Lioncross Abbey to Massington took a little over a day, and they'd received word late yesterday afternoon. That meant they could possibly arrive at any moment.

Feeling like a lamb to slaughter, Elysande was forced to obey her mother and prepare, at least outwardly. But she wasn't going down without a fight.

She had a little surprise planned for her betrothed.

CHAPTER THREE

"**S**OMETHING ELSE YOU'LL want to remember," Christopher said. "The du Nor family is from Brabant, as I mentioned, and Marius told me that they still have a good deal of family there. Considering the man is a *duc*, he commands thousands of Flemish soldiers. Should you ever need reinforcements, you can send for them."

Westley was unhappy. Not the usual *I do not wish to marry* unhappiness, but now he was enduring the shame of not being able to ride his warhorse. Christopher had him trapped in the de Lohr carriage, a fortified conveyance painted the blue and yellow de Lohr colors with a big lion's head standard on the sides, and it was something that his mother and sisters usually rode in. Men did not ride in a carriage.

But Christopher was forcing him to.

Westley knew why. It was his father's attempt to keep him off a horse that could be spurred down the road and into oblivion, escaping the marriage that he was so averse to. It was just him and his father, as his brothers had not come because Dustin felt it might agitate Westley further, and about eighty de Lohr soldiers.

No warhorse for Westley.

And no brothers for support, moral or otherwise.

He knew this was all a ploy to keep him contained so he couldn't bolt and, so far, it had worked. He had been a captive audience to his father's conversation for the entire trip, and even though the windows were small and barred, he had been trying to figure out how to remove the bars and squeeze his bulk through the window for the past three hours.

He felt like a prisoner going to his execution.

"And how am I to send for them?" he asked, leaning back against the carriage wall, one big leg up on the bench seat he was planted on. "With a messenger? There is a sea to cross, Papa. I would need vessels for that."

"You would have them," Christopher said. "Du Nor has a fleet of his own ships. Did I not tell you that?"

"Nay, you did not tell me that."

"Now you know."

Westley sighed heavily as he looked away. He hoped that was the end of the conversation, but it wasn't. His father seemed to want to tell him every detail of the title and lands he would eventually inherit all in a single day. Westley, in spite of his sometimes-immature behavior, was extremely bright. He had been very good in his studies, particularly with math. He was a very pragmatic thinker. Truth be told, out of all of the de Lohr siblings, he was perhaps the brightest. Therefore, the numbers his father was throwing at him made sense to him. He understood them.

But it didn't make the betrothal any sweeter.

"Something else I should mention," Christopher said, knowing the information about ships and ducal armies was weighing heavily in favor of the marriage. "Your neighbors at

Massington. Of course, I am your liege because we are still in Hereford, but you have Evesham to the east. That's Charles de Aldington's property."

"An ally?"

"Most of the time," Christopher said. "Do not forget that these old men remember the wars between Richard and John and even Henry, and back in those days, men took sides. Those sides still hold today."

"He was a supporter of John's?"

Christopher shrugged. "He was," he said, "until John seduced his wife, but then he tried to make up for it by giving him the demesne of Evesham, so I think de Aldington is torn about it. Still."

"That was more than thirty years ago."

"Not for some," Christopher said. "In addition to de Aldington, your own brother's properties are to the south at Cheltenham. Roi borders a good deal of your southern end."

Westley scratched his blond head irritably. "He told me that," he muttered. "Who is to the north?"

"Someone to be careful of."

"Who?"

"Samson Fitz Walter."

Westley cocked his head, showing some interest in the conversation for the first time. "I've heard the name but do not know much about him," he said. "Who is he?"

Christopher lifted his eyebrows. "It is an interesting tale," he said. "Your mother's mother was a Fitz Walter."

"Lady Mary?"

"Aye, Lady Mary," Christopher said. "You never knew her, West. She was a calm, serene lady, the complete opposite of your mother. I have no idea how someone like her had a daughter like Dustin."

Westley was laughing before his father was even finished. "You have mentioned that in the past," he said. "I'm sorry I never knew her."

"As we all are," Christopher said. "My point is that Mary was a Fitz Walter, a rather large family in and around Nottingham. One of their more famous sons was Ralph Fitz Walter, the Sheriff of Nottingham during the reign of King John."

"You knew him?"

Christopher sighed heavily. "Knew him," he muttered. "Fought him. Trust me when I tell you there was no love lost between us. Ralph Fitz Walter was a despicable man. He was also the son of Mary's father's brother. They were first cousins. The dark hair that Christin has? That is Fitz Walter. They're all rather dark and dreary. All except Mary, of course. She was a beautiful woman."

Westley thought on that. "And this Samson Fitz Walter is related to us, then?"

Christopher nodded. "Through Mary," he said. "He is the grandson of another Fitz Walter brother. There were several of them, evidently. I have known Samson for many years and he has nothing but hatred for me. Absolute hatred."

"Why?"

Christopher sat back against the wall of the carriage. "He blames me for the death of Ralph," he said. "The whole family does."

"Did you kill him?"

"He had abducted your mother and sister and intended to harm them. What do you think I would do?"

Westley nodded in understanding, in agreement. "Then he deserved it," he said. "You'll have to tell me about that adventure sometime. I do not think I have ever heard it."

Christopher thought back those many years, to that dark time when Ralph and John had abducted Dustin and Christin, who had been an infant at the time, and intended to use them both against Christopher. Quite honestly, he'd put that out of his mind because it had been such a traumatic event in his life that he simply didn't want to recall it. So much death and destruction. So much greed and wickedness. That was his past, his history, but some of it was still difficult to recall, even after all these years.

Even to the sons he loved.

"I will, sometime," he said after a moment, forcing himself to focus on the subject at hand. "The point is that Samson Fitz Walter is your neighbor to the north at a castle fittingly called Hell's Forge. The Fitz Walter family drained quite a bit from the Crown over the years, so they have wealth, and Samson has a good-sized army, but the most important thing he has is that castle—it is quite impenetrable."

"And you know this from experience?"

"I do," Christopher said. "Back in the days when John was moving his army across the country and attacking Richard's allies, Hell's Forge was a haven for them. The royal forces tried to breach it once and we couldn't. It's a big, beastly place of mostly walls and moats, or at least it was. I have no idea what it looks like these days, but my advice to you is to avoid Fitz Walter. Do not try to reach out to him and remind him that we are distant cousins. I do not think he wants to be reminded of that. Be on your guard with him, always."

Westley nodded as he thought on a distant cousin who was so hateful toward his family. "What about du Nor?" he said. "Is he allied with Fitz Walter?"

"That is a good question," Christopher said. "We are about to find that out. I am certain when you marry the lady, that alliance will more than likely be broken, if there even is one, but it is of no consequence. Massington has much more powerful allies in me and your brothers."

"What about Gloucester?"

Christopher grunted. "Richard?" he said. Then he shrugged. "You know de Clare. His loyalty is like the wind—it blows one way and then the other. The man is powerful and comes from a powerful family, so it is a shame that he is not more stable, but he and I have historically been friendly. He has given me troops when I need them and I have provided him the same. But is he someone to be counted on? Mayhap. Mayhap not."

Westley fell silent, thinking on the situation he found himself in. He liked his life and the freedom of it, serving his father and basically doing as he pleased, but that was all about to change drastically. To be truthful, he wasn't entirely sure he was ready for it. Ultimately, that was the basis of his resistance to the marriage. At thirty years and six, he was the baby of the family, but he was a man in his prime. A man who had never known real responsibility in his life. His father had, his brothers had, but not him.

But he was about to.

It was time for Westley de Lohr to grow up, and he wasn't sure he wanted to.

"And after this marriage," he said, "I am to live at Massington?"

Christopher nodded. "It will be yours someday," he said. "You must become accustomed to the place and its people. Nothing is worse than a liege who does not know those he commands. Moreover, du Nor lost his son a couple of years ago. He has no other male kin, so you would be assuming that role to a certain extent. Especially if you are to inherit."

That made Westley grossly unhappy. He'd spent his formative years away from Lioncross and been very happy to return. He loved working alongside his father and brothers, being the favorite uncle to his nieces and nephews. If he went to live at Massington, all of that would be gone.

His sense of family would be gone.

"Papa," he finally said, "I do not mean to cause further trouble, but I am not keen on living away from Lioncross."

"Why not?"

"Because it is my home," Westley said somewhat passionately. "My family is there. If you send me to Massington, what is there for me?"

"Your new family."

"People I do not know," he shot back softly. "A wife I knew as a child and her father, whom I do not know at all. Do you not understand? My family, my sense of self, is at Lioncross."

Christopher could comprehend what he was saying. "It is a rite of passage for most men, West," he said. "They marry and sometimes go to live with their wives' families. Roi did it, as did Myles and Douglas. They return home often enough. You will, too, but Massington will be your home from now on. It will be what you make of it."

Westley sighed heavily and turned away. Christopher knew he was brooding. But it only lasted for a few seconds before Westley stood up and opened the rear door of the carriage. The escort was all around the conveyance and Christopher thought Westley might ask for someone's horse, but instead, he hoisted himself onto the roof of the cab and made his way to the driver's bench. Christopher could see him plant himself next to the wagon driver, evidently unwilling to spend one more minute in the carriage with an unsympathetic father.

Poor Westley, he thought.

Poor Westley that he had a father who had been elderly when he was born. Westley had never known Christopher in his prime. He'd attended battles with him, but he'd never actually fought alongside him because Dustin had made Christopher give up fighting battles long ago. Truth be told, he'd never really been the same after receiving the near-mortal wound at Tickhill Castle many years ago. Oh, he'd made a good show of it. He'd pretended he was back in peak form for years afterward, but the truth was that the wound had greatly reduced his stamina. He became fatigued too easily, unlike the healthy warrior who had traversed the sands of the Levant at King Richard's side and who could fight in a battle for three straight days and never feel his fatigue.

That man had died when the wound was inflicted.

Consequently, he'd fought battles into his sixth decade, but at that point, he was command only. He'd never actually taken the field with Westley and wondered if that had contributed to his son's rebellion. Westley had indeed been the rebellious one, and he well remembered times when Curtis, his heir and eldest son with Dustin, or Peter, who was older than Curtis but had been born of a different mother, had taken Westley to task. It wasn't necessarily that Westley had wild ideas and was aggressively resistant. It was simply that he had his opinions and he stuck to them.

Stubbornly.

Like now.

He was sticking to them stubbornly.

The carriage lurched over a rut in the road, causing Christopher to grunt. His physic had frowned upon his making this trip, even as short as it was, but Christopher had ignored him. There really wasn't anything wrong with him but old age and increasingly severe headaches that hit him from time to time, sometimes blurring his vision. That was why he rode in the carriage these days—although he could still handle a horse, sometimes, it was just too exhausting for him, so he rode in his wife's carriage like a weakling. But he really didn't care because he'd put his time in as a warrior, riding horseback all over the country for decades. He'd earned the right to ride in style and comfort these days. And this particular journey promised to be an interesting one.

Have the wedding mass the very day he arrives.

That had been Dustin's command. Time would tell if Christopher could truly force Westley to do it without the support from his dictatorial mother.

For certain, they were about to find out.

CHAPTER FOUR

Massington Castle

I T WAS ACTUALLY quite impressive.

That was what Westley thought when Massington Castle appeared in the distance, a great, sandstone-colored fortress that sat gleaming in the afternoon sun. When Westley realized the scope of the size of the place, he began to show just the slightest bit more interest in the situation at hand.

But it wasn't just the fortress.

It was the land.

They had entered into an area that was particularly rolling. There were hills to the north and hills to the south, and toward the west there was an even larger series of hills that looked like mountains. Even the driver, an old soldier who had seen much in life, pointed out that on top of one of the taller hills was an old Roman fort. Since Westley had a fondness for the history of his country, he found that rather interesting and made a mental note to explore it someday. He wanted to walk where Roman generals had once walked, back when the Great Empire had tried to conquer Britain.

As he looked over the landscape, the carriage driver told

him that Massington had been built out of the stones from the old Roman fort, something that piqued Westley's interest further. Since his home of Lioncross Abbey was once an old Roman temple, he knew what treasures could be left behind and hidden within the walls. As a child, he and his siblings would explore the ruins of the old temple in the bowels of the castle, finding names carved in stone. Once, they'd even found part of an old dagger, or *rudis*, his father had called it.

That kind of thing had always fascinated him.

Feeling more interest in his new home, Westley mentally prepared himself for what was to come—at least, as prepared as he could be. Prepared to take a wife, prepared to one day assume command of what appeared to be an astonishingly remarkable fortress. As they drew closer, he could see berms and earthwork surrounding the castle, strategic small hills meant to slow down an enemy attack, but what he didn't see until they were nearly at the gatehouse was that the berms hid a series of moats. There were great ditches in between the earthworks that had been filled with water and sludge so that an enemy would have to not only mount the earthworks, but struggle through the moat before making it to the next berm.

It was truly ingenious.

Westley hated to admit how impressed he was. It weakened the foundation of his resistance narrative. Since he'd been told about this betrothal years ago, he'd spent all that time loathing the moment he would be expected to fulfill the contract, so the fact that Massington Castle wasn't an unimpressive fortress with unimpressive surroundings destroyed his rebellion. His father had spoken about how he would inherit the Ledbury title, but it had never meant anything to him until this moment.

He would be inheriting something quite substantial.

But he wondered if the price he had to pay would be worth it.

It was clear that the gatehouse was expecting the party from Lioncross Abbey because the substantial drawbridge was already down and the portcullises were lifted. There were two, and as they passed beneath them, Westley found himself looking up at the massive iron grates and noting how imposing they were. The gatehouse in general seemed to be quite strong, and once they entered what was an outer bailey, he began to get the full impact of the interior of the castle.

He didn't see anything he didn't like.

"My lord?" A knight with bright blue eyes and a Teutonic accent approached the carriage. "I am Harker of Kent, servant to Lord Ledbury. Are you Sir Westley?"

Westley nodded as he climbed down from the driver's bench. "I am," he said. "How long have you served here, Harker?"

"More than twenty years, my lord."

Westley was still looking around the sand-colored walls as if he could focus on nothing else. "This place is extraordinary," he said, sounding awed. "I've never been here. I cannot imagine why not. I had no idea this even existed."

He was so caught up in the sight of the castle that he failed to remember his father was in the carriage. One of the soldiers had to help him out, and as he came around the side, heading for the front of the cab, Westley caught sight of him. Cha-grinned, he went to meet him.

"My apologies, Papa," he said.

Christopher eyed him. "For what?" he said. "Ignoring me? You *should* apologize. I raised you better than that."

Westley was properly submissive. "You did," he said. "We

have been greeted by Harker of Kent."

He indicated the big man behind him, hoping that would deter some of his father's irritation. Fortunately for him, it worked. Christopher straightened the heavy, knee-length leather and fur coat he was wearing and approached Harker.

"I'm Hereford," he said. "Where is Marius?"

Harker bowed respectfully. "My lord," he said. "Lord Ledbury is indisposed at the moment and begs your forgiveness. His wife will receive you in the great hall, if you will follow me."

Christopher did. Westley was right behind him, but the man hadn't taken four steps when he heard what he thought was a shout behind him and, abruptly, an armed opponent was in his path. A sword, very real and very sharp, swung in his direction and he had to jump back to avoid being sliced in the belly by it.

Suddenly, the polite greeting at Massington wasn't so polite.

"Ella!" Harker shouted as he saw what was going on. "Cease this moment!"

The warrior slowed down but didn't come to a halt completely. He, or she, began to pace back and forth, sword leveled, blocking Westley from following his father or Harker. Westley wasn't sure what was going on, or who Ella was, so he backed up, snapping his fingers at the de Lohr soldiers, one of whom provided him with a broadsword. Westley wasn't wearing any protection or mail because he'd been riding in the carriage, but he didn't need it.

He was already sizing up his opponent.

"Ella!" Harker came rushing up, almost in a panic. "What are you doing?"

The attacker lifted the faceplate on the helm and Westley found himself staring into an utterly exquisite, absolutely female face. Somehow, the eyes seemed familiar to him—beautiful pale hazel eyes that he'd seen once before. A very long time ago.

Suddenly, it occurred to him who it was.

"Elysande?" he said incredulously. "Elysande du Nor?"

She looked at him, seemingly startled for a moment that he should remember her or say her name, but that surprise quickly vanished. "You still smell, Westley," she said. "I can smell you over here."

Westley frowned at the hostile response, looking between Elysande and Harker. "What is going on here?" he demanded. "What is the meaning of this?"

Before Harker could reply, Elysande answered. "Is that not obvious?" she said imperiously. "You intend to marry me and I intend to chase you off. I do not want to marry you."

Westley scowled. "And I do not want to marry you," he said. "None of this was my idea."

"But you are here."

"Because my father forced me to come," he nearly shouted. Then he looked her up and down. "Now that I see you again after all of these years, you've not improved in any fashion. You're still the same little gutter rat you were those years ago. I could do much better."

Elysande's eyes widened in outrage at the insult. "You're no prize, either."

"I'm more of a prize than you are."

"What a ludicrous statement!"

"At least my father is an earl," Westley snarled. "What's yours? A no-name warlord with a madwoman for a daughter?"

The emotion Harker had warned Elysande against made an appearance. With a growl, she charged Westley, who easily moved out of her way because she was heavy with mail and he wasn't. As she stumbled past him, he reached out a hand and spanked her, hard, right on the bottom. That caused her to lose her balance and pitch to her knees as a chorus of laughter rang up from the men around them, men who had been drawn to the conflict. They'd been watching the entire thing, and with Elysande being whacked, they found it amusing.

Elysande found her feet quickly as she faced Westley.

"You'll not say that about my father," she said through clenched teeth. "And there's nothing great about you except the de Lohr name. You haven't earned anything yourself except to ride on the achievements of your father and brothers."

That wiped the grin off Westley's face. "At least my father and brothers have achievements," he said. "What do yours have?"

Elysande's face was turning red with rage. "Prepare yourself, de Lohr," she said, lifting her sword. "You'll pay for that remark."

"No one is paying for anything." Christopher was suddenly between them, holding up his hands to prevent either one of them from charging. "You've both managed to get off some good insults at each other, but it stops now before things are said that cannot be forgotten. Lady Elysande, where is your father?"

Elysande faltered as a very big man thwarted her plans of vengeance. She knew who he was, however. Showing contempt to Westley was one thing, but showing contempt to his father was quite another.

She wasn't that stupid.

"In the keep, my lord," she said.

"What is he doing there when he has guests?" Christopher

asked.

Elysande looked at Harker, reluctant to tell the truth, but Harker could only shrug. *He'll find out soon enough,* the man's gaze seemed to say.

Elysande sighed with resignation.

"He is drunk, my lord," she said frankly. "He is sleeping off the wine."

"So your father is a drunk, is he?" Westley said, unable to keep silent. "I was right. A no-name, lowborn warlord with a no-name, lowborn daughter. I'd do better marrying a pig."

With that, he tossed the sword to the ground and stormed off, heading back into the carriage as Elysande stood there, embarrassed at the entire situation. She truly thought Westley would rise to her challenge and she could force him to retreat. A foolish thought, but she was desperate. She tried to assert herself to control the situation, but instead, she had only humiliated herself and her family as the tide had turned quickly against her.

She couldn't even look at Harker.

"Lord Hereford, my mother is waiting for you in the great hall, I believe," she said, unable to look at Christopher, either. "Mayhap… mayhap you would be kind enough not to tell her what I have done."

Christopher could see that the young woman was embarrassed. "How am I to explain Westley's absence?" he said. "If I do not tell her, West probably will. Or any one of the fifty men that witnessed the situation. It would be better if she heard it from you first."

Elysande's gaze lifted. Her eyes locked with his for just a moment before she reluctantly nodded. Without another word, she headed off toward the hall, passing Harker as she went. He made sure to confiscate the sword from her, which only embarrassed her further. Christopher watched her go before turning and heading back to the carriage. Trying the door, he found it locked.

"West," he said quietly. "Unbolt the door."

"I will not," Westley said from inside, his voice muffled. "I'm not coming out until we return home."

"That was not a request. Unbolt the door."

A few moments passed, during which the de Lohr soldiers glanced at each other apprehensively, before the door finally opened. That brought relief for the entire escort, but they were in a holding pattern before they could move. Either they were turning for home or they were proceeding inside for good.

Time would tell who had the stronger will.

Christopher or Westley.

The odds, at this point, were even.

But not as far as Christopher was concerned. He didn't feel any differently than he had when they first arrived. When Westley unbolted the door, Christopher shoved it open and hit his son with the force of his actions. He didn't even apologize.

He motioned Westley out.

"Come with me," he said.

But Westley stood his ground. "Papa, I mean no disrespect, but I am not going with you," he said. "It is clear the lady and I do not wish to marry."

"I do not care what you want."

"Would you truly cause me such misery?"

Christopher did something then that he rarely did with his children. He set his jaw and glared at Westley with an expression that had sent many an enemy to cower. The Defender emerged, the man who had been at King Richard's side throughout the Levant, the same Defender who had gone head to head with Prince John. He was an immovable man, one who wasn't about to let his youngest son refuse his wishes.

This was a man of legend.

"Listen to me and listen well," he said through clenched teeth. "This is the last time you are going to refuse my command. There will not be a next time because if there is, I will turn this carriage around without you in it and head home. You, my son, will not be welcome there. You will not be welcome at the homes of your brothers or sisters or any of our allies. I will ensure they know you are to be turned away, wherever you go, and that includes the royal household. All doors will be shut to you, including my own, and you can fend for yourself for the rest of your life because that is all you deserve. Your rebellion and refusals are no less than slapping me in the face, in public, and showing everyone how much you disrespect your own father. If that is the truth and you truly do not respect me or my judgment, then tell me now and let us get on with it. Tell me where I stand with you, Westley, so there is no mistake in my own mind. Well?"

Westley stared at him. Hard. He'd never known his father not to be a man of his word, so he took the threat very seriously. Was his future misery worth risking his relationship with his father? It wasn't. But in the years to come, when he was truly miserable, then his father would have to expect to shoulder all of the blame. Perhaps that would affect their relationship anyway, but in any case, their relationship as father and son was about to change forever. One decision would see Westley exiled.

One decision would see Christopher as the cause of his son's pain.

Either choice would make Westley extremely unhappy.

"As you wish," he finally said. "I will go with you. But in the years to come, when I am so miserable that I want to drive a sword through my own neck, remember this conversation. Remember what you did to me."

With that, he climbed out of the carriage and, in silence, followed his father to the hall.

Things had changed, indeed.

CHAPTER FIVE

"**H**E LOOKS HANDSOME enough, my lady. I could see him from the window."

Seated in her messy bower, with cats sleeping on the bed and two pet rabbits underneath a nearby table, Elysande listened to her maid chatter on about Westley. *Westley is so handsome,* she had said. *Westley is so strong! Westley looks like a god!* Elysande had to roll her eyes at her excitable maid.

"Enough, Freddie," she said miserably. "I do not want to hear your opinions again."

"Aye, my lady."

"If you like Westley de Lohr so much, *you* marry him."

"I am not betrothed to him, my lady."

But I am. That thought caused Elysande to hang her head in shame, in agony. She tipped back over, falling flat on her bed, staring up at the ceiling.

"What have I done?" she muttered. "Mama is going to be furious."

Frederica du Nor, or Freddie as she was known, continued to busy herself about the chamber. She was actually a cousin, orphaned, who had come to live with Marius and his family when she was quite small. Esther didn't like the girl's mother, however, so Freddie had been relegated to the life of little more than a servant, when the truth was that Freddie's mother had been meant for Marius many years ago until Esther's more powerful family edged the woman out. She'd married Marius' younger brother, but in the end, the jealousy was still there for Esther. She couldn't get past it. Marius, however, had always been kind to the girl, as had Elysande.

They were quite close.

"I could ask why you did it," Freddie said as she went for the broom. "Everything seemed to be going well before Hereford's arrival. Your mother had you properly washed and primped, but the moment she left and you changed into your usual clothing, I should have asked you why. I should have known you intended to do something. Resistance to this betrothal is all you've spoken of lately, so mayhap I should have tried to stop you."

As Elysande lay on her back, one of the cats on the bed saw their mistress and climbed up on the woman's abdomen. The kneading with sharp little claws began as Elysande winced.

"I am certain after this display, the betrothal will be broken, so mayhap it achieved its goal after all," she said, stroking the cat. "Mama will take her pound of flesh before she sells me to the nearest convent."

Freddie began to sweep some of the dried grass left behind by the rabbits who roamed freely in the chamber. "Certainly you knew that would be her reaction," she said. "Knowing this, you still went ahead and tried to attack your betrothed."

Elysande sighed heavily. "I could not have done much damage," she said. "You saw how big he is."

"Then you are a fool."

"I know."

Before Freddie could respond, the door swung open and Esther appeared. From the expression on her face, it was clear she knew what had happened. Someone had told her before Elysande could. Spying her daughter on the bed, she narrowed her eyes dramatically.

"*You!*" she spat.

Elysande knew that tone. She pushed the cat off her belly and stood up, preparing to run. "Mama, please," she said. "I know it was foolish. I know I should not have done it. But it is your fault for forcing this… this *travesty.*"

Esther was not in a forgiving mood. She'd been in the hall when Harker arrived ahead of Hereford and told her what Elysande had done. Bowing out quickly and leaving Harker to tend to their guests, she'd darted into the keep to confront her daughter. Grabbing the broom out of Freddie's hands, she wielded it like a club as she charged her child.

"How dare you shame this family with your actions!" she said, chasing her daughter around the room while swinging the broom at her head. "And you'll not cast the blame on me. You had a choice. As always, you made the wrong one!"

Elysande yelped as the broom missed her head by mere inches. "I am sorry I shamed you," she said, falling to the floor and trying to squeeze under her bed. "I thought I could force him to change his mind. I did not set out to deliberately humiliate you."

She wasn't fast enough in pulling herself under the bed because Esther was able to drop the broom and grab her by the feet. Giving a big yank, she pulled the woman out from underneath the bed and Elysande ended up on her belly, in the middle of the floor, as her mother spanked her on the buttocks with her bare hand.

"You will never disobey me again, do you understand?" she shouted as Elysande shrieked. "Tell me that you understand me because I can do this all night. *Well?*"

Her mother was getting in some good blows. "I understand," Elysande cried, trying to put a hand between her buttocks and her mother's palm. "I am sorry, Mama! Please stop!"

Esther came to a halt, standing up to straighten her dress and her wimple. She eyed her daughter severely as the woman sat up, blinking away tears.

"Now," Esther said, "you are going to dress appropriately and come down to the hall."

Elysande wouldn't look at her. "I do not want to go down there," she said. "I cannot face Lord Hereford and his son."

"You can and you will," Esther said firmly. "You brought this upon yourself, Ella. Take responsibility and greet your guests properly. If you do it well enough, they may forget about your idiocy."

Elysande wasn't so sure, but she nodded because she had no other choice. She didn't want her mother trying to spank her again, so there wasn't much more she could do. She kept her gaze averted until Esther departed the chamber. When the woman was gone and all was brittle silence, Freddie came out of the shadows.

"Come along," she said with quiet firmness. "You do not want to keep your guests waiting."

With a heavy sigh, Elysande picked herself up off the floor. God help her, she was going to have to face the man she'd tried to attack. Unless, of course, the floor opened up and swallowed her, which would have been preferable to facing Westley de

Lohr. She wondered how much more abuse she was going to have to take tonight as a result of her impulsive behavior.

She had a feeling she was about to find out.

Perhaps she wouldn't go to the hall after all.

ℭℨ

HE TOLD HIS father he was seeking the garderobe.

That wasn't exactly the truth. The reality was that Westley just needed a breath of fresh air. The longer he sat in that stuffy, smelly hall, the more he wanted to simply get out and breathe.

He wasn't exactly fighting the betrothal anymore, but he also still wasn't willing to make it incredibly easy for his father. After what had transpired this afternoon, he had a hard time believing his father was still willing to go through with it, but clearly, the man was. Westley was sure that the attack upon him was a window into his future, and he was furthermore certain that things like that were going to happen with great frequency. Perhaps one of those times his wife would get lucky and he would end up with a punctured belly.

Then his father would be sorry.

Maybe.

In any case, Westley felt sorry enough for himself for the both of them. He was on the north side of Massington's great hall, nowhere near the garderobe, but it was relatively quiet here and away from the noise and smoke of the hall. He'd been out here for about twenty minutes and knew at some point soon his father was going to come looking for him, so he was soaking in the last few moments of peace before heading back into that hall. Perhaps the banshee he was supposed to marry would be there. He seriously wondered if he needed to be on his guard in the hall.

He wouldn't be surprised.

Westley was sitting in the shadows of the wall, camouflaged by one of the flying buttresses that supported the northern wall. He was staring up at the sky, at the constellations, something he had shown great aptitude for during his school years. To him, the stars were nothing more than mathematics, and given that that was a gift he had, he found their arrangements fascinating. The priests taught that God made the heavens and the Earth, and he had to agree because certainly nothing short of God could create something so mathematically perfect. He had also been taught that the stars were nothing more than fixed points of light embedded within the celestial sky, but as a young man, he had studied those points of light and knew that they moved. Were they other heavens? Other suns? Other countries, like England?

Perhaps someday they would know.

As he was gazing up at a particular constellation, he caught movement off to the left. Servants were moving back and forth between the kitchens and the hall, so he wasn't completely alone out here, but he realized that there was someone else in the area nearby. A flying buttress was concealing the figure somewhat, so he watched with some curiosity as the figure moved out of the shadow and into the faint torchlight. Then it hit him.

It was the banshee.

Westley froze because he didn't want her to see him. Given what happened between them earlier in the day, he couldn't be sure that she wouldn't try to attack him again. He wasn't armed and he was fairly certain he could fight her off with ease, but he really didn't want to have to try. Perhaps if he stayed completely still, she would simply not see him and leave him alone.

That was the hope, anyway.

Unfortunately, it was not to be.

Elysande came around the corner of the buttresses and immediately spied Westley tucked back against the wall. She came to a startled halt and, as Westley watched, took a few steps back.

He braced himself for what was to come.

"I did not know you were out here," she said, sounding surprised. "If I disturbed your peace, my apologies."

Westley could hear the tension in her voice and it didn't help his sense of self-protection. "You did not disturb me."

She nodded and took another step back. She turned to leave but came to a halt again, hesitantly turning in his direction. *Here it comes,* he thought. He was expecting that this would be the moment she came after him again, and this time, there was no one to separate them. It could get ugly. He was prepared for that.

Already, he could feel his body tensing.

"I… I am glad to find you alone," she said after a moment. "I did not think we would have this opportunity."

He was wary. "Opportunity for what?"

She took a deep breath. "To apologize for attacking you this afternoon," she said after a moment. "Sometimes I tend to act before thinking, and… and I apologize for my actions and for my words. You were right when you said you'd do better marrying a pig. I am sure you wish to break this betrothal, and I completely understand. You should."

That wasn't what Westley had expected to hear. In fact, it put him more on his guard than before because he had no idea if the woman was being sincere. Perhaps she was trying to lull him into a false sense of security.

He was careful with his answer.

"Why should you apologize for something that came naturally to you?" he said. "You do not want to be married. You expressed that opinion."

"I did."

"So did I."

"Then why are you still here? Should you not be heading home?"

Westley eyed her a moment before sighing sharply and moving away from the wall. He faced her in the darkness. He couldn't tell if her apology was sincere or not, but she didn't seem angry or aggressive. Perhaps if there were any opportunity for honesty at this moment, he needed to take it.

He needed to get this over with.

"Because my father does not want to leave," he said. "If you are going to be angry about that, then do it now and be done with it. My father will not dissolve this betrothal. You are going to have to convince your father to do it."

Elysande snorted rudely. "My father will *not* break the betrothal," she said. "Nor will my mother. I think she is more adamant about it than he is. What about your mother?"

Westley rolled his eyes. "My mother threatened me if I did not go through with this."

"At least she only threatened you," Elysande said, sounding defeated. "My mother beat me."

Westley's brow furrowed as he looked at her. "She did?"

"Absolutely."

"When?"

"Not an hour ago."

He let his gaze linger on her, trying to get a closer look at her in the dim light. "It could not have been very hard."

Elysande's eyebrows lifted. "The woman took her open hand and whacked me on the arse, several times," she said. "If you think it was not very hard, then I'll have her do the same thing to you. You'll think differently then."

Westley put up a hand. "Keep her away from me," he said. "In fact, keep all mothers away from me. I want nothing to do with them."

"Me either."

"Fathers, too," he said, disgruntled. "I've had my fill of them."

"As have I," Elysande agreed. "It would serve them right if we ran off and never spoke to them again."

Westley shrugged. "I've thought about that," he said. "When I was a child, I even tried a couple of times. But my father always found me and brought me back."

"How long did you stay away?"

Westley cocked his head in thought. "The first time, it was a few hours," he said. "The second time, it was two days. My uncle actually found me hiding at a livery in Hereford and brought me back. My mother took a stick to me and I could not sit down for a week."

"Only two days?" Elysande said. "I ran away before my parents sent me to foster at Warwick and was gone for four days before my father's men found me."

"Did you fight them?"

She nodded. "Of course I did," she said proudly. "Well, as much as I could, anyway. It was winter and I'd fallen through the ice at the fishpond because I'd been trying to catch my supper. My legs were nearly frozen. I spent almost two months in bed recovering."

Westley grunted, folding his enormous arms across his

chest as their conversation grew oddly cordial. "That story could have had another terrible ending," he said. "You were fortunate they found you in the water. My father fell into a frozen river, once. We thought we'd lost him."

"Winter is nothing to be trifled with," Elysande agreed. "I learned that the hard way."

"I think there are many things we learn the hard way," Westley said. "That is nature's way of ensuring we are never foolish again."

"True," Elysande said. "Fortunately, I've not done many foolish things in my life."

"You've done at least one that I know of."

"What?"

"Attacking a man as he came through your gatehouse."

She looked at him, sharply, realizing he'd come back around to the source of her shame again. She was torn between defiance and surrender.

"I've apologized for it," she said. "Must I do it again?"

He shook his head. "If you are sincere, there is no need."

"I assure you that I am sincere."

"Then I believe you," he said. "But I do understand your reluctance toward the betrothal. If the situation had been reversed and you had come through the gatehouse of Lioncross to claim me, I might have attacked you also. I comprehend the logic."

Elysande stared at him a moment before shaking her head, baffled. "There *is* no logic," she said. "That is the problem. I was angry and frustrated and, truly, even though we've been betrothed for years, I thought our parents would grow weary of the wait and dissolve it. At least, I hoped my father would. But your father seemed to be most eager to maintain the integrity of it."

Westley scratched his shaggy head. "I can well believe it," he said. "I have no idea why. It is not as if you have anything great to offer."

Elysande almost flared at that comment, but when she thought about it, she knew he was right. "It is not as if we are great title holders, at least not in England," she said. "Though my father is a Flemish *duc*. Did you know that?"

Westley nodded. "I was told," he said. "Nevele, is it?"

"Aye."

"Have you ever been there?"

Elysande nodded. "Many times," she said. "Have you been across the sea?"

"Not to those lands, but I have been to Paris and other places."

She shrugged. "The land around Nevele is very green, very flat," she said. "The soil is quite rich."

"Were you born there?"

"Nay," Elysande said. "I was born here. My father inherited the lands from his father, but no du Nor has lived at Nevele Castle in about four generations. Massington is our home."

Westley pondered that. It also occurred to him that for the past few minutes, they'd been having a perfectly pleasant conversation. No attacks, no shouting. She was calm and he was calm. Although he'd known her long ago, he didn't remember the rich sweetness of her voice when she spoke. He'd also never seen the womanly curves she'd developed since the last time he saw her. It was difficult to tell in the dim light that they were standing in, but he thought she was rather lush. And she was tall, too. He hadn't remembered her being that tall. Most women were quite a bit shorter than he was, and it was rare to find one that came past his sternum.

But Elysande seemed to.

That was a pleasant surprise.

This entire conversation had been a pleasant surprise.

"I have some shocking news for you," he said after a moment.

She looked at him with concern. "What is it?"

He turned to look at her. "We have been carrying on an agreeable conversation with no hint of aggression for several minutes," he said. "Why do you suppose that is?"

Elysande stared at him a moment as if genuinely startled by his statement. After several moments, whereupon she seriously contemplated the question, she simply threw her hands in the air.

"I do not know," she said. "Mayhap we have both gone mad."

"Nay," he said, shaking his head. "We are too young. Bewitched, mayhap?"

She nodded. "Possibly," she said. "Did you bring a witch with you?"

"Nay," he said. "Do you have one here?"

"Nay," she replied as if still trying to find an answer. "Is it possible—now, I could be completely wrong—but is it possible we are actually reasonable adults and we are both reconciled to the future?"

She said it with some mirth, which he appreciated. He liked a woman with a sense of humor. But he looked at her, frowning, before shaking his head with vigor, as his shoulder-length hair wagged back and forth.

"Never," he said. "Not us. We're too..."

"Brilliant?"

"Aye," he agreed. "Brilliant. We would not fall victim to such a thing, no matter how much we were threatened."

She rubbed her bum. "Or spanked."

"Exactly," he said. "We are not so foolish."

She waggled her eyebrows and pointed to herself reluctantly. "Well… there was earlier…"

The attack came up again, only this time, there was humor to it. None of the horrible rage and angst attached. The entire mood was lightening, in fact. Westley quickly put up his hands as if to surrender to her reminder.

"True," he said. "But that has been forgotten."

That brought Elysande pause as she gazed up at the man. "Has it truly?"

He looked at her, a hint of mirth on his face. "You said your apology was sincere."

She nodded firmly. "It is," she said. "And not because my mother beat me."

The corners of his mouth twitched with a smile. "Then it has been genuinely forgotten," he said. "May we call a truce?"

"I suppose we should."

He grinned and held out a hand to her. "Take my hand and swear it."

Fighting off a grin, Elysande did, placing her soft, warm hand in his palm. "I swear it."

"So do I," he said, holding her hand a moment longer before letting it go. "Now, we are facing a larger question."

"What is that?"

"Do we tell our parents of this truce?"

"Why wouldn't we?"

He tapped his head thoughtfully. "Because if they think there is a hint of truce, they'll be hanging over us every minute, wanting to know if we have grown to accept one another."

Elysande made a face. "Awful."

He could tell she wasn't serious, but he nodded in agreement. "Completely," he said. "They will want to know every step of the way what we think of one another."

"Ghastly!"

"But if we do not tell them of the truth, they will think we are still at odds."

"And they will leave us alone?"

He shrugged. "Not really, but enough so that they will not be hanging over us every second of the day."

Elysande was trying to follow his train of thought. "And this is beneficial because…?"

"Because we clearly cannot get out of this betrothal," he said. "That has been established."

"It has."

He cocked an eyebrow. "Do you truly want your parents being present as we come to know one another?" he said. "If we keep up the ruse that we are not getting on, then mayhap they'll not be so keen to force us together. At least, not until we can calm down and become reasonable. In their eyes, anyway."

"Are you saying you are agreeable to this betrothal now?"

"Are you?"

"I asked you first."

He took a deep, dramatic breath. He still had mirth in his features, but there was something more as well. Possibly interest, although Elysande couldn't have seen it in the dark. The nuances of his expression were best seen in broad daylight.

But there was no mistaking the tone of his voice.

"Possibly," he said quietly. "You?"

"Possibly," she replied with equal softness. "And there is

something else I must confess."

"What is it?"

"You are not really smelly."

That made him chuckle. "And I would not do better marrying a pig," he said. "I am sorry I said that. I was angry and I often speak before thinking."

"Much like I act before thinking."

"God, what a pair we will make."

Elysande started to laugh. "If we do not kill one another first."

He couldn't disagree. "Let us hope it does not come to that," he said. He paused before continuing. "I am glad we have had this time, my lady. It is unexpected, but not unwelcome. I had just come out here to ponder my future when you appeared. It was fortuitous, I think."

"And I had come out here to avoid seeing you inside."

"Then the joke is on us."

She was still chuckling. "I would say so."

Westley could see her teeth in the moonlight, straight and white. Truth be told, she had a beautiful smile, something he didn't remember from those years ago.

"The last I saw of you was many years ago at Warwick Castle," he said. "Frankly, all I remember of you is that you tended to follow the squires around and play jokes on them. I remember being the butt of your jokes more than once."

Elysande shrugged. "That is possible," she said. "But I played jokes on a lot of squires, not just you. Truthfully, all I remember of you is that you were a big bully. I remember your shouting at the squires and pushing them around because you were a de Lohr and you were the biggest."

"Do you still think I'm a bully, then?"

"I've not seen evidence of that yet."

He snorted. "Then I will try not to do it," he said. "But that brings me to something else. My father expects me in the hall at this moment. He is not very happy with me."

Elysande looked up at the walls of the enormous hall with the steeply pitched roof. "And my mother is not happy with me, either," she said. "I suppose I should go in so she will not beat me again."

"And I should go in so my father does not berate me again."

"Do we tell them of our truce, then?"

He sighed heavily. "I warned you what could happen if we do."

"True," she said. "Would it be better if I chased you through the hall with a sword?"

He grinned. "Not if you think your mother would spank you again."

"She probably would."

"Then mayhap we should simply enter together and take our chances by making our truce known."

"Are you comfortable with that?"

"Are you?"

"Can you not simply answer a question, Sir Westley?"

He chuckled. "Possibly."

"You've given me that answer before."

"I possibly have."

She started to laugh again. "Now you're simply being annoying," she said, though she was smiling as she turned in the direction of the hall entry. "Is that how you wish to form my opinion of you?"

"I'd rather be annoying than a bully."

"How about you simply be Sir Westley and I will be Elysande?" she said as if it were a novel idea. "That seems the proper way to do this if we are truly come to know one another."

"As you wish, my lady," he said. "Let us be proper. But that is not very fun."

"You'd rather have fun?"

"Wouldn't you?"

She rolled her eyes and began to walk. "There you go again, not answering my questions."

Westley began to walk after her, watching her rounded backside in the simple red dress she was wearing. He rather liked the view. In fact, he rather liked this entire conversation.

"Sorry," he said, though he didn't mean it. "I'll try to stop answering questions with other questions."

She looked over her shoulder at him, suspiciously. "Why don't I believe you?"

With a grin, he shrugged. His lack of an answer told her what she needed to know. That only made her smile, but she turned around quickly so he wouldn't see it. Or so she thought.

But he did.

Holy hell, if he wasn't smiling, too.

And he wasn't the least bit distressed about it, either.

CHAPTER SIX

Seat of the Earl of Daventry

"**I** 'LL NOT CAPITULATE to your threats!"

Dustin was facing off with a surprisingly strong young woman. Cedrica de Steffan was a beautiful girl, fragile looking, with skin the color of cream and long red hair. She had been quite pleasant when Dustin and her daughters arrived, knowing they'd come on behalf of Westley and hoping this meant what she thought it meant—that Westley took her threats of a pregnancy seriously and they'd come to discuss a betrothal.

Given the situation and the time-sensitive nature of it, Dustin forwent the pleasantries and dived straight into the subject of Cedrica's alleged pregnancy. Her father, too, had hoped that the appearance of Lady Hereford meant a marriage proposal on behalf of her son, and when the pregnancy was brought up, he was certain that was why the woman had come.

He couldn't have been more wrong.

Dustin hadn't come to discuss a marriage. She had come to question the pregnancy and the very character of Cedrica. It only took a few moments of conversation for Cedrica to realize that Dustin didn't believe her. Even if the girl was pregnant, Dustin intimated that there could be other fathers than her son. Cedrica had tried to be pleasant, but it was clear that Lady Hereford had no intention of making this a polite conversation where her son's future was concerned, so the moment Dustin suggested that she would ask around to see who else Cedrica had slept with, the proverbial gloves came off.

Now, Dustin was facing off against an angry little devil.

"Why should you consider my suggestion a threat?" Dustin asked calmly. "If you have nothing to hide, then it should not be an issue. That is why I brought my daughters, so they can make inquiries about other partners you may have had. They will get to the bottom of this situation."

"My lady," Lord Daventry spoke up, red in the face and struggling with his manners. "You cannot possibly suggest that my daughter is unchaste? Surely you do not mean that."

"I intend to find out, my lord."

Daventry looked at his daughter in astonishment before returning his attention to Dustin. "But… but she was seduced by your son," he said. "He practically forced himself on her. Look at her—she is small and weak. Your son is more than twice her size. He could have easily overpowered her."

Dustin's eyes narrowed. "Are you suggesting what I think you are suggesting?"

Daventry cleared his throat loudly. "I am simply saying that he is a seducer."

"Your daughter could have refused."

Daventry was quickly losing his mannerly behavior. "In the face of an enormous de Lohr son? She would risk her life to do so."

Dustin didn't like the fact that they were trying to paint

Westley as a predator, or worse. "My son was raised to be respectful and mannerly with women," she said. "He would never do what you are suggesting—and, in fact, you are suggesting it to cover the tracks of a daughter who finds herself in men's beds. Often, I'm told. Do not think I've not heard of her reputation and how you cannot find a decent husband for her because of it. Now you seek to trap Westley into raising a child that is not his own. *If* there even is a child."

Daventry had all he could take. "You forget yourself, madam."

Brielle put herself between her mother and Lord Daventry. "*You* forget yourself, my lord," she said, jabbing a finger in his face. "My brother was seduced by your daughter, who has probably bedded half of your army, and now you try to foist other men's leaving upon my brother. You are in the wrong, my lord, and not my mother. You will not speak so to her again."

Dustin had Brielle by the arm, pulling her back. "Brie," she said softly, "get back, sweetheart. I am certain Lord Daventry did not mean to be disrespectful. I am certain he would not want such behavior to get back to your father, who would take it as a personal insult. Unless that is what Lord Daventry wishes?"

Daventry was cornered and growing increasingly furious. He eyed Brielle, who was as tall as he was, and the other daughter, Lady de Sherrington, whom he'd heard about. An assassin, some said, in her past. She was certainly married to the most fearsome assassin England had ever seen in Alexander de Sherrington. God's Bones, he didn't want that man down around his ears. He'd never survive such a thing. It was bad enough facing the de Lohr women.

He certainly didn't want to face the men.

"The fact remains that Westley bedded my daughter," he said, eyeing Brielle and Dustin as he backed away. "She carries his child."

"How do you know?" Dustin asked.

"Because she told me."

"And that is your only proof?" Dustin shook her head. "I am not so trusting when it comes to conniving young women. I require more than her word."

Daventry was outraged. "What do you want, then?" he demanded. "That it comes out looking just like your son? Will that be proof enough?"

Dustin turned to Christin, standing a few feet away. "Lady de Sherrington," she said, once again reminding Daventry whom her daughter was married to, "you will go to the commander of the army. Invoke your father's name and ask him to tell you which men have bedded Lady Cedrica. Do what you must to get your answers. Go, now."

Christin, her gaze lingering on Daventry in a way that suggested she was happy to prove him a liar, quit the chamber as Daventry tried to call her back. But she didn't return and, exasperated, he turned to Dustin.

"Lady Hereford, you are threatening a long-held alliance between Hereford and Daventry with your behavior," he said. "I will not tolerate your disrespect any longer."

Dustin moved toward the man, her manner swift and determined. She wasn't tall in the least, but her expression made her ten feet above Daventry at that moment. She got in the man's face, her gray eyes flashing.

"Listen to me and listen well," she hissed. "I will get to the bottom of this claim and you will not refuse me. Any refusal on your part will see my husband withdraw his alliance with you and, in fact, you will have made an enemy of the great de Lohr empire. You will not have Westley as a husband, either, because I will summon the Bishop of Hereford and tell him the story of your daughter's reputation. I will dispute Westley's involvement with her and I will summon every man she has ever bedded. I will put them all in front of a tribunal so that your daughter's secrets can be spoken aloud, for all the world to hear. If that is how you want the daughter of Daventry to be known, then continue your obstinance and your lies. Continue them and I will fight back by any means necessary. Is this, in any way, unclear?"

By the time she was finished, Daventry was glaring at her with a good deal of loathing. But he also knew he was beaten. If he continued pressing his daughter's suit, and her lies, then the tide would turn against him and he wouldn't be able to survive it.

"You are a nasty woman," he finally growled. "You have daughters yourself. What if this was one of your daughters? Would you still treat her so poorly?"

Dustin smiled thinly. "It would not be one of my daughters," she said. "I raised mine better than you have raised yours. Now, I must ask your daughter some questions. You may not wish to be present when I do, so it is your choice. Leave or go; it is all the same to me."

Daventry gave her a long look. "I'll not leave you alone with her," he said. Then he gestured at his daughter. "Ask her what you will. But be civil."

"I told you not to speak to my mother that way," Brielle growled, stepping up for her mother once again. "Behave yourself, Daventry."

Daventry didn't like being bullied by anyone, much less

women. He glared at Brielle. "Or what?" he said. "This is my home and I can do as I please."

Brielle smiled faintly. "As powerful and frightening as you think my father and brothers are, or even my sister's husband, you should be aware that I married a de Velt," she said. "Were you not aware of that? My husband and his brothers are the sons of Ajax de Velt. You know that name."

That brought Daventry pause as the news sank in. "Everyone in England knows that name."

"Then you do not want the de Velt war machine to come down around you, do you?"

Daventry wasn't stupid. No one wanted to tangle with the House of de Velt, an empire built on blood and terror. As powerful and intimidating as de Lohr was, a de Velt was even worse. He knew of Ajax de Velt and he knew that the man plowed through the Welsh marches many years ago, confiscating six castles and putting entire armies on pikes for all to see. Roads were lined with crucified soldiers. It was one of the more horrible legacies of warfare in England, but the House of de Velt was mostly in the north now and far more civilized these days.

But he didn't want to tempt fate.

Waving off the de Lohr women, he went to find a chair to sit in, weary and frustrated, as Dustin faced Cedrica.

"How far along is this pregnancy?" she asked.

Cedrica looked like a cornered cat, edgy and wide-eyed. "Far enough."

"Do you not know precisely?"

"I'm not sure."

She was being deliberately evasive, disrespectful in tone. Dustin could see the charade from a mile away. "Answer my question or I will summon a midwife and hold you down while she examines you," she said. "Now... how advanced is this pregnancy? And tell me the truth."

That terrified Cedrica because she had no doubt the woman would do what she said she would do.

"I... I do not know for certain," she said, a little less disrespectfully. "Months, at least."

"How *many* months?"

"I do not know, for certain. I—"

"I do."

The words came from the entry to the chamber where they were all gathered. Everyone turned to see Lady Daventry standing in the opening, her gaze on her daughter. Now, another player had entered the mix. Shaking her head in disgust at her daughter, the short and round Lady Daventry stepped into the chamber.

"This is why you sent me on a mission to the storage vault," she said to her child. "A mission that was impossible to complete because you requested pickled onions. Those are not in the storage vault, but in the kitchen, or so I have discovered because I was told you moved them."

Cedrica looked like a cornered cat. "Mama, I—"

"Quiet," Lady Daventry whispered loudly. "You sent me to the vault knowing fully that I would not find your requested item there. You did this so I would not know that Lady Hereford had come. You do not want me to speak with her and, I suspect, neither did your father. This was probably his idea more than yours, because you've never come up with an original idea in your entire life."

Cedrica stared at her mother, unable or unwilling to respond. That brought Daventry up from his chair.

"You needn't be here, my dear," Daventry said. "This conversation does not concern you."

It was clear that he was trying to chase the woman away, but Dustin stopped him. "Wait," she said, putting up a hand as she put herself between Daventry and his wife. "*I* wish to speak with her. Mayhap I can get a straight answer."

Lady Daventry focused on Dustin. "Of course I will tell you what you wish to know," she said, throwing a baleful glance at her husband. "I know I should support my husband and daughter in this matter, but I find that I cannot. Unfortunately, they know it, and that is why they deliberately did not tell me that you had arrived. They know that I cannot support their dishonesty in any fashion."

Dustin was very interested. "What dishonesty, my lady?"

Lady Daventry sighed heavily as if the weight of the situation was crushing her, body and spirit. "She is not pregnant, my lady," she said, her voice weaker. "What you see before you is a conspiracy. I am certain Westley bedded my daughter because she lets anyone with interest bed her, but she is not pregnant. My husband hoped to force a marriage based on a lie because once your son and my daughter were married and she became pregnant, she could simply say that the baby was born early. If she did not become pregnant, she could simply say that she lost the child. That is an old scheme, my lady, but I refuse to be part of it."

Dustin could see the entire story playing out before her as realization dawned. "And knowing you were against this plot, they tried to occupy you elsewhere when I came so you would not tell me the truth," she said.

"Exactly," Lady Daventry said, unable to look at her husband, who was standing a few feet away with his eyes closed as his plot was revealed.

But Cedrica was more vocal about it.

"Mama!" she said, bursting into tears. "How could you do this to me?"

"Because you are a stain upon this family's good name," Lady Daventry said with contempt. "You are an immoral child, Cedrica. I have tried to teach you well, but you take after your father too much. He has no sense of what is right or wrong and neither do you. Therefore, I have done something about it."

Cedrica looked at the woman in fear. "What have you done?"

Lady Daventry fixed on her only child. "I have spoken to the nuns at St. Augustine's Priory," she said. "I have made arrangements for you to become a postulate."

Cedrica's weeping grew louder as her future was revealed. "Nay, Mama! Please!"

"That is the only way to redeem our name, Cedrica," Lady Daventry said firmly. "You'll spend your life serving a God you've so richly sinned against."

Cedrica buried her face in her hands and wept. Lady Daventry dared to look at her husband then, but he had his back turned to her, moving away and perhaps contemplating a scheme gone wrong. Lady Daventry knew that he was panicked to get his daughter wed, but she also knew that Cedrica would make a terrible wife. She was vain and disloyal, a bad combination, especially if she married into a family that prided honor. With her husband and daughter in tatters, Lady Daventry finally turned her attention back to Dustin.

"I would offer you our hospitality, but I am certain you do not wish to stay," she said. "I do not blame you. I hope you do not think too badly of us, my lady. Every family has flaws, some more obvious than others."

Dustin understood. "You have redeemed your family in my eyes, my lady," she said. "And we shall be going now."

Lady Daventry moved aside to make the path to the door clear. "Please tell Westley that I am sorry for the trouble that has been brought to his doorstep," she said. "Assure him that it will not happen again."

Dustin forced a smile at the woman, who was genuinely contrite about her husband and daughter. It was too bad that the woman had to deal with vipers in her home, but as she said, every family had flaws. Some were just more obvious than others.

But thank God the woman had spoken up when she did.

And it had been exactly what Dustin had suspected.

Grateful, and anticipating a marriage with Westley and Lord Ledbury's daughter now without interference, Dustin and her daughters were on the road before the hour was up, heading back to Hereford and Massington Castle.

CHAPTER SEVEN

Massington Castle

T HEY'D BEEN PLEASANT to one another.

Not only that, Westley and Elysande had entered the great hall at the same time and gone to take their places at the dais with their respective parents without a word of complaint. No fighting, no arguing. Not even a nasty look. Westley told Christopher in confidence that a truce had been declared between the two of them, so the situation would be much more pleasant from now on.

Christopher could hardly believe it.

But the proof was before him. Not to say he doubted his son, because he trusted the man with his life, but in this situation, it seemed that this truce was all too simple. People didn't simply surrender years and years' worth of belief and resistance. It just wasn't that easy. Therefore, he sat through the feast feeling suspicious of every statement, every move. He was mostly suspicious of the young woman at the other end of the dais because from what he'd seen earlier that day, he didn't entirely trust her not to pull out a sword and come charging across the table.

That, he would have believed.

But this truce? It didn't seem convincing.

However, they managed to make it through the feast that night without an incident, which was encouraging, but Christopher couldn't help but notice that lady du Nor seemed almost as suspicious of the truce as he did. She, too, was watching her daughter carefully to make sure she wasn't trying to lull the entire group into a false sense of security before she went on a rampage. Christopher had to admit that he was watching her for the exact same reason.

When the feast was over and they'd retired to bed, Christopher breathed a sigh of relief. Westley had passed out on one of the two beds in the chamber they shared and had promptly begun to snore. He hadn't even taken his boots off as his long legs dangled over the edge of the mattress. It was Christopher who, with a heavy sigh, unlaced his son's boots and pulled them off his stinking feet. He had to laugh because Elysande had mentioned that she could smell Westley from where she stood when they first arrived.

Christopher was convinced she wasn't wrong.

She smelled his son's feet.

Stench aside, Christopher still managed to fall asleep and awake before dawn. The sounds of the fortress coming alive as the horizon turned pink wafted through the windows. Heaving his old bones out of bed, he washed and dressed and slipped out into the dawn to check on the escort and the horses. Once he made sure all was as it should be, there wasn't much for him to do, so he simply began to walk the bailey, looking at this enormous castle that would someday belong to Westley. He was over by some outbuildings when he noticed another person walking in his direction. It took him all of a split second to realize that Lady du Nor was coming in his direction.

He greeted her politely.

"Lady du Nor," he said, pausing in his walk. "A good morn to you."

Esther smiled weakly. "And to you, my lord," she said. "How did you sleep?"

"Well enough, thank you. And you?"

"Terrible."

His brow furrowed. "I am sorry to hear that," he said. "Should I summon a physic?"

Esther sighed sharply. "Nay," she said. "But you can help me."

"How?"

"You can tell me what your son said about this alleged truce between him and my daughter," she said. "Honestly, my lord, I am not sure if I trust her when she says it. It has kept me up all night. Even now, I fear she is plotting your son's destruction, so I must know. Do you believe your son when he told you of this peace accord between them?"

Christopher suspected that might have been her trouble. He could tell last night that she was having difficulty with the concept of an instant truce between two warring parties, just as he was. But she seemed to be far more suspicious.

Probably with good reason, since her daughter had historically been the aggressor.

"Mostly, I believe him," he said with a shrug. "At the very least, I believe he is being honest. But I share your concern. The two of them were so adamant about not marrying that this abrupt cessation of hostilities is... confusing."

Esther grunted. "Concerning is more like it."

Christopher eyed her. "Do you seriously think your daughter is lying about her feelings on the matter?" he said. "Have you spoken with her?"

Esther shook her head in exasperation. "Only at supper," she said. "She went to bed shortly after leaving the hall and I did not have an opportunity to speak with her further, but like your son, she at least conveys a belief in this so-called truce. I can usually tell when she is lying, but this time… I am not certain."

Two puzzled parents looked to each other for answers, but in this case, there were none to give. Christopher started walking again, this time with Esther falling in beside him. Nervous energy was working itself out as they paced the outer bailey.

"Let us review this logically, then," Christopher said. "Last evening, they somehow came together before the feast. That is established."

"But how?" Esther said. "I did not arrange it. In fact, I instructed my daughter to apologize to you and your son after I heard what she had done. I was expecting her in the hall."

"Then she must have seen Westley before she entered the hall and apologized," Christopher said. "He did not leave my sight until he stepped out to find the garderobe. Come to think of it, he was gone for some time. Mayhap he wandered and they happened to find one another?"

Esther shrugged. "Possibly," she said. "I have a suspicion she was trying to find the courage to enter the hall when she came across Westley."

Christopher nodded. "That must be what happened," he said. "They crossed paths and, knowing this is not something that will resolve itself without effort, had a conversation and came to a truce."

Esther didn't speak for a moment. "Does it not seem strange

that they have so suddenly stopped their hostilities?" she said. "They were mortal enemies until last night. Is it possible a simple conversation stopped everything?"

"Or they want us to *think* it stopped everything."

Esther came to a halt, her eyes wide at Christopher. "A ruse!"

"Anything is possible."

"Do you think that is the case?"

Christopher sighed heavily. "I truthfully do not know," he said. "Where is your daughter now?"

Esther gestured toward the south side of the castle. "Near the troop house," she said. "You may as well know that since her brother died, she has been training as a warrior. She spends her days with the knights."

Christopher frowned. "Why does she do this?"

Esther lowered her gaze. "My son's death devastated his father," she said. "The man has spent nearly every day since drunk because he cannot deal with the pain. Ella has trained as a warrior to somehow lift her father's spirits, to somehow be seen by him. He hardly acknowledges her. She does it to please him."

Christopher appreciated the insight into Elysande, something that was clearly not easy to speak of. "The death of a child is a shattering experience," he said. "Particularly an heir. I am sorry that your daughter feels a need to step into her brother's boots."

Esther shrugged. "Marius has made us all invisible since our son's death," she said, trying to appear brave about it. "Truthfully, I hope that Westley's appearance might bolster Marius. That he might return to the man he was before Emory's death."

"Does he even know Westley is here?"

"He knows," she said. "I told him yesterday when you arrived. What he does not know is that Ella attacked Westley upon arrival. In fact, this returns us to what we were just speaking of. Whether or not their sudden truce is a ruse."

Christopher grunted as the subject came around again. "I certainly intend to question West about the situation, to be sure. Or…"

"Or *what*?"

He held up a hand for patience. "Bear with me while I think this through," he said. "I promised my wife that I would see Westley wed as soon as I arrived. If we were to suggest an immediate marriage, that might show us the truth of any truce. If there truly is such a thing, then they will be amenable. But if there is not…"

"Then it shall come out in the open," Esther said with satisfaction. "Honestly, my lord, I can fight my daughter when I know what I am fighting. It is when she is hiding something that the trouble starts."

Christopher glanced at the hall behind him, the keep. "Then let us not allow them to start any further trouble," he said. "Summon a priest and we shall have the mass said in the hall tomorrow. Let us move forward with this marriage and be done with it. No more refusals, no more resistance."

Esther liked that idea. "Agreed," she said. "I will tell Ella. I am curious to see her reaction."

"As I am curious to see Westley's," Christopher said. Then he scratched his chin thoughtfully. "If there is not truly a truce, then the marriage may be just what they need. I will confess that my wife and I fought when we first met. Neither one of us wanted the marriage, but we were bound to it. We were forced into it. As it turns out, it was the best thing I've ever done. It is a hope that West and Elysande will feel that way, with time."

Esther shrugged. "Or they will kill each other and we will only have ourselves to blame."

Christopher snorted. "Let us hope it does not come to that."

Esther couldn't share his optimism, though she was trying. "Aye," she muttered. "Let us hope."

Christopher didn't think she seemed too convinced.

Truth be told, neither was he.

ᙯ

ODDLY ENOUGH, HE felt the same way this morning as he had last night.

That was surprising.

Westley hadn't been exactly sure if he would hold the same opinion of Elysande that he had last night, but he was shocked to realize that he did. He'd awoken to an empty chamber, as his father was gone, so he found himself lying there for several long minutes, pondering the conversation he'd had with Elysande the day before.

He could still hardly believe that it had happened.

She had been... *pleasant*. More than pleasant, she'd actually shown a sense of humor. She'd shown interest in his conversation. He was still having trouble believing that she'd been so compliant, but given the fact her mother had dealt her an evidently swift beating because of her earlier behavior, perhaps that had been enough to convince her that hostility would no longer be tolerated. He truly hoped that common sense was gaining a foothold with her because he honestly did not want to fight the woman for the rest of his life.

He could only hope that she felt the same way this morning, too.

Rising from his lumpy bed, he realized that he had fallen asleep in his clothing, but that was nothing new with him. He often wore the same clothing for weeks at a time, something his mother would constantly harass him about. *You smell like a goat,* she would say. Perhaps that was true, but it wasn't as if he had anyone to smell good for, and his friends certainly didn't care, so more often than not, he simply laughed at her.

Dustin had never taken well to that.

With thoughts of Elysande on his mind, he went to pull his boots on and caught a whiff of his feet, which made him stop and think. Yesterday, Elysande had mentioned that she could smell him from where she stood, and, given the stench coming from his boots, he realized what she meant. She wasn't wrong. He took a good, long sniff of each boot and realized just how bad they smelled. Then he began to sniff his tunic and his armpits and realized that he did, indeed, smell bad.

Perhaps his mother and Elysande hadn't been wrong.

He had to do something about it.

His father's saddlebags were in the small chamber, which was lodged into one of the towers close to the keep. Male guests weren't usually housed in the keep if there were women inside, so he took no offense to the fact that he and his father, a great earl, had been relegated to a neighboring tower. Seeing his father's possessions stored neatly under the bed, Westley pulled out one of the smaller satchels. He knew what his father usually traveled with and, as expected, came across hair combs, soap, and a razor, among other things. Westley had never traveled with those things and, quite honestly, wasn't even sure he owned a comb, but he knew that today was a day that he should probably use such a thing. He didn't want to look, or smell, like a goat any longer.

Pulling out the soap and the other things, he went to the door and summoned hot water.

He didn't have to wait long for the servants to bring him a basin and a couple of buckets of steaming water. Westley proceeded to strip down and wash himself in the hot water using his father's soap. It was some of the finest that money could buy, made in Castille, and it smelled strongly of rosemary and thyme. Westley scrubbed himself from top to bottom, hopefully removing all of that horrible smell, and that included his feet. He actually sat on the floor to wash his feet before dousing his entire body with one of the buckets of hot water.

He was fairly certain he had scalded the skin right off his body.

Next came his face. He always had a bit of a beard, like his father did, but in his case it was simply because he was too lazy to shave. Today, he was going to make an exception, and he used the soap and his father's razor to shave off a rather scraggly beard. He also proceeded to wash his hair, something he didn't do nearly as often as he probably should, and scrubbed until he was positive his scalp was bleeding before rinsing out the soap with the rest of the water. The wood floor was now covered with water, but he didn't care. He'd have the servants dry it up before his father returned. After combing his hair and feeling rather naked now he didn't have a beard on his face, he dried off using one of the linen sheets on the beds and then stole some of his father's clean clothing so he would have something fresh to wear.

And with that, he was ready.

For what, he wasn't sure, but he was ready for anything that came his way. Perhaps a certain young woman he'd only seen in the darkness last night, even in the great hall, or camouflaged in a helm and protection when she'd attacked him. Truthfully, other than shadowed views, he'd never seen her clearly in the light of day. He was rather curious to see if his first impressions of Elysande were correct.

Off he went.

The morning had a hint of haze in the air, although the sun was desperately trying to burn it off. The ground was wet and muddy from the damp night as the soldiers around him went about their business. The first thing Westley did was check on the horses that had pulled the carriage the day before, just to make sure there were no swollen tendons or other concerns. He found the animals, all four of them, in a small corral outside of the stables, eating from buckets of grain. A nearby stable servant told him that his father had already been there, so Westley continued on out into the bailey, looking for his father amidst the activity.

Although he didn't catch sight of Christopher right away, he did see something going on over near the south side of the bailey. Upon closer inspection, he could see men gathered around a pair that seemed to be fighting.

Curious, he headed in that direction.

As Westley drew nearer, he could see that it was more of an instruction than an actual fight. Harker of Kent was instructing a pair of warriors, at least one of them being a knight. Westley could tell by the way the man moved. He came to a pause and watched, realizing very quickly that Elysande was the other fighter. Harker was trying to convince her that emotion was deadly in battle, something that seemed elementary, but that she clearly thought would work to her advantage. She was arguing with the man strongly on it.

Westley thought it was all rather comical.

"He is right, you know," he said loudly. "Emotions in battle will get you killed."

All heads turned to see Westley standing back behind the gathered crowd, mostly taller than everyone else. He had a booming voice that carried a mile. But he was smiling as Elysande removed her helm.

"Can you not use them to your advantage?" she called back to him, unwilling to back down. "Emotions feed the soul. If you are in the heat of battle, the soul *must* survive. Can emotions not fuel that?"

Westley was still smiling as he shrugged, coming closer to the center of the action. "I understand what you are saying," he said. "But most men cannot control those emotions. They become reckless with them. That is what Harker is trying to teach you. If you are to use your emotions, you must manage them. Can you manage them?"

Elysande gazed up at him, lifting a hand to shield her eyes from the sun. "I can," she said confidently.

Westley grinned. In the light of day, she was absolutely spectacular. He couldn't remember ever seeing a woman of such beauty and brightness. There was nothing about her face that wasn't perfect, and coupled with that bright smile and long, glorious hair, he had to admit that he wasn't disappointed. Quite pleased, actually.

This wasn't the same runt he'd known those years ago.

"Let's see," he said, turning to the knight she'd been sparring with. "May I use your blade, my lord?"

The knight nodded, handing over the heavy weapon. "You may," he said. "Mayhap you will have better luck with it against her than I have had."

Westley snorted softly. "Somehow, I doubt it," he muttered.

"I do not mean to overstep, but it's apparent I must make my point. I do not mean to usurp whatever you were doing."

The knight grinned and removed his helm. "Not in the least," he said. "Mayhap you will have better luck with her. She does not want to seem to listen to me or Harker."

"Your name?"

"Olan de Bisby, my lord."

Westley simply nodded, turning to face Elysande as she fought off a smile. She was several feet away, fully armed, wearing protection that didn't exactly fit her, but she had tried to make it work. She was sweaty, and a little dirty, so it had been clear that she'd been out here for a while. He wasn't sure if this was work or play, but when it came to swords and battle, he took everything seriously.

"I do not recall that you trained with the men at Warwick," he said.

She shook her head. "I did not," she said. "But since the death of my brother, I have asked Harker to train me as a warrior."

"Why?"

Her smile faded. "Because I am the only du Nor left," she said. "If we have trouble, then I must be prepared to defend my family's home."

Westley looked at Olan, at Harker. "You have knights for that, do you not?"

She was beginning to get exasperated. "Are you going to talk or do you want to fight?"

Westley fought off a grin at her impatience, looking at the sword in his hand. "'Tis a fine weapon," he said, looking back at Olan. "Yours?"

Olan nodded. "It belonged to my father."

Westley took a second look at it. "Quite fine," he said. Then he turned to Elysande. "When it comes to emotion in battle, the only one you should have is courage. Courage is simply fear mixed with determination. Determination that you should not fail because if you do, you will die. Others will die. If you bring any emotion to battle other than courage, then you are risking everyone around you. Have you been taught that?"

His eyes flicked up to Harker, who was sitting on the perimeter of the group. The older man nodded slowly.

"I have told her," he said. "Mayhap you should reinforce it."

Westley's focus returned to Elysande. She was watching him, completely off her guard, listening to his words with a mixture of defiance and curiosity. From the brief conversation he'd heard between her and Harker, he could see how stubborn she was. Stubborn and confident that she was in the right.

"Lady," he said slowly, "if you are not listening to your trainer, then you are already dead."

Her chin went up. "I *do* listen to him," she insisted. "But there are things I do not agree with."

Westley cocked his head. "And you base your opinion on what?" he said. "Your endless years of fighting battles? Your already-extensive training? The fact that you have watched a man die on your sword?"

The men gathered around began to laugh, and Elysande's expression lost all humor, all defiance. Now, she was growing angry.

"It does not take vast experience or years of battle to know some things," she said.

"Like what?"

"Like… like motivation in battle," she said, her cheeks growing red with embarrassment because the men were still laughing. "I can use my fear and anger as motivation and it has nothing to do with courage. Anger *is* courage."

"How do you define that?"

"Because you use it as motivation to fight."

"Anger and fear will paralyze you."

"I do not believe that."

Westley didn't say anything. He was looking at his sword again. But suddenly, the sword was up and he was charging Elysande like a runaway bull. He had been about twelve feet from her, and by the time she realized he was moving, he was nearly upon her. She screamed in fright and lifted her sword, clumsily backing away and trying to escape a truly large man with a sword that moved like the wind.

Sword still up, but in a very precarious position, Elysande ended up tripping over her own feet. As she fell back, Westley was on top of her, sword arcing, and she gasped again as the blade came down right next to her head. She tried to roll out of the way, but the sword came down again on the opposite side. Furious, and terrified, she began swinging her sword at him indiscriminately, and all he had to do was take one good swing and knock it from her grip. Then he swung his sword over her head again, about two inches from her face, and she came to a horrified halt, frozen in fear, eyes shut tightly. She was waiting for the next strike to slice her. But there was no next strike.

Westley had made his point.

"That," he said quietly, "is what I mean by fear paralyzing you. I could have killed you and there was nothing you could have done about it. The point is that emotions do not help you. They hinder you. And in battle, you must suppress all of them except for courage. That is the only emotion that will do any good at all."

Elysande opened her eyes. Westley was standing over her, and she could see Olan and Harker come up on either side of him. Olan looked rather sad while Harker seemed to have no emotion at all. When Westley moved from his dominant position over her, Harker reached down and pulled her to her feet.

"Now do you see?" he said, his voice low and unsympathetic. "You do not listen, Ella. Do what I tell you to do and if you ever go into battle, you may survive."

Humiliated, and verging on tears, Elysande quickly moved away, heading back to the armory where she stowed her gear. Olan, wanting to be sympathetic to her embarrassment, turned away and dispersed the men, chasing them back to their duties. Only Harker was left with Westley.

"Although I do not know the circumstances as to why the lady was partaking in swordplay, I think she should know this is not a game," Westley said. "She could be seriously injured or worse if she does not listen to you."

Harker turned in his direction. "She has spirit," he said. "And she never thought it was a game. She is very serious about learning how to fight."

"Not serious enough."

Harker's brow furrowed. "How can you judge that?" he said. "You have been here less than a day. You do not know her enough to make that statement."

There was an edge to his voice. Westley could hear it. "I did not mean to offend," he said. "I simply meant she does not seem to take your advice seriously."

"You do not know enough to make that statement, either."

There was a bit of a challenge in that assertion. Westley had been trying to be kind, but he didn't like an old knight who wanted to tell him what he felt or what he knew. His polite manner was suddenly not so polite.

"I know enough to know that yesterday, she charged me the moment I walked through the gatehouse," he said. "It was a stupid move at the very least. Reckless was more like it. I could have seriously injured her if I'd wanted to. Her recklessness is because all of the men she spars with will take pity on her—and if you are serious about training her, then that is something that should be drilled into her head. Show no mercy and treat every man as if he wants to kill you. If you are going to train her, train her correctly."

Harker's bright blue gaze moved over Westley, studying him. "And you think that because you come from the House of de Lohr, you can dictate what is correct and what is not correct for all of us?"

That statement was most definitely a challenge. Harker had taken offense to Westley's words and manner, but Westley didn't have time for an old man who had his feelings hurt easily. Facing Harker, he took a few steps in the man's direction.

"Aye, I do," he said. "My father is the greatest knight of his generation and I have five older brothers who are all exceptionally accomplished. I know more about training and warfare than almost anyone in England, you included, so this is not an area I am inexperienced in. Moreover, no more training for Lady Elysande. We are to be married and I do not want my wife lifting a sword, so her schooling with you ends here. Thank you for your expertise, but your services are no longer needed."

With that, he turned away, heading in the direction that Elysande had gone and leaving Harker standing there with the remnants of his pride bleeding out into the dirt. He wasn't a great warrior and he knew it. Training and managing men was all he had. He didn't like the de Lohr whelp making it plain that he wasn't a better man than most.

The lines, between Harker and Westley, had been drawn.

CHAPTER EIGHT

Hell's Forge

"THAT IS WHAT my cousin tells me, my lord. De Lohr has arrived and rumor is that there is to be a wedding."

A cowering man stood in a small, circular chamber, with a fire blazing in the hearth that filled the room with smoke and cloying heat. He'd just delivered news that he hoped wouldn't set off the man seated near the hearth, a cup half filled with wine in his hand and sweating in the profuse heat of the chamber.

When it came to Samson Fitz Walter, anything was possible.

"Be calm, Alend," Fitz Walter said. "Truly, be calm. There is no need to be fearful. Start from the beginning and tell me how you came by your information."

Alend, short and wiry and bald, had served Samson for many years. He knew that tone and it terrified him. When Samson told him to be calm, it was a ruse. He wanted the man to relax so that when he finally did explode, the look of fear in Alend's face would fill him with joy. Some men took pleasure from food or drink or women.

Samson took it from fear.

"You know my cousin serves Marius du Nor," Alend said slowly, trying to show that he was calming down. "Olan is his name. You have paid the man in the past for information about Marius."

"I am aware of Olan."

Alend nodded nervously. "He sent word to me yesterday to meet him in Poolbrook, as it was an urgent matter," he said. "I met with him earlier today and he told me that the Earl of Hereford and Worcester arrived yesterday with his son. The rumor around Massington is that there is to be a wedding soon."

Samson simply sat there and chewed his lip. He was looking at Alend, but he wasn't seeing the man. He was pondering what he'd just been told, his mind elsewhere as he thought of the lovely daughter of Marius. The one he'd been denied. A louse bit him on the thigh, infesting the breeches he'd not had off his body in years, and he scratched it furiously. He scratched so much that he was perpetually covered in sores. All the while, through the scratching and grunting, he continued to gaze at Alend.

Thinking.

"So the man himself has come," he finally said, setting his cup down on the nearest table. "I do not believe Christopher de Lohr has ever been to Massington."

Alend shook his head. "I do not think so, my lord," he said. "We would have heard."

"Aye," Samson said. "We would have heard, indeed. But this time, he comes for the betrothal with the fair Elysande."

Alend watched the man stand up, an enormous fellow dressed in black rags—black breeches, black tunic, black robe that had seen better days. It had belonged to his father, a vicious man with a lump of coal where his heart should have been. That kind of man had turned Samson into a similar character, a wraith of a human who lived a solitary life and cursed the world around him because he could not control anything outside of Hell's Forge. The last of the glorious Fitz Walter clan was coming to an end in a most inglorious way.

With the lack of an heir.

It was slipping away before his very eyes.

"Is there anything to do, my lord?" Alend said. "To prevent the marriage, I mean. Could we send word to a magistrate and protest it?"

"On what grounds?" Samson said. "We would have to have serious grounds to protest it."

Alend shrugged thoughtfully. "We could lie and say that Marius promised you the girl," he said. "We could fabricate… something. It would be your word against his."

Samson shook his head. "You forget that he has Hereford on his side," he said. "All de Lohr would have to do is produce the betrothal contract between him and Marius and any magistrate would show us the door."

Alend sighed with resignation. "Mayhap," he said, still thinking on a way to help his liege. "Would it do any good to summon a priest and ask for their intervention?"

Samson shook his head again. "Again, we would have to have grounds for such a thing, and I have none," he said. "The only thing to do is to go to Massington and formally lodge my protest with Marius. At least I could delay the marriage. Mayhap it would give Marius time to consider my offer."

"What offer?"

Samson looked at him. "That I will not attack Massington if

he breaks the contract and gives Elysande to me."

Alend stepped back because Samson was pacing the room and he didn't want to get too close to the man, because things like fists and feet tended to fly around if he was particularly unhappy—and this subject was one that was bound to make him furious.

"But Hereford is at Massington," he said hesitantly. "You said yourself that he will support Massington. And his army is larger than ours. Much larger."

Samson was by the chamber door when he came to a halt and lifted his head as if an idea had just occurred to him.

"Yet this is one more thing Christopher de Lohr has stolen from me," he muttered. "He killed my uncle. Now, he steals the woman who will give me a son and continue my family line. The man is a murderer and a thief. Long have I vowed vengeance against him and his kind. I wonder... I wonder if Marius realizes the character of the man he has so willingly done business with."

Somewhere over by the hearth, an old raven awoke from the nap it had been taking and began to squawk, demanding food from Samson, who had tamed the thing long ago. It would bite anyone else but Samson, so Alend hated the creature. When it began to fuss, he moved over near the wall, away from it, as Samson made his way over to his pet.

"Even Morrigan knows this," he said as he petted the bird affectionately. "Did you know that our feathered friend is named after the goddesses of old who protected the warriors on the battlefield?"

"Nay, my lord."

"They also chose who would be slain," Samson said, finally reaching into a cup near the bird to give him a dried pea.

"Mayhap that is what needs to be done, Alend. I must go to Marius and make him aware that I will choose to slay him should he not break the betrothal with de Lohr. For certain, that is my only recourse now."

"How may I help you, my lord?"

"Summon my guards. We must plan our visit to Massington."

"As you wish, my lord," Alend said. But he paused before leaving. "And… my cousin? May I promise him a coin for this information?"

Samson glanced at him. "You may promise him that I will not kill him when I attack Massington," he said. "And I will not kill you if his information turns out to be correct."

Alend blanched. "Kill *me*?" he said. "But I've done nothing."

Samson snorted, a nasty sound. "Men like you are worthless," he said. "You cower at my feet and follow me around like a dog, eager for scraps. Why do you think you are here, Alend? It is because you have a cousin at Massington. Did you think otherwise?"

Alend wasn't sure how to answer. "I have been with you for some time, my lord," he said. "I am loyal to you."

"You are what I say you are. Now, go away."

Alend didn't push, nor did he ask further questions. Samson's answer had frightened him, but he knew the man meant it. He meant every word out of his mouth, including his hatred for de Lohr and his need for vengeance.

And that was what this was all about.

Revenge.

CHAPTER NINE

Massington Castle

H E'D FOUGHT HER.
And he'd won.

Elysande had retreated from Westley in humiliated silence, which had been difficult to watch. Olan knew she was a proud woman, and defeat at the hands of Westley was difficult for her to stomach.

It had been difficult for Olan to stomach, too.

Given that his vocation was the knighthood, it was strange that Olan didn't truly have an aggressive bone in his body. He simply did what he was ordered to do, when he was ordered to do it, and given that Massington was a relatively peaceful castle, he could only remember one serious skirmish in the entire time he'd served there. There had been a rather large band of outlaws in the forest north of Massington, and they'd attacked one too many travelers before Marius finally ordered the woods cleared.

Emory had taken great delight in organizing a death squad, Olan included, to clear out the woods, but the outlaws took exception to the attack, and the next day they'd launched flaming arrows into Massington's bailey, setting part of the stables on fire. Emory went after them again, with Olan and Harker beside him, and they'd finally managed to kill several of them.

After that, the outlaws scattered and never came back. That had happened several years ago and he'd not seen action since then, unusual in a country where warfare was a regular occurrence. But at Massington, that extremely heavily fortified castle, things were simply peaceful. Peaceful enough that Olan led a rather boring, if not safe, life and pined after his liege's daughter. He'd made it obvious how he felt about her, but she'd always been coy about how she felt about him.

At least she hadn't outright attacked him, like she had de Lohr.

Olan had sentry duty on this fine day, which was giving him a lot of time to think about the situation. Guards were walking the walls and he was supervising the gatehouse, which was quiet at this time, so his thoughts were centered on the turn his life had taken. He'd always known about the de Lohr betrothal, but he also knew that Elysande was so opposed to it that surely her father wouldn't make her go through with it.

But he had.

Olan had gotten some satisfaction after Elysande attacked Westley when the man had arrived, but since then, it seemed that things had calmed down a little between them. He was disappointed about it because he was hoping Elysande would keep up the hostility. He was hoping she would fight for what he wanted. Or, at the very least, what she didn't want. But the fight seemed to have gone out of her, which left Olan facing the fact that the woman he loved was going to marry another.

It hurt.

There was no denying that it was painful. But he wasn't an

aggressive man by nature, nor was he a hater by nature, so he couldn't bring himself to be hostile toward Westley, who, by all accounts, was in an unhappy situation just as much as Elysande was. They both had parents forcing them into the marriage.

Olan could have been bitter about it, or angry about it, but he wasn't either. He was simply... sad. Perhaps at some point that sadness would turn to resentment and rage, but for now, there was simply sorrow in his heart.

Great sorrow.

But there was something else with Olan, something more he kept buried deep. He wasn't hugely loyal to du Nor and hadn't been since he first became part of Marius' army. He'd only sworn fealty because Marius was in need of a knight and he was in need of a job. They'd met in Birmingham, of all places, after Olan had lost his position with an old lord who had died and the man's son had gotten rid of the men he considered too expensive to keep. That meant Olan was out on his ear, and he'd met Emory in a tavern, by chance, and Emory had introduced him to his father.

But there had never been great loyalty there, and most especially not since Emory died. Olan simply wasn't the loyal type. His allegiance could be bought, and at this time, it was. He had a cousin at neighboring Hell's Forge Castle, and the lord of Hell's Forge, Samson Fitz Walter, liked to keep an eye on his neighbors. The man had spies all over Herefordshire and beyond. When de Lohr had arrived, Olan had sent word to his cousin and the two had briefly met up in a neighboring village. It wasn't difficult for Olan to leave Massington unnoticed. He'd met with his cousin long enough to tell the man what he knew.

That the de Lohrs had come for a wedding.

By now, he was certain that his cousin had relayed the news

to Fitz Walter. Olan's agreement with Fitz Walter was to simply relay anything significant, any news that was deemed important, and he would be well paid for it. The visit of their liege was important, and the reason for his visit even more so. Olan knew that Samson had offered for Elysande's hand and had been summarily rejected, so the fact that Westley had come to marry the woman Samson wanted would be important news, indeed.

It wasn't as if Olan wouldn't take some satisfaction out of Fitz Walter stopping the marriage or, better still, chasing Westley off. Perhaps that was why Olan had been eager to tell the man—to have someone else who could do the dirty work of chasing Westley de Lohr away from the woman Olan loved. But he didn't think beyond that. Olan simply saw the immediate need of what was happening today.

He wondered if Fitz Walter would, too.

Westley de Lohr was there to take what they both wanted.

Elysande.

CB

"I OWE YOU an apology."

Elysande had been putting away her protection, fumbling with a joint in the shoulder that had caused her some discomfort, when she heard the words. She knew who it was before she ever turned around, and even when she did, she quickly turned back to what she was doing.

"No need," she said. "You were simply trying to teach me something I clearly have not grasped yet."

Westley could hear the indignance in her tone. She was offended and he knew she should be. Feeling rather bad about what he did, he came into the armory and perched himself on a bench near the door.

"You were correct when you said that I was a bully during my days at Warwick," he said. "I was the youngest of six sons. I had been pushed around and belittled and compared to my brothers all my life, so my way of dealing with that was to show my superiority at Warwick because I couldn't do it at home. But just now, I sincerely wasn't trying to bully you. I was honestly trying to help you."

Sighing faintly, Elysande turned around. "You were not wrong," she insisted quietly. "You showed me how fear can be paralyzing. I've just never had anyone do that to me before so, naturally, I argued the point. If it never happened to me, then how am I to know the truth?"

Westley smiled faintly at her, but with some regret. "That is because you are their lady," he said. "No one wants to hurt you or frighten you. They simply want to serve you and be kind."

"But not you."

He laughed softly. "I do not want to see you hurt or injured," he said. "The way I came on to you with the sword… That is a deadly move. If that had been in battle, you would be dead. And that would be most… regrettable."

There was something sweet in that statement, something that made her cheeks flush hotly. Horrified, she turned around and pretended to fuss with her protection.

"Are you certain you were not seeking some sort of vengeance for my having attacked you yesterday?" she said. "Just to teach me a lesson?"

He snorted. "Lady, I did not bathe and shave simply to come out this morning and teach you a lesson," he said. "You might have said you cannot smell me anymore… can you?"

Back still turned to him, she grinned broadly at his question. "And if I can?" she asked.

He began smelling his tunic, his armpits. "Can you really?"

She laughed softly and turned around again. "Nay, I cannot smell you," she said. "Why are you so worried about it?"

"Because I do not want to drive you away," he said. "This entire situation is precarious enough without my smelling like a goat."

"Who told you that you smell like a goat?"

He frowned and looked away. "My mother."

"I see," she said, noting that he did look well groomed this morning. His blond hair was clean, and possibly even still a little damp, and he'd shaved off that scruffy beard. The man cleaned up extremely well. "I suppose she would know. But I do not smell you, so that is a good thing."

He looked at her then. "A very good thing," he said. "I do not wish to offend you."

"You have not."

"Good," he said. But he eyed her a moment before continuing. "May I ask you a question?"

"Of course."

He threw a thumb in the direction of the area where they had fought. "Why are you having your knight train you?" he asked. "You do not really intend to answer the call to arms if needed, do you?"

She shrugged. "Why not?"

"Because being a warrior is not something you simply learn in a few lessons," he said. "Men are trained from childhood for such a thing. There is much more to it than squaring off against a knight who will not truly fight back. In fact, if that is all they have done for you, then they have done you a great disservice."

"Why would you say that?"

"Because they've not shown you the truth," Westley said. "If you think every man who goes up against you is simply going to hold a sword while you chop at him, then they have let you believe a lie."

She scratched her chin. "I just went up against a man who knocked me to the ground and nearly killed me," she said. "I am fairly certain I just got a real taste of what battle is like."

He grinned reluctantly. "Not even close," he said. "But better than what you've been taught."

Elysande pondered that statement for a moment before making her way over to him and sitting down on the same bench. There was a couple of feet between them, but she wouldn't look directly at him and he wouldn't look directly at her. They seemed to do a lot of side-eyeing, each one trying to figure out what the other one was thinking.

Or feeling.

Elysande finally broke the ice.

"You ask me why I want to train as a warrior," she said softly. "The truth is that I lost my brother a couple of years ago in an accident. He was my father's heir. Emory was the knight of the family, the shining star. My father put all of his hopes on Emory and in my marriage into the de Lohr family. He thought that Emory would produce strong sons to carry on the du Nor name, and he thinks that I will have at least a dozen de Lohr sons who will also bear du Nor blood."

"Only a dozen?" Westley dared to look at her, thinking that she was even more beautiful at close range. "That seems like a small number."

She looked at him in mock horror. "Is *that* what you expect?" she gasped. "No wonder I was so opposed to this marriage. Somehow, I must have known that is what you would want."

He grunted, lifting his shoulders. "Too many?"

She laughed ironically. "About six or eight too many."

He frowned. "Do you mean to tell me you will only bear four or six sons?"

"What if they are daughters?"

He shook his head. "I am not rich enough for all of those girls," he said. "They must be male."

She lifted an eyebrow. "I do not think I can choose what sex the child will be."

He was still looking at her, now biting off a smile. "We will pray heartily that they will be sons."

Elysande giggled. "I would wager that you will build a shrine dedicated to the prayers for male children."

"How did you guess?"

Her laughter grew, and he let his smile bloom. He studied her a moment, noting the dimples in her chin when she smiled and the way her nose wrinkled.

It was enchanting.

"You are beautiful when you smile," he said. "I do regret thinking you annoying those years ago. You have changed a great deal."

Her cheeks were starting to flame again. She was completely unused to compliments. "You should not have any regrets about that," she said, hoping he didn't notice the color of her face. "I *was* annoying. But I followed the squires around for a reason."

"What reason?"

"Because I missed my brother," she said, her voice softening. "Emory fostered at Norwich Castle, where my father fostered, but I was not allowed to go there. He found a place for me at Warwick where my mother fostered, but I did not want to learn what the young ladies learned. I wanted to do what the boys did. What Emory did."

Westley could see the emotion in her face as she spoke of her brother. "Then training to be a warrior is not something new to you," he said. "Even back then, you wanted to fight with the lads."

"I did," she said. "But they would not let me, so I was forced to learn feminine pursuits. And even upon my coming home, my mother insisted that I only indulge in ladylike tasks. She would not let me engage in anything Emory was doing. It was only after he died that I decided to follow in his footsteps. That is really all I was doing... trying to emulate my brother. I was even trying to please my father, who has been inconsolable since Emory's passing. That is why he drinks."

They had veered onto a subject of great emotion for Elysande, one that seemed to be a difficult admission for her. Given how Westley had said cruel things about her father and his drinking yesterday, he was coming to feel quite contrite about it.

He could see now that he'd been wrong.

"Forgive me for being unkind about your father yesterday," he said quietly. "Everything I said yesterday was unkind. My only defense is that I was angry. I've said it before—when I become angry, I speak before I think. But it was very harsh of me."

She waved him off. "You just had a woman attack you for no reason," she said. "I think you are entitled to a little anger and hostility."

"I did not mean what I said, any of it."

Elysande looked at him, eyes twinkling. "You are not the

bully I remember."

"And you are not the annoying little waif *I* remember."

"That is a good thing, is it not?"

He nodded. "Verily," he said. "It means that we can start fresh with our observations."

Elysande liked that idea and, truth be told, was relieved that he was willing to do such a thing. In her case, it also made the marriage almost palatable. She would be marrying someone she didn't know, but in her experience since yesterday, she would like to know him.

Perhaps Westley de Lohr would make a good husband after all.

"In the spirit of starting fresh, will you tell me something about yourself?" she asked. "Other than that you become angry and speak before thinking, I mean. We hardly know one another, and that is the truth."

He chuckled softly. "What would you like to know?"

"Anything. Anything at all."

He cocked his head thoughtfully. "Very well," he said. "I will tell you something if you will tell me something."

"Agreed."

He hunted for something that might be of interest to her. "My favorite dish is stewed chicken."

"Mine is carrots," she said, smiling. "I love carrots and on-ions, boiled together."

He nodded. "Tasty," he said. "Chicken and carrots and onions are even more tasty."

She laughed. "Now I know what to feed you to make you happy," she said. "But tell me of a vice you have. Something you cannot live without."

That didn't take much thinking on his part. "I am very fond

of horses," he said. "I have too many."

"How many?"

He shrugged. "Six warhorses," he said. "They are frightfully expensive, but I do not spend my money on anything else. I spend it on my horses."

"And you keep them at Lioncross Abbey?" she asked.

He nodded. "I have claimed one entire side of the stables as my own," he said. "My brothers and sisters all have their own homes, so I am the only one of my father's children still left at Lioncross. I suppose that means I can get away with more because I am the only one, although my mother is not afraid to deny me my wants. You'll understand when you meet her."

"Is she terrifying?"

Westley grinned, looking at her. "She's a tiny woman and looks quite placid, like a countess should," he said. "But then she opens her mouth and we all run."

Elysande burst into soft laughter. "I have a mother like that."

"Do you?"

She nodded. "I do," she said. "You met her last night."

"She seemed quiet enough," he said. "Although she really only spoke to my father, so I suppose I will have my own experience with her at some point."

"You will," Elysande said. "Just as I will have my own experience with your mother."

"She is coming here, you know."

Her eyebrows lifted. "Truly?"

Westley nodded. "She is coming to make sure I do not back out of this marriage."

"Do you plan to?"

"Do *you*?"

Elysande started laughing again. "Can you not simply give me a straight answer?" she said. "It is not difficult. Either you will or you won't."

He fought off a grin as he looked away. "I've not yet decided."

Her laughter came to an unnatural halt. "Is that so?"

He looked at her again, grinning. "I'm not going to admit anything until you do."

She turned her nose up at him. "I shall not admit anything either."

"Then we are at an impasse."

He was snorting. She could hear him. She was struggling hard not to grin when a figure suddenly appeared in the armory doorway. Because the sun was behind them, it was difficult to make out who it was.

Until it spoke.

"Here you are!" A man, older and smelling of ale, stumbled into the armory, glaring at Elysande. "I have been looking everywhere for you. Why did no one tell me Hereford and his son had arrived?"

Elysande stood up, followed by Westley. "We *did* tell you, Father," she said, irritation in her tone. "We told you but you were far gone with drink. We decided to wait until you were able to sleep it off before reminding you."

Marius du Nor scowled at his daughter. He was about to retort when it occurred to him that a very big man was standing next to her.

His scowl deepened.

"Who are you?" he demanded.

Westley remained cool in the face of the man's aggression. "I am Westley de Lohr, my lord," he said. "Shall I fetch my father for you?"

Marius looked him up and down as he realized who the man was. He seemed to calm down a great deal. "Christ, you're a beast," he muttered. "I saw you once when you were younger. You were a big lad, but not this big. So you've come to marry my daughter, have you?"

Westley's eyebrows lifted slightly. That was a question he and Elysande had been dancing around. They both knew that they were greatly opposed to this marriage. At least, they used to be. But the truth was that things had changed since yesterday. Westley still really didn't want to get married to anyone, but knowing he couldn't get out of this betrothal, he was rather glad that it was to Elysande. She wasn't as bad as his mind had made her out to be, and he hadn't thought he'd ever feel that way toward her, but he did.

Looking at Elysande, he answered.

"Aye, my lord," he said. "I have. Without reserve."

Elysande's eyes widened. "Truly?"

He took his attention off Marius to look at her. "Truly," he said, a smile spreading across his lips. "I hope that is agreeable."

Elysande's cheeks flushed the predictable red. She stammered over her words for a few seconds before letting out a chuckle of delight. "It is," she said. "If you are, then I am."

"Ella," Marius snapped, interrupting what was a touching moment between them, "go into the keep. Go in there and remain there. I must speak with Westley and his father and I do not want you present."

Elysande's expression became one of concern. "Why not?" she asked. "I am involved in this, Father. I have a right to know what is said."

Marius was displeased with her lack of obedience. "I told

you to go," he said sharply before turning to Westley. "Where is your father? Let us find him. There is much to discuss."

"Indeed, there *is* much to discuss," Christopher said, standing in the armory doorway with Esther beside him. "We saw you come from the keep, Marius. I was told you were not feeling well."

It was an unexpected appearance. Even Westley was surprised to see his father. Faced with Christopher de Lohr in the flesh, Marius seemed to falter in his reply.

"I do not know who told you such things, my lord," he said, his manner properly respectful. "I am well enough."

"Well enough and reeking of wine," Elysande muttered.

Marius heard her. Instantly enraged, he whirled on her. "What did you say?"

Elysande wasn't afraid of her father. For all of his anger and bitterness and posturing, he'd never once lashed out at her. He wasn't the hitting kind. But his rage could be quite intimidating at times.

"I said you reek of wine," she said. "It is not a secret that you have drowned yourself in barrels of wine since Emory's death, Father. If you think no one knows, then you are mistaken. *Everyone* knows. Lord Hereford arrived yesterday and you were sleeping off a binge in your solar and could not greet him. He had a right to know."

Marius was shocked and embarrassed. His face turned red and his mouth worked as if he wanted to say something, but nothing would come forth. It wasn't as if she'd said anything untrue. But he had hoped she wouldn't speak so openly of family business.

Especially when it involved Marius.

"I will not explain myself," he said, though he could not

look at Christopher. "We must all do as we must to live another day. But now that you are here, my lord, and your son is here, we have terms to discuss for this betrothal."

Christopher had some pity for a man who had lost his only son, so he didn't think too harshly of him and the fact that he really did reek of wine.

"The terms have already been established," he said. "You have asked me at least four times over the past several years if Westley was ready to marry and I have put you off. But I have decided this marriage will no longer be put off. It will take place tomorrow morning."

Of course, neither Westley nor Elysande had known that, nor did they know that it was a plot concocted by Christopher and Esther to see if the truce between Westley and Elysande was real enough. Westley appeared surprised at his father's announcement, looking at Elysande to see what her reaction would be, but she didn't seem to have much of one. When she caught him looking at her, she nodded. It was faint, but unmistakable.

That was good enough for Westley.

"We are agreeable," he said. "But shouldn't you wait for Mama?"

Christopher was pleasantly surprised that Westley was giving him absolutely no trouble at all with the coming nuptials. If that was the test of the validity of the truce, then it was evident that the truce was real. Westley, the man who had nearly beaten his brothers up when they tried to restrain him from running away from his wedding, seemed quite compliant about it, as if it was no trouble at all. And Elysande... She wasn't attacking anyone. She, too, seemed amenable to the idea.

Truthfully, Christopher was a little stunned.

"There is no telling how long your mother is going to be on her business," he said to Westley's question. "She instructed that you should marry immediately upon your arrival, so that is what we shall do. I am certain Lord Ledbury is agreeable also."

Marius looked at his daughter, who didn't seem rattled by Hereford's command. He'd been sober enough to know, at times, that she was opposed to the marriage, but her feelings were inconsequential to him. Still, he was hoping she wasn't going to put up a fight, but she was calm enough.

"Well?" he said, resigned and ill with an aching head. "If you have something to say about this, say it now and get it over with. Or are you going to let him do it for you?"

He was gesturing to Westley. Put on the spot, Elysande felt her cheeks threatening to flame again, but she fought it. Westley was looking at her, his eyes glimmering with warmth, and that gave her courage to do a complete turnabout in front of everyone who knew she was opposed to the marriage.

Westley included.

"I am agreeable," she said, as if daring anyone to disagree with her. "And if you must know, Westley and I have discussed things, Father. As we told Mother and Lord Hereford last night, we have come to a truce. There is no reason not to. It is not as if either of us can refuse this marriage, so we must make the best of it."

She smiled at Westley when she finished, which was a good thing. Otherwise, he might have thought her "we must make the best of it" comment suggested she really didn't want to go through with it after all. As if there was still some measure of rebellion there. But she seemed positive enough about it, so he didn't take offense. Truth be told, maybe there was still a tiny measure of rebellion in him, too, but every time he looked at her lovely face, it diminished just a little bit more. Soon, it would be nothing at all.

He was looking forward to that moment.

"Good," Christopher said, interrupting the soft expressions that Westley and Elysande were passing between them. "Lady Ledbury will send for a priest and we will have a prayer mass on the morrow. Marius, you and I must speak of your daughter's dowry and the title that is included for my son. I should like for him to be Lord Staunton by day's end tomorrow."

Marius, who was starting to feel a little sick now that the alcohol had worn off and his head was throbbing, simply nodded. "I have the necessary documents for it," he said, licking his dry lips and turning for the door. "Let us retreat to my solar to discuss. Bring your son."

Esther accompanied her husband out of the armory, followed by Christopher. Westley was supposed to follow but hung back, turning to Elysande.

"Well," he said, "it seems that it is done."

She nodded, her features tinged with warmth as she gazed at him. "Aye, it does."

"Are you happy?"

"Are you?"

He snorted. "Can you not give me a straight answer, woman?"

He was pretending to be irritated, but it was obvious that he wasn't. Elysande grinned. "I am not *un*happy," she said. "And you?"

"I am not unhappy, either," he said. "I must go with my father now, but I will see you when I am finished. Mayhap we can continue our conversation."

"I would like that," she said.

"Where may I find you?"

She shrugged, taking a step out of the armory and gazing toward the north side of the bailey. "Near the troop house, I suppose," she said. "I will be with Olan and Harker."

"Training?"

She nodded. "Aye."

He took a deep breath, looking as if he had something to say but hesitating to do it. He looked to the north, where the big troop house was, seeing men moving about.

"May I tell you something?" he finally said.

She looked at him curiously. "What is it?"

"I asked Harker not to train you anymore," he said.

Elysande was not pleased by that bit of news. "Why not?"

"Because I want to," he said. "My lady, I will not ask you not to do what you want to do, because clearly this is something you feel strongly about, but let me teach you properly. Will you at least let me do that? As your future husband, who wants the best for you?"

She wasn't truly upset when he put it that way. No one had ever truly wanted the best for her, and it was a rather good feeling. But she was curious about Westley's position on the subject.

"You do not think Harker is teaching me properly?" she asked.

Westley didn't want to disparage the man. "It is just as I told you," he said. "He serves you. I am afraid he may not be teaching you all of it in order to spare your feelings or keep you from getting hurt."

She opened her mouth to argue with him but thought better of it. "I was going to say that you are wrong, but clearly, you are not," she said. "After what happened earlier, you may be right."

"I do not think it is because they do not take you, or the training, seriously," he said. "But I do fear they are not teaching you like they should. If you are going to do this, you must do it right, because I would be greatly distressed were you to become hurt for lack of proper instruction."

Elysande thought his concern was sweet. "Very well," she said. "If you promise to teach me correctly."

"I will teach you correctly."

"And will you show me how to stand up to a man who tries to do to me what you did earlier today?"

"You mean stand up to a man who is charging you?"

"Aye."

He nodded, a glimmer in his eyes. "I will teach you how to use your mind and not your muscle," he said, tapping his head. "You can beat a man my size if you think it through. And that does not necessarily mean swinging a sword better than he can. It means outsmarting him."

Elysande liked the idea. "Then I will wait for you to finish with my father and we may proceed."

Westley nodded, prevented from replying when Christopher called to him, motioning him to follow. Westley glanced at his father, returning his focus to Elysande for a brief moment.

"Until later, Lady Elysande," he said softly.

"Ella," she said with equal softness. "You may call me Ella."

He flashed a smile. "Then you must call me Westley," he said. "Or West. I will answer to whatever you choose to call me, Ella."

"Even Goat?"

He burst out laughing. "Aye, even that, although I would be greatly insulted."

She was grinning. "Then I shall not call you that, I promise."

"Good."

With that, he gave her a wink and stepped through the doorway, heading after his father, leaving Elysande rather breathless with that display. The wink, the tone of his voice, was something she'd never experienced before.

And it had her heart racing.

With a grin, she sank back into the armory lest her men see her grinning like a fool. Knowing there was to be a wedding tomorrow—*her* wedding—had her thinking about things she'd never thought about before. Like clothing. She was to marry a de Lohr, after all. She couldn't wear her usual broadcloth. Unfortunately, she really didn't own anything very fine.

But her mother did.

With that in mind, Elysande headed for the keep.

CHAPTER TEN

"H E *WHAT*?" DUSTIN gasped. "He is actually… agreeable?"

It was just before sunset at Massington Castle and Lady Hereford had arrived with her two older daughters just as the sentries were switching posts for the coming night. Christopher, having been in the hall, was notified of his wife's arrival and met her carriage just as it came to a halt in the bailey. Truth be told, he found himself looking her over for war wounds, considering she'd gone to Daventry to do battle, and when she seemed sound and whole, he found himself looking his daughters over. Those two were even more prone to fighting than their mother was, but they, too, appeared unharmed.

He breathed a sigh of relief.

"Aye, he is agreeable," he told her. "Believe me when I tell you that I am as surprised as you are, but you'll not have to worry over him in this matter. With that established, I would like very much to know what happened with Daventry."

Dustin arched her back, stretching her muscles now that she was out of the carriage, but she waved off her husband's question.

"Nothing happened," she said. "Cedrica's mother confessed

that it was all a ploy to force Westley into marriage, so he is now free and clear of any impediments that might conflict with his marriage to Ledbury's daughter."

"A plot?" Christopher asked in dismay. "You're serious?"

"Completely," Dustin said. "But I had several uncomfortable and confrontational minutes with Daventry before his wife confessed. The man is a scheming lout, Chris. He is not a good ally and has little respect for me or for you. He was willing to do anything possible to ruin West's life, so we must make sure the man is treated as an enemy from now on. He is most definitely not an ally, but an opportunist."

Christopher's face hardened. "Thank God you discovered his plot," he said. "I do not know the man well, and he never struck me as ambitious, but he shall not be on my list of allies from now on."

Dustin lifted an eyebrow. "Tell him face to face," she said. "That will give me some satisfaction against the way I was treated."

"With pleasure."

Dustin could see he meant it. Her husband didn't like small-minded individuals, so he was ready to take them to task. He'd been doing it for over fifty years. Smiling, she wound her hand into his.

"Now," she said, "greet your daughters, for they were instrumental in helping me against Daventry. And then you can take us to the hall and feed us. I am famished."

Christin and Brielle were standing behind their mother, with Brielle helping Christin with a seam in her cloak that had come undone.

"Lady de Sherrington," Christopher said to his girls. "Lady de Velt. Tell me what truly happened. Given what I have been told, I suspect that, in reality, your mother took a club to Daventry, but you will tell me the truth."

Dustin rolled her eyes as Christin grinned. "Mama was fearsome, as always," she said. "But she is right—Daventry showed little respect for her. Brielle nearly clobbered the man."

"Ah." Christopher looked at his tall, blonde daughter. "My Valkyrie returns. We've not seen her in some time."

"You still did not," Brielle said, finishing fixing Christin's cloak. "Mama would not let me physically engage the man, so there was no violence. Only spoken threats. But it is over now, and I must say I am glad. Cedrica de Steffan is not someone we would want in our family. She was willing to lie straight to Mama's face about the situation."

Christopher waggled his eyebrows. "Then I daresay we are glad everything turned out as it did," he said. "Now, Westley shall marry Lady Elysande and hopefully all will be well. He seems to have changed his mind quite drastically about her, so she evidently has some appeal to him. Would you and your sister mind befriending her? If she is to be one of us, we may as well start somewhere."

Brielle and Christin nodded. "She is closer in age to my daughters than she is to me," Christin said. "But I am happy to do what I can."

Brielle had her hands on her head, fixing one of the iron pins holding her braided hair in its careful coif. "Speaking of children, I must return to Lioncross as soon as the wedding is over," she said. "My younger children have been with their nurse since my departure to Daventry, and they have a habit of bending the woman to their will. Armand and Rafe are particularly manipulative. We'll return to find they've taken over Lioncross and all is mayhem."

She was speaking of her younger sons, both of them under ten years of age, and both of them full of fire. Bright and creative and ruthless—unless their father got involved, and then they were not so brave. But Christopher loved those particular traits about them.

"What did you expect when you married de Velt blood?" he said. "Your children have very unique de Lohr and de Velt bloodlines and their grandfathers are two of the greatest warlords England has ever seen. In fact, Armand looks exactly like Jax, down to the shape of his eyebrows. Of course they will try to conquer Lioncross. I would expect nothing less, and neither would Jax."

Brielle looked at her father drolly. "Do you expect to get it back?" she asked. "If Armand is just like Jax, then you know he will take it and keep it, so do you really expect to have your property returned?"

"After much negotiation, I do."

Brielle broke down into soft laughter. "You are a dreamer, Papa," she said. "But let us speak of something other than your warmongering grandchildren. Has the wedding even been arranged yet?"

"Tomorrow morning," Christopher said. "You can leave afterward and ward off the conquering army."

"Good," Brielle said. "In fact, we should all probably leave. Westley has a new life to begin and will not want us hanging about."

Dustin was forced to agree. "That is true," she said, looking at Christopher. "He is going to live here, is he not?"

"It will be his property someday," Christopher said. "I told him he needed to spend some time here getting to know it."

"Did he seem agreeable?"

"Not at the time," Christopher said. "But I think that opinion has changed. At least, I hope it has. Now, come into the hall and I will find you food and drink."

No one argued with him. They were weary from a night sleeping in the carriage and almost a full day on the road from Daventry. Hungry, the women started to follow Christopher into the hall, but Brielle held her sister back. They waited until their mother and father were well ahead of them, out of earshot, before Brielle spoke.

"How does Papa look to you?" she asked her sister.

Christin turned her gaze toward the elderly couple entering the hall. "No worse than he has lately," she said. "No better, but no worse. Why?"

Brielle sighed, her focus shifting to her parents as well. "Because," she muttered, "you know that I brought the children to Lioncross in the warmer weather because Mama wrote to me and told me that Papa was not faring well, so I moved quickly to come."

"I know," Christin said quietly. "But let us be honest—he's not been well for the past ten years."

Brielle wasn't comforted by that comment. "I left my husband behind because he could not travel with us at the moment," she said. "I came running because of Mama's missive, and when I arrived, it was to Papa looking… exhausted. I do not think he was as bad as Mama suggested in her missive, but he did not look well. He looked worse to me. You live with him every day, Chrissy. You know what I mean."

Christin nodded. "I do," she said. "And Mama was not wrong in her missive. Papa has been worse this spring, plagued by terrible headaches and trouble breathing at times. He is a very old man, Brie. He probably should have passed on years ago, but still, he hangs on. Sherry and I have been watching him deteriorate, slowly, simply because of his age. But his mind remains sharp. So does his determination to do what our father has always done."

Brielle looked at her. "And what is that?"

Christin smiled ironically. "Be our father," she said simply. "The fact that he is here with West speaks volumes. He is going to oversee this wedding personally, as he has with all of ours. That means that a very old man must travel to see to it, and we could not have stopped him. Thank God it was not too terribly far."

Brielle shook her head at her father, a man who simply couldn't stay still when there was work to be done regarding his family. "Small mercies, I suppose," she said. "But I will admit it has been comforting to return home and see that Sherry is still in command of Papa's army and men. He takes such a burden off him and has for many years."

Christin nodded. "Over thirty years," she said. "Sherry came to Lioncross when we were first married because Papa asked him to. He knew that Sherry didn't have property or anything to inherit, so he made him another son, really. All of our brothers except for Westley have their own homes and commands, but Sherry... He is married to me, the eldest child of Mama and Papa's marriage. He was always content to serve at Papa's side when he knew our brothers had their destinies."

"But what happens when Papa passes on?" Brielle asked, feeling distraught even thinking of such an event. "Curtis will inherit Lioncross. Will Sherry stay? Will you stay?"

"It is my home," Christin said, smiling faintly. "I was born there, as were you. All of my children were born there. Curtis has already stated that he does not wish to leave Brython Castle, where his wife was born. He only just reclaimed it, in fact, after living at Monmouth for a few years. Elle is Welsh and their children are half Welsh, so he feels that it is important to remain at Brython for now. Lioncross will go to Sherry and I. It will remain our home and our seat. We will protect Papa's legacy."

Brielle didn't know if she felt better or worse about that. Alexander and Christin had spent all of their marital years living at Lioncross Abbey and Alexander, a very accomplished knight and agent, had remained with Christopher because of his wife. Or perhaps because he wanted to. Brielle was never sure, but Christin made it seem that it was Alexander's decision.

She wondered if that were really true.

"I hate that we are even discussing this," Brielle said. "I hate that we have moved into a time of life where our parents are getting old and death is inevitable at some point. Even now, as I look at Papa—he looks exhausted, but he also looks pale. His lips are very pale. He should be resting instead of dealing with all of this."

Christin lifted her shoulders weakly. "Then let us go into the hall, eat with him, and then force him to rest," she said as she turned toward the great hall. "If he refuses, we will hold him down, tie him up, and carry him to bed ourselves."

Brielle chuckled, following her sister into the great hall, where their parents had already taken seats at the dais and servants were beginning to set out the beginnings of the evening meal. The smell of fresh bread and roasting meat lured them like a magic spell, and they were eager to settle down for a decent meal.

But if it was peace they were looking for, this was not the night to find it.

Bad tidings were on the approach.

CHAPTER ELEVEN

WESTLEY KNEW HIS mother and older sisters had arrived toward sunset because he saw the carriage enter the bailey. They were traveling in the larger and more fortified de Lohr carriage, one that was like a prison on wheels. It was so heavily fortified that the "Rolling Fortress" was exactly what they called it. When one was traveling with women, however, that was the carriage to take.

Surprisingly, Westley had spent the day with Marius walking the perimeter of Massington alongside Harker and Olan. Marius was suffering through his first truly sober moment in nearly two years, ever since that horrible day when his son had been killed. It had happened near the gatehouse, so it was difficult for him to show Westley the structure and not remember seeing Emory astride the horse that threw him into a wall. Emory had laughed it off, but the truth was that he'd hit his head. Hard. Everyone thought he was fine until an hour later when he developed a horrible headache. Shortly thereafter, he'd lost consciousness and died the next day. A swollen brain, the physic had said. The hit on the wall had been hard enough to bruise his brain—and once that happened, there was nothing to be done.

God, how Marius hated that gatehouse.

But he'd taken Westley through it anyway.

Of course, Westley hadn't known any of that, and neither Harker nor Olan had mentioned it. That wasn't their right. They'd simply followed silently, each man to his own thoughts, which included one man greatly resenting the privileged de Lohr son because he would be marrying the woman he loved, while the other was thinking that de Lohr was too arrogant for his own good. Different men, different thoughts.

All of them in turmoil.

But it all became too much for Marius. His head was throbbing and he felt sick, so he begged off from any further conversation later in the afternoon and disappeared. Harker disappeared as well, but Olan remained for a short time, talking about the fine Belgian horses in the stables and how Marius liked to breed the mares with Spanish Jennets to create a more agile horse. He evidently sold them for a great deal, and Westley very much wanted to talk to Marius more about his horses because he, too, had a great deal of knowledge and affection for them. Their conversation was cut short, however, when Olan was called away, leaving Westley on his own to wander the grounds and inspect his future home.

A home that came with a woman he was increasingly interested in.

In fact, even though his mother and sisters had arrived, he didn't go to greet them. Not right away. He wanted to introduce his mother to Elysande, the woman he hadn't wanted to marry. The woman who'd caused him to fight his brothers for a chance to escape her. The woman he'd been ignoring for the past ten years. He wanted to see his mother's face when he introduced

Elysande without any reservation at all. He suspected his father would tell her first, but she probably wouldn't believe it until she saw it.

His mother was hard to convince that way.

Seeing that his father had met up with his mother when she entered Massington, Westley headed for the keep. He knew Elysande was no longer in the armory because he'd been there, so he could only assume she'd gone inside. He went to the keep entry but didn't enter because to do so without invitation, when women were in residence, was considered inappropriate. Therefore, he sent a female servant to seek audience with Elysande, and the servant returned with an invitation to enter.

Gladly, he did.

"Sir Westley?"

A disembodied voice called to him as he came through the door. He paused, looking around to see where it was coming from.

"Where are you?" he called.

The door to his left immediately opened and he could see a hand waving at him. "Here we are," Esther said. "Come in, my lord. Join us."

Westley went to the door, surveying the interior before he entered. It was a small chamber, with a festive hearth, and it looked very much like a woman's chamber. There was a loom, baskets of wool, and sewing kits among other things. A fat orange cat sat on a stool near the fire, dozing. Esther was sitting near the door in a comfortable chair while Elysande sat on the other side of the chamber with a mass of red silk in her hands.

And she didn't look happy.

"Since we are to have a wedding tomorrow, Ella thought she should wear something lovely," Esther said, fully aware of how much it was embarrassing her daughter to say so. "She doesn't have much of anything that is serviceable, as she would never allow me to make such a thing for her, so we are having to alter one of my gowns for her. Ella, show him."

Red-faced, Elysande held up the red silk. Westley could see the sleeves and a ripped seam. He could also see that Elysande's fingers were wrapped up with cloth, and he could see small pinpricks of bloodstains.

His brow furrowed.

"What happened to your fingers?" he asked.

Esther answered. "My daughter has many talents, but sewing is not one of them," she said. "She stabbed herself many a time with the needle as she worked."

Elysande let the dress drop to her lap as she rolled her eyes. "Mother," she said, "do you have to say such things?"

Westley wasn't the best at reading women, but he could sense that Elysande was mortified by her mother's comments. He went over to her, crouching down next to her as she avoided eye contact with him.

"It does not matter to me what you wear," he said quietly. "I suspect that you could make a peasant's dress look beautiful. Wear what makes you happy, not what you think you should wear."

She looked at him then, gratitude in her eyes. "You may as well know that I have never been one for fanciful clothing," she said. "I've never regretted that until now, so I asked my mother if she had something I could wear."

He shrugged. "If it pleases you, wear it."

"She was hoping it would please *you*," Esther said.

Elysande dropped her head again as her mother's bombardment of embarrassment continued. But Westley simply smiled.

"If she wants to wear her usual clothing to our wedding, then she should," he said. "I am marrying the woman, not her manner of dress."

Esther wasn't dense. She knew that her daughter was ashamed, but that was a good thing. Elysande never thought about clothing or jewels, but now that she was to become the wife of a great knight, those were things she would need to consider.

"That is true, my lord, but how she dresses will directly reflect on your ability as a husband to provide for her," she said. "She is no longer a maiden who can wear what she pleases and no one will take notice. She is to marry a de Lohr son and become a member of a great house. If she wants to reflect well upon you, she must wear clothing more appropriate to her station."

That was true. Even Westley knew that. He'd seen the knights at court and their bejeweled wives. The prettiest wives, the best-dressed wives, were often spoken of and admired. His brothers had all married beautiful and well-dressed women, very kind women who would be more than happy to help Elysande become acclimated. But, truthfully, he felt sorry for her. She was a free spirit, completely unaware of her beauty, and he admired that. He admired a woman who didn't care what others thought.

Even her mother.

"I want you to wear what makes you happy," he repeated. "I will be happy if you are happy. If you want to wear the red dress, then wear it. But if you do not, then don't let others convince you it is for the best."

Elysande looked up from her lap again, a weak smile on her

lips. "I do want to wear it," she said. "If a woman is going to look beautiful, then it should be on her wedding day."

"If you want my opinion, I think you look beautiful every day."

Her smile broadened and her cheeks turned the predictable shade of red. "How would you know?" she said. "You have only seen me since yesterday."

He put his hand over hers. "I only have to see you one day to know that your beauty does not give way in the face of a new day," he said. "But I will reiterate what I said—it does not matter to me what you wear. I will be happy with whatever you're happy with."

His words gave her confidence. "Then I shall try not to disappoint, I promise."

He gave her hand a squeeze before letting go. "Speaking of disappointment, my mother has arrived," he said. "She will, indeed, be disappointed if I do not bring you to meet her."

Esther, who had been listening to the rather sweet conversation, suddenly threw her sewing aside. "We have guests?" she said, standing up quickly. "Why did no one tell me? Ella, get upstairs and find something adequate to meet your betrothed's mother in. Hurry!"

They were flying out of the chamber. Elysande nearly bowled Westley over in her haste, and he had to steady himself as she fled. But he quickly found his feet, following her into the foyer as she began to take the stairs.

"You do not have to change your clothing," he called after her. "My mother will appreciate that you do not own anything fine. That means you are not after de Lohr money!"

The last few words were shouted because she had disappeared from his view. When she didn't answer, he knew she probably hadn't heard him. Or she didn't care. He was puzzled because he'd never said anything to her about the way she looked or the way she dressed other than to tell her to wear what made her happy. But given how her mother had responded to him and told him of the red dress they were altering for the wedding mass, he suspected Esther was behind Elysande's sudden preoccupation with clothing. Westley had developed a hearty respect for mothers in general from the day he was born.

He wasn't going to get in the middle of it.

As Westley sat down at the base of the stairs to wait for his betrothed to reappear in suitable clothing, Elysande and her mother had made their way into Elysande's chamber to comb through her limited clothing. Everything she had was stored in a big wardrobe, a heavy thing that had come from Nevele Castle and possessed the du Nor family crest, which was a sword with a decapitated head piked on it. It was carved into the doors, quite expertly done, but the artwork had faded over the years from hands grabbing the doors to open them.

Even now, Esther had flung open the wardrobe and begun furiously moving through the few things that were there. The only thing she had that would be remotely appropriate for an audience with a countess was a green linen overdress with a natural linen sheath underneath. Though linen wasn't usually dyed, this one had been by an old seamstress who used grass as the dye. It was a beautiful green color that had been made for Elysande when she was younger at the insistence of her tutor at Warwick. So many other fostering girls had fine clothing, and with Elysande dressing like a peasant child, the tutor had insisted the finer dress be made.

But it was too small.

Elysande had grown up and filled out, but that didn't matter to Esther. She couldn't loan her daughter unaltered clothing because she was too short and too full in the bustline, so the green dress would have to suffice until something new and finer could be made. Once the green dress was decided on, Esther fled down the stairs to greet Lady Hereford in the hall and wait for her daughter and Westley, who was camped out on the bottom step of the flight of stairs, to join them. Esther ran past him and told him to wait for Elysande, which he gladly agreed to do.

Meanwhile, Elysande proceeded to strip off the broadcloth she was wearing. The old leather girdle came off first, followed by the overdress with the bib and open sides. She had a dirty shift underneath, and just as she went to remove it, the chamber door opened and Freddie entered.

Elysande hissed at her.

"Help me," she said. "Lady Hereford is here and I must dress in something appropriate or she will hate me and the wedding will be ended before it even starts. Hurry!"

Freddie, who had come up to the chamber bearing watered wine and the small apples that Elysande liked to snack on, came rushing over to her, seeing the green dress on the bed.

"You're wearing *that*?" she asked, incredulous.

Elysande rolled her eyes. "That is all I have," she said. "My mother has insisted. Where is my soap? Is there any water that I can use to quickly wash? I was training earlier today and surely must have dirt on my face and neck. I cannot be introduced to Lady Hereford looking like a barn animal."

Freddie went to work, collecting soap and rags from the wardrobe and then running into the next chamber, Esther's chamber, to collect rosewater that had been brought up to the woman that morning. It was cold, and stale, but that didn't matter. It was good enough. As Elysande took a wet rag and soap and began to scrub her face, Freddie did the same with her neck and arms.

"The only thing Sir Westley has said about his mother is that when she opens her mouth, they run," Elysande said, eyes closed as she wiped the white, slimy foam over her forehead. "Something tells me that she is as terrifying as my mother is."

Freddie was scrubbing her left arm, which had dirt on it from the protection she'd been wearing. "I heard what happened this morning," she said. "Sir Westley pushed you down whilst you were training?"

Eyes closed, Elysande was scrubbing her right cheek. "He did *not* push me down," she said flatly. "He was showing me how a knight charges and I tripped over my feet. I am unharmed."

Freddie rinsed off her arm. "That is good, because I should not like for you to marry a brute, not when…" She abruptly stopped what she was saying and continued with something else. "I saw the de Lohr carriage arrive with its escort. Some of the men were in the kitchen, procuring food for the escort. They evidently left Daventry without any supplies."

Elysande grabbed for a clean, wet rag and rinsed off her face. "Daventry?" she said. "Lady Hereford was in Daventry?"

"Aye," Freddie said. "From what I heard."

Elysande finally opened her eyes as she continued to wipe down her face. "What were you going to say?"

"When?"

"When you suddenly stopped and began speaking on the de Lohr carriage?"

Freddie didn't answer right away, which caused Elysande to look at her. "Well?" she said. "What were you going to say?"

Freddie was scrubbing Elysande's right arm. "I thought not to tell you what I heard," she said, refusing to look at her. "But if you are to marry this man, then you should know."

"Know what?"

Freddie's scrubbing slowed. "I was in the kitchen replenishing the watered wine," she said. "I was there when the de Lohr men arrived and they were speaking of the journey to Daventry and why they were there."

Elysande shrugged. "They were there escorting Lady Hereford, I would assume."

Freddie nodded. "Aye, that is true, but she was there for a reason," she said. "Ella, do you remember Cedrica de Steffan?"

Elysande didn't hesitate. "Of course I do," she said. "You know that Daventry is not far from here. Her mother and my mother were friends, once, and Lady Daventry would come to visit and bring Cedrica when I was very young. I remember Cedrica always wanted to play in the kitchen yard, with the chickens."

"Why did your mother stop entertaining Lady Daventry?"

Elysande shook her head. "I do not know," she said. "Mayhap they simply lost touch with one another. They both had children, families to tend to. My mother has never said anything about her in a negative fashion, so I cannot answer your question. But why are you asking me so many questions about Cedrica and Lady Daventry?"

"Because Lady Hereford went to see Cedrica."

Elysande turned back to the water, rinsing out her rag in it. "Oh?" she said. "She knows Cedrica?"

Freddie hesitated. "She knows her," she said. "More importantly, Westley knows her. I heard… I heard that Cedrica is with child. *Westley's* child. Lady de Lohr went to Daventry to pay her money so she would not tell anyone and it would not interfere with your marriage to Westley."

Elysande froze, mid-wash. With wide eyes, she turned to Freddie.

"You heard that?" she gasped.

Freddie nodded fearfully. "The de Lohr soldiers must have told some of our soldiers, because our servants heard about it," she said. "The cook told me. You know how rumors spread like wildfire, Ella. But in this case, I thought you should know. You are to marry a man who has bedded another woman, and she carries his child."

Elysande stared at her. For several long and painful moments, all she could do was stare at her as she processed what Freddie had told her. When it finally sank in, she let go of the rag in her hand and dropped onto her bed, stunned.

"My God," she breathed. "Is it really true?"

Freddie set her own rag down and went to Elysande's side. "That is what they said," she said gently, seeing how upset her cousin was. "Mayhap you should ask him?"

Elysande felt as if she'd been hit in the gut. All of the air had drained out of her along with everything else. She felt ill. Nay… more than ill. Her chest ached. Her head hurt. The man who had pretended to show her so much attention and care had evidently shown that care and attention to others, too.

Perhaps that had been his game all along.

And she had trusted him.

She'd trusted him when he told her that he wanted to train her. She'd trusted him when he was kind to her, when he told her she was beautiful. He'd even winked at her and made her feel things she'd never felt before. All the while, she'd believed him. He'd rolled out a deception and she had willingly accepted it.

She'd accepted *him*.

She felt like a fool.

"Freddie," she finally said, her voice quivering, "I want you to do something for me."

Freddie nodded anxiously. "Anything you wish," she said. "What would you have me do?"

Elysande realized that she felt very much like crying, and it was an effort for her not to break down. "I want you to go into the hall and tell my mother what you have told me," she said steadily. "Tell her in private, where Hereford cannot hear. Then you will tell my mother to ask Lady Hereford if this is true. Let my mother deal with this situation, for I will not."

Freddie looked at her curiously. "What will you do?"

Elysande took a long, deep breath, struggling to keep her composure. "I will finish bathing and then I will go to bed," she said. "If anyone asks, my head is aching and I have gone to sleep. I am not to be disturbed, not by anyone. Not by my mother, not by Westley. I just want to… sleep."

Freddie nodded, seeing how truly distraught her cousin was. She knew Elysande enough to know that. She was sorry to be the bearer of such news, but as she'd told her cousin, Elysande had a right to know the character of the man she was to marry.

Even if it hurt.

Once Freddie departed the chamber and slipped down the servant stairs on her way to the hall, avoiding Westley in the entry completely, Elysande bolted the door behind her and also bolted the connecting door to her mother's chamber. Then she proceeded to finish bathing with the soap and cold rosewater before donning a heavy sleeping shift, combing her hair and braiding it, and then climbing into bed and pulling the coverlet over her head.

Then, and only then, did she allow herself the comfort of hot tears.

She wept.

CHAPTER TWELVE

L ADY LEDBURY HAD come into the hall and introduced herself to Lady Hereford before she had been called out again. It had been a brief appearance that could have been construed as rude, but Dustin wasn't offended by it. She was rather glad for it because that left her, Christopher, Brielle, and Christin at the dais alone, enjoying meat pies, warmed wine, and good conversation. It was a pleasant moment in an otherwise unpleasant trip thus far.

Marius' whereabouts were unknown, and men were just starting to trickle in for the evening's meal. While Dustin, Christin, and Brielle finished their meals and relaxed with some of Marius' excellent wine, the conversations revolving mostly around Christin's eldest sons and potential wives, Christopher had eaten very little because he wanted to wait for Westley and hopefully Marius. He had no idea where Westley was, and was wondering if he should send one of the de Lohr men out to look for him. He was pondering that very thing when Lady Ledbury returned, marching all the way to the dais.

And she did not look pleased.

Dustin caught sight of the woman.

"Ah, Lady Ledbury," she said, her belly full and quite possibly too much drink in her veins. "My daughters and I were just wondering if you had another daughter or a niece somewhere. My grandson is in need of a wife."

As Brielle burst into snorts of laughter, Christin moved quickly to circumvent her mother's matchmaking.

"Andrew is *not* in need of a wife at this moment," she said, mostly to Esther. "He has just celebrated his day of birth and is, mayhap, old enough to start considering a wife now."

"Old enough?" Brielle said, incredulous. "Chrissy, the man has seen thirty years and seven. He is older than West."

As Christin turned around to shush her mouthy sister, Esther focused on Dustin. "And it is about your son that I come, Lady Hereford," she said stiffly. "I must ask you a question, and I should expect an honest answer."

Finally, Dustin was starting to catch on to the woman's uptight attitude. She looked at her curiously. "I shall always give you an honest answer, Lady Ledbury," she said. "What did you wish to ask?"

"Did your son impregnate Lady Daventry's daughter?"

Brielle, who had been mid-gulp with her wine, nearly choked on it as Dustin eyed Esther. The mood around the table, peaceful and warm only moments before, now plummeted. Suspicion was in the air. Setting her own wine down, Dustin stood up to face the accusation.

"Nay," she said slowly. "He did not. And I would be very careful with what you say next when it comes to Westley. If it is anything unkind, you'll not like my reaction."

Esther was still clearly furious. "Then why did you go to Daventry?" she asked. "Word has reached my ears that you went to give Cedrica de Steffan money to keep quiet about her de Lohr bastard lest it impede your son's marriage to my daughter. What truth is there in this rumor?"

Dustin was growing angry. Angry and a little drunk, which was a bad combination. She was first and foremost angry with Westley for putting himself in this position, but she was also furious with the de Lohr escort because she knew the word must have come from them. It was not a coincidence that her party arrived from Daventry at the same time the rumor was going around. She knew that soldiers liked to gossip. That was simply the way of things, how news reached people. But in this case, this was not news to spread.

It was a struggle to fight down her rage.

"Cedrica de Steffan is a trollop," she said flatly. "She and her father conspired to coerce Westley into a marriage with Cedrica because no decent man will have her. So, they lied about Cedrica being pregnant. I went there to discover the truth of the matter and was told, by Lady Daventry herself, that her daughter and husband had lied. If you do not believe me, ask Lady Daventry. She will tell you. Is that enough of an explanation for you? Or should I use smaller words so you will understand?"

Esther's fury was cut short with Dustin's quite logical explanation, but it was sparked again by the insult.

"Where my daughter's life and future happiness is concerned, I have every right to ask the question," she said hotly. "You will notice I *asked* about it. I did not accuse your son of it, nor did I accuse you of hiding it. But you should have told me about this. Did you think I would not hear?"

Dustin sighed sharply. "I do not care what you hear," she said. "And you did, indeed, ask your questions in a most accusing and outrageous tone. Even if your words did not convey your belief in his guilt, the timbre of your voice most certainly did. And my journey to Daventry is none of your affair. It is between my husband, myself, and Lord Daventry. You are not part of that equation."

Esther wasn't going to back down. "Mayhap I am not, but my daughter is," she said. "Why would they accuse Westley of such a thing? Was he courting Cedrica when he was betrothed to my daughter?"

"He was not courting Cedrica, Lady Ledbury," Christopher spoke up. He had to or his wife was going to start throwing punches. "But, much like your daughter, he did not wish to be married. Your daughter attacked Westley the moment he came through the gatehouse, and I did not indignantly challenge you over the fact, though I could have. I understood the situation where it pertained to Lady Elysande, as you should understand the situation where it pertains to Westley. He was simply acting out. He did not court anyone, but I would be lying if I said there were not a few maidens who caught his attention. But nothing more than that."

Christopher's words calmed Esther down, but Dustin was riled up with the new information.

"Elysande *attacked* Westley?" she said to her husband, aghast. "When were you going to tell me this?"

Christopher held up a calming hand. "There was no reason to tell you," he insisted softly. "The situation has resolved itself. They are both agreeable to the marriage now, so it is of no consequence."

Dustin frowned, preparing to argue, but Christin spoke up. "Where *is* Westley?" she asked no one in particular. "And where is Lady Elysande?"

Christopher shook his head. "I do not know where he is,"

he said, turning his attention to Esther. "Is he with your daughter?"

Esther shook her head. "Ella is in her chamber," she said. "I was told that she has heard this rumor and was… upset."

Christopher grunted with regret. "Lady Ledbury, you may believe my wife when she tells you that the Daventry situation was simply a greedy man and his greedy daughter trying to trap West into marriage," he said, moving away from the table. "I suggest you go and tell your daughter that while I try to find Westley. If the two have had words, then there is no telling the state he is in."

"I will go with you, Papa," Christin said, quickly moving after her father. But she glanced over her shoulder at her sister. "Stay with Mama, Brie."

She held out her hand in a motion that suggested Brielle try to keep their mother calm. Sort of a tamping-down motion with her open palm, something that indicated the suppression of a rising anger. Brielle understood, moving between her mother and Esther to ease the two of them down and ensure they didn't fall out in any way.

It wouldn't do for the mothers of the bride and groom to perform fisticuffs.

Christin caught up to her father by the time he departed the great hall and headed out into the night. The bailey was lit up by the aura of dozens of torches as a cold, clear night descended. Men were on the walls, vigilant, and they were gathered at the gatehouse. That was usual at Massington, as the only real way to enter the place was, indeed, through the gatehouse because of all of the earthworks beyond the walls.

But Christopher wasn't looking at any of it. He was focused ahead, on the tower that housed visitors, where he and Westley had been staying. Christin walked alongside him, noting that his gait seemed slow. Now that Brielle had said something to her about him, she was noticing everything. Maybe he really *was* looking pale and poorly, and because she saw him daily, she simply hadn't noticed. Now, she was paranoid.

"Where are we going?" she asked him.

He pointed to the tower. "That is where West and I have been housed," he said. "We will look for him there first."

"And if he is not there?"

"Then we summon de Lohr men and scour the grounds for him."

That seemed like enough of a plan. The tower room turned up empty, however, and as they were heading back to the gatehouse to send a runner for the de Lohr escort, which was scattered, Christin happened to glance over at the keep.

"Papa," she said, pulling him to a halt. "Let's look in the keep. He might be there."

Christopher nearly refused but thought better of it. It wouldn't hurt to inspect it for his own peace of mind. "He should not be in there," he said. "His betrothed is presumably in there, which would make his presence inappropriate."

Christin shrugged. "It would not be the first time West has broken rules."

Christopher grunted, conceding the fact. "True."

They continued over to the keep in relative silence, although Christin could hear her father's breathing. He sounded winded. *Stop imagining things!* she scolded herself. The entry to the keep loomed before them, with wooden stairs leading to a first-floor entry above. That was fairly typical in most castles, as wooden stairs could be burned and the keep sealed in the event of an attack.

Christin led the way up the stairs, as her father seemed to be slowing down. In fact, it took him quite some time to get up the steps, and by the time he hit the top, he was nearly panting. Concerned, Christin opened her mouth to ask him how he was feeling, but Christopher spotted something through the cracked-open door.

"West?" he said.

Christin spun around to see her brother sitting on the bottom step of the mural stairs leading to the upper floors. The torches had been lit inside the keep, giving off a goodly amount of light, so it was no trouble at all to see him clearly. She followed Christopher into the keep, right up to Westley as he sat on the stairs.

"What are you doing here?" Christin asked before Christopher could. "We have been looking for you."

"Why?" Westley asked, seemingly unconcerned. "I am waiting for Lady Elysande to come down the stairs, though she has taken quite a long time. Do women always take this much time to dress?"

Christin and Christopher looked at one another in confusion. "Then... you have not spoken to her?" Christopher asked. "Recently, I mean?"

Westley stood up, stretching because he'd been sitting for so long. "I spoke to her before she went up the stairs," he said. "Why?"

Christopher wasn't sure how to answer him because the timeline of what he knew and what was happening didn't match up. "And you haven't seen Lady Ledbury?" he asked.

Westley shook his head. "Not for quite some time," he said. "Why are you asking these questions?"

"Because somehow, rumors of why Mama was at Daventry

have gone around Massington," Christin told him. "Lady Ledbury was in the hall just now demanding to know if Cedrica de Steffan was pregnant with your child and if Mama had gone to Daventry to pay the family off. She was quite upset about it."

Now Westley was showing some concern as he realized why his sister and father were asking questions.

"Damnation," he spat. "How did she find out?"

Christin gave him a wry expression. "How do you think?" she said. "None of us would say anything, of course. The escort must have spoken about it, and it not only got to Lady Ledbury, but also to Lady Elysande. Lady Ledbury said her daughter was most upset about it."

It occurred now to Westley why Elysande hadn't come downstairs. The more he thought about it, the more upset he became.

"Christ," he grumbled, running his fingers through his hair in a fraught gesture. "She did not know about it when she went to her chamber to change her clothing. I would stake my life on that. So she must have been told while she was dressing."

Christin, too, could see what had happened. "She undoubtedly had a maid helping her, a maid who would have repeated what she'd heard," she said. "I am sorry, West. I know that—"

Suddenly, Westley was bolting up the stairs with Christin running after him, calling to him and begging him to slow down. Christopher was moving slower, also calling to his son, pleading with him to show restraint. By the time Christopher finally reached the level where Elysande's chamber was located, Westley was at the door, knocking on it gently, asking her to open it. Christin, standing a few feet behind him, turned to her father and sadly shook her head. Christopher stood there for a moment, catching his breath, before going to his son and pulling him away from the door.

"Step back," he said quietly. "Back, Westley, back. Stay with your sister. Let me speak to your betrothed."

Westley wanted to argue with him, but Christin pulled him back, away from the door. When Christopher was certain that Westley wasn't going to try to charge again, he went to the door and stood near the seam where it met the frame.

"Lady Elysande?" he said loudly. "This is Lord Hereford. I realize my presence outside of your door is not entirely appropriate, but given the circumstances, I hope you will forgive me. We have just been informed that a rumor regarding Westley and Lord Daventry's daughter has reached your ears and that you are understandably upset. As I am a man of principle, and I do not lie, I hope you will believe my words when I tell you that the rumor you heard was, in truth, a plot by Lord Daventry and his daughter to force Westley into a marriage. She was not pregnant. What you heard was simply gossip and most of it was wrong. I swear this upon my oath."

He waited for some measure of a reply for a few moments, turning to look at Westley as he stood there with Christin. His son had an expression on his face that Christopher had never seen before, something between hope and fear. That truce that Westley had with Elysande seemed to be more than a truce at that point. Christopher had hoped for at least a peaceful existence between the pair even if they didn't agree with the betrothal, but the expression on Westley's face told Christopher that it was more than just a ceasefire.

Something more had been established.

Something... hopeful.

If that was the case, then Christopher felt sorry for Westley, who had never really had any one woman he was fond of. He loved women in general, of course, and had had his share of female companionship, but the woman he was to marry didn't seem to be part of that general crowd.

She was evidently different.

Realizing that, Christopher knocked on the door again. "My lady?" he said again. "Did you hear me?"

There was a long pause before a muffled voice came through the door. "I hear you, my lord," Elysande said. "Thank you for your explanation. I believe you."

"Will you open the door?"

Another pause. "Forgive me, but I am not feeling well," she said. "Please accept my apologies, to you and your lady wife. I will see you on the morrow, if I may."

Christopher moved away from the door and went to his son. "If you let her sleep on this news without explaining the situation from your perspective, any building trust might be lost," he muttered. "Tell her the truth, West. But be kind. This is a delicate situation."

Westley nodded and headed over to the door. Christopher pulled Christin with him toward the stairs, and they descended a few steps before Christopher came to a halt and Christin with him. Together, they monitored the situation from afar as Westley sank to his buttocks against the door, hanging his head as he pondered what he was going to say to Elysande now that his father had her attention.

This was an important moment.

He didn't want to make a mess of things.

"Ella," he said, lifting his voice, "I think it is fair to say that two days ago, we would have both welcomed this news as a way to break our betrothal. The Elysande who charged me when I came through the gatehouse would have been very happy to hear this. But I suspect the Elysande of today was not happy to hear it. I think it upset her greatly, and for that, I am deeply sorry. Please know that I would never deliberately hurt you, by deed or by word. That is the truth."

He waited a few moments for her to reply, but when it became clear she wasn't going to, he continued.

"I will tell you the truth of the situation because you deserve it," he said. "I will tell you here and now that I will never lie to you. That is dishonorable, and I am not a dishonorable man. What my father told you about the situation is the first time I've heard of the plot to trap me into marriage, but it makes sense given the circumstances. The truth is that I have spent the past ten years pretending our betrothal did not exist. I like women and they like me. Cedrica de Steffan was a woman I kept company with on occasion, but there was no deeper connection between us. She was lively, a little stupid, and pretty to look at, but that was all she meant to me. She and her father sought to trap me into marriage because I bedded her. I am sorry if that hurts to hear, but I did. I cannot lie to you about it. So, they had every reason to try to trap me into a marriage. My mother went to Daventry to get to the bottom of their claims and uncovered a plot, evidently. You know as much as I about that. But the truth is that there *was* an entanglement."

Over on the stairs, Christin frowned deeply, upset that her brother had told Elysande about the depths of his relationship with Cedrica, but Christopher silently eased her. He thought Westley was on the right path even if she didn't. As they were gesturing to one another, Westley continued.

"Ella, I cannot erase the past," he said. "I wish I could, but I cannot. I can only tell you how sorry I am, and if you are hurt, I will do all that I can to ease it. It is no secret that I did not wish to be married, nor did you, but that has changed. *You* have changed my mind. You are brilliant and beautiful and you make me laugh. I've never had anyone make me feel the way you do. I want to feel that way for the rest of my life, and I swear to you, from this day forward, that you will be the only woman I give my attention to. I've never given my heart to anyone, in fact. It is yours if you want it—if I earn the right to give it to you. You have my word on that."

He fell silent again, hoping she might say something, but she, too, remained silent. He could, however, feel the door move a little. That meant she was against the door, listening to him, and the realization made him smile. If he couldn't break her down with his apology, then perhaps he could break her down with something else. Anything to get her to open the door and forgive him.

He had to try.

"In my family, there is a saying," he said. "I have several brothers and everyone says that Curtis is the strong one, Roi is the smart one, Myles is the fearless one, Douglas is the wise one, and Westley is the lively one. Do you hear that? *I* am the lively one. I got that reputation for being entertaining in any given situation, I suppose. As a child, I used to make up songs to sing to my siblings, and I shall make one up for you now to prove to you that I meant what I said. Let me prove I have listened to you, that I am interested in you and only you. Although I hope you enjoy it, I will warn you to prepare for something inherently terrible."

At that point, he happened to glance at his father and sister in the stairwell. He could see their heads and little more. Christin was shaking her head emphatically, while his father seemed amused. Westley had sung many a silly song for his father as a child, off-key and clumsy, but Christopher had always loved them.

His father's expression gave him courage.

Lifting his voice, he sang slightly off-key to a rambling melody.

My admiration for you is like the most lovely carrot and your face reminds me of a charming horse.

Together, my dearest, we are like chicken and gravy.

Oh, my darling Ella,
My lovely carrot aficionado
My charming onion lover
The perfect companion to my chicken-loving soul.

On the stairwell, Christin clapped her hands over her face, mortified, while Christopher struggled not to laugh. Westley could see his father grinning and it spurred him on.

Oh, my darling Elysande,
Your feet are like sweet shoes on a summer day.
You are the most fearsome queen to every walk Massington.

Your charming horse face.
Your gravy soul.
Your sweet heart.
Your fearsome, queenly being.

How could I ever look at another when our lovely admiration for one another is so strong?

You are the perfect companion to my chicken-loving soul.

He ended the last verse rather loudly, beating out a drum

rhythm on the floor with his hands. Over on the stairs, Christopher grinned broadly, making an applauding motion, as Christin drew a finger across her neck in a gesture that suggested she wanted to slit her brother's throat. But Westley was grinning at them both, gearing up for another verse, when the bolt on the door was suddenly thrown. Christopher and Christin nearly killed themselves trying to move out of sight when the oaken panel opened and Elysande stood on the other side.

Westley had to face her on his knees because she'd opened the door so swiftly. He hadn't had the opportunity to stand yet. Elysande stood there, looking at him in disbelief.

"That," she said after a moment, "was the worst song I have ever heard."

Westley was properly contrite. "I am sorry," he said. "I never said I had any talent, only that I liked to create songs. I shall try to do better, I promise."

Elysande started at him grimly for a moment longer before breaking down into fits of laughter. She'd held it back as long as she could, but it was too much for her. She began to howl.

"We go together like chicken and gravy?" she gasped.

Realizing she wasn't angry with him, Westley climbed to his feet, smiling at her as she laughed. "Can you think of anything that goes together better than that?" he asked.

Tears were beginning to stream down Elysande's cheeks. "And I have a horse face?"

"A *charming* horse face. I told you I love horses. I meant it as an honor, truly."

She couldn't stop laughing. "God's Bones, Westley," she said, wiping at her eyes. "That truly was the worst song I have ever heard, but it is also the best one."

His eyes were gleaming warmly at her. "It was, mayhap, both," he said. "But it served its purpose. It opened your door."

She nodded as she struggled to calm down. "It was magic," she said. "No one has ever sung a song to me, much less a song like that."

She started laughing again, and Westley began to chuckle alongside her. "Give me time and I'll sing many more just like it," he said, but he quickly sobered. "I truly am sorry for the anguish and embarrassment the rumors surely caused you. Please know that."

Elysande was still wiping her eyes, but she sobered as well. "I believe you," she said. "Your father's testimony and your apology mean a great deal. If we are being perfectly honest about entanglements, then I have one of my own to confess."

He, too, was completely sober now, bracing himself. "Oh?"

She nodded. "You should know that Olan has a great deal of affection for me and I have not discouraged it."

"De Bisby?"

"Aye."

He tried not to feel territorial or jealous. "Thank you for telling me," he said. "Do you return his feelings?"

She shook her head. "Nay," she said. "I never have, but I deduced that if I had to marry someone, and that someone was not you, then I would marry Olan simply because I know him. He is gentle and kind and boring. But I do not have feelings for him."

Westley believed her. He could see that she was being earnest. "Then there is still a chance for me."

"After that song, there is every chance for you."

A smile spread across his lips. "Thank you," he said. "I appreciate the opportunity."

"And I do not have to worry about Cedrica coming between us?"

He shook his head. "Nay," he said, quickly frowning. "She was nothing more than someone to pass the time with. She cannot compare to you."

"Then we shall move forward with honesty between us."

"Always, Ella. I swear this to you."

"And I swear it to you, also."

"Will you come to the hall now and eat? My mother is anxious to meet you."

Elysande's smile faded. "May I beg off?" she asked. "I have nothing suitable to wear and my head really is aching. If we are to be married on the morrow, then I should at least like to be rested. I will meet her then."

"As you wish," he said. "May... may I bring you a meal and eat with you? I will sit out here on the landing and you may eat in your chamber. With the door open so you can see me on the landing, if you wish. But I should like to eat it close to you."

It was a very sweet plea, and Elysande didn't have the heart to refuse him. "Aye," she said. "But you do not have to bring my meal. I can summon a servant and..."

He was already moving for the stairs. "Nay," he said. "I will do it. I will return shortly."

He disappeared before she had a chance to reply. He was being eager and accommodating, relieved that something that could have been a barrier in their marriage had been worked through. Elysande understood that the man had had a life before her, much as she'd had a life before him. They were going to have to be accepting of that and move forward with the understanding that there would be no more suitors, no more ladies to keep company with.

Just each other.

And she was quite content with that.

But the chicken and gravy love ballad would be her favorite for the rest of her life.

CHAPTER THIRTEEN

"I THOUGHT I might find you here."

Harker had been in the guardhouse, gazing at the darkened countryside from the iron-barred window that showed the immediate area of the front gate. When he was in the guardhouse, the men were not because Harker chased them out. He believed they should be doing their duty, not gathering in a room, talking and laughing and drinking. Therefore, the small chamber was quite empty when Esther entered.

At the sound of her voice, Harker turned to see her heading toward the small hearth, holding her hands out to the heat. He watched her for a moment, a handsome woman with green eyes and her daughter's auburn hair color, though in her case she kept it wound up on her head and usually under a wimple. But not tonight. Tonight, she was without her headdress as she warmed herself by the fire.

"And so you have found me," he said, still by the window. "How may I serve you, Lady Ledbury?"

Esther shook her head. "There is nothing," she said. "I simply came to see how things were. Have you seen Marius at all?"

Harker nodded. "This afternoon," he said. "But he vanished toward sunset."

Esther grunted. "He is probably back in his chamber, drowning himself in another barrel of wine," she said. "He was sober today, you know. He dealt with Hereford and his son like the Marius of old until it all became too much for him. I did not realize how much I missed Marius until this afternoon. It was good to see him back in form."

Harker didn't want to hear that even though she had every right to say it. When one was in love with his liege's wife as long as he had been, he didn't want to hear her speak kindly or even affectionately about another man, even if it was her husband.

He'd given his heart to a woman he could never have.

That was his curse.

"And you?" he asked softly. "How are you feeling today?"

She glanced at him, knowing that tone in his voice. It was usually before he ravaged her and, quite honestly, he had been her rock during a very difficult time. The man was big and strong and warm and not shy about sharing himself with her. She found herself looking at the crotch of his breeches, knowing what they were concealing. She felt warm just thinking about it.

"Well," she said, looking back to the fire, "I feel... well. The marriage of Ella and Hereford's son will go forward tomorrow. Have you sent word to the priest at St. Andrew's as I asked?"

He nodded. "I have," he said. "I will send men to escort him here at dawn."

"Good," Esther said. "Then they shall be married and all will be well."

"And you are certain of that?"

She nodded. "I hope so," she said. "They seem to be tolerating one another well after their troubled introduction. After they are married, I am assuming Westley will live here, since he will one day inherit this place, and that means we must make him welcome. You will make room for him, Harker. He will be your liege someday."

Harker shook his head. "Not me," he said. "When Marius dies, I will return to Westphalia. I will go home. There will be no reason to remain."

She looked at him in surprise. "Not even for me?"

He turned back to the window. "You are not my wife," he said. "I will return home and find a young woman to bear me a son."

Esther was about to become upset when she realized she heard her own words in his statement. Long had she tried to talk him into finding a young wife so he could have children, but he had always refused. The two of them had engaged in a relationship for years, something Marius was probably unaware of, but even if he was, he'd never said anything. He probably didn't care. Esther knew it was wrong, but Harker offered her what Marius could not—

Warmth.

Warmth, attention, compassion. Everything Marius couldn't. But she knew Harker well and sensed that his mood was dark this night, beyond the comments of his returning home and leaving her. It seemed to Esther that something else was on his mind.

"Harker?" she said. "What is it?"

He was still looking out the window. "What do you mean?"

"You seem preoccupied."

He shook his head. "Not really," he said. "I was simply thinking about the future Lord Ledbury."

It took Esther a moment to figure out who he meant. "Sir

Westley?"

"Aye. Sir Westley."

"What about him?"

Harker didn't answer right away. "What do you think of him?"

Esther shrugged. "I do not know," she said. "I have not been around him very much. Why? What do you think of him?"

Harker paused a moment longer before turning around and looking at her. "I think he bears watching."

"Why would you say that?"

The man shrugged and moved away from the window, in her direction. "Because he is arrogant," he said. "He is a man who has had everything handed to him and he believes he is better than everyone else. That kind of man is difficult to live with. He has no humility."

Esther considered that. "He seems polite enough," she said. "Ella seems to like him, and that is truly all that matters."

Harker pulled up a stool, holding his hands out in front of the fire also. "I see a future where Westley de Lohr will wipe the name of du Nor from history," he muttered. "He will turn Massington into just another de Lohr property. Ledbury and Staunton will become his titles, no longer a du Nor title. Even the title Duc de Nevele will become a de Lohr title. That arrogant young fool will become the lord of everything."

Esther was watching him closely, sensing some jealousy in his tone. "There is nothing we can do about it," she said. "Why does it concern you so?"

Harker looked at her. "It does not," he said wryly. "It does not concern me because I've not lived here for many years. I've not served flawlessly, and when Marius dies, I shall receive everything. Won't I? Of course I will not. This fortress, which has become my home, will go to someone who already has everything in the world. Nay, lady, none of this concerns me. I will simply go home and rebuild my life once Marius dies. I could not have his wife. I could not have his castle. So, I will go home."

That was as much as Harker had ever said about his situation at Massington in all of the years Esther had known him. He'd always seemed content to her, and perhaps he had been, but he certainly wasn't content with Westley de Lohr here. She sensed bitterness and resignation, which was unlike him. Yet, on the other hand, she didn't blame him. Westley's arrival signaled the future of Massington, and it was something Harker didn't want to be part of.

There wasn't much she could say to him about that.

"Well," she said softly, gently touching his hand, "there is no use in dwelling over it. Life is never fair. If it was, we would be happy and we would be together."

Harker snorted softly. "If it were fair, I would be a great knight in a great house, with children by my side and the woman I loved," he said. "I would have money and power. I would have everything. But I learned that life is not fair a very long time ago. Mostly, it does not bother me, but there are times when it does."

"Like now."

"Like now," he agreed, his thoughts moving to darker places. "You are aware that Olan is in love with Ella, aren't you?"

Esther nodded faintly. "I know."

"De Lohr's arrival signifies the end of fairness for him, too," he said. "He must watch the woman he loves marry another man. The entire situation with de Lohr is disheartening for more than me. It affects Olan, too."

Esther sighed. "There is nothing I can do about that," she said. "Marius did not want a minor knight for his only daughter. He wanted a great house and that is what he got, so lamenting over it is useless. We must simply accept it."

We must simply accept it.

Harker didn't want to accept it. He was disturbed by it more than he'd thought he would be. Perhaps he wouldn't have been had Westley not tried to usurp his position by claiming to know more about training than he did, but he had. And Harker was growing increasingly discontented about it.

"You must accept it because your daughter is marrying into the family," he said after a moment. "But I do not have to accept it. In fact, I may leave tomorrow. I do not wish to serve under that arrogant arse."

Esther looked at him with concern. "Please do not leave me," she said softly. "I know this is not an ideal situation, but I need you here, Harker. If you are not here, I will surely go mad."

He looked at her, seeing a frightened woman, one he'd given much of his time to. It hadn't been a love match, but more of a power move. She was the Lady of Massington, after all. He was simply a knight. There had been times when she had submitted to his will. But he was fond of her. Perhaps even fond enough to stay.

Maybe.

"Do not trouble yourself," he said, winking at her. "I am angry, and when I am angry, I say things that are not always true. Let us see what tomorrow brings, my lady. Let us see how this marriage happens and what the future holds."

He said enough without really saying anything, but he was able to ease Esther. She smiled timidly, turning her attention back to the fire as Harker's attention wandered to the wedding on the morrow. He didn't feel any differently about the situation, or about Westley, but he was going to follow his own advice.

Let us see what the future holds.

For Harker of Kent, tomorrow would more than likely be a day of decisions.

CHAPTER FOURTEEN

TWO HOURS AFTER sunrise on the following day, Lady Elysande du Nor became Lady Westley de Lohr. There was no great celebration or fanfare, but simply the priest from St. Andrew's who had come at Harker's request with a host of Massington soldiers as escort. Christopher, Dustin, Esther, and Marius witnessed their children marrying at the door to the great hall, as was tradition, before moving everyone inside to the great feast that awaited.

A feast that went on all day.

The incident from the previous day was all but forgotten and, strangely, seemed to draw Westley and Elysande closer together. The both grinned through the entire wedding mass, and with the feast to follow, they remained with one another rather than separate. Westley remained by Elysande's side until the late afternoon when, suitably drunk on the fine wine that had kept Marius soused all these months, he wandered over to the table where the de Lohr escort was sitting and confiscated one man's citole. Then he returned to the dais and played a couple of songs for his wife, who had no idea he knew how to play an instrument. Not only was Westley an excellent musician, but he also sang one of his standard off-the-cuff songs that had his mother demanding he stop before he even got started.

The song, entitled "No Fragrant Cats at our Summer Wedding," was not a success for Dustin.

But Elysande loved it. She begged for the first verse and Dustin conceded, but warned her against any disappointment with the contents. As Westley held back laughter, the lyrics went something like this—

We are all enjoying my summer wedding,
No more fighting with my lady… for a week or two.
Full clouds and slippery arms at my summer wedding,
No more fragrant cats for me or for you.

Elysande clapped and cheered for his song, and even the de Lohr escort, who had been severely reprimanded for their gossip by Christopher, had stepped in to help him sing it. They were eager to make amends after the trouble they had caused. The song was bizarre and silly, which was usual with Westley, and he was laughing so hard by the end of the first verse that he couldn't continue.

Elysande thought it was all quite charming.

In fact, the day itself had been nothing that she had ever imagined her wedding would be. Though she always knew that she would wed, as all young girls knew, she had imagined her wedding to be something austere and serious. She had imagined a faceless groom and a murky future, and even when she knew of her betrothal to Westley, she still couldn't envision her wedding much more clearly.

Fortunately, the reality was much better than she could

have hoped for.

As Westley continued his cat song, even as his mother demanded he stop, Elysande thought back to the day before. It had probably been one of the most eventful days in her entire life. She'd become acquainted with the man she was to marry and they'd even suffered through their first crisis. How he handled that crisis told her a good deal of his character. He was honest to a fault, which was something she was very grateful for. He'd never tried to talk his way out of it or lie his way out of it and, in fact, went out of his way to clearly explain what had happened and why. She was certain that a couple of the things he mentioned weren't things that he had ever planned to tell her, like the fact that he had kept company with Cedrica regardless of their betrothal, but that was something that Elysande appreciated. Perhaps truth wasn't easy to hear sometimes, but it was truth and therefore welcome.

Difficult or not.

After that, the rest of the day went smoothly enough even though it had been early evening. She probably should have gone to bed right after she'd finished her meal with Westley, but instead, she had gone back down the stairs to her mother's solar, where the red silk dress was still lying in a state of disarray. She sat up half the night finishing the work she had started so that by morning, the dress was wearable even if her fingers were pricked to death. She wore the red dress to their wedding mass and would never forget the look of appreciation in Westley's eyes as he gazed upon her for the first time.

She'd never had a man look at her like that before.

Truth be told, it was quite possible that she was in a bit of a daze as the wedding feast went on around her. Even her father was in attendance, which was unexpected, but he was also quite drunk and isolated himself from the rest of the wedding guests. He simply sat at one end of the dais and drank cup after cup of wine as he watched the festivities. At some point, Christopher went to sit with him and tried to engage him in conversation, which was difficult because Marius became combative when drunk. Christopher eventually gave up and went back to sit with his wife and Esther, because the two of them still weren't getting along and Christopher was concerned that a wildfire could start between the pair at any time. Brielle and Christin were already heading home, back to husbands and children, so there were no daughters as a buffer.

It was, therefore, a very small group that celebrated the wedding, and that group did not include Harker or Olan. No one knew exactly why, and Marius couldn't give them an answer, so it was a big mystery. Usually, the knights of the house were considered an extension of the family and part of celebrations such as this. Only Esther seemed to give a moderately satisfying explanation, and that was the fact that both men were on duty during the daytime hours. At least that answer didn't offend Christopher, and Westley didn't care one way or the other if they were there.

His focus was where it should be.

On his new wife.

Frankly, he was glad that Olan wasn't around. Although the knight had always gone out of his way to be kind to him, after what Elysande told him about their semi-romance, he didn't want the distraction. He wanted his wife's focus on him, and his on her, as it should be. And his was solely on her, because from the moment she'd come from the keep in the brilliant red gown, he'd been unable to take his eyes off her. In his opinion, the woman seemed to become more beautiful by the day, but it was more than her physical appearance. It was evident in her conversation and manner, too. The way she looked at him when she spoke to him. All little things that were endearing the woman to him as no one ever had been before.

And now, they were married.

He could hardly believe it.

One of the de Lohr escort offered to play the citole so that Westley and Elysande could dance at their wedding feast, and he thought it was a marvelous idea, but Elysande flushed a predictably bright shade of red and refused to do it no matter how much he tried to coax her. Evidently, she couldn't dance, or didn't remember what she'd been taught, and even Westley's offer of teaching her as they went along couldn't convince her. Therefore, he started dancing in front of her as the men in the hall cheered him on, showing her how it was done.

"This foot goes forward and then it goes backward," he said, being quite sweet about it but also a little uncoordinated because he was drunk. "Then the person to your left will pass behind you and you must pass in front of them, like this."

He showed Elysande what he meant by demanding one of his soldiers play the female part of the dance, so between the two of them, they showed Elysande how it was done.

She simply sat there and grinned.

"How can I convince you that not only do I not remember how to dance, but that I have three left feet and all of them going in the wrong direction?" she said. "I am not graceful like you are."

Westley came to a halt and scowled. "I am *not* graceful," he said. "I am two hundred and seventy pounds of bull meat, and if I were to take my boots off, then you would see my cloven feet. Honestly, I am not graceful, but I try to be. Will you not at least try?"

Elysande didn't want to. She was terrified of humiliating herself in front of everyone. But she couldn't resist Westley's soft pleas, the gentle look in his eye that assured her he would never hurt her or shame her. He simply wanted to dance with his wife. Reluctantly, she put her hand in his and he pulled her to her feet, moving her away from the dais a little and instructing her on how to move as the soldier played the citole. They ended up twirling a bit before she tripped and they both started laughing.

From the middle of the dais, Christopher, Dustin, and Esther were watching closely.

"West was born a happy baby and he has always been a happy man, but I do not think I've ever seen him quite so happy as this," Dustin said. "To think that only days ago he was fighting his brothers because they would not let him run away from this commitment."

Christopher grunted in agreement as Esther looked over at her. "Why were his brothers involved?" she asked.

Christopher answered as he collected his cup. "Since your daughter tried to attack my son when he first came to Massington, I feel no shame in telling you that prior to our journey here, Westley was most intent to run off," he said, sipping his wine before continuing. "West has five older brothers, all extremely accomplished knights. I called upon them to help me keep West from running away, and it was literally a battle to keep him from doing so."

Esther wasn't particularly surprised to hear that as she turned her attention back to the couple. "He does not seem so apt to run now."

"Nor does she seem apt to attack."

Esther fought off a grin. "Children can be foolish."

"Foolish indeed."

Even Dustin was grinning. Esther noticed her expression, and, for the first time, their irritation with each other seemed to fade. They nodded at one another in agreement over foolish children. But Esther's smile faded as she looked to the end of the table where Marius was still sitting, very much alone. He was quite drunk at this point, leaning on the table to keep himself from falling over. She considered giving the man permission to leave the feast and retreat to his chamber. He didn't want to be here to celebrate anything joyful—and, in fact, watching his daughter and her new husband laugh at one another was probably doing more harm than good. Marius had lamented more than once about his son never marrying, never having children.

It was probably time to let him retreat into his world of grief once more.

Rising to her feet, she was heading over to the end of the table when Harker entered the hall. That brought Esther to a halt, but only momentarily. Any sighting of Harker had her full attention, but in this case, it was misplaced. There wasn't much she could do about it. It wasn't as if she could run to the man. Therefore, she continued to Marius, preparing to tell him that he should seek his bed, but Harker was heading for her husband.

His handsome face was tight with concern.

"My lord," Harker said, addressing Marius directly, "we have a visitor at the gatehouse demanding entry."

Marius was nearly unconscious with the amount of drink in his system, barely coherent enough to answer.

"Who is it?" he asked, speech slurred. "Who is demanding

entry to my home?"

"Fitz Walter," Harker said grimly. "Samson Fitz Walter. He said he has heard of Lady Elysande's marriage and demands entry or he will lay siege."

Christopher heard him. "Samson Fitz Walter?" he said with surprise. "He is here?"

Harker turned to look at him. "He is, my lord."

"And this is not a regular occurrence, I take it?"

"Nay, my lord," Harker said. "He has only come because he heard of the marriage."

Christopher frowned. "But how did he know about it?" he said. "More importantly, why should he care?"

"Because he offered for Ella's hand," Esther answered for her husband because his mind was too muddled to reply. "He has been steadily pressing for a betrothal even though he was aware she was pledged to Sir Westley, so I can only imagine he is here to create problems."

This was all news to Christopher. "I had not known he offered for Elysande," he said. "Why was I not told?"

Esther looked at Marius to answer, but the man was still lingering on the fact that Samson Fitz Walter had arrived and not *why* he had arrived. Frustrated, she answered for her husband again.

"It seemed trivial, my lord," she said. "Elysande has had other interest and we did not tell you of that, because it does not matter. Her betrothal is to Westley and now she is married to Westley. That is all that matters."

Christopher didn't agree with her. "If you know Samson Fitz Walter, then you know that he has an unnatural hatred of me, erroneously pointing the blame at me for things from the past," he said. "I have even cautioned Westley from straying to the north, near Hell's Forge, because Fitz Walter would like nothing more than to take his hatred out on my son. Realize, Lady Ledbury, that there is a problem with your neighbor and it has come to your doorstep."

Esther appeared both concerned and surprised. "What shall I do?" she said, looking at Marius, who wasn't coherent enough to comment. "What shall *we* do, my lord?"

Christopher came around the table to where Marius was sitting. He got in front of him so he was in the man's line of sight.

"Marius?" he said. "Are you listening to this? Trouble is at your door, man. What do you want to do?"

Marius blinked, looking up at Christopher as if only just noticing him. "Do what?"

"Samson Fitz Walter has arrived."

It took a moment for that news to sink in, and when it did, Marius frowned. "What does he want?"

"He knows your daughter was to marry Westley," Christopher said. "If you do not admit him, he threatens to lay siege."

Marius had to process that. The more he understood what was happening, the angrier he appeared. "Tell that bastard he'll not have my daughter," he said. "She is to marry Westley de Lohr."

Christopher sighed sharply, looking to Esther. "My lady," he said, "if you wish for me to take charge of this situation, then say so and I shall be happy to comply."

Esther nodded quickly, fearfully. "Of course, my lord," she said. "Do what you will."

With that, Christopher swung to Westley, who was still twenty feet away, dancing with his new wife and not paying any attention to the conversation over at the far end of the dais.

"West!" Christopher boomed. "To me. Now!"

That command had Westley looking at his father in confusion before moving swiftly to the man's side. One did not ignore a command like that. He had Elysande by the hand, however, as both of them ended up next to Christopher.

"What is it?" Westley said.

Christopher looked at him, his expression grim. "We have a problem," he said. "Do you recall I told you of Samson Fitz Walter?"

Westley nodded. "Of course," he said. "The man who blames you for his uncle's death."

"Exactly," Christopher said. "I have also just been told that he has been trying to solicit a betrothal between himself and your lady wife for quite some time, and news of your marriage has evidently reached his ears. He is, therefore, at the gatehouse demanding entry."

Westley's expression grew serious. "What does he want?"

"Entry," Christopher repeated. "He said that if he is not permitted to enter, he'll lay siege to Massington."

"Do you believe him?"

Christopher nodded without hesitation. "Very much so," he said. "Since Marius is incapable of making a decision in this matter, it has fallen to me."

Westley glanced at his father-in-law as the man slumped at the table. "Then it is good that you are here," he said. "What would you have me do, Papa?"

Christopher sighed heavily, looking at the women in the hall. His wife, Elysande, Esther... He didn't want them to be part of whatever was coming. He thanked God that Brielle and Christin had already departed, though he would miss their counsel. In any case, Fitz Walter's hatred was directed at him, and he didn't want the women exposed to it. Evidently, Samson thought there was something to hash out, so hash it out they would.

He lowered his voice.

"Send the women to the keep and have them lock it up tightly," he said. "They are not to open it to anyone except you or me or the Massington knights. No one else."

Westley nodded. "Agreed," he said. "Then what?"

Christopher paused a moment, thinking, before turning to Harker. "Once the women are secure, you will bring me Fitz Walter," he told the knight. "*Only* Fitz Walter. He is not allowed to bring anyone with him."

Harker nodded smartly. "Aye, my lord."

As Harker headed out, Christopher turned to Westley once more. "Send two of our men for Lioncross," he said. "They are to summon my army and any of your brothers still at the castle. I want the army immediately, as quickly as they can muster it. I have a feeling we may need a show of strength, so let's give it to Fitz Walter."

Nodding quickly to his father's command, Westley was on the move. He had to get his wife and mother and mother-in-law to the safety of the keep and, surprisingly, none of them argued with him as he relayed Christopher's orders. Not even Elysande. Before she could ask to fight with him, which he was fearful she might do, Westley asked her to take his mother and her mother to the keep and secure the structure. That gave her a sense of purpose for the moment, and a distraction, as he went to the de Lohr men and told them what his father's orders were.

Danger was looming.

And the de Lohrs were in charge.

CR

"HOW MUCH LONGER are you going to keep me waiting?" Samson demanded. "You *will* open these gates and admit me. I have business with Lord Ledbury."

Olan was at the gatehouse. A light rain had started, with clouds gathering low and creating halos of mist around the torches. Only one out of the two portcullises was closed and he was standing just inside the iron grate, Samson on the other side of it with about two hundred men, Alend included. Samson knew who Olan was after Alend reminded him, because he honestly didn't know the man on sight, but now that he knew who Olan was, he felt brave enough to make more demands.

"Do you hear me, knight?" he said. Then he lowered his voice. "Open this portcullis and admit me and my men or I will tell Ledbury that you spy for him."

That comment drove Olan away from the grate, which hadn't been Samson's intent. He began to call to him, shouting at him and generally creating a ruckus. It had been that way for the twenty minutes it took for Harker to go to the hall and return. By the time he came back, Fitz Walter was shouting something to his men that Harker couldn't quite hear. As Harker and Olan approached the portcullis, one of Fitz Walter's men must have told him, because he whirled around to face them.

"Well?" he demanded, nearly charging the portcullis. "Admit me immediately!"

Harker well remembered Fitz Walter from his visits to Massington when he was trying to convince Marius to break the de Lohr betrothal. He remembered the man's fits when Marius wouldn't do it. He didn't like the man or his manner, so it was a struggle to remain professional with him.

"Lord Hereford has granted you permission," he said. "But *only* you. Your men are to wait out here."

That wasn't the answer that Samson wanted. His face contorted in outrage. "Hereford?" he repeated. "Where is Marius?"

"Indisposed, my lord."

"What does *that* mean?"

"It means he is indisposed," Harker said, edged with sarcasm. "You may come in alone or not at all. Make your choice."

That caused Fitz Walter to bare his teeth. With a growl, he turned on his heel, marching away in anger before swiftly turning around and nearly running back to the portcullis. There was a good deal of nervous energy in his movements as he slammed a fist against the iron grate.

"Very well," he said. "Let me in. Do it now."

Eyeing him warily, because he didn't trust the man, Harker ordered the portcullis lifted about three feet. Enough for a man to slide under but not big enough for an army to come through. Samson was forced to crouch low and drag a knee in the mud before coming through, straightening up and furiously brushing at his clothing. Given that it was already dirty and torn, that was a ridiculous action, but he'd done it based on the principle of the situation. He shouldn't have had to duck under the iron grate. The portcullis was quickly lowered behind him as both Harker and Olan escorted him out into the rain, heading for the great hall.

Samson wasn't merely walking. He was marching. Marching straight to the hall to give Hereford, and any other de Lohr ally, a piece of his mind. He hadn't seen Christopher in years, so he was mentally preparing for such a meeting. He was prepared to take the upper hand. He was prepared to shout and curse and bully everyone until he got his way. But just as he reached the great hall entry, he was stopped from entering by a very big body in his path.

Hereford had made an appearance.

"You've not changed, Fitz Walter," Christopher said in a low voice. "Still spoilt and demanding and unwelcome. What possible business could you have with Ledbury that it requires the threat of military action?"

Already, the tables were turning against him as Samson found himself blocked from entering the hall as a soft mist fell on his face. For a moment, he studied the man before him. Enormous, imposing, a head full of neatly combed gray hair and a beard to match.

He'd recognize Christopher de Lohr anywhere.

"You, of all people, should understand the threat of military action," he replied after a moment. "Truthfully, I thought you would be dead by now. You're quite old."

"I will outlive you, Samson."

"I sincerely doubt that."

"We shall see."

"Aye, we shall." Fitz Walter paused, eyeing Christopher suspiciously in the torchlight. "This is not your home. Why do you block my entry?"

"I've come to ask you what your business is."

"That is between Marius and me."

"Marius is not in command at this moment," Christopher said. "I am, so state your business or I will have you thrown out."

"Where *is* Marius?"

"Indisposed."

Christopher wasn't going to give him any more answer than

that, and Fitz Walter's irrigation was growing. "My business with Marius is about a proposal I presented to him," he said. "It involves his daughter, so this is none of your affair."

The soft hum of a broadsword being unsheathed filled the air. It came from behind Samson, and, startled, he turned to see an enormous knight standing several feet behind him and behind Olan and Harker, who were still on either side of him. Since the torchlight didn't go that far, all he could see was an outline and the unmistakable glint of a metal blade.

Samson went for his own sword.

Harker and Olan were on him in a minute, confiscating the sword he tried to present. But not without a fight—Samson didn't want to relinquish it, so it turned into a bit of a battle until Olan finally got it away from him. But Samson was in fighting form now.

He was positively furious.

"You have a knight pull a sword on me, yet you will not allow me to defend myself?" he nearly shouted. "How dare you treat me with such contempt! My business with Marius is none of your affair! I have told you so!"

Christopher pointed to the shadowed warrior several feet away. "I would like to introduce you to my son, Westley," he said. "Marius' daughter is now his wife. If you have come about her, then you must discuss any business with him. And he does not seem to be too happy about your presence, so I suggest you state your business quickly."

Those words seemed to cool Fitz Walter off at astonishing speed. He stared at Christopher a moment before turning again to Westley, who hadn't moved. He was just standing there, sword in hand.

Waiting.

"The privileged son," he finally muttered. "The privileged son of a father who achieved his wealth and success through greed and murder. There are many men in England who will not shed a tear when your father dies, young Westley. I will be one of them."

Westley didn't say anything, but Christopher did. "That does not sound like business, Fitz Walter," he said. "State what you were so frantic to state and get on with it. The sooner you leave, the sooner we'll be able to get the stench of your visit out of our nostrils."

Fitz Walter nodded as if happy to comply. "Very well," he said. "Marius promised me that he would consider my offer for his daughter. He promised me that he would consider breaking your contract. I have a claim on the lady, you see."

Westley didn't wait for anything more to be said. He marched up on Samson as the man stood his ground, reaching out with his free hand and grabbing the back of his neck. Then he started to drag the man back to the gatehouse as Samson resisted. The fists began to fly.

Westley's sword clattered to the ground.

It was a brawl as Westley dragged Samson toward the gatehouse. Samson was tall, but he didn't have nearly the strength that Westley had. Still, he seemed to be holding his own in a fight against a muscular opponent. Harker, Olan, and even Christopher followed. Harker went to intervene but Christopher called him off. If Westley was to be lord of Massington someday, then the rules had to be established.

Westley had to prove himself unbeatable.

The soldiers on the walls were watching the fight as it unfolded. They saw, clearly, when Westley grabbed Samson by the hair and flung him in the direction of the gatehouse. The man hit the ground heavily and slid several feet in the muck. As he tried to get to his feet, Westley was on him again, grabbing him and continuing to toss him toward the gatehouse. The second time, however, Samson got to his feet faster and managed to land a heavy blow on Westley's face before Westley laid the man out with a devastating right-handed punch to the head. Samson went down and stayed down. Wiping blood from his nose, Westley ordered the portcullis lifted.

"Get him out of my sight," he said as blood and rain poured down his face. "Olan, you and Harker escort him back to his men and make sure they depart."

Harker nodded, grabbing Samson by one arm as Olan grabbed the other. Together, they dragged him underneath the half-lifted portcullis and dropped him at the feet of his stunned men. Harker went back inside the gatehouse, but Olan remained. He watched Alend and a few others pick Samson up and try to bring him around. When he finally regained his awareness, he began striking the men around him in anger, Alend included.

In order to avoid more embarrassment, Alend moved the army down the road so the men wouldn't see how soundly Samson had been beaten. That left Samson trying to shake the bells out of his ears with Olan standing a few feet away, monitoring the situation. When Samson caught sight of Olan, he jabbed a finger at him.

"This is *not* over," he snarled. "I will have my vengeance. Mark my words. And I will have your hide for your betrayal!"

Olan didn't react to the threat. "Leave now and there will be no more violence," he said steadily. "I am not entirely sure what you expected when you came as you did. You cannot take what you want by force, you know."

Samson was picking himself up off the road, shoving Alend aside when the man tried to help him.

"I have been betrayed," he said, coughing because Westley had somehow also managed to hit him in the throat during the struggle. "Marius knew I wanted to marry his daughter. I had presented the idea to him for a year—a long year—before he told me that she was pledged to a de Lohr. He led me to believe that a marriage between me and his daughter was possible. Did you know that? He misled me! And Hereford… The man has wronged me one too many times. He is a greedy, murdering bastard and deserves as much pain and anguish as God and his angels can deliver!"

Olan didn't know much about the dealings between Samson and Marius, but he did know that Samson had been a frequent visitor, once—at least every couple of months. He would bring wine and pretend to be a good ally when what he was really doing was trying to buy Marius' daughter. Buy her with wine and good behavior and pledges of taking care of the Massington properties. That much information had trickled down.

In truth, Olan felt guilty because he'd sent word to Samson about Westley's arrival. He was the one who had caused this scene, in essence. He'd hoped that Samson could separate the couple, or stop the marriage at the very least, but he'd come too late. The marriage was set. And the only way to separate Elysande from her husband now was death.

Westley's death.

Olan sighed heavily, glancing over his shoulder to see that everyone at Massington was standing far enough back that they couldn't hear the conversation. That was good, because he didn't want anyone to hear what he had to say. He had to make a choice now—either stay on the path of the morally righteous or head down the road of the damned. Unfortunately for Olan, the darker road was more attractive to him. He found himself heading down into the darkness because his love for Elysande was blinding him to the ways and means by which he could legally and morally have her. Or, at the very least, so she would be unattached. It was nothing personal against Westley.

He simply didn't want the man around.

"Will you bring your army and lay siege now?" he asked. "That is what you threatened if you were not admitted. Is that what you intend to do?"

Samson waved a hand at him, nearly throwing himself off balance. "I will *not* tell you," he said. "You will tell Hereford."

Olan shook his head. "I will not tell him anything," he said. "You may not be aware of the fact that I did not want Elysande to marry Hereford's son either. If anyone should feel betrayed, it should be me."

Samson scowled at him. "*You?*" he demanded. "Why?"

"Because I love her," Olan said simply. "I have loved her since the day I met her, yet she married another today. You do not love Elysande so you would not understand. But you do understand what it is when the person you want is taken by another."

Samson stared at him. A few long seconds passed before he cocked his head curiously. "You are in love with Marius' daughter?"

"Aye."

"Then you must want vengeance as much as I do."

Olan shrugged. "To be truthful, I was hoping you would stop this marriage today," he said. "But you came too late."

Samson conceded the point. "Why did you not stop it yourself?"

"Because I would not last long against Westley de Lohr," Olan said. "You saw how he handled you. He would break me in two."

Samson turned his face toward the mighty walls of Massington. "Oh, would I love to subdue that bastard," he muttered. "Subdue him and watch his father beg mercy for his son. I can do nothing against Hereford, but give me his son and I can control the man. My great nemesis. Hurt the son and you will hurt the man."

Olan could hear something in Samson's ramblings, something that sprouted a seed of thought. Samson hadn't prevented the marriage, but it was possible that there were other avenues to pursue that would separate Elysande from her new husband.

Hurt the son and you will hurt the man.

That gave Olan an idea.

"Your quarrel is with Hereford, is it not?" he asked.

Samson grunted, still looking at the walls of Massington. "He killed my uncle," he said. "Killed the man in cold blood. I would do anything to tear Hereford's heart from his chest and watch him bleed."

"And if I bring Elysande's husband to you, what would you do with him?"

Samson did look at him then. "Bring him to me?" he repeated, confused. "Why should you bring him to me?"

"So Elysande would be free."

"Free for you or free for me?"

"Me," Olan said. "But how badly do you want to hurt Hereford?"

Samson didn't have to think hard on that question. "Badly," he muttered. "My hatred of him is embedded into the very earth I walk upon, the very air I breathe. I cannot move without that hatred to give me strength."

"Then I will give you the son," Olan said quietly. "I care not what you do with him, or how you exact your revenge from Hereford, but Elysande is mine. That is the price you will pay for the vengeance you seek. And when I marry Elysande, you and I will be close allies."

He had Samson's attention. "How close?"

"I will give you the run of Massington and a portion of her wealth."

"And the duchy?"

"The title will be mine, but I will pay you a stipend from the properties."

If Samson couldn't have Elysande, then the deal Olan was offering was quite generous. Even he knew that. But the best thing of all was the ultimate vengeance against Christopher de Lohr. For his Uncle Ralph, the former Sheriff of Nottingham and close aide to King John, Samson was willing to agree to the terms, if only to satisfy his uncle's memory.

If only to satisfy that old blood feud.

His father would have been proud.

"Very well," Samson finally said. "Bring Hereford's son to me. Do what you must do in order to bring him to me, but do it immediately. I will be ready and waiting."

"And you will surrender any claims on Elysande?"

"I will. Providing you give me something in exchange."

Olan nodded. And with that, he waved both hands at Samson in a sweeping motion so that anyone watching would think he was chasing the stubborn man away. When Samson started limping down the road, where Alend was waiting far down the way, Olan turned back for the gatehouse. The portcullis lifted for him and he slipped underneath, all the while his mind working, thinking, churning.

Processing the deal he'd just made with the devil himself.

For Olan de Bisby, a rather disloyal creature and an apathetic knight, the future was about to take a deadly turn.

CHAPTER FIFTEEN

"**Y**OU HAVE BLOOD on your face," Elysande said. "Sit down and let me clean you."

Westley did as he was told.

This wasn't the way he'd hoped to end his wedding day, which had been a day of wonderful memories. He hadn't envisioned himself sitting on a bed while his new wife cleaned up the blood from his face and inspected him for damage, but the moment he'd returned to the great hall, with blood still leaking from his nose and dribbling onto his tunic, the festivities seemed to be over with.

Upset at the sight, and from the entire happenstance, Elysande insisted they retire to her chamber so she could tend to her bloodied husband while Dustin, greatly concerned at the sight of bleeding Westley, offered to help. Elysande politely declined, wanting to tend him herself, and Dustin backed off. The last Westley saw of his mother, Esther was pouring her a full measure of wine in the hopes of calming her down a bit. He had to smile at that because it was the first time Esther and Dustin weren't ready to throw fists at one another.

He was pleased to see it.

Christopher, however, followed the couple to the keep. He had seen the entire fight, but what he hadn't seen was Olan standing out on the road having a conversation with Samson. Others had, but everyone assumed it was Olan telling the man to go back to Hell's Forge and stay there. When Olan confirmed those observations, there was no reason to believe otherwise. Olan retreated to his chamber afterward, leaving Harker on watch as Dustin and Esther got drunk in the great hall alongside Marius, who was sleeping with his head on the tabletop.

The evening had ended with a bang.

"It is not that bad, I assure you," Westley told Elysande, watching her move around the room in search of rags and water. "I've received much worse, from my brothers, no less."

Elysande found rags, but no water to wash with, so she went to the door and called to the nearest servant for hot water.

"Your brothers are not brutes, are they?" she said doubtfully. "I am not entirely sure I like hearing that they beat you to a bloody pulp."

He grinned. "I never said they beat me to a bloody pulp," he said. "And nay, they are not brutes. Curtis is the eldest, the Earl of Leominster. Roi is the Earl of Cheltenham and also the chief justiciar for the king. He's very accomplished. Myles is next, as Lord Monnington, and Douglas comes after him. He is the Earl of Axminster. There is also Peter, who is from a relationship my father had well before my mother, and he is a great agent for the king. These are great men, Ella, every one of them. They are wise and generous and I am very fortunate to have them."

Elysande was still standing near the door, waiting for the hot water. "You are close to them?"

"All of them."

"Then why did they not come to your wedding?"

He lifted a hand to gingerly touch his nose, determining the extent of the damage. "Because my father did not want them to," he said. "He felt it would only create... trouble."

"What kind of trouble?"

He glanced at her. "I told you I fought them before I came here."

"You did."

"My father was concerned that their presence might incite me to more violence," he said. "I am the youngest. I love my brothers, but they have been known to tease me and, if the mood strikes, be hard on me. After what happened at Lioncross, my father didn't want to take the chance that their presence at Massington would aggravate me. He thought it might make things worse."

"Ah," she said in understanding. "But your father's fears were for naught."

"Thankfully," Westley said. "Mayhap not when I first arrived, but it was easier for me to settle into the situation without an audience."

"What do you mean?"

"My brothers would have encouraged me to accept the situation," he said. "Being stubborn, I would have refused because I will not always do what they tell me to do, so without them around, it was simply easier for me to make my own decision about our situation."

"A good decision, I hope."

"The best."

The door was pushed open before she could reply, and a small woman with dark hair and big, dark eyes stepped in with an earthenware bowl. She was followed by two serving women carrying buckets of hot water, all of them looking at Westley and his bloodied face rather fearfully as they moved to set everything down. The servants slipped out of the chamber, but Elysande grasped the woman with the dark eyes.

"This is my cousin, Frederica," she said to Westley. "Freddie, this is my husband, Sir Westley."

Freddie dipped into a quick curtsy. "My lord," she said. "Welcome to Massington."

"Thank you," Westley said, eyeing the woman. "I was not aware that Elysande had a cousin living here."

Elysande answered for her. "Aye, she does," she said. "Freddie and I are inseparable, so you will see her quite a bit."

He nodded. "It is good that you have someone so close," he said. "It was a pleasure to meet you, Lady Frederica."

Freddie nodded and fled before another word could be said. As Elysande closed the chamber door and bolted it, Westley looked at her curiously.

"What's wrong with her?" he said. "Is she afraid of men?"

Elysande made her way over to the steaming buckets of water, picking one up to pour a measure into the earthenware bowl. "She lives in fear of my mother," she said, carefully pouring the water in. "Her story is a strange one."

"Why?"

Elysande finished with the water and set the bucket back on the ground. "Her mother was pledged to my father long ago," she said. "But my mother's family was powerful, and wealthy, and somehow they broke the betrothal and instead my mother married my father. Freddie's mother ended up marrying my father's younger brother, who died some time ago. In fact, both of her parents died some time ago, but when my mother sees Freddie, she thinks of her mother. I think… I think there may be a little guilt in my mother's heart for what happened, but there is also jealousy."

"Why?"

"Because my father loved Freddie's mother."

"He does not love your mother?"

Elysande shrugged. "He has never been wholly affectionate with her," she said, coming to the beside with the steaming bowl of water and rags. "He was kinder to her when Emory was alive, but after he died, the rest of us ceased to exist."

Westley lifted his eyebrows in sympathy. "Grief is a terrible thing," he said. "It can do terrible things to a man's soul. I've seen it for myself."

Elysande had him tip his head back so she could get to work. She lifted the warm, wet rag but paused before using it, looking him in the eye. "Do you want to know something?"

"What?"

"My mother has been having a love affair with Harker," she said softly. "She thinks that I do not know, but I do."

Westley grunted sadly. "Mayhap your father's behavior drove her away."

Elysande began to gently clean around his nose. "They were lovers before Emory died," she said. "She loves Harker and I think he loves her. He's a good man, Westley. He is deserving of your respect even though I suspect you do not think much of him."

Westley sat stock-still as she mopped up the blood from his face. "I do not know the man," he said. "But I do not think he likes me very much."

"Why not?"

"I'm sure he views me as a usurper."

Elysande rinsed out the bloodied cloth, wrung it, and went to clean his chin. "Things are changing," she said. "No one likes change very much. I tried to attack the man who had come to change my life."

He smiled faintly. "You certainly did."

She met his eye, grinning. "I did not succeed."

"Regrets?"

She paused. "Not so far."

"Good," he said, reaching up to take the rag from her hand. "And now you are finished with this task."

She looked him over. "There is still a little blood by your ear."

He handed her the rag again. "Then clean it."

She did. Once that was gone, she looked him over completely and put the rag back into the bowl. "You are finished," she said. "But your nose is swelling where you were hit. I can make a compress for it."

He shook his head. "Do not bother," he said. "It will go away in a day or two. But I am more concerned now that you and I have another task to complete."

He tilted his head in the direction of the bed, and she knew exactly what he meant. The familiar flush crept into her cheeks.

"I suppose we do," she said as he took the rags and bowl over to the table where the cooling buckets were. "I… Well, clearly, I've not done this before, so you'll have to tell me what to do."

He set the stuff down and looked at her. "Gladly," he said. "May we speak freely about what is expected of us? Or does it embarrass you to speak of it?"

She sat down on the bed rather stiffly. She looked nervous. "It does not embarrass me," she said. "Should it?"

He shrugged. "If you've never done it before, it might."

She thought on that a moment. "I… I suppose it is a *little* embarrassing," she said. "But we are married now, so we should speak of it."

Westley tried not to smile because he knew this was a serious matter. He sat down on the bed next to her. "It is really nothing to fear," he said. "Everyone who is married does it. Even people who are unmarried do it, though the church frowns on that. But it's something that can be very pleasurable, so men—and women—believe it is worth the risk."

She was watching him closely. "Have you done this a lot?"

He cleared his throat quietly and averted his gaze. But he caught sight of her hand and picked it up, holding it in his big mitt.

"I've done it enough," he said. "It is different for men, Ella."

"Why?"

"It just is."

"*Why?*"

She wasn't going to let it go without an answer. "Because men have stronger urges than women do," he said. "Men are animals. Women are civilized creatures. They can control their urges better than men can."

"The urge to do what?"

He shrugged. "Procreate, I suppose," he said. "Relations between men and women are as old as time itself. Animals do it to procreate. People do it for the same reason, only we derive some pleasure from it."

She contemplated that. He was being factual and kind, which she appreciated. But something occurred to her as she looked down at his hand holding hers.

"This is all we have ever done," she said.

He wasn't sure what she meant until she lifted her hand to show him. "Hold hands?" he said.

"Aye," she said. "We have never even kissed, not even at our wedding because we went inside the hall so quickly after the blessing that there was no chance. And now we are to do... do this... and we have never even truly touched one another. Not an embrace or anything."

He couldn't tell if she was distraught or not. She definitely sounded perplexed. Lifting up her hand, he kissed it tenderly, watching her face as she did so. When he saw the faint blush creep into her cheeks, he gently cupped her face with one hand and leaned forward, kissing her cheek sweetly. It was a soft cheek and he kissed it again and again before making his way to her mouth, where he gently kissed her lips.

He felt a bolt rush through Elysande, shaking her entire body.

"Did you like that?" he said, grinning. He was still very close to her, so he kissed her on the lips again, this time a little longer. "And that? Was it pleasant?"

She was staring at him, blinking rapidly. "Aye," she said, her voice husky. "Olan kissed me once. It was not like that."

He dropped his hand and sat back, giving her an expression of disbelief. "A man does *not* want to hear about another man when he is trying to seduce his wife," he said. "Do you understand?"

She nodded quickly. "I am sorry," she said. "I do not know why I said that. It was stupid."

He fought off a grin. "You can think it, but you cannot say it," he said. "How would you feel if I brought up another woman just as I was kissing you?"

"I would not like it."

"Nay, you would not," he said. "So no more comments about Olan, ever, or the next time I see him, I might cut off something vital to punish him for trying to steal what rightfully belongs to me."

She was waiting for him to tell her what rightfully belonged to him, hanging on his words, when she realized he meant her. "Me?"

He rolled his eyes. "God's Bones," he muttered. "Aye. *You.*"

"Will you continue now, or are you cross with me?"

His grin broke through then. "I am not cross with you," he said. "But I am hurt that you would think of Olan when I kissed you."

She shook her head. "I was not thinking of him," she insisted. "I only meant that he is the only one who has ever kissed me other than my father or mother. But his kisses were like a sunrise. Bright, but otherwise cold. Your kiss… It is as if I am standing on the sun."

His smile broadened. "Lass, if you are trying to seduce me, then you are well on your way."

He leaned over and kissed her again, his lips to her cheek before he kissed her chin and then tilted her head away from him so he could kiss her neck. Her skin was warm and soft and her feminine musk filled his nostrils, putting cracks in his carefully held control. But he kept his restraint, being gentle with her, trying not to overwhelm her with his size and power.

But it was oh-so-difficult.

He wanted to relax her enough that she would be compliant with anything he wanted to do to her or with her. That was a trick he'd learned from his older brothers, in fact—being very gentle but persistent with a woman, showing her how good a kiss or a touch felt, how non-threatening it was. Douglas was particularly good at it, or at least he had been. He was married now and had finished coaxing all of the women he was ever going to coax except for his wife. But Westley had learned his lessons well, and they'd served him when he met a woman he wanted to get close to.

Like now.

But, much like Douglas, this was going to be the last woman he would ever coax, too.

"God, you're beautiful," he breathed as he finally pulled back to look at her. "Should we retire to the bed? Do you feel comfortable enough to do so?"

Fighting down flaming cheeks yet again, because they seemed to flame easily when Westley was around, Elysande glanced at the bed and nodded.

"Aye," she said. "I… I think so."

"We can wait to do this until you feel better about it, you know," he said. "We've only known each other a couple of days. The truth is that we barely know each other at all. If you are uncomfortable, I understand."

Elysande thought on that. Everything was moving with lightning speed, that was true. "It does not matter if we wait or if we do not wait," she said. "We are married. It is not as if we can annul it. My mother would not allow it and neither would your father."

"Do *you* want to annul it?"

She shook her head. "I did not mean it the way it sounded," she said. "I simply meant that this is something we must do to consummate the marriage."

"It is."

"This is what will truly make us belong to one another."

"It will make it legal in the sight of the church and the law, for certain."

"May I ask you something?"

"Anything."

"Why was Samson Fitz Walter here tonight? You did not tell me."

That was not the question he'd expected. Westley's fire of passion was starting to burn deep in his belly, and after all of the kissing he'd just done, his manhood was semi-aroused, so he was ready to get into bed with her and she was asking questions on a completely different subject.

He tried not to show his annoyance.

"You want to speak of that *now*?" he asked.

She shrugged. "I thought there might be a simple answer," she said. "But if you do not wish to discuss it, we do not have to."

It began to occur to him why she had asked. *She's nervous,* he thought. She was trying to delay the inevitable in spite of her brave talk. Talk of Olan was one delay, and now talk of Samson was another. Understanding that, he wasn't going to push her.

But he was going to show her what she was missing.

"He came to protest our marriage," he said, standing up from the bed. "He says that he has a claim on you. Do you know anything about that?"

He was pulling off his clothing as he spoke, very casually, watching her face when he pulled off his tunic—or more correctly, his father's tunic—and tossed it aside. His big muscles and broad chest were revealed, and Elysande stared at his naked flesh as she struggled for an answer.

That had been his plan.

"Well?" he said. "Do you?"

"Aye," she finally said. "I think so. My father said he had suggested a betrothal, but when he was told I was already betrothed to a de Lohr, he went mad. Honestly, I do not know why. I do not know the man. My father said he spent time trying to ingratiate himself, which led up to the suggestion of a betrothal, but it is not as if he is a strong ally. He's not."

Westley grunted as he sat down to pull his boots off. "He's more than likely an enemy now," he said, yanking off a boot and feeling somewhat relieved that his feet didn't smell horrible. He went to work on the other one. "I chased him off with the understanding that the woman he seeks is already married. To me."

The second boot came off and hit the floor. Westley stood up and unfastened his breeches, sliding those down his thighs as he heard Elysande gasp. His breeches were around his ankles, his buttocks in full view, and he looked at her upside down as she sat on the bed with her head turned away.

"What's the matter?" he asked her.

"Nothing is the matter," she said, though her head was still turned. Quickly, she stood up and headed over to her wardrobe. "I... I suppose I should don my sleeping shift."

He chuckled to himself as he pulled his breeches off and tossed them over a chair. Nude, he went to the fire, banked it, and then returned to her bed. It was a rather large bed for a young woman, a good size for the two of them. As he climbed in, Elysande stood over by her wardrobe and tried to use one of the doors to block his view of her undressing. Truthfully, he felt a little sorry for her, so he pulled the coverlet over his head.

"I cannot see anything," he said. "You may undress in confidence, my lady. I will not look, I promise."

Over by the wardrobe, Elysande turned to see that he had the blanket over his face. Truthfully, that did bring her some relief. He may have been comfortable stripping down in front of her, but she wasn't comfortable in the least undressing in front of him.

"I do not mean to be prudish," she said. "But I do not usually dress with an audience."

"Not to worry," he told her. "Since we are to share this chamber for the time being, I will purchase a dressing screen for you so that you may have some privacy."

She pulled the red surcoat over her head. "That sounds as if it may be expensive," she said. "I will not ask you to do that."

"It is no trouble at all," he said. "Hereford has a woodworker, in fact, that made such a screen for my sister. It was carved with lions on it and is quite nice."

"If you think it is for the best."

"Unless I want to spend the next six months with blankets over my head whenever you dress, it is for the best," he said drolly. "I might suffocate this way."

Suddenly, the bed gave way and Elysande jumped in, quickly covering herself up. Westley pulled the coverlet off his head, smiling as he looked over at her. She had the coverlet pulled up to her chin as she sat there, wide-eyed, looking at him. He felt rather sorry for her because she appeared absolutely terrified. Laughing softly, he cupped her face and kissed her cheek.

"What would make you feel more comfortable about this?" he said softly. "Shall I explain what I am going to do? That way, there will be no surprises, no questions?"

She nodded. "Aye," she said. "If you can just tell me what to expect."

He sat back against the pillows, his bare chest glorious and nude in the soft light of the chamber. Reaching out, he began to toy with tendrils of her silken hair.

"I will start by kissing you," he said. "You may kiss me in return if you wish. You see, in order to make this a success, we must both become aroused. For me, it means their manhood becomes hard so it can penetrate your body. For a woman, it means that her body becomes… wet."

She cocked her head curiously. "Wet?"

He nodded. "Down there," he said, motioning to her lower regions. "You will become wet so my penetration will be easier. A woman's body must be prepared so it does not hurt her. So I will kiss you and touch you and that will help your body become prepared. Do you understand so far?"

Elysande nodded. "I do," she said. "Then what?"

"Then we will couple."

"And that's all?"

He nodded, fighting off a grin at the simplistic view she had of it. "That is all," he said. "May I proceed?"

"Will you tell me what I need to do?"

His eyes twinkled warmly at her. "Just lie there and enjoy it," he murmured. "That's all you need do. For now. Can you do that?"

"Aye."

"And if, at any time, you wish for me to stop, just tell me. Will you do that?"

She nodded. "Aye."

"Good," he whispered. "Now… just lie there and enjoy this. Trust me, Ella. Just… trust me."

With that, Westley indicated for her to slide down in the bed and lie down, which she did. He followed. But the moment he lay down next to her, he realized that she was naked, too, and that fed his lust like nothing he'd ever known. He'd fully expected her to be bundled up in a suit of armor disguised as a shift, but she wasn't. Realizing that, he pulled Elysande against him and his mouth came down on hers, so firmly that he accidentally drove her teeth into her lip. He kissed her deeply, firmly, tasting her sweetness along with the faint taste of blood. There was passion and lust in the kiss, sensations that made him gather her more tightly against him. Her arms went around his neck, timidly, and her breasts, soft and warm, were pressed against his chest. Their naked flesh touching for the first time spurred Westley to another level of desire.

Rolling over, he pulled her underneath him.

Westley loved the feel of her soft, nubile body beneath him. He moved his mouth down her neck to the exposed cleavage, tasting her collarbone so very gently. She didn't stop him, so he continued, running on instinct. Gently, he lifted her arms, trapping them above her head, as he began to move his free hand very carefully. He very much wanted to acquaint her with his touch, something he hoped she would learn to crave.

But this was all so very new to them both.

He'd only known her such a short time, but somehow, this moment didn't feel wrong or awkward. It felt right within the progression of their relationship, a most intimate act establishing trust and a foundation for what they were building between them. His mouth trailed away from her lips, down her neck, and to her breasts. Using his knees, he pushed her legs apart and wedged himself in between them. He was very careful about it. Releasing her arms over her head, he felt her hands settle on his shoulders as he continued to kiss the swell of her breasts. But he moved lower, to her puckered nipples, and took one in his mouth. As he suckled gently, feeling her twitch and buck, he moved one hand to the delicate heat between her legs and stroked her gently.

Elysande shuddered.

"Are you well?" he whispered, his mouth against her right

breast. "I can stop if you want me to. Tell me if this is uncomfortable in any way."

Elysande shuddered again when he touched her, and something that sounded like a moan escaped her lips. "N-nay," she murmured. "It is not uncomfortable."

"May I continue?"

She could only nod. Carefully, he thrust a finger into her and she cried softly, her hands against his shoulders as if to push him away, but that was only momentary. He left his finger there a moment so she could become used to it before finally moving it in and out, slowly, mimicking what he would soon be doing with his thoroughly engorged member. The woman had him so hot that he could barely contain himself. At the same time, his mouth found a nipple again and he suckled firmly.

Instinctively, Elysande's knees came up.

She grunted every time he thrust his fingers into her tight, wet heat, her eyes closed as she experienced everything he was doing to her. He'd told her to simply lie there and enjoy it, and that was exactly what she was doing, only the things the man was doing to her were making her lightheaded. She kept forgetting to breathe. It wasn't long before her body started to quiver, the beginnings of her first release, so Westley quickly removed his fingers and thrust his manhood into her as she began to throb with pleasurable convulsions.

Elysande was so highly aroused that the introduction of his manhood into her body seemed to propel her to a higher level of passion. It was briefly uncomfortable, but she was mid-climax when he did it, so the pleasure-pain was wildly satisfying. For his part, Westley could feel her body pulsing around him as he thrust into her, telling her how much she was enjoying this. Her gasps of pleasure filled the air until he slanted his mouth over hers, kissing her with the power of the attraction he was feeling for her. In fact, he was so highly aroused that he released himself sooner than he had anticipated, spilling deep into her nubile body.

He'd never climaxed so fast in his life.

The sounds of Elysande's gasping filled the air as Westley slowed his thrusts, finally stopping completely as he struggled to catch his breath. Beneath him, Elysande lay with her eyes closed, arms flung out to her sides, her bare breasts reflecting the firelight. Westley watched her, thinking he'd never seen anything more beautiful.

His wife.

Was this what he had railed against? Was this what he'd berated his father for? He couldn't even remember doing it, but he knew he had. All he could see before him was something he never knew he wanted, but now didn't want to be without. How an act he'd done for recreation, for pleasure, with no real emotional connection, could suddenly be so incredibly binding was a mystery to him. But here he was, and what he was feeling for Elysande was very, very real.

He was astonished.

As he lay on top of her, still embedded in her, she moved her arms, her hands coming up to grip Westley's arms, and her breasts moved in the light. The sight was enough to arouse him again, and he started thrusting in and out of her again, very slowly, as his manhood began to twitch back to life. Westley had his face buried in her neck, inhaling her scent, as his hips gyrated slowly to the ancient, primal rhythm.

"Westley," Elysande gasped as he hit a particularly sensitive spot. "Oh, God… *Westley…*"

Her legs were far apart, but her hands found his taut buttocks. It was a timid touch as she acquainted herself with his body, his movement, but it was an invitation to him. She wanted more of his touch, and he responded by covering her mouth with his, his kisses hot and sweet. He rubbed himself against her as he thrust, rolling his hips in a circular motion against her woman's core, and when he felt her tremors begin again, he thrust into her more firmly as she climaxed once more in a burst of stars. It wasn't much longer before he was able to do the same, perhaps weaker than before, but no less satisfying.

The fire in the hearth snapped softly as heavy breathing filled the room. Westley lay beside his wife, his body still joined to hers, thinking that this moment had been one of the most impactful of his life. He began to kiss her gently, familiarizing himself with her scent and taste, while a hand went to her breasts, tenderly fondling her. He was quite enjoying himself, hoping she was also, but her soft snores began to fill the chamber and he smiled, thinking that she was utterly adorable when she snored. But he continued to kiss her, and touch her, until he, too, drifted off to sleep for a time, only to awaken deep in the night with another erection that demanded satisfaction.

Elysande was more than happy to comply.

It went on until morning.

CHAPTER SIXTEEN

"**H**AS ANYONE SEEN them this morning?"

The question came from Dustin.

Seated in the great hall of Massington, she sat alongside her husband and Esther, and that was the extent of the people in the hall other than the senior officers of the de Lohr escort. The soldiers were on duty or still in the troop house, and both knights were outside with the men. In response to Dustin's question, Esther shook her head.

"Nay," she said as a servant poured her a measure of hot, watered wine. "I have not seen them. But I did… hear them."

Esther's chamber was right next to her daughter's, where the newly married couple had taken up residence. When Dustin looked at her questioningly, Esther simply waggled her eyebrows in a suggestive manner, and Dustin took her meaning immediately.

"I see," Dustin said, perhaps a little surprised. "But… in a good way? No yelling or fighting?"

Esther shook her head slowly. "None," she said. "I believe we may have a successful marriage, after all."

That was a huge relief to Dustin and Christopher. They

looked at one another, Dustin smiling timidly as Christopher breathed a sigh of relief.

"Given how West was behaving even just a few days ago, I find that surprising," he said. "Pleasing, but surprising."

Esther smiled. "I agree with you," she said. "I am assuming he will stay here for the time being? And not return with Ella to Lioncross?"

Christopher shook his head. "I told him that he should remain here and become acquainted with the castle and the land," he said. "If he is to inherit all of this someday, he will need to know it."

Esther nodded, sipping on her wine, which was too hot to drink, so she set it aside. "Harker and Olan will be able to tell him much," she said. "They are good men, though you've not had the opportunity to see that for yourself because they have made themselves scarce. They are quite vigilant in their management of Massington, and I am grateful. Given that Marius does nothing these days, it is good to have their alertness."

"Where is Marius?" Christopher asked quietly.

Esther forced a smile. "Probably in his solar, sleeping off yesterday's binge," she said. "That is usual. You will not see him today, of all days. I believe that the advent of Ella's marriage will plunge him further into depression, knowing he will never see Emory's wedding. He mourns what has been lost, what will never be."

Christopher was listening with some sympathy. "I can understand that," he said. "But when the time is right, mayhap you will remind him that he will have grandsons through his daughter. And since West will inherit the duchy of Nevele, I will encourage him to keep the du Nor name. Mayhap that will give Marius some comfort."

Esther looked at him in surprise. "You would do that?"

"I believe it is the right thing to do."

She shook her head in wonder. "That is extremely generous, my lord," she said. "Thank you."

"My pleasure."

Esther went to collect her cup of wine, now cooling off. "Speaking of pleasure, it has been a great pleasure having you both here," she said. "I hope you will stay as long as you like."

Christopher tried to stifle a yawn, as it was still fairly early. "As much as we appreciate your kind invitation, we shall be departing on the morrow," he said, looking at his wife for her agreement. "I feel that we should stay one more day to ensure this marriage is, indeed, a peaceful one, but if it is, there is no reason for us to remain."

"I understand," Esther said as Dustin nodded to her husband's statement. "I hope you can return to visit us often, then."

Christopher chuckled. "I am not entirely sure West would appreciate that," he said. "He might think I am coming to check up on him, so for the first several months, at least, I will stay away. West needs to learn to stand on his own feet now. I can no longer be a crutch."

Esther cocked her head curiously. "Do you feel you have been?"

Christopher shrugged. "Westley is our youngest son," he said. "I am certain there was some amount of coddling going on, probably up until yesterday. He is very attached to his mother's apron strings."

Dustin scowled. "He is not," she said to him before looking at Esther. "But he can be immature at times. With five older brothers constantly making the decisions, what chance does he have? I agree with my husband—we will not be visiting him anytime soon. Let the man find his own path, his own voice."

Esther understood. The entire situation was delicate for them all. As she changed the subject and engaged Dustin in a conversation about purchasing a finer wardrobe for Elysande, since that had been a topic in the past, Christopher finished up his meal. The two women seemed to be getting on much better, and as the discussion devolved into a women's conversation, Christopher felt confident enough to leave them alone and excused himself. There were a few fine stallions in Marius' stable that he wanted to get a look at and possibly purchase, so as the main topic in the hall became silks and fabrics, Christopher wandered out to the stables.

Already, it was a good day.

But it would be the last good day for some time to come.

○3

"ARE YOU AWAKE?"

Westley was lying facedown in the bed, one leg hanging over the side. He'd been dreaming about a little cottage near a lake on his father's lands and how he always wanted to have the chamber that faced the lake when he'd been a child. Curtis and Roi would take it over, however, and kick him out, but his dream was about him reclaiming that chamber.

Until a soft voice filtered into his dream.

"Westley? Are you awake?"

He peeped an eye open, seeing a chamber he didn't recognize until he quickly remembered whose chamber it was and why he was there. A sleepy smile spread across his face and he rolled onto his back, finding himself gazing up at Elysande. She was wearing the green linen with the white shift underneath, her hair pulled into a braid. She was smiling in return, and he reached out, grasping her by the wrist and pulling her down to him on the bed.

"Good morn to you, *cherie*," he murmured, kissing her on the lips. "How did you sleep?"

He was pulling so forcefully that Elysande had to put her hands on his chest to keep from falling into him. "Well," she said as he kissed her face repeatedly. "And you?"

"Well," he said. "What there was of it, anyway."

Her cheeks turned their predictable shade of red. "It is at least two hours after sunrise," she said. "The castle is up and moving. I am certain our parents are up and moving. Should we go and see them?"

He stopped kissing her and sighed. "Must we?"

She snorted. "Why not?"

"Because I would rather stay here with you."

Elysande was completely unused to flirtation or any manner of love talk, and her red face continued to get redder. "We cannot stay here all day, Westley."

"Why not?"

She didn't really have an answer for him other than she was embarrassed by the idea. More than likely because if they did stay there all day, everyone would know what they were doing. While he didn't care and, in fact, would be rather proud of it, she did and probably wouldn't. She was still a delicate maiden in mind even if her body wasn't. Her body had responded quite spectacularly to her new husband. Westley tried not to think of that because he was going to become amorous all over again.

"Very well," he said, tossing off the covers and sitting up. "We shall go see the parents. But we are going to eat in this chamber tonight and spend all night and mayhap even all day tomorrow here. I think we have that right."

Elysande picked up a horsehair brush and began brushing the ends of her braid. "What right?" she said. "To become recluses?"

He frowned. "Do you not wish to spend time alone with me?"

She smiled bashfully. "Of course I do," she said. "But we have the rest of our lives to do that. If you do it too much now, won't you become weary of me?"

He stood up, his naked body in full view. "Of course not," he said as if that were the most foolish thing he'd ever heard. "How can you even suggest such a thing?"

She noticed he was nude and kept her back turned to him, though she wasn't as shocked as she had been last night when he first stripped down. She'd spent the entire night attached to that body one way or the other, and she rather liked it. She noticed that he was grabbing for his breeches, but she stopped him.

"Are you not going to wash this morning?" she asked.

He froze, looking at her strangely. "Why?"

"Because... because of last night," she said, refusing to look at him as she gestured to her pelvic area. "There was a lot of... Well, there was perspiration and... it was sticky and... Well, are you going to wash it off?"

Her last few words came out quickly, like a plea, and he smiled as he put the breeches back where he found them. "I take it you like a clean husband?"

She shrugged. "Not really," she said. "It is not that. But there is much of... me on you."

He came up behind her, wrapping his arms around her and burying his face in her hair. "Would it be wrong of me to say that I like smelling you on me?" he said. "It will remind me of you."

Elysande didn't say any more, mostly because his body against hers had her heart racing. She could smell him, too, and it was not unpleasant. But the truth was that things had gotten a bit sticky last night, and proof of her virginity, faint though it may be, was still on him and still on the bed where body fluids had run. She was embarrassed by the whole thing, but not so embarrassed when he held her close. She reasoned that it was something she had to become accustomed to.

His body smelling like hers.

Her body smelling like his.

"Then get dressed," she said. "I will not complain if you want to smell like me all day."

He kissed her head, lightly spanked her bottom affectionately, and returned for his breeches. In little time, he was dressed in the same clothing he had worn the day before. He pulled the horsehair brush out of her hand and ran it through his hair a couple of times, something he didn't normally do, but he figured that a woman wanted a husband that was at least moderately groomed. Perhaps he'd even buy a brush for himself at some point. He thought he was finished and set the brush down, going to the door to wait for her, but she grabbed him by the hand and pulled him back over to her dressing table. Picking up a comb this time instead of the brush, she began to drag it through his locks.

"Honestly, Westley," she said, "your hair looks like a nest for birds."

He frowned. "It does not!"

"I noticed it from the first."

He tried to look at her as she yanked the comb through his

hair. "That is the first thing you noticed about me?" he said. Then he winced when she hit a snag. "Och, lady. Be careful with that thing."

Elysande struggled not to laugh. "You have a big knot at the back of your neck," she said, trying to work on it. "When is the last time you combed your hair?"

"That is none of your business."

"You know, if you are not going to brush it, then you should simply shave it off."

He quickly darted away from her, putting his hands on his hair. "How dare you suggest such a thing," he said without force. "I am like Samson of the Bible. My hair is my strength. You stay away from me, Delilah."

Elysande started to laugh at him, the silly lad, but her smile quickly faded. *Samson,* he'd mentioned.

That brought her thoughts around to Fitz Walter.

"Do you think he'll come back?" she asked softly.

He wasn't sure what she meant. "Who?"

"Samson Fitz Walter."

He lifted his eyebrows. "Ah," he said. "Truthfully, love, I do not know. Possibly."

"How is your nose this morning?"

He touched it gingerly. "A little sore," he said. "Is it bruised?"

"A little."

Reaching out, he took her hand, bringing it to his lips for a sweet kiss. "Do not worry about him," he said, softly but with confidence. "He cannot hurt us. He cannot get to you. I will kill him if he tries, so I do not want you to worry. Understood?"

She nodded, but was clearly still upset. "Understood," she said. "But are you simply going to leave things the way they are?

With your giving him a beating and his retreating home?"

He tucked her hand into the crook of his elbow as he led her to the chamber door. "What would you have me do?"

She shrugged. "You will be Lord Ledbury someday," she said. "Fitz Walter is a neighbor, like it or not. We cannot live the rest of our lives in fear of his attacks."

"Do you want me to apologize to him?"

"Nay, not apologize," she said as he opened the door for them both. "But... ease the situation somehow? Mayhap speak with the man and try to be diplomatic? I have a feeling you would make a very good diplomat. You know how to speak to people."

He looked at her as if impressed. "Flattery, Lady de Lohr?" he said with a wink. "Well done."

She giggled as they headed out of the chamber and toward the stairs. "It is not flattery if it is true," she said. "But mayhap you should consider trying to at least make peace with Fitz Walter. I fear what a conflict with him will do to Massington. To us."

They hit the stairs and Westley went down first, holding her hand as he went. "If that is your wish, then let me speak to my father about it," he said. "Fitz Walter's animosity is toward my father. Let me see what he thinks and form a course of action. Fair enough?"

She nodded. "Fair enough," she said. They came to the bottom of the stairs with the entry to the keep looming in front of them. "Thank you, Westley. For listening to my concerns."

He smiled and kissed her hand. "I will always listen to your concerns, my lady," he said. "Your opinion means a great deal to me."

"You would not have said that three days ago."

"Three days ago, I was a fool."

Holding hands, they quit the keep, heading out into the bright, if somewhat brisk, morning. As soon as they exited, Elysande caught sight of Freddie over near the kitchen yard and, begging leave of Westley, headed off in the woman's direction because Freddie seemed to be wrestling with a large basket in her arms. That left Westley continuing on to the great hall alone.

Or, at least, he thought he was alone.

Suddenly, Olan was beside him.

"My lord," Olan said. "May I congratulate you on your wedding yesterday? I've not had the chance to offer my best wishes."

Westley came to a halt, facing the young knight. "Thank you," he said. "And for your help last night with Fitz Walter, you have my gratitude as well."

Olan nodded quickly. "In truth, I was hoping to find you alone this morning," he said. "I had a conversation with Fitz Walter on the road as he left Massington last night. I wanted to speak with you about it but did not want to do it in front of Lady Elysande or your father. What I have to say is for your ears alone. Is it convenient now?"

That was a question Olan had been waiting to ask since last night, since he made his deal with Fitz Walter and the man had staggered home. Olan had been up most of the night, planning what he would say to Westley, planning how he would get the man to do what he wanted him to do. The immediate need was all he was concerned with.

The far-reaching consequences of his actions were of little matter.

He needed to get Westley alone.

"I suppose so," Westley said. "I think Ella is over in the kitchen yard, so you may speak now. What is it?"

Olan looked around. He didn't want anyone, like Christopher or even Elysande, interrupting them. On the wall, Harker was looking right at them, and Olan didn't want the man seeing more than he should. He motioned for Westley to come with him.

"Let us find some place private to speak," he said, gesturing to a small tower directly ahead. "The armory should suffice. I do not want anyone else hearing what I must tell you."

"It must be important."

"It is."

Westley followed him to the armory but was hesitant to go inside. He'd just married the woman that Olan loved and, not knowing Olan at all, wasn't sure if the man was trying to lure him into an enclosed room to ambush him, so he stood at the door, with it wide open, as Olan stood inside and looked at him.

"Come inside and close the door, my lord," Olan said.

But Westley begged off. "You'll forgive me if I am not comfortable doing so," he said. "There is no one around to hear us. What did you wish to speak about?"

Olan seemed surprised at first, but then it occurred to him what Westley meant. He'd never shown any animosity toward him and, in fact, had gone out of his way to prove otherwise, but Elysande must have said something.

He could see the mistrust in Westley's eyes.

"My lord, I will give you no trouble, I assure you," he said. "The lady was meant for greater things than me. That is all I will say about it."

Westley's gaze lingered on him for a moment, but he didn't come inside. He remained in the doorway. "You followed Fitz

Walter out of the gatehouse last night," he said. "Tell me what happened."

Olan nodded. "That is what I wanted to speak with you about," he said. "This is not for your father's ears, my lord. Only you."

Westley frowned. "Why me?"

"As the next Lord Ledbury," Olan clarified. "I have been acquainted with Samson Fitz Walter several years now. He is a man who prefers solitude, and he is not the friendly type. From what I know, he does not have any friends in the area. I do not even think he entertains. But he came to Marius a few years ago and the subject of a betrothal between him and Elysande came up. That much you know."

Westley nodded. "I do."

"Clearly, Fitz Walter knows that the marriage has taken place," he said. "He knows that the lady is married and that is the end of his pursuit. But he made many threats against your father as he left last night."

"What *kind* of threats?"

Olan shrugged. "The usual," he said. "He wants the man dead. He kept calling him a murderer. For whatever reason, he views Elysande as a stolen bride. He threatened to steal her back."

"He did, did he?"

"He made a lot of threats last night, most of them aimed at your father," Olan said. "But I was able to calm him a little. He feels he's been grossly insulted by Marius, by your father, and by you. Still, he was not without reason. He understood that the fight was his doing. He came, he threatened, and you reacted. He did not blame you, strangely enough. In fact, he said that he was willing to… talk."

"Talk about what?"

"He wishes to speak with you but does not want your father present," Olan said. "My lord, I do not know what longstanding hatred is between Fitz Walter and your father, but it runs deep. He seems much more amenable to speaking with you and you only, especially if the two of you are to be neighbors."

Westley looked at him dubiously. "Why does he seem amenable to me?" he said. "I am my father's son."

"But you are not your father," Olan said. "It is my sense that the man feels terribly insulted by everyone, and that is not going to be eased if no one discovers why. If there is no peace settlement now, Fitz Walter will keep up his attacks on Massington. Your wedding to Elysande seems to be fueling some rage in him. He wanted to marry her but she was promised to you. He has threatened to bring his army and attack Massington, but if you are able to convince him otherwise, it would mean that we could all live in peace."

"You think he is serious?"

"I do," Olan said. "Most of all, he's serious about Elysande. I am certain you do not wish for her to be in danger for the rest of her life."

"Of course not," Westley said. "But what can I do to convince Fitz Walter not to attack Massington as he has threatened? I thrashed the man within an inch of his life, de Bisby. I cannot believe he would simply overlook that and ask for a parley."

Olan shrugged. "You said it best yesterday morning when you saw Ella training," he said. "Emotions will get you killed in battle. They make a man reckless. I got the sense that Fitz Walter was being fed by his emotions, and, consequently, he was reckless. I also got the sense that he regretted that."

Westley wasn't so sure. But, then again, he didn't know Fitz Walter. All he knew was what his father had told him and now what de Bisby was telling him. Was it possible the man really had acted on impulse and then, after a sound beating, regretted his actions? Of course it was. Westley had been through that very thing in his life before, more than once. He'd gotten too arrogant, taken a pounding, and was sorry for it afterward.

It happened all of the time.

It was very possible it had happened now.

Something else Olan said had his attention. Did Westley want Elysande to be a target for Fitz Walter in the future? Did he want her life at risk from a man who thought he'd been wronged? Of course he didn't. He knew, as he lived and breathed, that he would do anything to protect her. Anything to remove any danger from her life. Odd how the only women he'd ever felt that strongly about were his mother and sisters, but now he was feeling it with Elysande, and he'd never felt so strongly about anything. He'd kill anyone who threatened her, but short of killing them to remove the threat, it was possible there was another way.

A discussion.

Westley had never been the great diplomat, in spite of what Elysande had said. He had brothers who were far more diplomatic than he was. He'd rather speak with his weapons. But what if it was possible to end a forty-year hatred for his father? What if he could end that, too? Would he be willing to try, for his father's sake?

Of course he would.

There was no question.

"Then what do you want me to do?" he finally asked Olan. "Do I take an army to Hell's Forge and parley with Fitz

Walter?"

Olan cocked his head. "If you want to enrage the man, then that would be a way to do it," he said. "My lord, the only way this will work is if you go alone. I will go with you if you wish because I know Fitz Walter. He does not hate me. You and I will go and you will speak with the man and see if there is some accord you can come to. Some peace. Wouldn't that be far better than living with angst and tension, fearful that every time Elysande goes beyond the gates, danger is waiting for her?"

Westley considered that. "I should tell my father," he said. "He would be very angry if I went to speak with Fitz Walter and made a bigger mess out of the situation."

"He will also tell you not to go," Olan said. "Worse still, he will want to go with you. Ultimately, your father is why Fitz Walter is so angry. If he comes with you, that is more dangerous than you can imagine. Why would you expose your father to a man who hates him so?"

"True," Westley said, pondering the situation. Olan had made some very good points. "Very well, then. I'll go, but you will come. It's important that I do not go alone. How far is Hell's Forge from here?"

"Almost a day," Olan said. "Shorter if we ride faster."

"Should I not at least tell my wife?"

My wife.

Olan felt as if a knife had just sliced through him. His body shuddered, imperceptibly, but it was enough to jar him. He hadn't heard those words where they pertained to Elysande yet, and they only served to reinforce that what he was doing was right and necessary. This had to happen. Westley had to go.

He had to be the sacrifice to Fitz Walter.

"Do not tell her," Olan said after a moment. "She never

could keep a secret, and if she tells your father, he will come after you and you will have a very old man facing an enemy who hates him desperately. Again—you should not subject your father to that. But I will tell Harker so at least someone knows where we are if we do not return. Not that I am concerned over that, but just in case."

Westley didn't like any of this, but Olan had made a strong enough case. Perhaps this was just another step in the maturity of Westley de Lohr, the youngest de Lohr brother, the man who needed to grow up. He had a wife now. He had the opportunity to protect her and his father at the same time. Dialogue with an enemy whereby they would at least come to a truce. If that was the best Westley could hope for, he would take it.

"When do you want to leave?" he finally asked. "And even if I do not tell Ella where I am going, I need to tell her something. She will notice if I'm gone for hours."

"True," Olan said. "Then tell her that you have a task to attend to. Mayhap hint that you want to buy her a wedding present. Something that will take you away from Massington for the day."

"Just the day?"

"I do not think this will take too long," Olan said. "Either Fitz Walter will be receptive or he won't. And do not tell her you are going with me. That will make her suspicious."

"Why?"

"Because you are taking a man you hardly know to help you purchase a wedding gift?"

"You know her better than I do. It could happen."

Olan shook his head. "I would not chance it," he said. "Mayhap you should not tell her anything at all. She'll wonder where you are, but I do not think she will panic about it. She'll probably assume you have business elsewhere."

"My father knows I do not."

"Then they will wonder where you went, and when you return to tell them that you have brokered a truce with Fitz Walter, they will be pleased and relieved."

Olan seemed to have all of the answers. Since Westley didn't know the man particularly well, he couldn't have known that this was unusual for him. Being *too* helpful, *too* full of suggestions. Since Olan had served at Massington for years, and Elysande trusted him, he would trust him as well.

And that would be his most grievous mistake.

Before the hour was out, they departed through the postern gate, undetected, and headed north for Hell's Forge.

And Harker saw everything.

CHAPTER SEVENTEEN

Two days later

H IS HEAD WAS killing him.
That was the first thing Westley was aware of. A throbbing, dull, sickening ache. When he tried to open his eyes, one eye would open but the other one wouldn't. He seemed to be blind in his left eye.

And he had no idea why.

He didn't even know where he was.

Where in the hell am I?

It was a question with no answer.

"So?" came a voice from the darkness. "You are finally awake? I was wondering if you ever would be."

Westley shifted around, finding it difficult to move because his head felt as if it weighed more than a horse. He could hardly lift it. But with his good eye, he could see that he was on a floor. Somebody's floor.

He grunted in pain.

"Where am I?" he rasped.

"You are with me," a man said. "Do you recognize me?"

Westley could hardly keep his good eye open. "I cannot see

you," he said. "Who are you and where am I?"

The man came around to the front of him. Westley could hear the footsteps. "Think, de Lohr," the man said. "What is your last memory?"

Westley genuinely had no idea. He lay there, on his back, eyes closed and his stomach lurching. He bent a knee up, changing the position of his right leg to take some of the strain off his back, as he lay there and suffered.

"I do not know," he said, sighing heavily. "Massington. I was at Massington."

"You were married."

"I was." Suddenly, Westley was struggling to sit up in a panic. "My wife. Where is my wife?"

Someone kicked him in the left shoulder, shoving him back to the floor. "She is not here," the man said. "If she were here, she would belong to me, not you. You stole something from me."

Westley was in agony. He hit his head again when he fell back, and stars were dancing in front of his eyes. Both eyes, so he knew he still had sight in the eye he couldn't currently see out of. His mind was muddled, but it was working. He lifted a hand to touch the closed eye, realizing he had blood or mud or something caked on it. All the while, however, he was thinking on the man's words.

You stole something from me.

That gave him a final clue as to where he was.

"Fitz Walter," he said after a moment. "I'm at Hell's Forge."

"You are."

"I was told you wanted to speak with me," Westley said. "What is the meaning of all of this? What have you done to me?"

Samson gazed down at Westley, sprawled out on his solar floor. "You have figured out who I am," he said, avoiding the questions. "I wondered if you would."

"What am I doing here?"

"Isn't it obvious?"

"If it was, I would not have asked."

Samson grunted. "Then you are as stupid as your father," he said. "He is a murderer and a thief, you know. I should not be surprised that his son is also a thief."

"What did I steal?"

"My wife."

"I did not steal Elysande," Westley said, struggling with his temper. "She was never yours to begin with."

Samson drew back a booted foot and kicked Westley in the left thigh. Westley grunted, but he didn't flinch. He simply lay there, listening to Samson move around him.

"My offer to Marius was fair," Samson said, sounding irritated. "But he tricked me. I think he used my offer to coerce a more lucrative offer from your father."

Westley groaned as he sat up unsteadily, waiting for another boot to come flying at him. "I will not speak of your betrothal offer," he said, hand to his aching head. "I want to know why I am here. I was told you wanted to speak with me and I was told you wanted a truce. That you regretted your actions at Massington. I came to your gatehouse and…"

"And I dropped a stone on your head," Samson said.

Now things were starting to make sense. "So that's what happened," Westley muttered. "I remember riding up the gatehouse and then… nothing."

"That is because we saw you coming and were prepared."

"To kill me?"

"To capture you."

There was a long pause as Westley digested that. "Then you lied to Olan to get me here."

"Nay," Samson said. "Olan lied to *you*."

Confused, Westley tilted his head back to look at him. "*He* lied to me?"

Samson eyed him. "He does not want you married to Lady Elysande any more than I do," he said. "After you so unfairly beat me at Massington, Olan promised to bring you to me. He wanted you away from the lady, and I was happy to comply. I want you away from her, too."

Now, everything was laid clear to Westley. He could see what had happened and silently cursed himself for being so bloody stupid. He'd trusted a knight he didn't know—a knight he knew to be in love with his wife, no less—and tried to give the man the benefit of the doubt. Olan had seemed sincere, as if he truly wanted to help Westley protect Elysande against Fitz Walter's threat.

But he didn't want to help Westley at all.

He wanted to hurt him.

Damn...

Now, Westley was in a bind. He was a prisoner of a man who hated his father and had for many years. More foolish still was the fact that he'd walked right into it. He'd been too gullible, which wasn't a trait he usually possessed. He'd developed a keen sense of caution over the years, one that had served him well, but in this case, he'd let a knight talk him into something he was unsure of to begin with.

He should have gone with his gut.

Damn!

If he was going to survive this, he was going to have to think of something and think fast. He was going to have to be cleverer than the people who'd duped him, although given where he found himself, that might be a monumental task because he'd walked right into this with his eyes open. Now, he was going to have to think like they did—or try. He was going to have to get himself out of a situation that could very well mean his end.

"So I am away from her now," he finally said. "Give me some water to wash off the blood before you decide what to do with me. At least let me see death when it comes."

Samson's gaze lingered on him for a moment before he motioned to Alend, who had been standing by the door the entire time. The man went darting off to find water for the prisoner as Samson stood over by his table, by the raven who had been watching the event with its beady eyes, and watched Westley struggle.

"Now," Samson said, "you and I are going to have a serious discussion."

"What about?"

"About you signing your death confession."

Westley frowned, tilting his head back to look at the man. "What confession?"

Because Westley was looking at him, Samson picked up a cup of wine and took a healthy swallow. He knew Westley must have been very thirsty, and hungry, so he was going to make it hurt.

"A confession that you deliberately stole Elysande from me," he said. "A confession that your father colluded with Marius to steal her from me."

"What do you need something like that for?"

Samson took another swallow. "To take to the king," he said as if Westley were an imbecile. "I want the king to see how the great Earl of Hereford and Worcester wronged me and wronged my entire family. My hatred for your father goes way back, Westley. Far, far back. I want the king to know the character of the man he trusts so much, and from his own son, no less."

Westley thought the man sounded deranged. Samson Fitz Walter wasn't a rational man. He was speaking of old grudges and imagined thievery, which meant Westley couldn't really contest him. It would only drive the man to anger and perhaps even something desperate. Westley had to recover a little before he could take Samson on physically, which meant he had to stall. Perhaps he even needed to feed the man's fantasies, anything to keep him from going mad and trying to kill him.

Westley had one thing in his favor—he wasn't in the vault. He was in a chamber, unguarded, and he intended to keep that status. He was going to have to do what he needed to do in order to survive.

He hoped his father and wife would forgive him.

"Thank God," he muttered.

Samson eyed him. "Why are you thanking God? He has done you no favors by allowing you to end up here."

Westley grunted, long and deep. "I thank Him because you see what I see," he said. "No one ever sees what I see, but you have. Truthfully, I did not even know about you until I was forced to come to Massington. Forced into a marriage I wanted no part of. Why did you simply not abduct Elysande and marry her? If you had, I would not have had to."

Samson stared at him for a few moments, warily. "What are you talking about?"

"Just that," Westley said loudly, smacking his hand against the floor. "It is your fault I had to marry Elysande. I never wanted to. I tried to run but my brothers captured me, and then I was transported to Massington in a fortified carriage I could not escape from, where I was forced to marry Ledbury's daughter. I never wanted that!"

He was speaking so passionately by the time he was finished that Samson was mildly taken aback. But he was also greatly suspicious.

"Do not lie to me," he snarled.

"I am *not* lying," Westley insisted strongly. "If you do not believe me, ask anyone at Massington what happened when I arrived. Elysande attacked me with a sword. She tried to fight me. Do you think I want to marry someone like that? If you think so, you would be mad. Nay, good sir, you are more than welcome to Elysande. Let me escape to France or Flanders, and you can tell everyone you killed me and then marry her—but I warn you, she is not worth the trouble. She will try to kill you when you sleep because the woman is mad."

Samson eyed him unsteadily. "Is this true?" he said. "I can easily find out if this is true."

Westley jabbed a finger at him. "Then I suggest you do," he said. "All of it is true. I was brought to Massington in a cage and Elysande attacked me when I arrived. Whatever source you have at Massington, because clearly someone is giving you information, ask them. They will confirm what I have said."

Samson was slowly sliding into confusion. He had not expected this kind of reaction from a man he'd just abducted. Westley seemed more than happy to let him have Elysande.

Nay, he hadn't expected that at all.

Alend chose that moment to return bearing a bowl of water and rags. He tried to hand them to Westley on the floor, but Samson ordered him to put Westley at the table. Alend put the water and rags on the table before pulling Westley to his feet and helping him stagger into a chair. As Westley picked up the rag and began cleaning his face off, Samson stood back by his raven and frowned.

"Then I shall discover the truth," he said, watching Westley use the water to soak away the crusted blood on his eye. "If you have lied to me, your punishment shall be swift."

Westley looked up at him, the rag over one eye. "And if I am telling you the truth, I would be more than happy to bring Elysande to your doorstep," he said. "I never wanted this to begin with. I've got another lady I'm fond of over in Daventry, and she's the one I would rather wed."

Alend was standing nearby—Westley could see him out of the corner of his eye. He thought that, perhaps, he'd better show that he was sincere and in control, not cowering and hoping Samson would believe his lies. He had to play the game. With a growl, he threw the water bowl in Alend's direction, spraying water all over the wall.

"Get me clean water," he demanded. "And bring me some food!"

Given that Westley was big, and muscular, and the least bit frightening, Alend fled to do as he'd been ordered. But Samson remained over by the table that contained his writing kit, empty cups, junk, and that old raven. He simply stood there and watched, trying to figure out if Westley really was lying to him.

Trying to figure out if he should kill the man where he sat.

But he wouldn't. At least, not now. In spite of his doubts, Samson was rather interested in how Westley reacted to all of this. In fact, a thought occurred to him as Westley painfully peeled off some of the dried blood from his eyebrow.

"If you did not want this marriage and all is as you say, why did you attack me when I came to Massington?" he said. "I had come to speak to Marius. You did not need to involve yourself."

Westley winced as he pulled away a rather large blob of dried blood. "Because you were threatening my father," he said. "In spite of the marriage, he is still my father."

Samson absorbed that statement. Westley was more agitated than he had been, his faculties returning along with his rage. And perhaps even his fear. Samson touched his jaw where Westley had hit him back at Massington, feeling the familiar ache and remembering the pledge he'd made after he was beaten and humiliated.

I can do nothing against Hereford, but give me his son and I can control the man.

Hurt the son and you will hurt the man.

Now he had exactly what he wanted in front of him. He had the son of his nemesis, and if Westley was to be believed, there was a crack in the foundation that was Hereford. The youngest son, possibly rebellious against his father? It had been known to happen. Kings often had sons that were against them. So did great earls, evidently.

It *was* possible.

Perhaps this would be better than Samson had planned.

CHAPTER EIGHTEEN

"**H**E DID NOT run away," Christopher said. "I refuse to believe he ran away. He was happy with this marriage and with his new wife. The day of his marriage, he was happier than I have ever seen him. He did *not* run away."

He was facing off against Marius and Esther in Marius' cluttered, smelly solar. Marius was surprisingly sober and Esther was distraught. Elysande had been crying steadily since the day before, and Dustin had already sent word to Lioncross, summoning the sons they'd left behind to make haste to Massington.

Westley is missing.

That was what the missive said.

But no one wanted to truly believe it.

Least of all Christopher.

"If he did not flee, then where is he?" Marius demanded. "He has married my daughter, assumed a title, and now he is gone? Mayhap that was his intention all along!"

Christopher eyed Marius with a great deal of displeasure. "It was not his intention," he said. "Your daughter agrees that they were happy. The marriage was agreeable. But somewhere between the morning after the wedding and this very moment, Westley has vanished. His horse is gone, but his possessions are still here. Would a man flee and leave his possessions?"

Marius didn't have an answer for that. He was upset and hungover, a bad situation for him to be in, so he stood up and went in search of the wine that was like mother's milk to him. As he found a half-full pitcher of it on a nearby table, Esther looked to Christopher apologetically.

"I do not believe he fled, either," she said quietly. "He left his things. He left Ella. What could have happened to him?"

Christopher didn't know. All he knew was that the more time passed, the more panicked he became. It wasn't like Westley to run off like this, much less run off without telling anyone. Wearily, he rubbed his forehead.

"I do not know, my lady," he said. "My soldiers have asked everyone at Massington if they have seen him. Your knights, Olan and Harker, are searching for clues. The rain yesterday has washed away any trace of hoofprints, so we cannot track his horse. My men have been out on the road for two days, looking for clues. I even sent them into Ledbury and Hereford to look for him, but no one has seen him. My wife sent a missive home to Lioncross, so if he has gone home, I will know about it soon. We *will* find him."

Christopher rubbed his head again, suffering through another one of the terrible headaches he'd been prone to for the past few years. No sleep and plenty of stress weren't helping. Esther noticed that he was rubbing at his temples.

"Mayhap you should lie down, my lord," she said. "I will send warm wine with willow bark in it. That will soothe your head."

Christopher forced a smile at her, knowing she was trying

to be kind. "Mayhap I shall," he said. "I do not think I've slept much over the past two nights."

"Go," Esther said, eyeing her husband. "I will stay with Marius. Where is your wife?"

Christopher grunted as he stood unsteadily. "She went to the kitchens to find something to tempt me," he said. "I've not eaten much in the past two days, either. I have been a good deal of trouble to you and to my wife."

Esther smiled. "No trouble at all," she said. "If I hear anything, I will send word to you right away."

"Thank you, my lady."

As Christopher lumbered out, heading for the mural stairs that led to the upper chambers because Esther had moved him and Dustin into a room in the keep, his wife was down in the kitchens because the cook was making stuffed boiled eggs at her request. It was the one thing Christopher would go out of his way to eat, so she wanted to have something for him that he could not refuse. He hadn't eaten much lately. The cook at Massington was a man who had served the House of du Nor since the days of Marius' father, and he had an excellent recipe for stuffed eggs. Dustin watched him make them, a dish she wanted to take back to Lioncross with her.

Essentially, the hard-boiled eggs were cut in half and the yolks extracted. The yolks were mashed with vinegar, cream, salt, minced pickled onions, dill, a little cheese, and then some chopped egg whites. They were then folded back into the egg halves, rolled in flour, and fried in lard. Dustin had one as soon as it was finished, and it was utterly delicious, so she confiscated about a dozen for Christopher. The cook piled them into a basket, and she took that and a pitcher of watered wine, heading back to the solar to find her husband and see if she could tempt his appetite.

Given the stress of the past two days, it could go either way.

The kitchens of Massington were in a separate outbuilding, tucked into the kitchen yard and about halfway between the great hall and the keep. There was a little alleyway between the great hall and the wall of the kitchen yard that provided a nice, protected pathway between the locations, and she was in this passageway, shoving an egg into her mouth, as she swiftly moved for the keep. Just as she drew near the small yard that surrounded the keep, a shadow stepped out from the gateway that led to the great hall.

"My lady?"

It was Harker. He startled Dustin and she nearly choked on the egg, coughing as she tried to swallow it and not spray it all over the ground. Hand covering her mouth, she managed to choke it down.

"Harker, is it?" she said, coughing out the last little bit. "My apologies. You startled me."

"Forgive me, my lady," Harker said. "I did not mean to. But I wanted to speak with you alone."

Dustin looked at him curiously as she wiped the egg crumbs off her mouth. "Why?"

Harker sighed heavily, looking around as if hoping no one would see them. "My lady, I must tell you something," he said quietly. "But first, you will promise me that you will not tell your husband where you received your information. If he knows, he may want to interrogate me, and I am not the one to be interrogated."

Dustin's curiosity began to shift into something suspicious. "What do you mean?" she said. "What information are you speaking of?"

Harker hesitated, looking around again, before continuing. "On the day your son disappeared, I saw him speaking with Olan," he said.

Dustin's eyebrows lifted. "Olan?" she repeated. "I do not know who that is."

"The other Massington knight," Harker said. "My lady, forgive me for saying this quickly, but I must before someone sees us in conversation. When Samson Fitz Walter was chased from Massington, Olan was tasked with ensuring he and his men departed. I came back into the bailey, but Olan remained on the road with Fitz Walter for quite some time. When he finally returned, he went straight to bed. He did not speak with me or anyone else that I am aware of."

Dustin wasn't quite following him. "Why is that an issue?"

"It would not be, under normal circumstances," Harker said. "I am not explaining this well, but I believe that Olan has a loyalty to Fitz Walter."

"Why should you think that?"

"Because his cousin serves Fitz Walter," Harker said. "I believe he sends the man information from time to time. He does not think I know, but I do. I have for years. He pays a soldier to run to Hell's Forge. He also pays him for his silence on the matter."

Now, Dustin was starting to catch on. "So you think that Fitz Walter coerced Olan to do something?"

Harker shook his head in a helpless gesture. "All I know is that Westley was last seen with Olan," he said. "I saw them together myself. Then they both disappeared, only Olan returned in the middle of the night. He does not think I am aware of his return, but a servant told me. It is my belief that Westley and Olan left together, and mayhap Olan tricked him somehow and turned him over to Fitz Walter, to whom Westley had just given a savage beating. Do you understand what I am telling you now?"

Dustin did. Her eyes widened and she gasped. "You think Westley has been taken by Samsom Fitz Walter?"

"The only way you will know that is if you interrogate Olan," he said. "But you must not tell your husband that I told you this, because he will want to speak with me—and if Olan senses that I saw him with Westley, he may try to run. He may even try to kill me to silence me. There is no knowing. When a knight goes bad, he will do anything to keep his secret. Therefore, your husband must not know it was me. No one must."

Dustin was starting to quiver. She was absolutely terrified by what she was hearing. "My God," she breathed. "There is a viper at Massington and he has struck my son."

Harker wasn't sure how to respond to her. He had said all he intended to say, something he'd wrestled with for two days. He was positive that Olan had something to do with the disappearance of Westley, but given that Harker didn't like Westley very much, he'd kept his mouth shut. He was glad that Westley was gone, but that lasted for about a day. Then his conscience started to get the better of him. Even if he didn't like Westley's arrogance, his disappearance was concerning, and hurting, a great many people.

They had to know what he knew.

"Tell your husband, Lady Hereford," he said. "I will go back to my duties, but you must tell him now. And you must not let Olan know that you know until you can cage him in a room and not let him leave. If he flees, you'll never know what happened to your son."

Dustin had never been so frightened in her entire life. "Thank you," she whispered.

And then she was gone.

Harker went back to his duties, hoping he'd done the right thing.

And he could only hope he had done it in time.

ଓ

"CHRIS?"

Dustin entered the small, warm chamber she and her husband were sharing, setting the basket of stuffed eggs on the nearest table as she scurried over to the bed.

"Chris? Are you awake?"

He wasn't. It was the first real sleep he'd had in two days, especially after Esther's wine had arrived, but Dustin's hissing had brought him around. The chamber was dark, the oilcloths pulled and embers glowing in the hearth, but he could see her outline in the dim light.

"I am awake," he mumbled. "But I was not when you came in."

Over near the bed, Dustin struck a flint and stone and lit the taper at the bedside. When she knelt down next to the bed, Christopher could immediately see that she had been weeping. More awake now, he reached out a hand and gently cupped her face.

"Do not cry, sweet," he said softly. "We will find Westley, and when we do, I shall kill him for giving us all such a scare. You needn't worry."

Dustin shook her head firmly. "Listen to me, please," she said. "He has been abducted by Fitz Walter."

Christopher frowned and sat up in bed. "What are you

talking about?"

Dustin was trying very hard not to sob. "Chris, I was sworn to secrecy about the source of the information I am about to tell you, but I find I cannot keep it from you in good conscience," she said. "You must not do anything about it. You must not contact the person who gave me this information. You must focus on the information itself. That is the best chance of us finding Westley alive."

She wasn't making any sense, and he took her hands in his, giving them a squeeze. "Breathe, love, breathe," he said quietly. "Now, tell me what you know. What has happened?"

Dustin took a deep breath. "As I was coming back from the kitchens, Harker stopped me," she said. "You know Harker—the Teutonic knight."

Christopher nodded. "I know of him."

She continued. "He told me that he saw Olan and Westley leave Massington two days ago, only Olan returned and Westley did not," she said. "Harker says that Olan is loyal to Fitz Walter because he has a cousin who serves him. Harker believes that Olan took Westley to Fitz Walter and that Westley is now his captive."

Christopher was stunned. "My God," he gasped. "But... why? Why would he do such a thing?"

"Because Olan is sweet on Elysande," Dustin said, wiping a tear that had trickled out of her right eye. "He did this out of jealousy or spite. Who knows? Chris, what are we going to do?"

She was starting to cry, and he pulled her onto the bed, into his embrace. He held her tightly as his mind whirled—*what are we going to do?* Truthfully, he didn't know. It had already been two days. There was a very real possibility that Westley was already dead, but Christopher wasn't going to say that to

Dustin. She was probably already thinking it, but he wasn't going to voice it. Not now.

Now, he had to focus or all would be lost.

His son would be lost.

Forever.

"You already sent word to Lioncross, did you not?" he asked.

Dustin nodded, pulling her face out of his chest and wiping her eyes. "As soon as we realized that Westley was missing," she said. "We should be hearing something soon."

Christopher thought on that. "Very soon if they moved swiftly," he said. "When we left, Curtis and Roi and Myles were still there. Douglas was heading home. And Peter was at Ludlow."

"Then mayhap Curtis and Roi and Myles will come," Dustin said hopefully. "But can we truly wait for them? Olan must be interrogated immediately. Every second that passes is a second that Westley is in danger."

Christopher rubbed her arms, soothing her. "I know," he said. "But we must plan well for this. We cannot simply run off in a panic."

"I am not panicking," she insisted. "But we cannot wait. Westley needs help."

Christopher could see how upset she was, seized with the urgency of the situation. There was a time when he could have taken on Olan quite easily and interrogated the man to death, but the truth was that he was an old man with health issues now. He was still big and strong, but could he take on a man like Olan, who was younger and more agile? Possibly. He had about eighty de Lohr soldiers with him, including some senior sergeants who could quite easily take Olan into custody and contain him while Christopher interrogated him. He had thought to wait for his younger, strong sons, but perhaps Dustin was right—perhaps Westley didn't have that kind of time.

But he would need his sons to march on Hell's Forge.

God, he hated the thought of Westley in that place.

He hated the thought of trying to breech it even more.

Well did he remember those many years ago when John was tearing across England, wreaking havoc, and the siege of Hell's Forge to force Ralph Fitz Walter's older brother to surrender the bastion. The man was Samson's father, and it was possible that Samson remembered that siege also. It was bloody and long but, in the end, Hell's Forge held. Christopher was terrified that if he laid siege again, it would continue to hold.

With Westley inside of it.

But he couldn't relay that fear to his wife. She was already upset enough. Now, he was going to have to move and gain information before he could plan a successful campaign. Hopefully, reinforcements from Lioncross would be there soon, because there was no time to waste.

"You're right," he finally said. "He does."

He pushed her out of the way so he could rise from bed, going in search of his clothing as Dustin watched anxiously.

"What are you going to do?" she asked.

Christopher pulled off the heavy sleeping robe he was wearing. "To find Marius," he said. "If the man isn't sober and I have to force boiled fruit juice and eggs and honey down his throat to help him regain his senses, then that is what I am going to do. I need him and he *will* comply. I will not accept anything less."

He pulled a tunic over his head as Dustin rushed forward to

help him dress. "He started this by being deceptive about not telling us that Fitz Walter had made an offer for Elysande," she said. "And his knight is the one who has betrayed Westley. When we regain our son, I will advocate that you lay siege to Massington, oust Marius, and place Westley in command. How dare that man cause us such grief!"

She was moving swiftly and angrily in helping him dress, which meant Christopher eventually stood there while she did everything for him. When she pulled the ties on his breeches too tight, he grunted and put a hand over hers.

"Sweetheart, I realize we are not having any more children, but if you make that any tighter, something you and I both greatly value may be restricted to the point of death," he said, watching her grin. "Ease up, my love. I am not the enemy."

She started laughing. "What are you waiting for?" she said, pointing to the door. "Marius is waiting for you."

A smile flickered across his lips, the first one in two days. "Aye, general," he said. "Anything else?"

The grin faded from Dustin's face as she looked up at him. "Just bring my little lad home," she said, tearing up. "My Westley. He was such a difficult birth, Chris. I would be destroyed for him to survive only to be cut down by Ralph's nephew."

His mirth faded as well. "I know," he murmured.

"Ralph tried to destroy us once. He is still trying, even from the grave."

A deadly gleam came to Christopher's eyes. Like the Defender of the Realm of old, a title he had held for years, Christopher de Lohr was not to be trifled with.

Not even from beyond the grave.

"Not if I can help it," he rumbled. "I killed him once. I can do it again."

Leaving his wife wiping away tears, Christopher went in search of Marius.

CHAPTER NINETEEN

S HE'D HEARD EVERYTHING.

Two days of believing Westley had lied to her and run out on her were summarily shattered when she heard her father and Christopher in conversation.

Westley had been given over to Fitz Walter by Olan.

Truly, Elysande hadn't meant to eavesdrop, but she hadn't slept in two days and had barely eaten, and she had been reverting to her life before Westley entered her world. She was returning to that nearly feral creature who liked to dress in old broadcloth and breeches, the one who wanted to learn to fight, and this day had seen her preparing to go out to the troop house and resume her training with Harker. She wanted to forget about Westley de Lohr and all of the sweet lies he'd told her, but her determination to resume her training had come to a halt when she heard her father and Christopher speaking in her father's solar. Mostly, she'd heard Christopher's angry tone and her father's resigned responses.

Westley hadn't run. He'd been abducted.

By Olan.

With that realization, everything in Elysande was filled with rage. Wild, unadulterated rage. She'd slumped against the wall next to the solar door, listening to her father and Christopher plan how they were going to get Westley back, alive.

Alive.

To think of Westley in such danger drove her to tears. Hot, painful tears, and she had to slap her hand over her mouth to keep from sobbing aloud. For two long days she'd thought the worst of him, cursing him and hating him so much that she refused to sleep in her bed because he'd been there. It still smelled like him. Instead, she'd slept on the floor and Freddie had slept next to her, trying to give her some comfort. But there was no comfort to be had.

Until now.

Now, she knew she'd been wrong.

Slumped against the wall, she could hear Christopher speaking on the fact that his sons would soon be here with his army and they could rise to Fitz Walter's threat, but in the same breath, he was lamenting the fact that Hell's Forge was impenetrable. Evidently, he'd fought there before, and he knew how difficult it was to penetrate. Westley's life was hanging in the balance, but he couldn't get to him immediately.

That brought up the subject of Olan.

Christopher blamed Marius for harboring an immoral knight, in love with his daughter and willing to do anything to ensure her marriage was destroyed. As Elysande listened to that, she began to realize that she had been at the core of Olan's betrayal. He couldn't have her, so he didn't want Westley to have her either—so much so that he gave the man over to Christopher's deadly enemy, who also happened to want her. The more she listened, the more appalled she became.

The common denominator, for the entire situation, was

her.

It was horrifying and sickening. She could hear them discussing it further, discussing how to deal with Olan, who was apparently oblivious to the fact that they were onto him. Christopher wanted to wait to confront him until his older sons arrived, but Marius wanted to address it with Olan at that moment. He wanted an immediate confession out of the man.

So did Elysande.

She wanted the truth.

And then she wanted to kill him.

As she stood there and debated what to do, her father called from the solar, summoning the nearest servant. Elysande darted into the shadows, underneath the stairs, as a servant came forth from the passage that led to the stores. Marius sent the man for Olan, so Elysande made the decision to stick around. She wanted to hear the interrogation, too, but she knew if she asked to be part of it, her father wouldn't allow it. He'd never had much faith in the judgment of women, nor did he ever include her in any business, so she knew she would be denied. Therefore, tucked under the mural stairs in the entryway, she crouched down and prepared for Olan to appear.

Waiting...

CHAPTER TWENTY

"ROI! CURT! I'M going to find Papa!"

Having just come in through the gatehouse of Massington, Myles was already off his horse, already heading for the keep. The de Lohr army, as much as they could muster in a short amount of time, had arrived, and in one day and one full night, three thousand de Lohr soldiers, ten wagons, a variety of archers on horseback, and three heavily armed knights made the journey to Massington Castle because the Countess of Hereford and Worcester had asked them to.

The Earl of Leominster, the Earl of Cheltenham, and Lord Monnington had arrived.

All they knew was that Westley was missing. Given the last time they'd seen their brother, and the fact that their father had told them not to come to Massington for the wedding for fear it would only antagonize Westley, they had been confused by Dustin's missive.

Westley is missing. Summon the army and come with all due haste to Massington.

But the confusion hadn't lasted. They knew that Dustin wouldn't have asked for the army if Westley had simply run away. The tone of the missive, and the messenger who delivered it, intimated there was foul play involved, and that had the men at Lioncross scrambling.

Now that they were here, they were desperate to know what had happened.

Which was why Myles was walking very quickly toward the keep. As he was heading there, a knight in partial protection was heading in the same direction. They looked at one another and the man smiled politely.

"My lord?" he said. "You are with the House of de Lohr?"

Myles came to a halt, nodding. "I am," he said. "My mother has summoned us. Do you know where I may find her?"

The man pointed to the keep. "I was just heading in there myself," he said. "I have been summoned by my lord. I am Olan de Bisby. I serve Lord Ledbury."

"Myles de Lohr."

Olan nodded in greeting. "A pleasure, my lord," he said. But his features sobered. "I am very sorry about your brother. We have been looking everywhere for him."

Myles nodded, acknowledging the effort, then pointed at the keep. "Are my parents inside?"

"As far as I know," Olan said, quickly moving toward the keep and gesturing for Myles to follow. "Come inside, my lord. I did not mean to delay you."

"You did not," Myles said. "We just arrived. My brothers should be right behind me."

Olan took him up the stairs and into the keep. The heavy entry door creaked back on its hinges, admitting Myles into a two-storied entry chamber that smelled heavily of dust and smoke. To his left was a chamber off the entry, and he could hear voices.

He recognized one of them.

"Papa?" he said, charging into the chamber because he knew his father was in there. "We are here. What has happened?"

Christopher was in the process of heavily watering down Marius' wine. The man wanted desperately to drink, and the only way Christopher would let him was if the wine was cut with boiled water. He'd sent for it from the kitchen but it had arrived hot, as they always had a supply of simmering water on hand for washing and other things, so Christopher was cutting the wine with hot water, making it hot wine. Myles coming through the door saw him spill some of the water on to the floor in surprise.

"Myles," he said, breathing a sigh of relief. "You have come."

Myles went up to his father, putting his hands on the man's shoulders. "Of course I have come," he said. "Mama sent for us, so we are here. Brought half the damn army with us. What in the hell happened with Westley?"

Given Olan was in the chamber, too, it was all Christopher could do not to charge the man or, at the very least, point accusing fingers at him in front of Myles. Instead, he grasped for words.

"Gone," he finally said. "Who came with you?"

"Curtis and Roi," Myles said. "Sherry remained at Lioncross with Adam, but he sent Andrew, Gabriel, and Nicholas."

Andrew, Gabriel, and Nicholas were Christin and Alexander's eldest sons. Adam was another older son, a very capable commander much in the vein of his father. But Christopher felt a good deal of relief already knowing that his grandsons, fully fledged and very capable knights, had come.

"Who else?" he asked.

"Curtis brought Chris," Myles said. "You know he has only seen eighteen years, but he has already been knighted. Curtis wanted him with us. Arthur is with him, too."

Christopher nodded, accepting the fact that Curtis had brought his two eldest sons with him, mature young men and excellent warriors, even if they were only eighteen and seventeen years, respectively.

"They'll be of help," he said. "Where is Douglas?"

"He had already gone home by the time we received Mama's missive," Myles said. "We've sent word to Axminster for him to return. I do not know how long it will take."

"What about Brie's sons?"

"Max is in the north with his father, as you know," Myles said. "But I've brought Rhodes with me. He's so much like Jax, Papa. Truly astonishing to watch him bellow orders to the army. It's like watching Ajax de Velt all over again."

Christopher smiled faintly, greatly relieved that he had so many sons and grandsons to help him hunt for Westley. But the idea that help had arrived somehow weakened him, giving him enough comfort that he felt he could let go, just a little. He wasn't going to have to do this on his own.

But he was still highly aware of Olan in the chamber.

Now, things were going to get interesting.

"Please bring Andrew and Gabriel and Nicholas inside," he said quietly. "Rhodes, too. I have need of them."

Myles nodded, looking at his father strangely. "And the rest of us?"

"Leave Chris and Arthur with the army," Christopher said. "But the rest of you… I have a task for you."

Myles didn't press him. His father looked horribly pale and

drawn, and it seemed that even that short conversation had taxed him, which was concerning. But he moved swiftly to do his father's bidding. As he headed out of the chamber, Christopher turned to Olan, who was still standing politely near the hearth. He was unarmed, but there were plenty of iron implements for the hearth within reach, and Christopher didn't want to give the man the ability to arm himself if he knew the tides were about to turn against him. That meant Christopher had to put the man at ease until he was ready to make his move. Crooking a finger, he motioned Olan to him.

Olan came promptly, looking eagerly at Christopher, waiting for an order.

"You have been here since the death of Emory," Christopher said in a low voice.

Olan nodded quickly. "I have, my lord."

Christopher eyed Marius as the man sucked down the watered wine. "Have you ever had any reason to keep Marius sober in all that time?"

Olan couldn't help but look at Marius too. "Not really, my lord," he said. "Why?"

"Because I need help keeping him sober," Christopher said. "Beyond watering his wine, what would you suggest?"

Christopher hoped that he was putting the man at ease so he wouldn't be suspicious when six burly de Lohr men entered the chamber. His intention was to have Roi and Myles interrogate Olan, and the others would just be muscle. Myles, in particular, was good at such things because he was an Executioner Knight, an agent for the Crown, and he'd been trained in such unsavory tactics.

And Christopher wanted answers. Meanwhile, he was keeping Olan busy as the knight thought on Christopher's question.

"I know that, in the past, Lady Ledbury has cut the wine with fruit juice," he said. "I also know that she has had the cook boil the wine to remove what makes a man drunk. She'll cut his wine with the thicker wine that has been boiled, and that has helped."

Before Christopher could reply, voices began to fill the entry. Myles and his nephews were starting to filter back into the keep, entering the solar. Christopher could see his two older sons, Curtis and Roi, entering as well.

So much for keeping Olan occupied.

It was time to strike.

"Thank you, Olan," he said evenly. "Please wait here."

Olan did as he was told. He was standing in a corner of the chamber where there were no weapons or implements. Not even a window to jump out of. He stood there, watching attentively, as Christopher went over to Curtis and Roi and hugged them. His grandsons also put their arms around him, hugging their grandfather. It was clear that there was a good deal of love and camaraderie among the de Lohr men. When Christopher was finished greeting everyone, he spoke to the crowd.

"Now," he said, rubbing his forehead wearily, "you have come at your mother's summons because Westley is missing and we need help looking for him. Since the missive was sent to you, however, we have discovered what has become of him."

Everyone looked at him in surprise. Everyone except Marius, who was trying to drain watered wine out of a cup. He was beyond caring. But Curtis put his hand on his father's arm, his expression full of confusion.

"You have?" he said. "Then he really has disappeared?"

Christopher nodded. "He is being held hostage by Samson

Fitz Walter of Hell's Forge Castle," Christopher said. "Hell's Forge is to the north, almost a day's ride. Andrew, Nicholas, Gabriel, and Rhodes? Will you do something for me?"

The four well-built young knights came forward. "Whatever you wish, Taid," Andrew said, using the name they'd always called Christopher, the Welsh name for grandfather. "How may we be of service?"

Christopher looked across the chamber to Olan and pointed. "Restrain that man," he said.

The four grandsons didn't hesitate. Suddenly, they were charging across the chamber and Olan barely had time to hold up his hands to defend himself before they grabbed him. He decided he should probably fight back at that point, but it was a short struggle. Rhodes de Velt, in particular, was built like a bull and got him around the neck, bending his arm behind his back so he couldn't move, while the others restrained other body parts. Unable to move, Olan began to panic.

"Why have you done this, my lord?" he cried. "What have I done?"

Christopher walked up to him and looked him in the eye. Then, in a shocking move, he slapped him across the face, open-palmed, as hard as he could. It was a loud, nasty crack that sent Olan's head sideways. Blood from a cut lip and his nose sprayed out onto Andrew, who was on his right side.

"Does that shake your memory loose?" Christopher snarled. "That is for letting Westley fall into Fitz Walter's hands."

Olan's face was pale with shock. "My... my lord," he stammered. "I would never... I would never do such a thing!"

Christopher didn't have time for his lies. "Then explain to me how you left Massington with Westley but returned without him," he said. "In the middle of the night, no less. Before you try to deny this, know that you were seen coming and going. Well? What lies are you going to tell me now?"

Olan's features slackened. He had a wide-eyed, panicked expression, but realizing what Christopher knew had caught him off guard. He was in a room full of lions, and the expression on his face suggested he knew that he was about to be eaten.

"Who has told you such things, my lord?" he said. "One of the soldiers? Would you truly believe a lowly soldier?"

Christopher wasn't going to engage him. He turned to the group of knights standing behind him.

"Myles?" he said. "Attend me."

Myles was at his father's side immediately. "My lord?" he responded formally.

Christopher's baleful gaze lingered on Olan for a moment longer before he turned to Myles. He leaned toward the man and lowered his voice.

"Find out what he did with your brother," he said. "And make it hurt if you must. Your brother may already be dead for all we know, so make sure Olan feels our anguish."

Myles understood the assignment. "As you wish, my lord," he said, a gleam in his eye. "I will discover everything."

As Myles went over to Olan, who had a look of terror on his face, Christopher went to close the solar door. He didn't want anyone hearing the sounds that were about to come from Olan, but he also didn't need to be there. He'd been present for hundreds of interrogations over the years, and in this case, he simply didn't want to hear it. If Olan knew that Westley was dead, Christopher didn't want it screamed out at him. He would rather have the news delivered by Curtis or Roi, calmly, to him and his wife when everything was over.

He just couldn't bear to stick around.

Therefore, he quit the solar, closing the door behind him. With great effort, as he was greatly fatigued and fighting a horrible headache, he made his way up the stairs, up to the chamber he shared with Dustin. She was still there, napping on the bed because she, too, hadn't slept in two days. He was loath to wake her, but she had to know her sons had arrived.

"Sweetheart," he murmured, rubbing her arm gently until she came around. "Wake up, love."

Dustin yawned and rubbed an eye. "What is it?"

Christopher sat on the edge of the bed, pulling off his boots. "The de Lohr army has arrived," he said quietly. "Curtis, Chris, Arthur, Roi, Andrew, Gabriel, Nicholas, Rhodes, and Myles are here. They are interrogating Olan as we speak."

Dustin sat up. "They are?" she said, more alert now. She tossed the coverlet off. "I must go to them."

He put a hand out to stop her. "Nay, you will not," he said. "I do not want to be part of that, and neither do you. They will tell us what they discover once it is over. But trust me when I tell you—this is not something you want to witness."

Dustin didn't look particularly convinced, but she didn't argue with him. "Very well," she said reluctantly. "What do we do now? Simply wait?

"Simply wait. And rest."

Dustin wasn't sure she could go back to sleep, knowing her sons were here. "As you wish," she said. "What about you? How are you feeling?"

He sighed heavily. "Weary."

"Are you hungry?" she said, pointing to the parcel on the table. "I brought you some lovely stuffed eggs, but they are cold now. I can have the cook warm them up."

He peered over at the basket she was indicating, the one she'd brought in when she told him what Harker had told her and they'd both forgotten about the food. He held out a hand, and she got out of bed, collecting a couple of the eggs, and put them in his palm. He stuffed both of them in his mouth, grunting happily because they were delicious. Dustin stood there and shook her head.

"You are going to choke someday the way you eat those things," she said. "You really should be more careful."

He shrugged, chewing happily. "It would be a delight to die with my mouth stuffed with eggs."

"It would be embarrassing."

He tried not to laugh and spray egg out all over the bed. He chewed a few more times before swallowing. "Those are delicious," he said. "They are better than yours."

She gasped in outrage. "How can you say such things?"

"It's true."

"I will never, ever make stuffed eggs for you again."

"You won't need to. I am going to hire Marius' cook."

Feigning insult, Dustin grumbled as she climbed back into bed. "Ungrateful," she muttered. "Get your own stuffed eggs next time."

He lay down on the bed, grabbed her, and pulled her to him. "You know I am only jesting with you," he said. "I could not live without you or your stuffed eggs."

She was stiff in his embrace. "Do not try to speak sweetly to me now," she said. "It will not work."

He pulled her closer, nibbling on her cheek. "Is it working now?"

She struggled not to laugh. "Nay," she said, putting a hand over his mouth. "Be still and go to sleep. You are positively exhausted. I would wager that your head is still hurting, too."

He stopped nibbling and settled down, closing his eyes. His head was, indeed, throbbing. It had eased up a little when Esther sent him the wine and willow drink, but that was short-lived. The pain was back again.

He just wanted to sleep it off, if only for a short time.

"I will sleep," he mumbled. "Sleep with me. It might be the last bit of sleep we get before the heavens open up and chaos descends."

Dustin snuggled up against him. "Just for a little while," she said. "Then we must find Westley."

Christopher thought of his youngest son. Visions of the man came to mind, the way Westley defied him, the way he hugged him, the way he laughed when Christopher was annoyed. He hadn't really allowed himself to feel genuine fear until this moment, knowing that Fitz Walter wanted an eye for an eye at the very least.

A son for an uncle.

And that scared him to death.

"The night West was born was the most terrifying night of my life," he muttered. "You did not have an easy time with him."

Dustin could hear his heart beating steadily in her ear as his words took her back all those years to that moment in time. "My first son and my last son were the most difficult births for me," she said. "It took Curtis two days to come and it took Westley two and a half. And when he finally came, he was backward. His arm was behind his back, too. He was a mess."

"*I* was a mess," Christopher said softly. "Every other child you gave birth to seemed to come easily except Curtis and Westley. But they came and they thrived. I've always felt that because their births were so difficult, it was because they were meant to be here. They were meant to accomplish something great."

"There is time still," Dustin said. Then she sat up and looked at him. "I know you have been entertaining the idea that Westley is already dead, but I am telling you that he is not. I would know if my son was dead. I would feel it. But I do not feel it. He is alive and he is waiting for help."

Christopher popped an eye open to look at her. "And we will give it to him," he said, reaching up to cup her face. "Your missive to Lioncross called down the thunder, and it has arrived on our doorstep. It is down below us even now, discovering what has become of their brother. The thunder *is* here, sweetheart. Along with thunder comes lightning, and soon West will be back safely."

Dustin nodded, lying back down again. "Have you even spoken with Elysande?" she said. "About what we've discovered, I mean. Have you told her about Fitz Walter?"

"Nay," Christopher said. "A conversation for another time. She was so distraught at Westley leaving, I think she thought he abandoned her."

"Then I will tell her when we go back down the stairs," Dustin mumbled, feeling her fatigue. "I do not want her thinking Westley ran away and left her."

Christopher's arms tightened around her as they both fell into a deep, restful sleep. Dustin did, anyway.

But Christopher's sleep turned out to be the stuff night-mares are made of.

CHAPTER TWENTY-ONE

H IS CONVERSATION WITH Samson didn't go as planned. Now, he was locked up.

After his initial introduction to Samson, Westley had remained in the chamber with the man for quite some time. Samson spoke very little because Westley was trying to convince the man that he'd never wanted to marry Elysande in the first place, but Westley was starting to think he'd laid it on too thick. He'd been too obvious in his resistance to the marriage. He'd overplayed his hand and Samson had caught on.

After too much conversation and even some arguing, Samson had left the chamber sometime before dawn, taking the raven with him, and he'd bolted the chamber door once he left. That left Westley in that cold, cluttered chamber with no fire, no food, and no bed. He also needed a physic to tend the wound on his head because it was swollen and his head ached a great deal. All he wanted to do was sleep.

Lying on the floor, he tried to get comfortable.

Sleep came.

But for how long, he didn't know. He was awakened by the sound of the bolt on the outside of the door being thrown, so he struggled to push himself into a sitting position to face what was possibly another round of Samson's demented gloating. The man clearly had a huge hatred for Christopher, and it was difficult for Westley to sit through that and not react, but he was trying to present the image of a well-behaved captive because, chances were, Samson would let his guard down at some point.

He could only hope.

The door opened, sticking on its old and rusted hinges, revealing the other man who had been in the chamber with Samson. Westley didn't know his name, but he did remember throwing water at him. Therefore, he eyed him warily.

"What do you want?" he asked.

The man stood by the door, ready to run and slam it in case he needed to. "I came to see to your head," he said nervously. "Fitz Walter does not want you to drop dead just yet."

Westley snorted softly. "Just *yet*, is it?" he said, pushing himself into a sitting position against the wall. "He is saving my death for something more spectacular?"

The man didn't reply, just entered the chamber. He was carrying a tray with a collection of items on it and set it down on an old, leaning table near the hearth. Just as he was organizing the things on the tray, a poorly dressed servant entered carrying a bucket of what turned out to be kindling and peat. As the servant tended to the hearth and started a meager fire, the man carrying the tray handed Westley a compress.

"Put this on your wound," he said. "It will help."

Westley looked at the compress, a tightly folded cloth. It was damp and heavily rubbed with something. He could see the bits of petal and leaf. He sniffed it.

"What is this?" he asked.

The man gestured at Westley's head. "A paste of golds," he said, referring to a medicinal flower that was commonly used for wounds. "Put it on your injury."

Westley did. He figured he had nothing to lose at this point. Gingerly placing the compress on the wound, he held it there, watching the man as he fussed with things on the tray. An odd sort of silence settled, one of apprehension and perhaps even a little fear. There was something heavy in the air, something that made Westley uneasy.

The unknown always did.

"What will happen now?" he asked.

The man picked up a cup. "You will eat."

"That is not what I meant."

The man handed Westley the cup, which turned out to have some kind of stew in it. Westley didn't recognize the meat, but he didn't care. He was starving and began to slurp it down. As he was doing so, the servant who had been at the hearth slipped out, closing the door behind him. That left Westley alone with Samson's man.

A man who moved closer to him now that they were alone.

Westley noticed his movements and was mentally preparing to defend himself. He had no idea why the man should move closer to him, but he could guess. Perhaps he was an assassin. As Westley anticipated taking the man's legs out from beneath him and then pouncing on him, the man came to a halt just outside of the range of Westley's feet. He simply stood there, watching.

Waiting.

Westley tensed, preparing for what was to come.

"Listen to me and listen well," the man whispered. "I want to know that if I help you escape, will your father see to it that I have a position of safety within his house?"

Westley stopped slurping the stew. He was still tense, still waiting for the first blow in a fight, but the seconds ticked away and nothing was forthcoming. After several long seconds of pause, he resumed eating.

"Whatever you are doing, it will not work," he said.

"What will not work?"

"I will not agree to let you help me escape only for Fitz Walter to be waiting for such an attempt," Westley said. "It would give him an excuse to execute me."

The man shook his head. "He will not know," he said with quiet urgency. "I know you do not trust me, but I beg you to at least listen to me. My name is Alend. I have served Fitz Walter for many years, and each day of my life that I spend in his presence could be my last. I want to leave as much as you do. Probably more. I have never had the opportunity to leave, but with you, I see that opportunity. Will you assure me of a place within the de Lohr household if I help you escape?"

Westley finished the stew and set the cup down. "As I said, I will not fall for your trick."

"It is not a trick, I swear."

"Go back to Fitz Walter and tell him I am not as stupid as he thinks I am."

Alend sighed sharply. "If you want to live, you will listen to me," he said. "Fitz Walter has an unnatural hatred for your father and your family. He fully intends to kill you in revenge for your father killing his uncle many years ago. He views it as a reckoning. An eye for an eye, as it were. And then he intends to lay siege to Massington and collect your wife as a spoil of war."

"I am not listening to you."

"If you do not, you will die."

The man said it with some conviction, enough that Westley looked up at him. His position was starting to waver, just a little, mostly because he had no other choice. He was locked up deep in a castle he didn't know and there was no one else to help him. He was alone.

Except for Fitz Walter's servant.

Still, he was quite wary.

"So you want to help me escape if I will promise you a position with my father when we leave?" he said.

"Aye, my lord."

Westley smiled thinly. "What a perfect way to plant a Fitz Walter spy next to my father."

Alend's eyes widened at the implication. "Nay, my lord, that is not what I mean at all," he said. "I do not have to serve with your father. I can serve anywhere in the de Lohr household. I can even serve with an ally so long as the man is fair."

Westley waved him off and turned his head away, effectively ending the conversation, but Alend was desperate. He'd been thinking of this proposal ever since the visit to Massington when Samson was badly beaten by Westley. Alend had to admit that he'd found fiendish delight in every blow Westley delivered to Samson. When Westley was captured, with Olan's help, no less, Alend saw an opportunity. He was so tired of living in fear and in filth, serving a madman. He was afraid he'd never have another chance like this.

If only he could convince Westley that he was sincere.

"My lord," he said, hoping desperately to catch Westley's attention, "I was trained as a knight. My father was a very minor nobleman, so my opportunities were limited. I trained at a small castle in Cornwall, Trematon. It is a relatively insignificant castle in the grand scheme of things, which meant when I earned my spurs, my choices were limited. I met Fitz Walter in London, at a church festival. I did not know him, or what he was like, and when he offered me a position, I took it instantly. I did not even think about it. And that has been the greatest regret of my life, because Samson Fitz Walter is an evil man with evil intentions. I have lived with the threat of death hanging over my head since I swore fealty to the man. I do not know if I can ever live without fearing my liege, but I want to try. I cannot live like this any longer. I am asking for your help."

By the time he was finished, Westley was listening seriously. Alend was trembling, his voice quavering and his eyes welling. The man looked like a nervous wreck. Either it was extremely good acting or it was the truth.

Westley's stance was wavering further.

Given the fact that he was the captive of someone who hated his father deeply and made no secret of it, he knew he was in a bad position. And, frankly, Fitz Walter didn't need an excuse to execute him. He already had an excuse, given the fact that Westley was Christopher de Lohr's son. That made his theory that Alend's help would lead him into a trap a moot point. Given that logic, perhaps the man *was* serious.

It wasn't as if Westley had any other choices in escape routes at the moment.

"Why haven't you left before if it was so terrible here?" he asked. "Why not return to Cornwall, where you trained?"

Alend seemed surprised that his plea had elicited an actual response that didn't include a refusal. "I... I suppose I could return to Lord de Vautort," he said. "I simply wanted to do something bigger and better than a small castle in a wild land."

"So you came to Hell's Forge."

"I did, my lord."

Westley paused a moment, wondering if he could trick the man into betraying his true intentions, to reveal if Fitz Walter really was behind this little scene. He might not have any other escape choices, but he still didn't trust this short, rather meek knight. Truthfully, he couldn't believe a man such as this actually *was* a knight.

He seemed like more of a slave.

"If you are so fearful here, then why did you not leave long ago?" Westley said. "If you feel as if Fitz Walter is going to ram a sword into your chest every day, why stay?"

Alend shrugged. "Because I was happy to be here, at first," he said. "My cousin serves at Massington and I could be near him. We could be proud in our service together, side by side with allied castles. My father could be proud. If I ran, my father would be shamed and so would my family."

"Who is your cousin?"

"The man who brought you here. Olan."

Westley's eyebrows lifted. "De Bisby?" he said, feeling his anger rise. "Olan de Bisby is your cousin?"

"Aye, my lord."

Westley snorted rudely. "The man betrayed me," he said. "What makes you think I will trust his cousin?"

"I did not have to tell you that he was my cousin, my lord."

Alend had a point, but Westley was still feeling his rage. "When I see your cousin next, I am going to kill him," he said. "Now are you still so eager to help me escape?"

Alend nodded. "I am," he said. "Because I would escape with you and serve at a house far greater than anything Olan could serve. My lord, you know why he betrayed you, don't you?"

"Because of my wife."

"Exactly," Alend said. "Because of a woman. *Your* wife. Olan has been in love with Lady Elysande for a very long time. Of course he did not want you around. Fitz Walter gave him the opportunity to rid himself of your presence and he took it. I have no such need to be rid of you."

He had another point, but Westley was still wary. "I trusted your cousin and it was a mistake," he said. "I cannot say I am in any hurry to trust you."

Alend nodded. "I realize that," he said. "But if you do not, you will die. Every second that ticks away is a second where Fitz Walter may decide to kill you and send your body back to your father. I am certain your father would not react well to that."

That vision settled Westley down a little. "Nay, he would not," he agreed quietly. "Nor would my mother. Or my wife, I suspect."

Alend turned and went back to the tray on the table, collecting a cup. He returned to Westley, crouching down in front of him as he extended the cup.

"I know you do not want to trust me," he said quietly. "I do not blame you. But I swear to you upon my oath as a knight that I mean what I say. We can escape together and return to your father. I am trusting that you will advocate on my behalf for your father to accept my fealty. Westley, we must both trust each other if we are to survive this."

He addressed Westley informally, giving his final plea some impact. If Westley didn't trust him, then the future probably short and bleak. But if he did...

There was a chance.

"Very well," Westley muttered, reaching out to take the cup of watered wine. "What did you have in mind?"

Alend told him.

CHAPTER TWENTY-TWO

E LYSANDE HOPED SHE never heard sounds like that again. Sounds coming from a human body, no less. The sounds coming from her father's solar as the men from Lioncross interrogated Olan were truly horrifying. Elysande had been under the stairs the entire time, and very close to the solar door, so she heard the initial defiance of Olan followed by refusals, denials, anger, accusations, and finally groans of pain that were reduced to screams.

Screams from the man who had betrayed her.

She should have put a stop to it. She should have rushed in and demanded that they leave him alone, but she couldn't bring herself to do it. Olan had allowed Westley to fall into Fitz Walter's hands, so with every snap, or sharp noise, or scream of pain, she cheered.

God help her, she cheered.

When they finally dragged Olan out of the chamber a few hours later, there was blood running out of his mouth, onto his tunic, and leaving a trail behind him. She heard one of the younger knights say something about teeth. Evidently, someone had systematically removed each one of Olan's teeth for his refusal to confess until he only had a few left. Pain and exhaustion and fear had seen him admit to everything he'd done.

They hauled him down to the vault, nearly toothless, until they could determine what to do with him. Worse still, Marius had been in the solar the entire time, choking down the watered wine Christopher had made for him, horrified at what was happening and wondering why he wasn't getting drunk enough to block it all out. Once they dragged Olan out of the solar, Elysande could hear her father vomiting.

It had been a ghastly situation altogether.

But Elysande wasn't sorry for Olan, nor had she been particularly put off by a screaming man. For all she knew, Samson Fitz Walter was doing the same thing to Westley at that very moment, so she didn't feel the least bit of sorrow for the knight she had once considered a friend. She didn't consider him anything now. As the de Lohr knights trickled out of the keep and went about their business, she came out of hiding, but not until she made sure everyone related to de Lohr was gone. Timidly, she stuck her head into the solar to see if her father was still there.

He was.

Elysande stepped into the solar, watching her father as the man sat near the hearth with his head hanging and vomit at his feet. She took her gaze off him long enough to look around the chamber, at the blood on the floor, and as she peered closer, she could see bloodied teeth scattered around.

It didn't even turn her stomach.

"Father?" she finally said, returning her attention to the man. "Marius, can you hear me?"

Marius' head moved. Eyes that had been closed now

opened. Slowly, he lifted his head, seeing his daughter standing several feet away.

"What are you doing in here?" he said in a raspy voice. "Get out, Ella. You should not be here."

"And yet I am," she said, coming closer. "Are they going to rescue Westley now?"

Marius' gaze remained on her for a few tense moments before he looked away. "I do not know," he muttered. "I do not have any control over anything they do, so how should I know this? They just tortured Olan right in front of me. Ripped his teeth out until he screamed. *Screamed!*"

"He deserved it," Elysande said coldly. "He is the one who delivered Westley to Samson Fitz Walter. He deserved everything they did to him."

Marius looked at her in surprise. Then he simply shook his head. "It starts with you and ends with you," he said, looking around for his wine bottle. "Fitz Walter made an excellent offer for you, but you were already betrothed to Westley. Had I accepted his offer, none of this would have happened."

"You would have condemned me to a terrible life."

He found a nearby pitcher and peered inside only to see that there was nothing left. "We all have our private hells, Elysande," he said. "Why should your life be any different from mine?"

The words hurt her. "Is that what you wish for me?" she said. "A private hell?"

He tossed the pitcher aside. "Where is your mother?"

"I do not know."

"Find her!" he suddenly shouted, agitated. "Find her and send her to me immediately!"

Elysande didn't reply. Marius was in his own private hell, as he'd said. A hell where wine was his lord and master and nothing else mattered. Perhaps that was fine for him, but Elysande didn't want a private hell. She'd had a glimpse of a private heaven with Westley, and that was all she could think of. She'd had a day and a night of sheer bliss, and that wasn't something she was willing to give up on.

She had to do something.

Her father was right—this started with her. A man's life was at stake because of her. Samson Fitz Walter wanted her, so why not give the man what he wanted? Perhaps Lord Hereford would negotiate a trade—her for Westley—but even as she considered that proposal, she knew it was stupid. Christopher de Lohr would never exchange a woman for his son.

Instead, he had called forth his other sons and an army, and they were planning on... something. Marius didn't know, or didn't remember, but it would be a big operation. Christopher de Lohr never did anything on a small scale. More than likely, the de Lohr war machine would march over to Hell's Forge and lay siege to the place. They'd huff and puff and beat their chests and kill men, but Westley would still be inside Hell's Forge unless they managed to get him out somehow. There was the very real possibility that Fitz Walter would kill him before they could get to him. *Unless...*

Unless a deal could be struck.

Perhaps *she* would be the deal.

With an epiphany, Elysande knew what she needed to do.

Leaving her father hunting for more wine, she departed the solar and headed up the mural stairs. While everyone was trying to come up with a plan, she was actually going to do something. In just the few short days that she had known Westley, the man had shown her a glimpse of life that was like nothing she'd ever imagined. A life where she had a handsome husband who lived with her and laughed with her and... loved her? Was it possible he could love her someday? Because she was fairly certain she could love him.

Perhaps she already did.

She wasn't going to let that go.

Perhaps her determination to make a deal with Fitz Walter put that admiration, that love, into action. She wasn't even worried for herself. She was only worried for Westley. How did her life even matter in the long run? Elysande was the daughter of a lesser noble, as Westley had once put it. She wasn't anything great, meant to go on and do great things with a name that was greatly respected by all of England. Nay, that wasn't her at all.

But it was Westley.

He had every right to life. Even if she had to sacrifice herself so he could. She had been training for two years as a warrior, and even if Westley didn't think she had learned much, she was going to prove him wrong.

When it comes to emotion in battle, the only one you should have is courage.

Well, she *had* courage. And she was going to prove it. While everyone else was standing around, she was going to set Westley free. Perhaps it was the only great thing she would ever accomplish in her life, but she was going to do it.

Elysande du Nor de Lohr had picked her moment to shine.

CHAPTER TWENTY-THREE

"**W**HAT'S GOING ON with Taid?" Gabriel de Sherrington was speaking to an anxious collection outside of Massington's keep. "The physic has been with him for hours."

No one had an answer for him.

It was after sunset on the day that saw Olan lose his teeth and the de Lohr army prepare for war. They'd been so busy, in fact, that no one noticed Elysande slip into the stable and collect her horse. No one even noticed when she passed beneath the gatehouse because there were three thousand men coming in and out at the time, crowds of men that masked her escape. Not even Harker noticed, as he'd been inside the bailey trying to find a place for the de Lohr troops.

Now, she was gone.

But no one knew.

Not even the de Lohr grandchildren, who were all gathered at the base of the keep in a worrisome bunch. Andrew, Gabriel, Nicholas, Rhodes, Chris, and Arthur had been equally busy in managing the army, blending the Massington troops with the de Lohr troops, adding to the stores they carried from Massington's supplies, and so on. It had been a perfectly normal, perfectly busy day until Curtis was urgently summoned to the keep.

That was when things turned dark.

So very dark.

Something had happened to Christopher, though no one knew what. Curtis was the only one who knew, and he wouldn't say. He simply sent his sons for the physic in Hereford, who knew Christopher and knew of his health issues over the years. Chris and Arthur rode at top speed to Hereford, grabbed the physic, and then forced the man to endure a harried flight back to Massington. Fortunately, Hereford was close, so it took hours instead of days to fetch the man. The moment the physic arrived, Curtis, and also Roi, rushed the man up to their parents' chamber, where he'd remained to this very minute.

It was an anxious little group that waited below.

"Naina should come tell us something soon," Rhodes said, referring to Dustin by the name all of the grandchildren called her. "Or, at the very least, Uncle Roi should tell us. He knows we have been waiting."

"What do you think it is, Andrew?" Chris asked quietly. "His heart? His stomach? He has had trouble with both in the past."

Andrew, the eldest of the group, was a wise man, much like his father. In fact, he wished his father were there to help calm their nerves. Alexander had a manner about him that was always confident, always calm. Andrew had inherited that trait from his father, but he had two brothers and three cousins looking at him now as if he had all the answers and, frankly, he was stumped. Anything he could come up with wasn't good.

He was trying not to panic.

"I do not know," he said truthfully. "But we must all keep in mind that Taid is a very old man. Most men of his generation died years ago, so we have been very fortunate to have him as long as we have. We must remember that he had a very good life and he was much loved."

"God," Nicholas, Andrew's younger brother, groaned. "You think he's dead, don't you? You think he has died!"

Andrew shook his head. "If he had died, we would have been told already," he said. "And stop saying things like that. You'll panic everyone else, and then Naina will box your ears if she's mad enough."

"She is always mad enough," Gabriel muttered.

Six heads nodded in agreement. Dustin wasn't afraid to punish or demonstrate her annoyance if anyone disobeyed or displeased her. As the six of them stood there, wondering, waiting, their Uncle Myles suddenly bolted past them and up the stairs. He had been in a neighboring village, negotiating for some additional stores to take on the battle march, and someone must have told him about his father. He ran into the keep before the nephews could stop him.

That had all of them looking at each other nervously.

"No word yet?"

They heard a voice coming from the bailey and turned to see Harker heading in their direction. The big knight's gaze was on the keep, on the illuminated windows high above.

"Nay," Andrew said. "No word."

Harker came to a halt, his gaze still on the keep. "Whatever it is, you will know soon enough," he said, finally lowering his focus to look at them. "You can just as easily wait in the great hall where it is warm and there is food."

"We know," Andrew said. "And your hospitality has been greatly appreciated. But we would rather wait here, if you do not mind. I do not suppose we could eat anyway."

Harker understood. "If you change your mind, you know where the food is," he said. He paused a moment before continuing. "I do not suppose any of you have seen Lady Ledbury or Lady de Lohr."

"Our grandmother is in the keep with our grandfather," Andrew said.

But Harker shook his head. "I meant Lady *Westley* de Lohr."

The group shook their heads. "Truthfully, we've not met her yet," Andrew said. "Mayhap she is in the keep."

Harker excused himself with a nod as he turned back for the great hall. The problem was that he'd been to the great hall in search of Esther and Elysande but had come up empty. He'd also been to the kitchens with no luck. He could only assume that both Esther and Elysande were in the keep, as Andrew had said. He knew that Elysande was extremely upset about Westley's disappearance. He'd seen her weeping over it. Esther, he was sure, was dealing with whatever was happening inside the keep.

Like a good knight, Harker went to the hall to oversee things.

It was the least he could do.

As the big Teutonic knight walked away, the de Lohr grandsons went back to worrying. Andrew, who had his eye on the entry door, decided enough was enough. With a growl, he headed up the stairs.

"I'm not waiting out here any longer," he said.

His brothers started to follow. "Can we come?" Gabriel asked.

"I do not care what you do!"

That meant Gabriel and Nicholas followed and charged up the steps after their brother. By the time Andrew was throwing open the entry door, Chris and Arthur and Rhodes brought up the rear. All six of them barged into the keep and, realizing that the activity they were concerned with was taking place on the upper floors, stampeded up the steps until they came to a second set of stairs that led to the third floor. They were halfway up when a figure appeared at the top.

"What in the hell are you lot doing?" Myles demanded. "I could hear you coming inside like a pack of wild animals."

Andrew came to a halt, as did everyone else behind him. "We do not want to wait outside any longer, Uncle Myles," he said. "We want to know what happened as much as you do, but no one has told us anything."

Myles could see how worried they all were. Honestly, he had enough worry of his own, but he wasn't unsympathetic. He knew how much they loved their taid and he didn't disagree with them—they had a right to know.

Myles had to figure out how to tell them.

"Uncle Myles?" Rhodes asked from far back in the pack. "Please—what has happened?"

Myles waved a hand at them, indicating for them to go back down the stairs. They did, trying not to trip and fall on one another in the tight space, until they reached the landing at the top of the mural stairs. Myles came down behind them.

"I am going to tell you what I know," he said. "I want you to listen to me and keep silent. Can you do that?"

Six heads nodded seriously and Myles looked at them all pointedly.

"Naina does not need your questions or weeping or any-thing else," he said. "You must be calm and quiet or I swear I'll throw you out the window personally. Understood?"

Again, the group nodded. "What is so serious?" Andrew asked, a hint of pleading in his tone. "What has happened to Taid?"

Myles sighed softly. "You know this situation with Uncle West has been taxing on him," he said. "And then this morning with Olan and Marius... Taid was greatly exhausted by it all, so he took what sleep he could this afternoon. When he awoke, he could not move the left side of his body. He can barely speak. The physic is trying to assess what, exactly, happened. And that is all I know."

The young knights looked horrified. They all wanted to ask questions, questions of concern or desperation or fear, but Myles had asked them not to. Tucked back behind his older brother, Arthur, the youngest of the group, was starting to tear up.

"Is he dying, Uncle Myles?" he asked.

Myles looked at the young man. He wasn't a knight yet, but he would be soon. Another proud de Lohr knight. In fact, Myles had sons of his own. His older boys, Sebastian and Evander, were fostering at Derby Castle like their grandfather had many years ago. But he had several smaller children at home and his wife was due to give birth to their seventh child next month. Therefore, he was sympathetic to the emotions of youth. He was surrounded by them at home and, not strangely, had learned to be patient. Myles was a paradox of a man, so capable of brutality, yet so capable of understanding.

"I do not know, lad, and that's the truth," he said softly. "Now, you may come upstairs and wait with me, but you are not to make a sound. No questions, no conversation. Agreed?"

The young men nodded, so he turned around and headed

up the stairs with the six of them in tow. Reaching the level where Christopher's chamber was, they could see that the landing was empty, so they went to stand against the wall, silently, as Myles had asked. When Myles slipped into Christopher's chamber, they all strained to catch a glimpse inside, but they couldn't. The door had opened and closed too fast.

Therefore, they waited.

ↈ

"Get up."

Someone was kicking Andrew's foot. Startled, he lifted his head to see Myles standing over him. Blinking, Andrew looked around and saw that he was on the landing outside of Christopher's bedchamber, slumped against the wall along with his brothers and cousins. They'd settled down to wait at the end of an extremely busy day and ended up falling asleep.

All of them.

"Andy, get up," Myles said again. "Gabe, Nick—wake up. Come on, lads. There's news on Taid."

The young men bolted up, rubbing their eyes and yawning, but they were alert. They followed Myles into the rather large bedchamber that Christopher and Dustin had been sharing. It was warm inside, a snapping fire in the hearth and banks of candles lit up so the physic could see what he was doing.

But it also smelled dank.

Like death.

Dustin was on the far side of the bed, wrapped up in a shawl, her features pale and drawn. Curtis and Roi stood at the bottom of the bed while the physic leaned over Christopher, his hand on the man's chest to feel his respiration. When he evidently had the information he needed, he stood up straight and sighed faintly.

"I've seen enough," he finally said. A younger man with black hair pulled into a knot at the back of his head, he opened up his medicament bag and began putting things away. "Lord Hereford and I know each other quite well. For a man of his advanced years, his health has been remarkable. Even when he is ill, he still manages to come through. That is a testament to how strong he really is. But... he has something now that will be very difficult to recover from. I must tell you that I have seen people with this affliction before."

"What affliction?" Curtis asked, sounding strained. "We've watched you for hours and you've not said a word. Sometimes you just sat and stared at him. *What* affliction?"

The physic looked at him. "I will not lie to you, my lord," he said. "He has had an attack of the brain that we call apoplexy. Something happens inside the head and it affects the body. As of now, Lord Hereford cannot move the left side of his body. He can barely speak. He has lost control of some bodily functions. When I arrived and realized what it was, I was able to force a willow potion down his throat. That sometimes helps in something like this, but it is not a cure. There is no cure, I am sorry to say. He will never fully recover. If the next few days show no real improvement, then I am afraid we will lose him."

There it was. What they'd all been dreading. One could hear a collective gasp go up from the grandsons, but Curtis and Roi and Myles remained silent, looking at their father with various expressions of sorrow. Curtis was tearing up and roughly wiped at his eyes.

"Is he dying, then?" he forced himself to ask.

The physic looked at him, trying to be sympathetic. "It is difficult to say," he said quietly. "Possibly. His breathing is irregular and that concerns me."

"If you have seen this before, then how have others weathered the affliction given the same symptoms?" Dustin asked. Her voice was faint and tremulous. "Have you seen others survive something like this?"

The physic sighed and looked to Christopher, who was unconscious. He thought the man might be sleeping because of his erratic breathing, but he could not be sure. He also could not lie to the family on his experiences with such attacks.

"If it were my husband, my lady, I would send word to anyone of importance to him," he said as gently as he could. "Let things be said now that need to be said to him. Make any preparations you must make. Usually, when an attack this bad happens, it is more often than not followed by another attack that will kill. I wish I could give you more hope than that. I am sorry I cannot."

Dustin nodded. Then her eyes welled up and tears spilled over. Her lower lip trembled as she sat on the edge of the bed, looking at her husband as he lay there. Reaching out, she took his hand, turned her head, and began to weep silently.

With a heavy sigh, Roi went to his mother and sat down at her feet, taking her free hand and holding it tightly. He was trying very hard not to tear up himself. Curtis, unable to hold back the tears, looked to the physic and whispered his thanks as Myles simply stared at his father and ground his teeth together. The man was clenching his jaw so hard that he was close to breaking teeth.

"What brings on an attack like this?" Myles asked, hardly able to get the words out because he was gritting his jaw so tightly. "Is it worry? Is it concern or heartache?"

The physic lifted his slender shoulders. "No one knows," he

said. "But great and terrible events have been known to cause such things. They cause an imbalance in the body, a tightening of the heart or lungs, and that can bring on these attacks."

Myles snorted ironically. "Great and terrible events," he muttered. "Like his youngest son being abducted. Of course that caused this. Olan de Bisby has caused this."

With that, he stormed for the door, but Curtis dashed after him, grabbing him before he could leave.

"Wait," Curtis said, holding his angry brother. "Where are you going?"

Myles was furious. "Where do you think?" he growled. "I am going to visit our friend in the vault. *He* caused this, Curt. If you think I was cruel to him earlier today, watch what I shall do to him now."

"Roi?" Curtis called over to his other brother. "I need your help."

Roi was on his feet, nearly leaping over the bed to get to Curtis and Myles, who were now starting to struggle. Roi grabbed Myles, trying to keep the man from getting through the door.

"This does *not* help Papa, Myles," he said, grunting when Myles inadvertently elbowed him in the gut. "Calm yourself. Show your nephews how a man of wisdom and experience handles a devastating situation."

Myles had a different personality than his older brothers. Both of them were more diplomatic, calmer in dire situations, while Myles was a man of action. He was fearless, something that had served him well as an Executioner Knight. As the group struggled at the door and the younger knights watched in concern and confusion, a noise came from the bed.

It was low and mournful but loud, startlingly so. In fact, it made the hair on the back of their necks stand up, as if something otherworldly and dark had just entered the room. The brothers stopped tussling as all eyes looked to the bed. Another noise came again, not as loud as the first, as Christopher lifted his right hand slowly.

"Myles," he said, but the word was barely understandable. "To me."

Shocked, the brothers moved back to the bed, with Myles putting himself in his father's line of sight. Or so he hoped. Christopher's right eye was open, half-lidded, while the left eye remained closed. But he was most definitely awake. How alert he actually was remained to be determined, but Myles and Curtis and Roi and even Dustin leaned over the bed, watching Christopher as he lowered his right hand.

"Myles," he said slowly, sounding like he had a mouth full of sand. "No... more."

Myles looked at Curtis to see if his brother had any clue as to what their father meant before returning his attention to Christopher.

"No more, Papa?" he said gently. "No more... you mean leave Olan alone?"

Christopher's right eye closed, as if the mere act of talking had taken everything out of him. "Aye," he whispered.

Dustin sat down on the bed next to him, taking his right hand in hers. "You've had a bit of a mishap, my love," she said softly. "The physic says your brain is being difficult and has made it so you cannot move your left side. He has seen this before. Are you in any pain?"

Christopher squeezed her hand but didn't reply right away. The left side of his face was droopy and immobile while the right side was relaxed and pliable.

"Nay," he finally said, though it was extremely difficult to make out what, exactly, he was saying. "West... Westley?"

Curtis came around to stand next to his mother. "We are mobilizing the army, Papa," he said quietly. "We will retrieve Westley, I promise."

Christopher took a long, deep breath. "Hell's Forge is... difficult," he mumbled. "Do not... waste time on... gatehouse. Too strong. Target... walls."

Curtis nodded. "We will," he said. "We will be successful, I swear it. But what can we do for you? Are you comfortable?"

Christopher sighed again, a sound that implied exhaustion and defeat and sorrow. Before he could reply, however, Andrew came between Curtis and Dustin, going to his knees beside the bed. Reaching out, he took his grandfather and grandmother's hands, still intertwined, and held them tightly.

"We love you, Taid," he said, his voice breaking. "We are here—me and Gabriel and Nicholas, and Rhodes and Chris and Arthur. We are all here and we love you."

Tears streamed down his face as Dustin put her free hand on the young man's head in a comforting gesture. "They are all here," she confirmed. "You know they would not stay away when they heard you'd taken ill. Your lads love you very much."

Suddenly, the younger men were rushing the bed, all of them crouching or going down on their knees. Hands reached out to touch Christopher as he lay there, incapacitated. Arthur, the youngest of the group, began to weep softly. If Christopher could have been healed by love alone, the adoration filling that chamber at that moment would have healed him a thousand times over. In response to his distraught grandsons, Christopher pulled his hand free from Dustin's grip and put it on Andrew's dark head.

"I… am not dead yet," he said. "Who is weeping?"

Andrew looked over at Arthur. "Artie is, Taid," he said. "Do you want me to slap him?"

That brought laughter from the entire group. Even the right side of Christopher's mouth twitched. "That is not… necessary," he said. "Be kind to your cousin. He is… just a lad. Curtis?"

"I'm here, Papa."

"Find Westley," Christopher said, his right eye opening to fix on his eldest son. "Find my son. And I want to go… home."

Curtis nodded. "We will make sure of both, Papa," he said. "You needn't worry."

Christopher's eyes closed again and the hand that had been on Andrew's head lowered back to the bed. After several long moments, his breathing evened out and he started snoring softly. His weary body had gone to sleep. With a sad and lingering look at his father, Curtis motioned everyone out of the chamber.

Silently, they moved.

Leaving Dustin and the physic in the chamber with Christopher, the de Lohr men gathered on the landing outside of the chamber. Curtis was the last one through, shutting the door quietly behind him before turning to the group.

"Now," he said with quiet firmness, "we have a siege to plan, a brother to rescue, and a father to take home. We will all have roles in this because there is much to do. Roi, you will be in charge of moving Papa home. As much as I want your sword in battle, I would rather have you responsible for Papa. That is going to be a difficult enough task and, aside from saving West, it is inarguably the most important. Will you see to it?"

Roi nodded. "Aye," he said, glancing at the group around

them. "Give me Artie and Chris. That means you take the more experienced men to battle with you."

"Agreed," Curtis said. Then he turned to Myles. "You must be the army's eyes and ears. You are the best one suited for intelligence and strategy. Pick your men and send them to Hell's Forge to gather information so we know what we are facing. The army will move on your plans."

Myles nodded. "I'm taking Andrew with me."

"Go."

Andrew made the most sense, since both of his parents had been Executioner Knights and he, too, was an operative for the guild. As the two of them headed down the stairs, Curtis turned to the remaining knights—Rhodes, Gabriel, and Nicholas. Young knights, but all highly trained. Rhodes in particular was worth his weight in gold in battle. The three of them were looking at Curtis eagerly, awaiting orders. Like any man with de Lohr blood, they lived for a good fight.

And this one promised to be one of the most serious they had ever faced.

"Rhodes," Curtis said, "you are in charge of mustering the army. I realize that everyone has been working all day to prepare, but the moment is here. Movement is imminent. Go to the bailey, inform Harker, and be ready to move."

Rhodes nodded smartly, heading down the stairs with the rest of the young knights in tow, Chris and Arthur included. That left Curtis and Roi alone on the landing, struggling to digest all that had happened and all that needed to happen.

It was up to them now.

"This is not how we had planned this day," Curtis muttered, running his fingers wearily through his blond hair. "I suppose I always knew we would face this moment with Papa, but now that it is here… I feel as if I am wholly unprepared."

Roi nodded. "I know," he said quietly. "Curt, what do we do if we get to Hell's Forge and Westley is already dead? Do we tell Papa?"

Curtis shook his head slowly, with great sadness. "I do not know," he said honestly. "But my instincts tell me that he must know. I've never lied to Papa in my life and I do not want to start now by lying to a dying man."

Roi nodded with resignation. "Then let us hope it does not come to that," he said. "But I will say one thing."

"What is it?"

"If Westley is dead, then I am unleashing Myles and I hope he obliterates the entire House of Fitz Walter. I will goddamn help him."

A deadly gleam came to Curtis' eye. "So will I, brother," he muttered. "So will I."

CHAPTER TWENTY-FOUR

E LYSANDE HAD NEVER been out of the castle walls in the darkness, and she'd certainly never traveled all night before, so the journey to Hell's Forge had taken time. Perhaps too much time, because she traveled cautiously.

But she was determined to get there.

She knew where Hell's Forge was because her father had explained it to her, once, after a visit by Samson and his subsequent tantrum when he found out Elysande was betrothed to a de Lohr. It was actually quite simple to find. Literally, all she had to do was take the northern fork in a road that was about a mile west of Massington and follow it until she ran into an imposing fortress that was perched on the edge of a gorge. That gorge bordered the entire west and north side of the castle, which was part of the reason it was so difficult to breach. But Elysande didn't see any of this until sunrise.

Then she felt as if she had arrived in another world.

The landscape surrounding Hell's Forge looked as if it had been picked clean. The trees were dead or broken and the land itself looked cluttered and dreary. As she drew near, coming in from the southeast, he couldn't help but think how forbidding the place looked. Tall walls surrounded by a ditch with steeply pitched sides so anyone falling in couldn't escape. She could see the top of a circular keep peeking over the wall, but the gatehouse itself was about the size of the keep.

It was positively enormous.

The land was wet from the dew the previous night. It had been a clear night, with a half-moon, but damp. It had been enough for Elysande to see by, but she'd traveled so slowly that it had taken her all night to reach a destination that, under normal circumstances, would have only taken her several hours at most. But she didn't really know the land and didn't want to fail before she even reached the castle, so her arrival at dawn was the best she could manage.

Now, she was here.

Fearful she would be seen by the guards on the walls, she plunged into the overgrown, broken bramble. The horse she'd chosen was a small mare and very fast. She was gray in color and blended in with the foliage. Heart beating in her throat, Elysande moved parallel to the road, approaching Hell's Forge as best she could until the road veered off to the north and ended in the gatehouse. But even from her position in the bush, she could see the triple portcullis entry through the gatehouse— a fearsome thing, indeed.

As the moments passed, the more fear she began to feel. Truthfully, she had been feeling no apprehension as she rode north. She could only think of Westley and saving him and nothing more. Now, as she faced that enormous castle that seemed to bleed something ominous into the very air around it, that courage was wavering.

She was feeling real fear.

But to think of Westley in that terrible place balanced out

her courage again. She could feel it rising, overcoming the anxiety that was trying to take hold of her. The trade-off with exchanging herself for Westley, of course, was the fact that she would have to endure that awful place. But she was willing to endure it if her sacrifice would save him. Her life had never stood for much.

Now, it did.

It stood for a man's freedom.

The very man she adored.

Feeling fortified, Elysande had to make plans. If she was going to present her offer to Fitz Walter, she had to make sure not to end up trapped inside with Westley still a captive. It wouldn't bode well for both of them to be prisoners, so she tethered her little horse and began to do some intelligence gathering of her own. There was a field directly behind her, behind the undergrowth, and it stretched off to the south until it came into line with a small forest. The road she'd traveled on was down there, somewhere, because of the way it had wound through the landscape. Since the horse she'd come on was so swift, she was certain she could make it to those trees in little time if Fitz Walter decided to chase her. If there was no place to hide, then she'd simply get on the road and head home.

She was confident she could outrun anyone.

It wasn't much of a plan, but it would do. It was straightforward. Also, it was all she had. The trick would be to capture the attention of Fitz Walter and stay far enough away from the portcullises and the walls that she couldn't be hit with an arrow or grabbed by someone at the gatehouse until her deal was accepted and Westley was released. From her position in the foliage, she could see men on the walls and inside the gatehouse, moving around.

Taking a deep breath, she decided she would make her move.

There was no time to waste.

Elysande was clad in the garments she wore when Harker trained her—heavy linen breeches, two tunics, including a padded one, boots, arm braces, and her hair tied back in a tight braid. She had a sword hanging on at her side, the one Harker had given her, one used to train pages and squires. It wasn't a big broadsword like most knights used, but much smaller.

Yet it was still sharp.

And she could still kill.

Coming out of the bush, Elysande headed toward the road, her eyes fixed on the gatehouse. Step by step, foot by foot, she moved. She came up out of the grass and onto the rocky road. Her heart was pounding in her ears and her mouth was dry, and she realized it was because she was very nearly panting. She'd never been so frightened in her entire life.

Courage!

She had to do this.

About twenty feet from the gatehouse, she came to a halt.

"You!" she shouted. "You there! Are you deaf? Aye, I'm speaking to you!"

There were at least two or three soldiers inside the portcullis and several more on the wall walk overhead. The guards in the gatehouse paused to look at her strangely, and she unsheathed her sword, pointing it at them.

"You will send for your lord immediately," she said. "Do you understand me? I have business with Samson Fitz Walter!"

There was some conversation going on but no one seemed to be taking her seriously or even listening to her. She was a curiosity more than anything. Elysande did at that moment what she should not have done—she moved closer to the portcullis, well within range of any archers that could launch at her from the wall overhead. But she was being ignored and that didn't sit well with her.

"Listen to me and listen well," she shouted at them. "If you do not send for Samson Fitz Walter immediately, you will be in a good deal of trouble when he discovers who I am."

One of the men poked his head through the slats on the portcullis, which was wooden with great iron rivets, and peered at her lewdly.

"And just who are ye, love?" he asked.

Elysande wasn't planning on giving her name so soon, but the buffoons at the gatehouse were ignoring her. She needed them to do as she wished, so she had little choice as she saw it. Those years of Harker and Olan not training her as they should had given her a false sense of control in what was a very dangerous circumstance. Westley had been right—they'd lied to her, and even though she was showing bravery in this situation, one she thought she could control, the reality was that she'd placed herself in a potential fatal position.

And she didn't even realize it.

"Samson and his army came to Massington Castle a few days ago," she said. "If you are part of his army, then you know it is true. You also know that Samson took a beating by a knight you currently have inside your fortress. Olan de Bisby brought Westley de Lohr to Fitz Walter. Do you understand me so far?"

The lazy smile vanished from the soldier's face. In fact, men were starting to gather at the portcullis, including an older man with a scar across his mouth who stuck his face through the portcullis and scowled at her.

"Who are ye, wench?" he demanded. "How do ye know

this?"

Now Elysande could see that she had their attention, and she experienced a surge of panic. She wanted their focus, but now that she had it, it was terrifying.

Courage, girl, courage!

"I am Lord Ledbury's daughter," she said for all to hear. "I am also Westley de Lohr's wife. Tell Samson I've come to bargain with him. Do it now!"

The soldiers at the portcullis whispered furiously amongst themselves. They were pointing at Elysande and to the keep, hissing like the steam from a fire. Finally, someone went running off, presumably to notify Samson.

When Elysande realized that, it was all she could do to keep from running herself. Perhaps this wasn't such a good idea. Perhaps she was going to get herself and Westley killed. Worse still, she might end up Fitz Walter's captive and all would be lost. Was she doing the right thing?

Was she?

She was about to find out just how much courage she really had.

☙

"DE LOHR?"

Westley heard his name, but he was having a hell of a time opening his eyes. It was pitch black in the chamber and he was sleeping on the floor because there was no bed. He was in the same chamber he'd been in since his arrival at Hell's Forge and now, someone was hissing at him. He caught a glimpse of a taper, a feeble point of light against the darkness.

"De Lohr, can you hear me?"

Westley took a deep breath, coughing as he tried to sit up. "I hear you," he grunted.

"Good." It was Alend and he was putting something into Westley's hand. "Take this and eat it. You will need your strength."

Westley's head was killing him, throbbing as he managed to push himself into a sitting position. His eyes were becoming accustomed to the light a little, and he could see Alend as the man looked at him with an anxious expression. He also noted that the man had pushed bread into his palm. Without hesitation, he shoved it in his mouth and took a huge bite.

"What is amiss?" he asked, chewing. "Why do I need my strength?"

Alend motioned for him to stand. "Because Samson is still sleeping and it is time for us to go," he said. "There is a postern gate near the kitchens, where the cook conducts business, and we must depart before Samson awakens. The sentries are changing guards right now, so no one will be watching the postern gate. We must hurry."

Westley didn't need to be prompted any more than that. He stood up, swaying dizzily because he'd either been on his back or seated for the past few days, so he had to reclaim his equilibrium before he was able to start walking. Alend had him by the arm as he led him out of the chamber and silently shut the door behind him.

Since Westley had been unconscious when he was brought in, he didn't recognize anything. It was a darkened entry, low-ceilinged, and the only light was from the flame Alend was holding, which turned out to be an oil lamp. Westley was trying to walk and eat the bread at the same time, which proved tricky. He didn't seem to have much coordination. As they neared the entry door, Alend had Westley stand back against the wall as he opened the door to see if their way to the postern gate was clear.

Unfortunately, it wasn't.

The sun was just starting to rise, casting pink and purple streaks in the sky, and Alend caught sight of a soldier running toward the keep. He motioned to Westley to slink back into the shadows as the soldier bolted up the steps. Alend stood in the doorway to prevent the man from entering.

"What do you want?" he asked the soldier.

The soldier was breathing heavily from his run. He pointed in the direction he'd come from. "At the gatehouse," he said. "There's someone demanding to see Lord Fitz Walter. He must come."

Alend's brow furrowed. "Why?" he said. "Who is it?"

The soldier shook his head. "She didn't give a name," he said. "But she knows about the fight at Massington. She said that she's Lord Ledbury's daughter."

A bolt of shock ran through Alend. "L-Lord Ledbury's—?" he stammered. "But—that's purely madness. She must be lying!"

The soldier shrugged. "That's what she said," he told him. "The sergeant on duty told me to fetch Fitz Walter."

Alend didn't know what to do other than nod that he acknowledged the request. As the soldier headed back the way he'd come, Alend went to shut the door, but Westley was on him. The man was trying to throw the door open, trying to get out of the keep, and Alend had to push him back out of sight.

"*Stop,*" he hissed. "What are you doing?"

Westley looked as if he'd seen a ghost. "My wife is here," he said, his voice trembling for the first time since Alend had known him. "I must get to her!"

He pushed, and Alend shoved yet again, keeping him away

from the door. "Are you mad?" he said severely. "What do you think is going to happen to you if you run to the gatehouse? Do you actually think fifty Fitz Walter soldiers are going to stand by while you have a touching reunion with your wife? Nay, they will *not*. You'll end up dead!"

The last word was like a slap to Westley's face. *Dead*. Just what he'd been trying to avoid. For a few brief moments, he simply hadn't been thinking. He was exhausted and injured and not in the right frame of mind, but the thought that Elysande was actually here had driven him to momentary madness.

And he was scared to death.

"Do you know her on sight?" he asked, sounding desperate. "You must go to the gatehouse and see if it is her. She has long hair, dark red in color and beautiful, and the most magnificent hazel eyes. She is a beautiful woman in all ways. You *must* find out why she is here!"

Alend nodded, hands still on Westley's chest to try to keep him from charging out of the door. "Listen to me," he said, thumping Westley on the chest when the man seemed unable to focus. "Westley, *listen*. I will go to the gatehouse, but you must go to the postern gate."

"But—!"

"Go to the postern gate or you will die," Alend said, giving him a shake. "Westley, I cannot save you if you are going to be stupid. Do you understand me? Do not be stupid! Go to the postern gate and flee into the nearby trees. There is an entire line of trees that runs the length of the castle and along the road, so you cannot miss it. I will find you there, and if your wife truly is at the gatehouse, I will get to the bottom of it. Do you truly think she came alone? I would be willing to wager she has knights with her, men who have come to save you."

That gave Westley something to think about. He blinked, digesting what Alend was suggesting, before nodding his head. "You are correct," he said. "My family would not let me languish here. She must be a decoy."

"I will find that out," Alend said. "Meanwhile, go down the stairs and then turn to your right. Run along the length of the wall until you enter the kitchen yard. Inside the yard is the postern gate. Unlock it and follow the path out, but stay low so the men on the walls will not see you. If this is truly a diversion, then we must not waste it while their attention is on the gatehouse."

Even Westley understood the logic of that plan. They had an opportunity with the guards diverted. He couldn't help Elysande if he was dead, and unless he did as Alend said, he could very well end up that way. With an unsteady nod, he agreed, and Alend returned to the entry door to make sure no one was around before waving frantically to Westley.

It was time for his escape.

Alend watched Westley dash down the stairs and race over to the wall, staying flush against the stone as he began to run the length of the wall as Alend had told him. When the man entered the kitchen yard and disappeared from sight, Alend stepped from the door and was preparing to go down the steps when he heard his name. Startled, he turned around to see Samson emerging from the stairwell.

"Alend?" Samson said irritably. "Did you not hear me calling to you?"

Alend's heart was pounding in his chest at the close call he'd just had with Westley on the loose. "Nay, my lord," he said. "I was just speaking to a gatehouse sentry. It… it seems there is someone here to see you."

Samson tugged on the tunic he was wearing, scratching at the vermin that lived in it. "Who is here?" he said, frowning.

Alend hesitated. If he told him, no doubt the man would run to the gatehouse himself to see if it was true. But if he didn't tell him... Truthfully, he knew he didn't have a choice. He had to tell him because Samson would find out from someone else, and then Alend would be punished. He'd told Westley to run, and hopefully the man was already outside of the wall in the trees somewhere, waiting. Alend could only surmise that Lady de Lohr was here as a decoy while three thousand de Lohr soldiers were waiting to pounce. The gatehouse was the only point of weakness at Hell's Forge. If they could get the triple portcullises open, then they had a chance of taking the castle.

And Alend had a chance of escaping after all.

"I'm told Lord Ledbury's daughter is here," he said after a moment. "I was just about to see to her myself."

Samson stopped scratching and looked at him in surprise. "Ledbury's daughter?" he repeated. "Lady Elysande?"

"So I am told, my lord. Should we proceed to the gatehouse together?"

Samson was off and running without another word.

CS

THE LONGER SHE waited, the more apprehensive she became.

No one was saying anything. They were all simply watching her, either through the portcullis or from the wall overhead. Elysande didn't like the idea of being scrutinized, but she tried to shake it off, focusing on the bigger picture.

Westley's freedom.

Truthfully, the more she thought on Westley and his freedom, the more confident she became. Certainly there was lingering fear and doubt, but it no longer made her feel as if she was doing the wrong thing. She knew she was doing the right thing. She was securing her husband's release from a man who would be quite happy to kill him, and that was something she couldn't live with.

It all came down to that.

She couldn't live without Westley.

In the short time she'd known him, she felt as if she'd lived a lifetime. More than that, she felt as if her life was only getting started. Before Westley came, she didn't really know what, or who, she was. She was simply a daughter of a lesser lord, struggling to fill the hole left by her brother's death. It never occurred to her that trying to fill that hole was futile. She always thought she could, and she always thought that her father would come around at some point and appreciate her efforts.

It never occurred to her that he wouldn't.

Life at Massington had been more of an existence than an actual life. They existed. They didn't really *live*. They went from day to day doing mundane things, thinking mundane thoughts, and laboring through a reality that was unpleasant at best. Elysande had tried to fill that existence with a purpose, and that purpose had been to learn how to fight, to step into her brother's shoes to the best of her abilities. Her father's existence had revolved around a bottle and her mother's existence had been trying to fill the void where her heart and soul used to be. It had started even before Emory's death, and Elysande had known for years about her mother and Harker. That affair had been born out of a lack of affection in her parents' marriage. Emory's death only made it worse. Therefore, her family simply existed. Rather than come together and draw strength from one another after her brother died, they had fractured.

A family in pieces.

Strange how she only realized that after Westley had arrived and she had seen how parents interacted with a child that was loved. When Westley had been abducted, his brothers and an army had shown up to help, and that further opened her eyes to the purpose of a family. It was to support one another and love one another, not ignore each other and become lost in one's own world. Westley's arrival had opened her eyes to many things, and that was how she knew that what she was doing at this very moment was right.

This was what a family did.

It defended each other.

Lost in thought, Elysande didn't see Samson or Alend until they were standing at the portcullis, studying her. When Samson let out what sounded like a gasp of glee, she was jolted from her reflections and spun around, finding herself gazing at the man who had wanted her so badly that he'd abducted her husband in retaliation. She knew there was more to it, but her perspective up until her marriage to Westley had always been that Samson had wanted her very much.

Perhaps he still did.

She was counting on it.

"Lady Elysande," he said, purposely addressing her as a maiden woman rather than a married one. "To what do we owe the honor of your visit?"

Elysande hadn't seen Samson since the day he was told her betrothal with Westley de Lohr was unbreakable. The day he'd pitched an epic tantrum. Already, she remembered why she didn't like the man.

"I think you know," she said. "You have something I want returned to me."

Samson's eyes were glittering at her. "I do not know what you mean."

"Then I shall be plain, since you are playing stupid," Elysande snapped. "I want my husband's freedom. I know Olan brought him here. Give him back to me."

Samson's manner cooled. "Why should I do that?"

"Because I am here to offer you something you want more in exchange."

"What might that be?"

"Me."

All of the lasciviousness or excitement present on Samson's face drained away, leaving shock and suspicion in its wake.

"You?" he said. Then his brow furrowed and his manner turned rough. "*You?* What do you mean by that?"

Elysande was trying to gauge his reaction but honestly couldn't tell which way he was going to go. Was he pleased? Angry? Offended?

"Just what I have told you," she said. "You took my husband. I want his freedom. What is more valuable to you than my husband? That would be me. You are willing to go to war over me. Release my husband and I shall turn myself over to you."

That didn't seem to clear things up for Samson, who couldn't decide how he felt about the whole thing. He frowned and grunted, looking to others around him to see what their reactions were, but they were looking at him instead. No one seemed willing to give him a response.

Except the man next to him.

He spoke up.

"It is not a simple situation, my lady," he said loudly. "We cannot simply open the portcullis and let you in. We are not fools."

Elysande recognized the man because he'd come to Massington when Samson had. He was, in fact, Olan's cousin, but it took her a moment to remember that.

"You are Alend de Bisby," she said. "Olan's cousin."

"I am."

"You convinced him to betray me and my husband."

Alend shook his head. "I did nothing of the kind," he said. "Olan made his own decisions. Now, you will leave. Go back into the bushes where you belong. Go, now. Into the foliage. Get out of Lord Fitz Walter's sight."

She had no idea that he was trying to get her into the greenery where Westley was supposed to be. The line of trees behind her stretched the length of the wall and beyond. It was about thirty or forty feet from the castle, giving the area good clearance, but if Westley had made it to those trees, he could easily be somewhere near the gatehouse by now. But there was no way Elysande could have known that Alend was trying to drive her straight to her husband and away from danger. In fact, his dismissive attitude only served to anger her.

"My proposal is for Lord Fitz Walter, not *you*," she snapped before returning her attention to Samson. "Well? Do we have a bargain?"

Alend opened his mouth to snap at her again, but Samson stopped him. "Why do you not come inside and let us discuss it, my lady?"

"Come out onto the road and we will discuss it here."

"Do you not want to see your husband?"

That brought Elysande pause. She may not have been experienced, but she was smart enough to see that he was trying to manipulate her. Also, she didn't want to visit her husband *inside* the castle.

She wanted to see him outside.

"Release him now and I will see him," she said.

"Do you not wish to speak with him first?"

"Nay," she said flatly. "I want to see him as he walks away from Hell's Forge. You have no right to keep him here, Fitz Walter. Until you came to Massington and threatened everyone, he never did anything to offend you."

"He thrashed me."

"He was defending us!"

Samson was becoming annoyed because he couldn't seem to force her to do what he wanted her to do, so he tried another tactic.

"You said you came here to exchange yourself for your husband," he said. "Did you consider that I may not want to let him go?"

Elysande sighed sharply. "Why not?" she said. "He means nothing to you. Your quarrel is with his father."

Samson snorted rudely. "How little you know about the ways of men," he said. "It is a good thing you are lovely to look at, because you are as stupid as a shovel."

"So are you."

"I would not push me if I were you," Samson said. "I can bring you inside, and you and your husband will both be my prisoners if I wish it."

Elysande was becoming increasingly frustrated with him. "You would have to catch me first, and I can run faster than you can," she said. Then she shook her head at the man and his arrogance. "You spent two years lying to my father, coming to visit and pretending to be an ally, only because you wanted to marry me. Now that I am standing before you, you have no interest in me?"

Samson shook his head. "So stupid yet so beautiful," he muttered. "Must I truly explain this to you?"

"Evidently."

"Very well," Samson said. "It was not you I wanted, but your father's lands. His titles. You were simply a means to an end, lady. Did you truly think I wanted to marry you because I was madly in love with you? I do not even know you. The only thing of value you have is your inheritance."

"You knew my brother would inherit, so your words are false."

"And your memory is lacking," he said. "I made the offer to your father *after* he died. 'Tis a good thing he did, because he saved me the trouble of killing him, but nevertheless, you were never my goal. Massington was."

In days past, that might have upset her. The mention of killing Emory definitely upset her, but she didn't show it. She didn't want to give Samson the satisfaction of knowing he had unsettled her. As it was, she saw his words as the opinion of a fool that held no weight with her, and she almost said so, but she had to remind herself that she was here to negotiate Westley's release and insulting Samson would not work well in her favor. Therefore, she had to bite her tongue.

Sort of.

"That is reasonable," she said steadily. "Any woman is only worth her inheritance, as any man is only as good as his property and title. Other than this beast of a castle, you do not have anything to offer, but still, I offer myself in exchange for my husband. If it is only the money and the lands you want, then an annulment can be achieved. If you marry me, everything will be yours."

Samson looked at her dubiously. "An annulment on what grounds?"

Unfortunately, Elysande hadn't thought that far ahead. In fact, the annulment comment was purely off the cuff. She didn't mean any of it but wanted Samson to think she did. Anything to gain his trust and his agreement. Therefore, she said the first thing that came to mind.

"Surely Westley will have the marriage annulled once I take up with you," she said. "If a man can prove his wife is an adulteress, the church will grant him an annulment. It is not difficult."

That was true. If a man could prove his wife betrayed him, the church would allow an annulment. Samson just stood there, watching her, hopefully mulling over what she'd said. She couldn't tell if he believed her or not. The wait began to grow longer and longer, and she began to feel more uncomfortable as he stared at her. Perhaps he was waiting for her to crack or give some sign that her presence here was some kind of trick.

Finally, he chuckled.

"If you are so willing to allow the marriage to be annulled, why have you come to seek your husband's release?" he said. "Your very presence would imply he means something to you."

It was Elysande's turn to chuckle. "I tried to kill him when he first arrived," she said, wondering just how much Westley had told the man about their relationship. "The moment he came through the gatehouse, I attacked him. I do not think that speaks of love and affection."

Samson seemed to agree with that. "He told me you fought when you first met," he said. "Do you know what else he did?"

"I am certain you are going to tell me."

Samson leaned against the portcullis, grinning the most

hideous grin. "He suggested that I let him run off to France or somewhere east," he said. "With him gone, you would assume he was dead and I could marry you. He *wanted* to leave you, my lady."

Elysande tried not to visibly react to that. She was certain that Samson was lying simply to hurt her. "And will you let him?" she asked.

Samson's smile faded. "Probably not," he said. "But if you do not care if he runs off, why are you here to secure his release?"

"Because I admire his family," she said. "Even if Westley and I have no interest in one another, his parents have been kind to me. And my father has no use for me. So... I am expendable. Mayhap I can do one good thing with my life by returning a son to parents who are worried."

She probably shouldn't have hinted that Christopher was upset over Westley's disappearance, but she couldn't take it back. Moreover, surely Samson would have known that. A missing son was a grave thing. But Samson's smile was completely gone by the time she finished and it was very clear that he was trying to determine if she was lying.

He couldn't quite seem to work it out.

"Are there a thousand men in those trees behind you, waiting for me to open the portcullis?" he finally said. "If they are using you as bait, they are clever. But not clever enough."

He seemed quite suspicious, perhaps *too* suspicious. That wasn't the direction she wanted him to go.

"No one is using me as bait," she said. "I have come of my own accord. You are holding my husband hostage and I want him released, so badly that I am willing to sacrifice my entire life so Westley can walk free. Mayhap our marriage is not a happy one, but I will tell you this—he does not deserve what you have done to him. Release him and I promise I will stay with you. I will not go back on my word. But if you do not release him, there are four thousand de Lohr men at Massington at this moment and they are preparing to attack you. They want Westley back and they will take him by force. I suspect you will not let them take him alive. Therefore, I beg you to take me instead. Let me do one good thing in my life, Fitz Walter. Let me be a sacrifice."

It was a rather passionate speech, one that had Samson's attention. Standing next to him, Alend simply hung his head. He could see how emotional Elysande was, and it was heartbreaking to watch. She was young and relatively naïve and really had no idea what she was asking, but still, she *was* asking.

But she was playing with fire.

If Westley had done what he was told, then he was already in the trees in the stretch of forest to the south. But something told Alend that Westley was watching what was happening at the gatehouse, seeing his wife standing there and more than likely planning to charge out of the trees and grab her at any moment. That was what Alend was hoping for. He was hoping that someone would save this girl from herself.

But then Samson did something unexpected.

"Raise the portcullis!" he shouted.

Men began to turn the enormous wheel that lifted the portcullis. It lifted slowly, the massive chains groaning under the weight, until it was about six feet off the ground. Not all the way up, but easy for a man to get through and easy to drop if the trees suddenly came alive with soldiers ready to attack.

"My lord," Alend said, trying to fend off whatever Samson was planning, "we must be cautious with a woman. All women are known liars."

Samson's gaze was on Elysande. "You worry too much," he said quietly. "Look at her—she is starting to cower. She knows I have control. Where is Westley?"

Alend had been prepared for that question. He'd decided that if Samson asked for Westley, he would dutifully look for him only to come up empty-handed and then swear to find him and go on the hunt outside of the walls. But when he found Westley, instead of going back to Hell's Forge, they would run all the way to Massington. It was simple, really. No reason to panic.

But knowing what Samson was capable of, the question made him feel sick.

"The last I saw him, he was in the solar where we left him," he said. "I took him a compress for his head this morning. Why? Should I fetch him?"

He was proud of himself for sounding so terribly normal, as if he weren't harboring a dangerous secret, but Samson shook his head.

"Nay," he said quietly. "But I do want to bring the lady closer."

"Why?"

"So you can snatch her."

Oh, God, Alend thought. But he nodded, posturing as if absolutely preparing to capture the woman, and Samson took a few steps under the portcullis.

Elysande backed up.

Seeing this, Samson came to a halt and crooked a finger at her. "Come here," he said. "No one is going to hurt you."

Elysande shook her head firmly. "I will not."

Samson cocked an eyebrow. "Yet you want me to trust

you?" he said. "How am I to trust you if you will not trust me?"

Elysande had seen Samson whispering to Alend. She might have been naïve, but she wasn't stupid in spite of what Samson had called her. The two of them were planning something and she wasn't going to walk into it. Oddly enough, her fear and doubt in the situation had fled completely. She was going to force this situation to be what she wanted it to be no matter what Samson said. No matter what names he called her.

No matter if he was trying to trick her.

"Trust goes both ways," she said. "If you want me to come closer, then you must do something for me."

"And what is that?"

"Release my husband," she said. "Release him and let me see that he is free. Then I will do whatever you wish."

Samson didn't seem pleased with that. He assumed a stance that suggested how annoyed he was and crooked his finger at her again.

"Just a little closer," he said. "I do not want to shout at you for all to hear. Come close enough so I do not have to shout, please."

Elysande still had her sword in her hand. It gave her a false sense of protection, as if she could fend the man off if he tried anything. Unless he charged her like Westley had when they first met, but she didn't think Samson was going to do that. She hoped not, anyway. With a sharp sigh, she took about six or seven steps closer to the open portcullis.

"There," she said. "Now, you will release my husband. If you want things to go your way without the violence of a battle, then release Westley and I am yours."

But Samson shook his head. "Closer," he said. "My throat and neck are still sore from the beating your husband gave me, so you'll have to come closer so I do not have to shout."

Elysande lifted the sword. "I will, but I will cut you if you try anything," she said. "You have been warned."

She took two more steps and came to a halt, but before Samson could say anything, a shout rose up from the trees back at the bend in the road, where Elysande had tethered her horse.

"Ella, *stop!* Get away from him!"

All eyes turned to the source of the shouting only to see Westley standing at the edge of the trees, his arms extended imploringly. Elysande, seeing him emerging from the bramble, gasped in shock.

"Westley?" she said, incredulous. Then she shouted frantically. "Westley, go home! *Go!*"

Samson and Alend were watching the exchange with a good deal of astonishment. In Alend's case, it was horror. Pure horror. But before he could make any move at all, Samson was running for Elysande. Westley's appearance had distracted her enough that she'd turned her back on her mortal enemy, and, like a good hunter, he had pounced. The next thing Alend realized, Samson had Elysande in his arms and was dragging her, kicking and screaming, back underneath the portcullis. More men were jumping to help him as Alend watched helplessly, but he knew he had to act. He had to think quickly or all would be lost.

God help me!

"I will go after de Lohr," he told Samson. "I do not know how he escaped, but I will bring him back!"

Without waiting for a response, he ducked underneath the portcullis as Samson ordered it lowered. That left Alend running down the road, alone, as the men at the gatehouse scrambled and prepared for an attack. They had no way of knowing if the lady really was, or wasn't, a decoy, so the sergeants in command were ordering their men to prepare for battle. It was chaotic at best.

And Alend kept running down the road.

By the time he entered the trees, he could see that Westley was mounted on a small mare. The man was turning the horse in the direction of Hell's Forge, clearly to save his wife, but Alend waved his arms in front of the animal and startled it as Westley struggled not to be thrown.

"Get out of my way," Westley said, clearly ill and gray in pallor. "What in the hell was she doing? Why did you not stop her?"

Alend could see that Westley was in a bad way. The head wound was wreaking havoc with him and he looked as if he were going to collapse at any moment. Alend grabbed the reins of the horse, steadying it, as Westley tried to pull away.

"Westley, listen to me," Alend begged. "You must go back to Massington. If you go to the gatehouse, there are a hundred men who will gladly kill you. You cannot fight them all. Do you understand me? *You cannot fight them all!*"

Westley heard him. God help him, he heard. And he was barely able to stay on horseback because the world was rocking and he was feeling horribly weak. "I went to the trees as you instructed," he said, his voice sounding as if it was about to crack. "But I had to see for myself if Ella was truly at the gatehouse. I could not hear what she said, but I saw her. I saw her move closer. Mayhap I should not have shouted to her, but he was going to take her!"

"And now he has her, thanks to you," Alend said angrily. "You should not have called to her. You should have left it alone."

"I know," Westley said, struggling with what he'd done. "But I often speak or act before thinking."

Alend wasn't going to scold him now. There wasn't time. "What is done is done," he said. "What you saw is Lady Elysande offering herself in exchange for your freedom, and Samson accepted her offer, so you must leave. You must not let her sacrifice be in vain."

Westley had a horrible feeling that might have been the case. Something told him that Elysande wasn't simply standing at the gatehouse for conversation's sake. She'd come to bargain, only he didn't think she would bargain with herself.

"My God," he said, horrified. "She... she offered to become his captive if he released me? I cannot believe it."

"You must," Alend said. "Because it is true and there is nothing you can do about it now."

Westley didn't like his answer. Of course there was something he could do about it. "To the devil with you," he snarled. "I will return and offer myself in exchange for her freedom. She should have never done this!"

"Yet she did," Alend snapped softly. "You cannot offer yourself in exchange for her. Samson will not release her, but he would gladly capture you again, and God only knows what he would do to you. In fact, Samson thinks I am trying to recapture you as we speak, so you must hit me on the jaw."

In the midst of his turmoil, Westley frowned at the very strange request. "You want me to *what*?"

"Hit me on the jaw," Alend said, moving to the saddle and pulling Westley off the horse. "If I am trying to capture you, it will not look real if there is no evidence. I will return without you, clearly having fought with you, and that way, I can keep an eye on your lady."

"But I want to—"

"Nay, you do *not*," Alend said sharply. "This is the only way. If you want to help your lady, hit me in the jaw and ride for Massington as fast as you can. I will do what I can to help her, but you must go. Do you understand me?"

Westley did, and every bone in his body was screaming against Alend's advice. He wanted to save Elysande. God only knew what was happening to her at the moment. But he could not save her if he was dead.

It was a devastating realization.

"Please," he finally murmured. "Just let me—"

"Nay," Alend said, cutting him off. "You ruined it the first time. If you want the lady, and you, to remain alive, you will do what I've told you to do. Hit me!"

The last two words were emphasized by Alend grabbing Westley by the hair. In response, Westley struck Alend in the chin and sent the man to the ground. But even in his distress, he knew that Alend was right. He knew what the man was trying to do. He didn't want to leave Elysande, but if he was going to fight another day, he would have to.

God help him, he had to.

"Help her," he whispered tightly, tears stinging his eyes. "Please... please, just help her."

Alend, on the ground, could hear the pain in the man's voice. "I will do what I can."

There was nothing more either of them could say. Swinging himself back onto the saddle, Westley charged south, across the field, heading toward the road that led to Massington. Alend picked himself off the ground, watching the man go before making his way out of the trees. He could feel something at the corner of his mouth and wiped at it, pleased to see that it was blood. That would be most convincing to Samson. But first, he had to make it back to the castle and hope the lady wasn't injured in the scuffle.

With blood on his mouth, he ran all the way back to the gatehouse.

Straight into hell.

CHAPTER TWENTY-FIVE

"**A**RE WE READY yet?" Curtis asked impatiently. "What is the delay?"

It was midafternoon on the day after Christopher's diagnosis. He'd made it through the night, but the physic was certain that he wasn't going to survive much longer. That meant everything the de Lohr sons were doing was sped up to accommodate the situation as well as the march to Hell's Forge.

But for Curtis, it wasn't moving fast enough.

He'd been supervising the situation in a general sense, and when the army was ready, he went to find Roi to see how their father's escort home was progressing. He found the situation not as advanced as he would like, and it was difficult to keep the annoyance out of his tone.

"We've had an issue with one of the wheels," Roi said. He wiped the sweat off his brow, pointing to a gang of soldiers and a wheelwright as they worked on one of the fortified de Lohr carriages. It was the largest carriage and the only one capable of accommodating Christopher for his homeward journey. "The wheel is iron-reinforced, but the wooden portion underneath was cracked. Westley and Papa must have had a rough journey here, because it takes a good deal of force to crack those wheels."

Curtis watched the soldiers place the wheel on the axle as the wheelwright hammered it into place. "But everything else is ready?" he said.

Roi nodded. "Everything," he said. "Hopefully we will be departing on the morrow if the physic deems Papa well enough to travel. We should reach Lioncross in a couple of days if we move slowly."

"Is the physic going with you?"

"Aye," Roi said. "I demanded it. I do not want Papa on the road for two days without assistance. Oh, and Mama has already sent word to Uncle David and Uncle Marcus, among others. She did what the physic told her to do—if there was anyone who needed to have words with Papa, she was to summon them."

Curtis sighed faintly, trying not to let the situation get to him. "This is going to be devastating to Uncle David."

"And Uncle Marcus."

Curtis nodded, thinking of the two men he'd grown up with in David de Lohr, his father's brother, and Marcus Burton, who was simply a very old friend. Men who had been very close to his father all his life.

"We should send word to Lioncross, too," he muttered. "To Christin and Brielle so they know what to expect."

"I already have," Roi said, noting his brother's depressed manner. Curtis was the deep feeler while Roi tended to be a little more pragmatic. "Meanwhile, our nephews have done an excellent job at mustering the army and preparing it to move out, but we are still waiting for Myles and Andrew to return with their information about Hell's Forge. Once we have that, the army can move."

He was trying to take the focus off their grief and onto the situation at hand, which Curtis thankfully responded to. "Why wait?" he said. "We can get the army on the road and Myles can find us there. Honestly, Roi, I do not want to wait any longer. We *must* get to Westley."

Roi tilted his head in the direction of the gatehouse. "Then go," he said. "Everything is ready. But have Rhodes as your second-in-command. He bellows orders like Jax de Velt did and everyone in the damn country will hear him."

Curtis laughed softly. "I miss the man."

"As do I."

"How many years has it been since we lost him?"

"Thirty-three."

Curtis lingered over that. "It seems forever ago," he said. "I never fought with him, you know. Too young."

"Nor did I," Roi said. "Peter did, once. He said he's never seen anything so frightening."

The de Lohr carriage suddenly settled heavily on the wheel that had been repaired. The entire conveyance rattled and shook. Curtis and Roi looked at the thing, watching the wheelwright continue to adjust the wheel. Gabriel and Nicholas were hovering over the man, telling him that a man's life depended on how well he could repair the wheel, and the old wheelwright simply took it in his stride. Young, bossy knights were amusing and he'd dealt with enough of them. Just as Roi was thinking about chasing his nephews away, there seemed to be some commotion over near the gatehouse.

Both Curtis and Roi turned in that direction, trying to see what the fuss was about but assuming it meant Myles and Andrew were returning. They began to make their way toward the gatehouse as Andrew abruptly charged in through the open portcullis. The horse was badly winded and Andrew nearly fell on his face as he tried to dismount. Harker was there to steady him, and the horse, but the moment Andrew caught sight of Curtis and Roi, he began to shout.

"We found Westley!" he said, running toward his uncles. "We found him on the road!"

Curtis and Roi looked at him in shock. "*Found* him?" Curtis said, incredulous. "Slow down, Andy. *Where* is West?"

Andrew threw an arm in the direction of the gatehouse, pointing. "With Uncle Myles," he said. Then the young man put his hand next to his head. "He has a wound on his head, a bad one. Uncle Myles says he needs a physic."

Curtis pointed to the keep. "Fetch the physic with Taid," he said. "Bring him immediately."

Andrew bolted for the keep. Meanwhile, Curtis and Roi ended up running the rest of the way to the gatehouse. By the time they reached the structure, men were crowding inside of it. They could see Myles and Westley just entering, trying to fight through the crowd, and Curtis and Roi began shouting to clear everyone out. With four de Lohr brothers bellowing, men cleared out quickly enough. When Westley came through the gatehouse and into the bailey, Roi stopped his horse and practically yanked his brother out of the saddle.

"Christ, West," Roi said, nearly holding his brother up once his feet hit the ground. "You have no idea how thrilled we are to see you."

Westley smiled wanly. "Same, brother," he said. "Truthfully, I wasn't sure if I would ever see you again."

Roi hugged him tightly as Curtis and Myles joined them. They all ended up in a big hug, so very glad to see their youngest brother. But they were all acutely aware that he had a visible injury, and Curtis grabbed hold of his head, taking a close look at the damage.

"You've got a nasty wound there," he said. "What happened?"

Westley sighed heavily, wearily. "I've escaped from Hell's Forge," he said. "But before I get into the tale, where is Olan?"

"In the vault," Roi said. "We figured out what happened, West. Mama sent word to us when you disappeared, asking us to bring the army to Massington, presumably to search for you. But Harker saw you and Olan leave Massington, and he only saw Olan return. When we realized he was responsible for your disappearance, we interrogated him. He confessed everything."

Westley couldn't even nod his head because it was paining him so much. "Good," he muttered. "Give me some time to tend my wound and then I'll join that bastard in the vault and show him just what I think of his betrayal."

"You probably do not need to," Roi said quietly. "Myles has been at him. It's not a pretty sight."

Westley looked at Myles, who was absolutely unrepentant. "Thank you," he said with more enthusiasm than he'd shown since he returned. "I do not care what you've done to him because whatever it is, I approve heartily. Because of him, I was nearly killed and Ella is now a captive of Fitz Walter."

That drew a reaction from the group. "Lady Elysande is at Hell's Forge?" Curtis said, bewildered. "How in the hell did that happen?"

Westley grunted unhappily. "'Tis a dreadful story," he said. "But your response tells me that you did not even realize she was missing."

Curtis shook his head. "We've not seen her, but we were

told that she was holed up in the keep."

"By whom?" Westley wanted to know.

Curtis shrugged, looking around the bailey until he spied the big Teutonic knight. "By Harker," he said, pointing. "We took him at his word."

Westley's gaze moved off toward Harker, watching the man as he dealt with some soldiers. "It is possible he may not even know she is gone," he said. "It seems to me that he has always been very tolerant of her and her wants. She wanted to train as a warrior, so he indulged her, albeit poorly. He thinks she simply wants to remain locked up in her chamber, so he hasn't made the necessary inquiries to confirm that, nor has he checked on her himself."

"Possibly," Curtis said. "He hasn't said a word about Olan. I would assume the two have served together for some time?"

Westley nodded. "Years, as far as I know," he said. "I'm assuming he knows about Olan's betrayal?"

"He knows," Curtis said. "But, as I said, he hasn't said a word about it."

Westley simply lifted his eyebrows. "I do not know the man well, but my experience with him suggests he's a brooder," he said. "In any case, I do not wish to waste my time discussing him. My wife is a captive of Samson Fitz Walter and I intend to raze the place to get to her. It looks to me as if the army is ready to march."

Curtis nodded. "It is ready to march to Hell's Forge for you," he said. "Now we shall go and retrieve your wife."

"Indeed, we shall," Westley said. "And I will lead that attack."

Curtis shook his head and grasped Westley by the arm. "Not until the physic looks at that head wound," he said, looking off toward the keep in time to see Andrew and the physic, who bore the odd name of Moonie, emerging from the entry. "There he is. Come with me, West."

Westley allowed himself to be pulled along as Roi and Myles followed. "Why is a physic here?" Westley asked. "Who is ill?"

That brought Curtis to a halt. He looked at Roi, at Myles, knowing he had to tell Westley about their father. The truth was going to be painful, but they could not avoid it, especially if Westley was asking a direct question.

"The physic is here for Papa," Curtis said, his voice quiet.

Westley didn't like the expression on his brother's face. "Why?" he said warily. "What happened?"

Curtis fixed him in the eye. "Shortly after you vanished, he went to sleep, and when he awoke, he could not move the left side of his body," he said. "He can hardly speak. The physic says it is apoplexy, an attack of the brain, and it has greatly affected him."

Westley stared at him. "He… he cannot move?"

"Not on his left side."

"Will he heal?"

"The physic does not think so."

Westley had to digest that information, struggling to keep down the emotions in him that erupted so freely. "What is being done for him, then?" he said, unable to keep his agitation at bay. As the physic drew nearer, he put out a hand as if to wave the man off. "I do not need him to look at me. Send him back to Papa. He needs to heal Papa!"

Curtis cupped Westley's face, forcing his brother to look at him. "Papa will not be healed, West," he said. "We've all had time to understand that, so I am sorry to tell you out here in the middle of the bailey with the world going on around us. Roi is preparing to take Papa back to Lioncross. He wants to go home so he can lie in his own bed."

Westley looked at him, horrified. Then he looked at Roi and Myles, who seemed particularly subdued. Grieving, even.

That told Westley all he needed to know.

"He wants to go home to die," he whispered. "Isn't that it?"

Curtis couldn't respond. None of them could. Westley stared at them as the news sank in and all he could feel was denial. Denial and rage and grief, all rolled into one. It was bad enough that his wife was the prisoner of a madman. Now he'd returned to Massington only to be told that his father was dying.

He just couldn't believe it.

Westley abruptly broke free of his brothers and started to run. He blew past the physic, past his nephew, and ran to the keep, barreling up the stairs. By the time he hit the entry, he was calling for his father, loudly. He then rushed up the mural stairs with his brothers racing after him, up to the floor where his parents' chamber was located. He was still shouting for his father, so when he finally reached the landing where Christopher's chamber was, Dustin was standing there. She'd heard him coming. One look at her youngest son with his bloodied head wound and she threw her arms around him, holding him tightly.

"Thanks be to God and his saints," she said, squeezing the life out of Westley. "My son has returned. My baby has returned. Let me see what they've done to you, West."

She pulled back to get a look at that black, nasty gash on his head, but Westley was trying to push past her.

"I must see Papa," he said. "Please let me see Papa."

He was starting to break down. The tears were coming and he couldn't stop them. Dustin put herself in front of the door, blocking him from going in, as Curtis and Roi and Myles held him back. Westley began to weep, so very painfully, as his mother cupped his face.

"You have been through so much, West," she murmured. "Although I thank God for your return, I am so very sorry you had to come back to this."

Westley could hardly speak. "I want to see my papa," he said. "Please… let me see him."

Dustin was struggling with her tears as well. "You can," she assured him, wiping at his cheeks. "But he is in a fragile state. Please do not burden him with more troubles, West. Let him see you strong and well. Can you do this for him?"

Westley was nodding even as he continued to weep. Tears and mucus were running down his face. "I-I'll try," he said.

"Try very hard," Dustin said softly. "I know this is difficult for you, but it is important that you not cause him further stress."

Westley took a deep breath to calm himself, or at least tried to. "I will not, I promise," he said, wiping at his leaking face. "May I go in now?"

Dustin nodded reluctantly. "Aye," she said. "But I'll send the physic in with you and he can tend to your wound while you talk to your father. He is difficult to understand because the attack has made the left side of his face stiff, but his mind is still there."

"I understand."

He was calmer now than he had been. Dustin took the sleeve of her garment to dry what remained on his face as he struggled to stop all hint of tears. She softly encouraged him to take deep breaths, and he did, finally relaxed enough to move forward.

She opened the door.

Christopher was supine on the big bed, his eyes closed as Westley and the others entered the chamber. Dustin took Westley's hand and led him around to his father's right side.

"Chris?" she said softly. "Are you awake?"

The right side of Christopher's body moved a little. His foot twitched, as did his hand. Dustin leaned down and kissed him on the cheek.

"Wake up," she murmured. "It is time to rejoice. Westley has come home."

That brought more of a reaction. Christopher twitched again and something that sounded like a groan came out of his mouth. His right eye opened, half-lidded, and the left eyelid opened a little as well.

"W-Westley?" he said.

So much for being brave. At the sound of his father's mumbled, jumbled voice, tears popped from Westley's eyes even though he tried to smile.

"It's me, Papa," he said. "I've returned."

Christopher's eye opened a little wider and he lifted his right hand, which Westley took quickly. The moment their flesh touched, however, Westley's face crumpled. He went to his knees beside his father's bed, holding Christopher's hand against his cheek.

"I am so sorry this happened, Papa," he said. "I did not mean to worry you so. You know I would never do that intentionally."

"It's as we thought, Papa," Curtis said, standing at the end of the bed. "Olan betrayed Westley to Samson Fitz Walter."

Christopher's eye was fixed on Curtis before returning to Westley. "Your... head," he said. "Did he... do that?"

Since Westley didn't seem too keen to settle down to let the physic tend his wound, Dustin pulled the physic over to the right side of the bed so he could work on Westley as the man knelt on the floor. Westley's tears faded as the physic examined the wound.

"Aye," he said to his father, wiping at his face with his free hand. "He dropped a stone on my head. I was unconscious for a couple of days, I think. I believe that Samson intended to kill me to even the score with you for the death of his uncle. He's not a well man, Papa. He reeks of madness. But I would not have been there at all had it not been for Olan de Bisby. He betrayed me."

Christopher grunted, closing his eye. "De Bisby has been... tended to," he mumbled. "As for Fitz Walter, the... family is mad. He did not... hurt you further, did he?"

"Nay," Westley said, wincing as the physic and Dustin began to clean the dried blood from his head with water and wine. "Mama and the physic are doing worse than Samson did."

Dustin grinned, glancing at her husband, knowing he was probably grinning inside as well.

"Quiet, Westley," she said. "You always were a complainer."

That brought a smile from Westley. His tears were gone now that he had seen his father and heard his voice, so in spite of the dire situation, that gave him some comfort. But given the stress of his wound and the past few days, his emotions were more brittle than usual.

"Forgive me, Mama," he said, suffering through the physic digging into his wound to remove some debris. But his focus was on his father. "Papa, the entire reason I'm here is because of

Elysande. She went to Fitz Walter and offered to exchange herself for me. I know our army was poised to march on Hell's Forge to reclaim me, but now we must do it for Ella. She sacrificed herself so that I could be free. I cannot leave her there. I need help getting my wife back."

Christopher squeezed his son's hand. "She was upset that you were gone," he said, sounding a little clearer. "But I've not seen her in days."

Westley snorted. "No one has, evidently," he said. "She decided to go to Hell's Forge herself to seek my release. It makes me think of a conversation I had with her when we first met."

"What was it?"

A look of adoration crossed Westley's features. "She and I had a discussion about courage," he said. "I told her that courage is simply fear mixed with determination. She told me that fear is anger, and she uses her anger to motivate her courage. Stubborn, that one is. Like Mama."

Something that sounded suspiciously like laughter came from Christopher's mouth. "Then you deserve her," he said. "But I did not know she had gone to seek your release. That was very brave of her."

Westley had to close his eyes when the physic finished cleaning out the wound and wiped it down with wine, which stung like mad.

"Papa," he finally said, "we cannot leave her there, though I have hope that one of Fitz Walter's men will help keep her safe until I can return. Fitz Walter has a knight by the name of Alend de Bisby. He is Olan's cousin."

"Is that how Olan communicated with Fitz Walter, then?" Myles asked, interrupting. He was over by the door, leaning against the jamb. "We knew there had to be some communication between Fitz Walter and Olan, but it makes sense if there was a connection with a cousin at Hell's Forge."

"Exactly," Westley said, looking over at Myles. "I realize it is probably stupid to trust another de Bisby knight, but if it were not for Alend, I would not be here. He's the one who actually helped me escape."

Curtis entered the conversation. "I would not trust him again, and certainly not with Elysande's life," he said, frowning. "We are ready to march on Hell's Forge when you are."

Westley was on his feet, much to the annoyance of his mother and the physic, who were still working on his head.

"*I* will lead this army," he said in a tone that didn't invite any argument. "This is my wife. Fitz Walter has now sinned against me. This is no longer Papa's fight, but mine. Are we clear?"

"You are not going anywhere until your wound is tended," Dustin said, pulling him into a chair so they could resume working on his head. "And your father will decide who leads his army. That is not your privilege."

"But it is *my* wife," Westley said as they went to work on his wound once more. "Papa, is this not my right? My fight?"

Curtis went to the bedside, kneeling down and taking his father's hand. "What is your wish, Papa?" he asked, smiling. "Should we turn the army over to Westley and watch the bloodbath?"

Christopher gazed at his firstborn son with Dustin with surprising lucidity. "Fitz Walter... has become Westley's enemy now," he muttered. "There is a reckoning to be had. If Samson had your wife, what would you do?"

Curtis' smile faded. "I would kill him."

"And that is what... Westley wishes to do," Christopher

murmured, his speech hesitant and difficult to understand. "He has seen Hell's Forge. It is the most difficult… castle I ever tried to breach. Let your brother have a seat at the command table, Curt. This is his wife. His life."

The last few words faded off and Christopher closed his eyes, exhausted from the short conversation. But his youngest son was back and he could rest far easier now. Even if his sons were preparing to attack the most impenetrable castle he had ever faced, he was confident in their abilities. They were of de Lohr stock.

They would get the job done.

Seeing his father drift off to sleep again, Curtis stood from his kneeling position beside the bed. But his gaze lingered on his father, and he felt such a hollow sense of sorrow at this mighty man cut down and betrayed by his own body. It was a painful grief, like his guts had been clawed out.

They all felt it.

"Roi," Curtis said after a moment, "as soon as the physic approves of Papa being moved, take him home immediately."

Roi, at the end of the bed, nodded faintly. "And you still wish for me to go with him?"

"One of us should."

Roi wasn't too thrilled about his brothers going to battle without him, but he understood. His job, taking his father home, was monumentally important. Myles, having remained largely silent throughout the entire conversation, pushed himself off the wall and approached the bed.

"Andrew and I have observations of Hell's Forge and, I think, a viable plan," he said. "I'll gather everyone and we can meet in the great hall."

Curtis looked at him. "Why not the solar downstairs?"

"Because Marius is lying on the floor, sleeping off his drink."

Curtis waggled his eyebrows in understanding. "I see," he said. "Does he even know his daughter is missing?"

"He does not."

The voice came from the doorway, which was partially open. Esther stood there, and by the look on her face, it was clear she'd heard everything. As she stepped into the chamber, her gaze moved to the men in the room. Warlords that controlled England and warlords who were now facing something unimaginably difficult.

Something that frightened her to death.

"I am sorry to intrude," she said. "But I heard that Westley had returned and I came to see him. I did not mean to listen in on a private conversation, but the door was open and I heard what you said. That my daughter is at Hell's Forge. I feel as if I should have known she was going to do something like that. She was devastated when Westley disappeared. I should have... known."

She looked rather sick at the idea of her daughter in mortal danger. Westley, in the process of having a few stitches put into the gash on his head, spoke up.

"We will reclaim her, Lady Ledbury," he said. "I swear to you that I will not leave her there. I will get her back."

Esther smiled weakly. "I know you will," she said. "I am grateful."

Dustin, leaving the physic to finish with Westley's head, went to Esther. The two of them may not have always gotten along, but at this moment, Dustin didn't feel any irritation with the woman. Only sympathy.

A kinship.

"Elysande has the de Lohr army on her side," she said reassuringly, reaching out to take Esther's hand. "Please do not be troubled. Soon enough, your daughter will be back in your fold. All will be well."

Esther was trying hard to be brave. She held Dustin's hands tightly. "I lost one child," she said. "I could not stomach losing another. Not Ella. She has tried to be both daughter and son to Marius and me. Since her brother died, she has tried so hard to be everything. I... I never told her how much I appreciated that. I would like to have the chance to do so."

Dustin squeezed her hands before turning her around, putting an arm around her shoulders. "She is a very good girl," she said. "She must be very special for Westley to be so fond of her. Let's go down to the kitchens and see to the evening meal, shall we? I fear your cook has been left to his own devices and he cooks for an army of men, not guests with more delicate stomachs."

As Dustin took Esther away, distracting the woman from the ominous situation, the physic finished up with Westley's head.

"I managed to clean most of the blood from your hair, my lord," he said. "You have five stitches in your scalp, so be mindful of them. Do not get them wet. Try to keep them dry and douse them with wine once a day for the next few days to keep away the poison."

Westley eyed the man as he gingerly touched the wounded area. "I am going to battle," he said. "I will be wearing my helm."

The physic shook his head. "No helm," he said. "It will cause poison to seep into your wound before it heals."

Westley frowned, looking at his brothers. "No helm?" he

said. "I am to go into battle with my head exposed?"

The brothers shrugged to varying degrees, unwilling to go against a skilled physic. Westley stood up, still touching the wound, as Curtis pointed toward the door.

"Everyone out," he said. "Papa must have peace, so let us leave. Myles, we'll meet you in the great hall."

Myles was already heading down the stairs, as was Roi. Curtis followed with Westley bringing up the rear. But instead of following his brothers to the great hall, he first retreated to Elysande's chamber. He was in filthy, torn clothing and he wanted to clean the dirt of Hell's Forge off him.

More than that, he simply wanted to retreat to the chamber he shared with his wife.

Just for a moment, he wanted something that reminded him of her.

The moment he walked in the door, he was hit with the smell of her. Not an unpleasant smell, but something musky and sweet. It smelled like her hair. Moving over to the bed, he found himself smelling the pillows, inhaling deeply, and tears came to his eyes. He simply couldn't believe she would put herself in such danger for him. God, he wished he'd known what she had planned and had found a way to stop her. As he'd told his father, he'd once questioned her on whether or not she knew what courage was.

He was coming to think she did.

Maybe he did, too, in a different way.

A sound at the door startled him and he turned around to see Freddie standing there. The cousin who kept herself so scarce stood in the doorway with wide eyes, surprised to see that Westley was there. Truth be told, he'd heard a rumor that his cousin, Nicholas, had struck up a relationship with the woman, but he'd never really met her or had a chance to ask about it. When she abruptly turned to stumble out, he stopped her.

"Wait," he said. "Freddie? Please come in. You do not have to leave."

Freddie entered the room, but she was looking at him quite fearfully. "I... I did not know you were here," she said. "I thought you were... gone."

He smiled wryly. "I was," he said. "But I am back. Now, Ella is gone. Did you know that?"

Freddie looked puzzled. "Gone?" she said. "Where did she go?"

"Then she did not tell you of her plans?"

"What plans?"

That answered his question. He simply shook his head. "I thought you would know," he said. "Doesn't she tell you everything?"

Freddie shrugged. "She used to," she said. "You came and we have not really spoken. She's been quite busy with you."

He studied her for a moment. "And that troubles you?"

Freddie shook her head. "I am very happy for her, truly," she said. "But may I ask you where she has gone? She did not sleep in her bed last night. I thought she might have slept with her mother."

"Why?"

"Because she was upset that you had gone away," she said. "When she was younger, she and Lady Ledbury were quite close. You could find Ella in her mother's bed often."

"Ah," he said, learning something he didn't know about his wife. "Nay, she did not sleep with her mother last night. She decided to do something very brave and now I must go and help her. That is, mayhap, the simplest way to describe the situation."

He averted his gaze, his thoughts lingering on Elysande, and Freddie dared to come closer. She noticed his wounded head and the fact that he seemed exhausted. Truth be told, she had heard about Westley's disappearance. She'd also heard that Olan had something to do with it, though no one seemed to know what it was. The rumor mill at the castle had been oddly lacking in facts this time around, but she also knew that something had happened to the Earl of Hereford. That information, too, had been kept tight. So much was happening at Massington that was confusing, now with Westley returned and Elysande missing.

Quietly, she made her way around the bed.

"What did she do?" she asked softly.

Westley looked at her, debating on what to say. He opted for the truth.

"Do you know the situation with Samson Fitz Walter of Hell's Forge Castle?" he said. "He offered for her hand in marriage."

Freddie nodded immediately. "He was very angry when he was denied."

"Exactly," Westley said. "Fitz Walter also hates my father. I disappeared because I was betrayed and given over to Fitz Walter as a hostage. When Ella discovered this, she went to Fitz Walter and offered herself in exchange for my freedom. And that was incredibly brave."

Freddie's features creased with worry. "Is she in danger, then?"

Westley didn't really want to answer that, mostly because he hadn't let his mind go to that dark place, to the extreme danger she was in.

"My father's army is mobilizing now to go to Hell's Forge," he said. "I am going to retrieve my wife and burn that castle to the ground."

Freddie pondered that declaration. It both gave her comfort and frightened her. With a sigh, she moved over to the wardrobe, which had been her original destination. There were some things that needed washing inside, and she pulled them out. But her movements were slow, her mind pensive.

"It seems that so much has happened since you arrived," she finally said. "We live in a very small world here at Massington. It is rare that we go outside that world. Ella has always been bold and brave, but only here. Only where those who knew her could see. But now... now, it sounds as if she has been brave outside of our world."

"Verily," Westley said. "I am proud of her. It was a great sacrifice."

Freddie fell silent, but only for a moment. "I do not think I have ever heard anyone say that they were proud of her," she said softly. "When you see her next, make sure you tell her that. Ella has worked all of her life for her mother and father to be proud of her, but I do not think they ever told her that."

Westley smiled faintly. "I will tell her when I see her."

Freddie nodded, pleased by that. She was still carrying the dirty laundry, heading for the door, but she came to a halt as she passed the table that Elysande used to store her toilette. It was cluttered, which was typical of Elysande, and there wasn't much on it. But there was a brush that had her hair in it.

Freddie set the laundry down.

Cleaning the hair out of the brush, she took a thread from the shift she was taking to the laundry and tied it up in a bundle. As Westley still sat on the bed, Elysande's pillow in his hands, Freddie approached and timidly extended the hair bundle.

"Here," she said quietly. "This is Ella's hair. Mayhap... mayhap it will give you strength for what is to come."

Westley looked at the hair, looked at her, and back to the hair again. Reaching out, he took it from her and held it to his nose, inhaling. From the expression on his face, it was clear that the scent of his wife meant something to him. He smiled at Freddie.

"Thank you," he said sincerely. "I will carry it next to my heart."

Freddie smiled in return. "You are welcome, my lord," she said, warmth in her eyes for the first time as they bonded over someone they mutually adored. "Now, I must go and have her shifts laundered. They will need to be clean for her return."

Westley simply nodded, his smile fading as she collected the laundry and scampered from the chamber. Alone in the room once more, he held the bundle of hair to his nose and inhaled again, closing his eyes and drawing strength from it. Such a small thing, but so very powerful. For a marriage he'd never wanted in the first place, he was willing to do everything in his power to ensure it continued. Odd how in just a few short days, it had become the most important thing in his life.

She had become the most important thing in his life.

Lowering his head, he did something that he hadn't done in years.

He prayed.

CHAPTER TWENTY-SIX

HARKER KNEW HE was down here.

He had seen the de Lohr brothers dragging Olan out of the keep and across the bailey, leaving a trail of blood behind him. Many people had seen it and the soldiers were whispering about the situation at large. Since the House of de Lohr arrived, it seemed that Massington was riddled with mysteries. No one seemed to be able to get the full story.

But Harker knew.

And he knew what needed to be done.

The army had departed about an hour earlier, heading north to Hell's Forge and the battle that awaited there. A battle that would have been completely preventable had it not been for a jealous knight and his turn to the dark side. But now that the army was gone and there was just one brother left with a small escort that would be returning to Lioncross Abbey on the morrow, or so he'd been told, it was time to carry out his plan.

It was time to right a wrong.

Harker had mostly stayed out of the way since the de Lohr army arrived. He had been very helpful and done as he'd been asked, but he hadn't taken a lead role in anything because it had been clear from the start he hadn't been needed. At first, that hurt his pride, but as the days went by, he was glad that he wasn't responsible for what was going on. Harker had come to Massington so many years ago and had assumed a quiet post that he cherished. He was never meant for the bigger battles or the higher chains of command, so taking a secondary role in the situation at Massington had been right for him.

But there was something he wasn't going to take a secondary role in.

And that was Olan.

He knew what Olan had done. He had seen it all. Although he never knew the man to be shifty or treacherous, he knew that Olan had a secretive underbelly that he liked to keep hidden. It was that secretive underbelly that came into the light when Olan had actively participated in betraying Westley de Lohr. The truth was that Harker felt greatly slandered by Olan's behavior because Olan was under his command. And every commander was responsible for the behavior of his subordinates.

That meant Harker was responsible for Olan's actions.

Not that anyone blamed him, because no one did. He had briefly seen Esther in the great hall, stealing a moment of private time with her where she had told him everything that had gone on since the de Lohr army's arrival. She spoke of Westley's return and Christopher's health, things she had been privy to. That was how Harker knew everything that had been whispered about. But he wouldn't spread rumors or participate in gossip. That wasn't his style. But given what he knew, and everything he'd been told, he viewed Olan's actions as a mark upon his record as the knight in command.

Olan's stain was his stain.

He simply couldn't stand for it. That was why he was heading over to the vault entrance at this very moment. The vault of Massington had been built under the gatehouse of the castle. The ground had been very rocky and hard, so the vault was uneven and narrow in places. Some du Nor ancestor had built the castle and Harker remembered Marius telling him once that building the vault had taken as long as building the castle itself because of the hardness of the ground.

These days, the vault was akin to the outer levels of hell because of its living conditions. It was cold and dank and, at some point, groundwater had seeped into it and created great blooms of mold on the walls and on the floor. Olan was down there, in the cell that was the least damp of all of them, with only a small torch on the outside of the cell for light. There wasn't even a fire for warmth, though the man had a couple of woolen blankets for comfort.

But that was all.

And Harker didn't feel bad about it.

In fact, he didn't feel bad about anything that had to do with Olan, not even what he intended for the man, so he entered the gatehouse and went straight to the door that led down to the sublevels. The stairs were carved out of the rock and, due to the humidity in the vault, very slippery with growth that the soldiers cleaned off on occasion. There were nineteen steps from the top of the vault to the bottom, with a severe drop from the top of the flight to the ground below.

Harker stayed to the right side of the stairs where the wall was, his hand on the wall to steady himself as he made his way down. In his left hand, he carried an iron key for the lock on the cell doors. Once he reached the bottom, he took the torch from the wall and used it to light his way to the first cell, which was reached via a small, low-ceilinged corridor. It was isolated from the other cells and not in sight of the stairs.

As Harker drew near, the smell of human habitation hit him. So did the smell of rot. Peering into the cell, he could see the bucket for waste, damp straw over the ground, and a pile of old straw in the corner with blankets on it for a bed. Sitting atop the old straw and blankets, Olan turned his head slowly in Harker's direction. Because of the dim light he'd been forced to sit in, he had to shield his eyes from the torchlight until they became accustomed to it. When he finally saw who it was, he gave a wry, toothless smile.

"What do you want?" he asked, muffled because of his torn-up mouth. "Have you come to finish what the de Lohr bastards started?"

Harker had no sympathy for the man he'd once considered a friend. "If it were up to me, they would have done worse," he said. "When a knight turns bad, he taints everything around him. You tainted me, Olan. You have made them suspicious of me."

"Nonsense," Olan said. "Their anger is at me."

"Whatever you did, I hope it was worth it."

Olan shrugged. "Time will tell," he said. "Why?"

"Because Westley has returned."

That brought a reaction from Olan. He looked at Harker in shock. "How is that possible?" he gasped. "Fitz Walter would not let him escape!"

Harker remained emotionless. "He did not allow him to escape," he said. "Elysande knew what you did and went to Hell's Forge to free her husband. Your treachery, your jealousy, may very well bring her death. Now tell me how your betrayal was worth it."

Olan's toothless mouth popped open in shock. He staggered up from his straw bed, the blankets falling away as he made his way over to the rusted cell door.

"What is happening?" he said, bloody saliva spraying from his lips. "Is she still at Hell's Forge?"

Harker was insulted at the level of concern Olan was showing. "What is it to you?" he said. "You caused this."

"I caused it to de Lohr, not to her!"

"She has fallen in love with her husband," Harker said, knowing Olan's feelings for her, so it was a dig at the man. "Anyone could see that. Why else would she go to Hell's Forge to secure his release?"

Olan was beside himself. He was sick, injured, and had been without any kind of care at all. His mouth was one giant blood clot. He only had three teeth left, on the bottom, and in the front. The vicious de Lohr brother had started with his molars, and Olan gave up any resistance toward the end. He should have given up at the beginning, but pride and a sense of righteousness had prevented him from doing so.

Now...

Now, he was a mess.

He had *caused* a mess.

"Oh, God," he muttered, a hand to his head. "Ella is at Hell's Forge, at the mercy of a madman. What has she done?"

Harker had had enough. He was growing increasingly disgusted watching Olan lament the situation. Putting the key in the lock, he turned the tumblers and yanked the cell door open.

"Come with me," he said.

Olan looked at him in surprise. "Where are we going?"

Harker simply crooked a finger at him, luring him out of his cell. It didn't take much, truthfully. Olan was ready to go.

Without a word, Harker headed to the stairs with Olan close behind, skittish because he thought Harker was removing him from the cell with the intention of hiding him from the de Lohr brothers. Given that they had served together for so long, that would have been the right thing to do. They were comrades. They were even friends. Harker knew why Olan had done what he did and, in some small way, surely supported it. No one wanted to see Elysande married to that barbarian of a son of the Earl of Hereford.

Certainly not Olan.

They were heading up the treacherous stairs. Harker was in front and Olan was tucked in behind him, hiding from the light that was trickling in from above.

"Where are you taking me?" Olan asked. "If I am seen by anyone from the de Lohr family, they might throw you in the vault, too. You must hide me."

Harker didn't say anything until they neared the top of the stairs, when he suddenly came to a halt and faced Olan.

"I do not plan to hide you," he said.

Olan looked at him curiously. "What do you plan to do?"

"Kill you."

With that, he shoved Olan back by the face and the man had no chance to save himself. With the steep angle of the stairs and the severe drop to the floor below, he tumbled backward, striking his head. It knocked him out because the rest of the fall was as if he had no bones, flailing and flapping and smacking all the way to the bottom. He ended up falling off the bottom of the stairs, tumbling the last five or so feet to the hard ground below with his head twisted all the way around on his shoulders so he was facing backward.

Clearly dead, he lay in an unmoving heap at the bottom.

Slowly, Harker made his way down the steps until he was standing over Olan's battered body. There was no remorse in his expression, no sense of loss, no hint of sorrow.

Just a cold, dead stare.

"When a knight goes bad, he reflects on the other knights around him," he repeated quietly. "You have reflected on me badly. You have endangered the family you have sworn to protect. Most of all, you have created chaos at the place I love. The place I have spent most of my life at. I will protect Massington and its family at all costs, and this time, the cost is you. Consider your punishment to have fit the crime."

With that, he headed up the stairs, his face upturned toward the light that was shining in the darkness. A light coming from the sun over Massington, illuminating the way for a man who had just dispensed justice.

And wasn't the least bit sorry about it.

But he had other plans, too.

Before the hour was through, Harker of Kent packed his belongings and departed the gatehouse of Massington Castle, heading back to the land of his birth where he would find a good woman and have many sons. That was what he'd told Esther, once.

It was time for him to find his happiness.

Finally, he was going home.

CHAPTER TWENTY-SEVEN

Hell's Forge

I T WAS MORNING.

Elysande awoke on her stomach, on a bed that was horribly uncomfortable, in a chamber she didn't recognize. It was cold because the fire had gradually reduced during the night until all that was left was embers.

Just embers.

Just like her life.

She felt like her entire life was reduced to this moment, smoldering embers that would soon be black and cold. There were three lancet windows in the chamber, none of them with any covering, so the icy chill of morning mixed with the smell of smoke from the morning fires was blowing in through the opening.

Cold was everywhere, body and soul.

Slowly, she lifted her head, wiping the drool off her chin. She squinted in the morning light, pushing herself up into a sitting position and wincing when she moved her right arm and it greatly pained her. She thought she might have broken it in the fight with Fitz Walter, although she could still move her fingers. Everything seemed to be moving well enough even if it did hurt.

But she was here now.

And here she would stay.

Yawning, she stood up and tried to peer from the window. It was a little too high, so she pulled her bed over and stood on it. She had a view of that enormous gatehouse from here and the fields and trees to the south. Trees that had covered Westley's escape, thank God. Never once had she doubted that her actions had been right and true. Westley was safe and that was all that mattered to her.

Now, she had to face the consequences of what she'd done.

Yesterday had been a battle. After Samson grabbed her, she'd fought fiercely enough that he brought in reinforcements, and by her count, at least ten soldiers came to his aid. She kicked and punched and even bit until Samson dumped her in a chamber that looked like a solar, with books and a table and clutter. There was even a raven on a perch, screaming at her. Samson locked her in that chamber for a couple of hours, and when he returned, it was with the news that Westley had evaded recapture.

When he told her that, she wept.

After that, the situation seemed to calm. Westley was on his way back to Massington and, as she'd promised, Elysande became Samson's prisoner. Truth be told, he didn't seem too sure about it. He had what he wanted—he had her—but he couldn't marry her legally as long as Westley was alive, and given how the exchange of prisoners went and the chaos that ensued, he wasn't entirely sure how Westley was going to respond. If he didn't want a wife, as he'd said he didn't, and she didn't want a husband, there was no telling what Westley would do.

A strange situation grew stranger.

But what wasn't strange was the fact that Elysande wasn't content to simply be a prisoner. It wasn't natural for her to be submissive, in any situation. Certainly, she'd exchanged herself for her husband, but Westley was free and she didn't want to stay at Hell's Forge. She considered Samson Fitz Walter a man without honor, so for certain, she didn't see a need to keep her word, or any part of her bargain, with him.

Now, all she could think about was escape.

She wasn't exactly sure how Westley got out, but if he managed to do it, then she could do it, too. Perhaps there was a gap in the wall or a friendly soldier to bribe. Whatever it was, and however he did it, she was going to do it, too.

She wanted to get home to her husband.

Her sword had been dropped in the chaos of her capture, so she didn't have a weapon. She'd been moved out of the solar last night sometime and placed in the chamber she was currently in, which had a bed, a small table and a chair, a taper, and a hearth. There was nothing else. Nothing to really make a weapon out of unless she used the chair or the table leg, and she didn't rule it out, but once she'd used it and escaped the chamber, she had nowhere to run.

No, that wouldn't work.

But perhaps chaos would.

It had before.

The chaos at the gatehouse yesterday had worked in Samson's favor. It had also worked in Westley's. The chaos of her diversion allowed Westley to escape and Samson to capture her. She began to think seriously on the chaos that had allowed everything to happen as it had and wondered if she could create that chaos again, this time to give her the same opportunity to escape.

Perhaps it could work for her.

But just *how* to create chaos eluded her. And how to get out of the castle once the chaos started was another problem. She was standing on the bed, watching the bailey below and pondering her next move, when she heard the bolt on the exterior of the door being thrown. Startled, she jumped off the bed and quickly moved it back to where it was, sitting down just as the door lurched open.

Samson was standing in the doorway.

"Ah," he said, a feigned smile plastered on his lips. "You are awake. Good morn to you, my lady."

Elysande's first instinct was to snap at him. She wanted to slap the grimace off his face, but she took a moment to calm herself. Fighting the man would get her nowhere. It wouldn't create a diversion or chaos or anything else she wanted in her quest to escape, so perhaps she needed to do what she most definitely didn't want to do.

Be polite to him.

Lull him into a false sense of trust that she would be compliant.

"And to you, my lord," she said, sounding like she didn't mean it. "It seems like a cold day outside."

Samson stepped into the chamber followed by Alend and a servant bearing a bucket of kindling for the smoldering hearth.

"I would not know," Samson said. "I've not been outside. But it is cold in here, so I've brought you a fire this morning."

"It is appreciated."

"I've also brought you something else to wear."

That caught her attention, and she looked at him oddly.

"What is it?"

He looked to Alend, who held up a shockingly beautiful garment of yellow silk with elaborate embroidery around the neckline and down the sleeves.

"That," Samson said simply. "I do not know if you are aware, but when I was trying to talk your father into a betrothal, I came to Massington bearing gifts for you. This is one of the gifts that your father turned away."

The dress was truly stunning. Elysande nodded her approval. "It is lovely," she said. "I do not own any such clothing."

"Pity," Samson said. "You should. I would have provided you with much. A woman with your beauty should be dressed in the finest."

"I thought I was only worth the inheritance I bring."

He looked at her, perhaps with a hint of disdain, as he heard his words in her comment. "True," he said. "But that does not mean you cannot present a lovely picture. No man wants to look upon a wife who dresses like a servant."

Elysande looked down at herself and her rugged clothing. "I did not exactly dress for a party when I came here," she said.

"I realize that," Samson said. "But I do not want to be offended looking at you, so you will put on this garment and then Alend will escort you to the hall, where we will enjoy a morning meal."

With that, he turned and left the chamber, taking the servant with him and leaving Alend behind. He'd given her an order and she knew it. As her focus lingered on the door, she caught sight of movement in her periphery.

Alend laid the gown on the bed.

"How are you feeling since yesterday, my lady?" he asked. "Were you injured in your capture?"

She looked at him, a man who bore a faint resemblance to Olan. They were both fair, with round heads. The sight of the man dredged up all of the horrible events from the past few days and she shook her head in disgust.

"You are Olan's cousin," she said.

He nodded. "I am Alend, my lady."

"I know," she said, looking at him with contempt. "It was your cousin who caused all of this. When I see him next, I will kill him."

Alend lifted his eyebrows in agreement. "I think your husband will already see to that when he returns to Massington."

Elysande didn't have much to say to that. She saw that the kindling was still sitting next to the hearth. The servant had simply brought it and left, so she got up and went to the hearth, stirring up the embers so she could restart the fire.

Alend watched her carefully.

"My lady," he said, his voice low, "I tried to stop this."

Elysande laid the kindling on the embers, blowing on them gently so a flame would catch. "Stop what?"

"You. Here."

"What are you talking about?"

"I tried to convince you to run back to the trees," he said quietly. "Do you not recall that?"

She sighed heavily. "Just get out," she said. "I do not want to see you."

"Did you stop to think how Westley escaped an impenetrable castle?"

That brought her pause. Slowly, she turned away from the fire and looked at him. "*What* are you talking about?" she asked again. "Be plain about it."

Alend's expression was serious. "I will tell you what I told your husband," he muttered. "If you tell Samson, I will deny it and he will believe me, so think not to betray me in retaliation for what my cousin did. I had no part in that. But your husband promised me that if I helped him escape, he would find a position for me with his father. I will hold him to that promise, more so now that I will help you escape, also. Do you understand me?"

It was as if a revelation had been revealed. Elysande had been wondering how Westley ended up outside of the walls of Hell's Forge, and now she knew. She'd been thinking about a friendly soldier who took a bribe, but as it turned out, it was evidently a knight who wanted to make a bargain.

She looked at him with new eyes.

"*You* helped him?" she said, incredulous. "And... now that I think of it, you did tell me to run for the trees."

"That is because I knew he was there," Alend said. "I was trying to help you."

A great many things were becoming clear and Elysande had to sit down and absorb them all. It was a most unexpected conversation, but one that made a good deal of sense. Still, she was wary. Olan, a man she'd known for years, had betrayed her trust. She wasn't too keen on trusting his cousin.

Even if he was possibly her only hope.

"Your cousin and I were friends for years," she said. "In the end, he tried to ruin my happiness. I am not in any hurry to trust his cousin, a man I do not know at all."

Alend nodded. "I know," he said. "And I do not blame you. But as I told your husband, I am a lesser knight serving a lesser house. I live in fear that every day will be my last, and I am tired of living that way. If you know anything about Fitz Walter, then you know I speak the truth. The man is brutal and unpredictable. He kills easily and sometimes without reason. It is a very hard way to live and one, quite frankly, without honor. I am a good knight, my lady. I deserve better."

He sounded logical and reasonable. But, then again, so had Olan. *I had no part in what my cousin did,* he'd said. Perhaps that was true. And perhaps everything Alend was saying was the truth, but it was very difficult to trust him.

Still... it wasn't as if she had a lot of choices.

"So you want to serve the House of de Lohr, do you?" she said. "You think that will help you reclaim your honor?"

Alend shrugged. "It will not erase my years of service to Fitz Walter, but it will at least give me a chance to redeem myself."

"And my husband agreed to this?"

"He did."

"What about all of that talk of Westley going to France so Samson could marry me?"

Alend conceded the truth. "I did not hear him say so," he said. "Fitz Walter could be lying to you about that, but I did hear your husband say that he would bring you to Samson's doorstep and that he never wanted to marry you."

Elysande tried not to appear hurt by that. "He said so, did he?"

"Aye," Alend said. "But I am convinced he was trying to throw Samson off the scent of the truth."

"What truth?"

"That he is glad he married you," Alend said. "I got the overwhelming sense that he was doing, or saying, anything he could to keep himself alive."

Elysande thought on that. "I did the same thing," she muttered. "If you think I did not want to gouge Samson's eyes out when he walked into this chamber, you would be wrong.

Instead, I was polite."

Alend got the sense that her walls of self-protection were coming down, just a little. "My lady, all I want is to escape this place, as you do," he said quietly. "I have not had the opportunity until now. Certainly, I could have left at any time in the past, but I had nowhere to go. No position to assume. And there is the matter of my family, who would have been ashamed had I merely walked away. But your husband has assured me that he will find me a place within the sphere of de Lohr, so I have every reason to help you, to prove that I can be trusted. And if you do not take me on a little faith, then I cannot say what your chances of survival are here. Fitz Walter could lock you up in this chamber for the rest of your life and you will die here, old and neglected and alone. I am certain that is not what you want."

Elysande shook her head. "It is not."

"Then trust me," Alend insisted softly. "Trust me and we will both escape this hellish place. If you will indulge me, I have an idea."

Elysande believed him. Perhaps she shouldn't, but he was offering her what she wanted. It was better than trying to figure something out on her own. But the sole reason she was willing to trust him was because he'd pointed something out that she'd been wondering herself—how Westley made it outside of the walls of Hell's Forge. Someone had to help him do that.

That someone was standing in front of her.

God… please let this man be telling the truth!

"Very well," she finally said. "Tell me what you want me to do."

He did.

CB

HE WAS FEELING more satisfied than he thought he would.

Samson had thought he might feel rather empty with only Elysande in his custody and not her husband as well, but he realized it was better this way. It had been a very long time since he'd had the company of a woman, even one who was violently opposed to him, and he intended to make the best of it.

It didn't matter that he couldn't marry her, at least not now.

He was still going to take advantage of her.

In fact, he was going to do it today. He was going to mark her so that Westley would never want her back. He was going to rub his scent all over her, fill her with his seed, and carve his name into her chest. Elysande was a beautiful woman, so it would not be a difficult task to be aroused by her, but he was certain she wouldn't cooperate.

That was why God had created rope.

And he planned to tie her down with it.

This morning meal was meant to establish the rules of the lady's existence at Hell's Forge. Samson intended to tell her what her duties were, and other than warming his bed, he hadn't really determined them. Perhaps she would become his chatelaine and manage his kitchens and keep. Right now, Alend did everything, and Samson knew he felt it beneath his station.

Perhaps he'd relieve Alend of those shameful tasks.

Samson had left instructions that the meal this morning should be a good one. He'd asked for beef and eggs and other things he found delicious, and the servants were still bringing dishes out. Eggs were prepared several different ways along with beef that was boiled, or in pies, or mixed with dumplings and gravy. Everything was smelling so good that Samson didn't wait for his new captive. He was halfway through his meal when she finally appeared with Alend gripping her arm so she wouldn't run away. As soon as they entered the hall, Samson stood up to greet them.

"Ah," he said. "My lady, come and sit. I have had this great meal prepared to welcome you to my home. Come, come."

He was waving them over, noting that Elysande was clad in the yellow silk garment and looking absolutely magnificent. Her hair was gathered at the nape of her neck and secured, giving her an exquisite profile. The appreciation in his eyes was obvious.

"My lady, you are positively resplendent in that gown," he said. "I have others that I purchased for you, but after your father rejected my suit, I tossed them aside. I will have to find them now and give them to you. Alend, do you know where they are?"

Alend was indicating a place for the lady to sit. "You burned most of them, my lord," he said. "Do you not recall shoving them into the hearth? This yellow dress was one of the only ones to survive."

The glee faded from Samson's face as he recalled that moment. "I suppose I did," he said. "But there were others that survived. You must find them."

Alend simply nodded, taking a seat next to Elysande under the guise of being her guard and restraining her should she attempt to run.

But that was far from the truth.

In fact, Elysande was on edge, not because she was sitting across from Samson, but because the hall made her uneasy. She swore it smelled like fire and brimstone. Everything about it seemed dark and gritty and shadowed. But the cavernous great hall was the heart of the castle, and as she entered, she had seen exactly what Alend had described—dead, filthy rushes covered the floor. Some had probably been there for years. The walls were covered with tapestries that the Fitz Walter family had collected for more than a century—and, according to Alend, many were stolen from castles that Prince John, before he was king, had stolen and given over to Ralph Fitz Walter, Samson's uncle and the very man Christopher de Lohr had killed for abducting his wife.

In fact, it was an extremely cluttered great hall, a shrine to a family's greed, and Elysande had never wanted to leave a place so badly in her life. Alend's plan had given her some hope, hope that all of this would soon be a terrible memory, but she needed it to happen soon.

Before Samson could get his hands on her.

She didn't like the way he was looking at her.

There were several wooden tables with benches in the great hall and one massive, heavy table where the three of them were sitting. Overhead, Fitz Walter standards hung from the beams supporting the thatched roof, and they were long enough that they were halfway to the floor. As she was gazing up at them, servants brought out trenchers for her and for Alend. Samson was well into his meal already as he pointed to various dishes around the table.

"Try the beef pie," he said, mouth full. "It is delicious. As are the eggs."

Since there were several egg dishes, Elysande wasn't sure which one he meant, so she took a little of everything. Servants were hovering, helping them fill their trenchers, and the wine in her cup was refilled every time she took a drink. But she didn't want to get drunk, so she asked a servant for some boiled water to cut the wine.

Samson heard her.

"Is the wine not to your liking, my lady?" he asked, insulted. "It is very good wine."

Elysande sent the servant on his way before replying. "It is good," she agreed. "But it is too early in the day for my head to swim. I usually only drink boiled fruit juice or boiled milk during the day."

Samson frowned. "How dull," he said, as his sense of indignation hadn't improved with her explanation. "I have presented this lovely display for you to show you the hospitality of Hell's Forge. You would do well not to insult it."

"It wasn't my intention to insult it," she said. "How is asking for watered wine insulting your hospitality?"

The conversation threatened to turn into an argument. Samson sat back in his chair, waving her off as he made a point of drinking deeply from his cup. Because he'd started his meal early, the wine was already going to his head. It was wine that could get a man drunk in a half-hour, very powerful wine he'd purchased specially from a Portuguese merchant in Bristol.

"I will permit you to have the wine your way this time," he said. "But not again. This wine comes from Lisbon and is much coveted. It is also quite expensive."

Elysande didn't reply. She simply focused on her food as Samson pitched his little tantrum and overcame it. Once he drained the last of his wine, he motioned for more and set his cup down.

"Permit me to tell you how things will be from now on," he said, fixing her with an unhappy gaze. "You will be my chatelaine. Your husband has abandoned you to me, so essentially, you will be my wife, if not in name, then in body and soul and spirit. Do you understand me so far?"

Elysande's instinct was to throw her wine cup at his face and then leap over the table and throttle him, but she kept her temper in check. A glance at Alend gave her some comfort and confidence that even though Samson would make such a declaration, none of it would come to fruition. But the demand that she be his in body got under her skin. The only man who had ever touched her that way had been Westley, and she would kill herself before allowing another such intimate access.

But still… she held her tongue.

"I understand," she said. "What else?"

Samson was perhaps the least bit surprised that she hadn't balked at his command, because he seemed a little surprised as he continued.

"You will do as I tell you," he said. "If I say crawl under this table and pleasure me, you will do so. If I say walk naked in the bailey, you will do so. You are mine to control, lady. Tell me you understand that."

Elysande had no idea what he meant about crawling under the table to pleasure him, but she knew it was awful, whatever it was. She couldn't help the fact that he was raising her dander now, rage building up in her that she was trying desperately to keep tightly controlled.

"I told you I understood from the start," she said. "All you speak of are things that involve the body, but what else do you want from me as your chatelaine? Shall I manage the stables? Do you want me to plant a garden? How clean do you want the keep? These are all things you must tell me."

Samson was looking at her as if he'd never once considered any of that. He hadn't considered anything beyond the woman in his bed or as a slave to his desires. But he didn't like the way she seemed to be challenging him. She was here at *his* pleasure. She had made a deal and he intended that she should keep it.

"Stop eating," he said.

Mid-chew, Elysande looked up from her trencher. "Why?" she asked.

Samson had a fresh cup of wine in his hand, his third that morning. He was certifiably drunk. Lifting a hand, he flicked his wrist in the direction of the hearth.

"Go over there and dance for me," he said.

Elysande nearly choked on the food in her mouth as she tried to swallow it. "Dance?" she repeated, horrified. "I do not know how to dance. I was never any good at it."

"That is no concern of mine. You will dance for me."

Shocked, Elysande set her spoon down. She looked at Alend, perhaps for support, but he threw a thumb in the direction of the hearth.

"You heard him," he said. "Dance."

She had no choice. She couldn't be entirely sure Alend was even on her side, but she had to talk herself into the understanding that he was doing this for show. He was doing it because his life depended on it.

And so did hers.

With a heavy sigh, Elysande stood up and made her way over to the hearth, which had a bright fire burning in it. It was a big hearth, easily able to accommodate five or six men in it. There were a few dogs around who didn't move when she came close, so she shooed them away. The dead rushes were catching on the bottom of her garment, so she pushed them away to have a clear floor to move in.

Pushed them toward the fireplace.

And there was a reason for that.

In truth, Samson's command was fortuitous. As Alend had told her before they came down to the hall, his plan was to create a situation that kept Samson diverted while Alend sent Elysande to the postern gate. It would have to be the following morning, as he'd done for Westley, when the guards were changing their posts, but Elysande didn't want to wait that long. Therefore, Alend thought that a small fire in the hall would be enough to clear Samson out, and while the servants were cleaning it, and Elysande was overseeing them—because she would offer to do so—she could, instead, slip out with Alend and he would take her through the postern gate himself. Together, they would flee south, to Massington, and Samson probably would not know about it until they were already safe.

Therefore, Elysande would start a small fire in the hall, enough to smoke up the room, enough to drive Samson out and to the safety of the keep.

That was the hope, anyway.

She was going to do her best.

"Dance!" Samson boomed.

His voice startled her from her thoughts, forcing her to focus on what needed to be done. She wasn't a good dancer, but she supposed she could spin around just like anyone else, so that was what she started to do. She simply put her arms up and began to twirl, kicking the dried rushes closer to the hearth with every spin. Then she stopped spinning and simply walked in what she hoped was a graceful circle. She spun again when she came near the hearth, kicking some of the dead rushes into the blaze.

It surged.

If Samson noticed, he didn't say a word. He was watching her dance, feeling the alcohol in his veins, thinking he hadn't been with a woman in a very long time, and there was a very beautiful one right in front of him, dancing with all of the grace of a newborn colt. It was a travesty, really.

He wondered if she'd be better in bed.

Setting his cup down, he stood up.

Elysande didn't see Samson move from the table. She was only aware of it when he grabbed her from behind, his mouth on her neck and his arms wrapped around her torso. One hand ended up clamping over her right breast, and he squeezed, hard, as he bit into her neck.

The fight was on.

Elysande turned into a wildcat. Samson was holding her with the same grip from the day before, a surprisingly unyielding grip that was difficult to shake. When she started to fight, he only held her tighter and the hand on her breast turned painful.

"You are mine, lady," he said. "Stop fighting and this will be pleasurable. Fight me and I will throw you to my men."

The threat terrified her. But being compliant to Samson terrified her more. She continued to fight as he bit down on her neck, hard enough that she screamed. But it took the fight to an entirely new level as she violently pulled away from him, or at least tried to. Unfortunately, she only managed to turn a little in his arms, so his mouth wasn't by her neck, but the second she saw his face, she rammed her fingers into his eyes.

Samson howled in pain and loosened his grip, but as she tried to get away, he managed to catch her hair and yank hard. Elysande stumbled backward, toward him, and he grabbed her by the back of her head.

"That," he said, "will be your greatest mistake, you foolish bitch. Now you have incurred my wrath."

With that, he tried to kiss her, smother her with his mouth, but she brought a knee up and rammed it into his privates. That caused him to scream in pain and cuff her on the side of the head. As Elysande went down, he pounced on her, grabbing her around the throat. His body weight was pinning her down, so she couldn't get her arms up to protect herself as his hands began to tighten.

"I hope you are right with God, because you are about to meet him," Samson snarled in her face, saliva trickling onto her chin. "I am going to kill you and send your body back to your husband in pieces."

Elysande was starting to see stars. He was squeezing hard. Her life began to flash in front of her eyes and the darkness was beckoning. She truly thought this was the end.

But then, something surprising happened.

Suddenly, Samson was lurching off her. Someone had him by the hair and by the neck, and as she struggled to roll away from the fight, Samson ended up in the hearth, in the middle of the flame. Thrown on the blaze like a new log for a fire.

Alend had put him there.

"Go!" he bellowed. "To the postern gate! *Run!*"

"You must come!" she cried.

Alend had started to reply when Samson propelled himself out of the fire and grabbed on to Alend. Given that Samson was already in flames, Alend tried to break the man's grip but was unable to. Samson fell back into the hearth and took Alend with him. The last glimpse Elysande had of Alend was of his hair going up in flames.

She fled.

Weeping, because she was truly terrified, she staggered to her feet and began to run. Out of the hall, blindly running because she had no idea where the postern gate was. All she knew was that they were usually near the stables or the kitchens, so she headed toward the stables, which were near the gate-house.

But no postern gate was there.

In a panic, she ran in the other direction, heading west, past the great hall and the keep. There were servants about, and soldiers, but no one tried to stop her. They were simply watching her, curiously, as she ran aimlessly. Every second that passed was a second that could see her recaptured, so she flew around the corner of the keep only to see the kitchen yard tucked up against the southwest side of the wall.

And a small postern gate was there.

Racing into the yard, Elysande kicked a couple of chickens accidentally, but she didn't stop to see if she'd killed them. She just kept running, stopping long enough to throw the bolt on the postern gate, which had an enormous lock on it. But it was unlocked, thankfully, and she yanked the gate open and tore through it.

The deep ditch was on the other side, but a small path wound around it, leading to a wooden bridge that crossed the bulk of it. Elysande charged down the path, over the bridge, and into the clearing on the other side. She ran straight into the trees as fast as she could, trying to orient herself so she could find the road south. But she didn't stop, fearful that men were close on her heels. Fear fed her, giving her the strength to continue running.

And run she did.

Through the trees and into a field, she continued running, realizing that she was paralleling the road south. She had no idea how far, or how long, she had run, but that didn't matter. All that mattered was that she get on that road and run home.

All the way.

As she neared the road, her exhaustion finally had the better of her and she ended up falling onto her already-tender right arm. She scored the yellow dress up with grass and mud, but she got her feet and, holding her arm, dared to turn around to see if anyone was following her.

The field was clear.

Back above the tree line, however, she could see the top of the Hell's Forge keep. She could also see great clouds of black smoke billowing into the air, a clear sign that the fire in the hall had gotten out of control. With all of the dead rushes and tapestries, she wasn't surprised. Alend had called it a tinder box, and he'd been right. Surely, all of the soldiers were trying to put it out, which meant there was no one to follow the escaped captive. The castle was burning and all hands were needed.

Realizing she wasn't being followed and why, Elysande burst into tears. Tears of fear, of exhaustion, and of the stress of the entire situation. There was another tree line in front of her, between her and the road south, and she headed for it, half running, half stumbling. But the will to live was strong.

She was going to make it.

Bursting through the trees, she could see the road stretched out before her, miles of it, and upon that road she saw something she recognized. An army heading north, flying blue banners.

De Lohr.

The same army that had been mustered to rescue him was now mustered to rescue her.

Westley had returned.

The tears returned in force. Still half running, half stumbling, she began to move down the road, keeping her eye on the army, knowing that, at some point, Westley would see that she was coming. Hopefully, he would recognize her. Who else could be running down the road from Hell's Forge? She'd run about another quarter of a mile when a charger broke off from the army and headed toward her at breakneck speed.

Her husband was coming.

Knowing this, Elysande started running faster. She drew on the last bit of strength she had, deep down, the strength that told her she was meant for the man she'd married, the one who would become her all for living and breathing. That deep, powerful, warm sense of strength that could never be broken, not by captors or bitter knights. Nothing they could do would crush the strength that came from the heart.

The strength of everlasting love.

Westley reined his horse up within a few feet of her, kicking up rocks and dirt as he did so. But he was off his horse before Elysande could come to a halt and she literally ran into his arms. Gasping, running, head swimming and all, she fell right into his embrace.

Now, she was finally safe.

Shortly thereafter, everything went black.

CB

"WE WENT IN through the postern gate," Andrew said. "No one was guarding it. In fact, the entire castle was in upheaval. Servants were packing up things from the keep and taking them out on carts. They are picking it clean."

The de Lohr army had stopped where Elysande fainted. Westley had her cradled in his arms, sitting on the side of the road, as Curtis, Roi, and Myles were crowded around. The nephews had been sent ahead to Hell's Forge because they, too, had seen the smoke. Thick black columns of it. Andrew and Rhodes had managed to get in the postern gate while the others went in through the gatehouse, which was open because the servants and soldiers were leaving. Now, the report was back and the older men could hardly believe what they were hearing.

"But where is Samson?" Westley said. "And where is the fire?"

"The great hall," Rhodes said, his face smudged with ash because he'd gotten too close to the blaze. "The entire hall is burning. The servants said that Samson and another man, named Alend, were inside, as was a woman."

Westley looked down at Elysande, who was starting to stir. "She's not in there now, God be praised," he muttered. Then he gently stroked her cheek. "Ella? Can you hear me, love?"

She sighed deeply and her eyes rolled open. It took her a minute to orient herself, staring up at Westley, but quickly, she came around.

"My God," she said, struggling to sit up as Westley propped her into a sitting position on the ground. She blinked, trying to clear her muddled mind. "Did I faint?"

Westley smiled. "Only for a moment," he said. "You've had quite a substantial morning."

Elysande nodded, smiling weakly at him, as she looked around at the knights standing over her. "I'm quite well, I assure you," she said. "May I stand?"

"Are you certain?"

"I am. Please."

Westley stood up and pulled her to her feet. Curtis helped steady her because she seemed quite shaky. Elysande's gaze moved to the black smoke belching up into the sky, and she pointed.

"Hell's Forge," she said. "It is burning!"

Westley nodded. "It is," he said. "Andrew says the great hall has gone up in flames. Do you know what happened?"

She nodded, trying not to throw herself off balance as she did so. "Samson attacked me," she said of the memories that had her shaken. "He was trying to kill me and Alend stopped him. He pushed him into the hearth. The last I saw, the two of them were going up in flames. Both of them. And I... ran. I ran until I found you."

Westley pulled her close because she was growing distraught. "But you are well?" he asked gently. "He did not hurt you?"

Elysande relished her husband's embrace, pressing herself up against him. She felt as if had been a thousand years since he last held her, and it was something she never, ever wanted to be without again. For a woman who had never known emotional security in her life, it was a feeling that she was finally home.

Finally safe.

Finally loved.

"Nay," she said, eyes closed as he held her head against his chest. "He did not hurt me. At least, nothing I will not quickly recover from."

As they stood there, two more young knights came charging down the road. Gabriel and Nicholas seemed terribly excited about something.

"The castle is for the taking!" Gabriel said. "Fitz Walter is dead. His servants and soldiers are fleeing. Uncle Curtis, should we secure the castle and claim it for the de Lohr empire?"

Curtis looked at Myles. "What do you think?" he said. "Can we hold it?"

Myles nodded. "Aye," he said. "We can hold it and Roi, as

England's chief justiciar, will ensure that we keep it. Spoils of war, brother. It's the least Fitz Walter can do for the anguish he has caused Papa. The score will never be even, but it's a start."

Curtis looked to the four excitable knights who had done the initial reconnaissance. "Very well," he said. "Andrew, you are in command. Take half the army with you and secure Hell's Forge. Clean the damn thing out. Anything, or anyone, that is part of Fitz Walter's army or house is to be corralled. Empty the keep and everything else, and make sure that fire is out before it spreads. The place will be flying de Lohr banners by nightfall."

"Aye, my lord," Andrew said sharply, trying to contain his excitable horse because his brothers were already racing back to the bulk of the army to collect some men. "What do we do with Fitz Walter's body if we find it?"

"Burn it until there is nothing left," Westley said, deadly serious. "But Alend de Bisby will be there, too. If he is indeed dead, then we will bury him appropriately. Were it not for him, I would not have escaped."

"Nor I," Elysande said. "He sacrificed himself so that I could escape, too."

Westley smiled at her, lifting a big hand to smooth back her hair. "Then he is due all great honors of a burial."

She thought on his words. "It's appropriate you should say that," she said. "He told me that he had served Fitz Walter for so long that he wanted to regain his honor by serving with de Lohr. I think he meant it."

Westley nodded. "He said the same thing to me," he replied. "Unlike his cousin, who has no honor, it would seem that Alend had a good deal."

"Fitz Walter did not deserve him."

"Nay, he did not."

As they stood there, wrapped up in each other's arms, the men around them began to disperse. Curtis and Myles headed back to the army while Andrew, Rhodes, Gabriel, and Nicholas headed on to Hell's Forge in the company of about three hundred soldiers. Plenty of men to clear out a castle and secure it. But, as it turned out, there was no need.

Hell's Forge surrendered without a fight.

As for Westley, he took his wife home. As she rode in front of him in the saddle, she couldn't remember ever seeing the sky brighter. The birds had never sung more sweetly. Everything seemed bigger and brighter and better now that she was with Westley.

And that included the rest of her life.

For a young woman who had tried to chase her suitor away on that first day to the contented wife wrapped in the arms of her beloved, the future had never looked so positive or hopeful.

A future that almost never happened.

And a dream that almost never came into being.

For Westley and Elysande, their dream was only just beginning.

Together.

CHAPTER TWENTY-EIGHT

Lioncross Abbey Castle
A week later

T HE CHAMBER WAS dark, smelling of peppermint and clove. Some physics thought the scent warded off the bad spirits and cleansed the air, but he found it cloying. To him, it was the smell of death because he'd seen, and smelled, many bodies in the Levant that were pungent with the spices that had been rubbed on them or stuffed into them. As he approached the bed, he half expected to see Christopher stuffed and rubbed with those strong-smelling unguents.

But he wasn't.

He was simply an old man, lying in bed.

Marcus Burton hadn't seen Christopher in about a year. His seat of Somerhill was a three-day ride from Lioncross, or at least it used to be when they were younger and could travel at a swifter pace. The past twenty years or so, it was a five-day jaunt. And then six. But Dustin had sent him a missive about Christopher's condition and Marcus had made this trip in record time, once again, even though his bones were aching and his back was permanently stiff.

It didn't matter.

What mattered was this moment.

He had to get to his friend.

Silently, he made his way to the bed, that enormous bed that Christopher and Dustin had shared for the duration of their marriage. It was early morning and a hint of gray light was coming in through the oilcloth. But it wasn't enough light to see by, and Marcus went to strike the stone and flint on a nearby table, lighting a solitary taper that gave off a glow to stave off the darkness. Seeing a bank of half-burned tallow tapers a few feet away, he used the single taper to light those.

Warm light began to fill the chamber.

"Has... my wife made you a servant now?" Christopher mumbled from the bed. "You ought to not let her do that. We have people... who can light the tapers."

The words were hesitant and barely understandable, as if the man had a mouth full of rocks. Marcus had to steel himself at the sound, the shock of those first few words from his friend's mouth. It was worse than he had imagined. But he finished lighting the last taper, forcing a smile as he put the original taper back in its holder.

"I did not realize you were awake," he said, sitting on the edge of the bed and studying the man lying before him. "You are supposed to be a very sick man. You may tell me if you are pretending just for sympathy. I will not give you away."

Christopher's right eyelid opened. The left one was permanently frozen because of the paralysis on his face, but the right one could move. The eye moved in Marcus' direction, and Marcus shifted so Christopher could see him better.

"I do not want to... admit that I am ill, but I suppose I have seen better moments," Christopher said. "This is only temporary."

"Is it?"

"Of course it is."

Marcus nodded, trying to keep the grief he felt off his face. The strongest man he knew was lying before him, paralyzed on one side, his usually eloquent and articulate speaking reduced to a low mumble. The man who had belted out commands in some of England's greatest battles had been felled by a brain fit that had taken over half of his body.

Apoplexy, Dustin had said.

It was overwhelming.

With Marcus having known Christopher since they were squires, their friendship had seen decade after decade. Christopher was the one constant in his life, the one thing he could completely depend on, and to see the man stretched out before him was devastating.

Beyond devastating, actually.

Marcus struggled not to burst into tears.

"Then I shall believe you if you tell me this condition is finite," he said after a moment. "But in order to heal, you must rest. I know idleness has never been your strength, but in this case, I do not think you have a choice."

"Nay, I do not," Christopher said. His speech was a little better now and not so labored. "But it is good to see you, Marcus. It has been too long and we are not getting any younger."

A half-grin creased Marcus' lips. "Speak for yourself," he said. "I *am* younger than you."

"Two years."

"It is still two years," Marcus said. "Actually, not quite two years. More like nineteen months."

"It does not seem like much in the grand scheme of life, does it?"

"Nay," Marcus said, leaning back to get a better look at Christopher's face. "Now that I am here, tell me how you are really feeling. Are you comfortable enough?"

Christopher lifted his right hand, waving him off. "I do not wish to speak of me," he said. "Tell me how your children are. And your grandchildren."

He was avoiding the subject. Marcus could tell. Rather than badger a sick man, he simply went with the shift in focus. "I think I almost have as many as you do," he said.

"No one has as many as I do," Christopher muttered. "I have an entire herd."

Marcus chuckled. "True," he said. "You and Dustin were quite prolific in breeding, and so are your children."

"You and Gabrielle did not do too badly."

Marcus shook his head. "Nay," he said. "We had the twins and then three sons to follow. By the time the youngest came around, I was an old man. Much like you were when Dustin had Westley and Olivia."

"Charlotte," Christopher said. "I named her Charlotte."

"Your wife named her Olivia."

Christopher started to chuckle. Or, at least, it sounded like it. That was an old argument that was well known in the family. Dustin had given birth to a very late baby when Westley had been about two years of age, a little girl that Christopher wanted to name Charlotte. Dustin wanted Olivia, so the baby went by Olivia Charlotte, both names, for most of her youth.

Amusing moments that were part of their fabric of memories.

"I will not go through this again with you," Christopher

said. "Her name is Charlotte and that is final. But I would like to know how you are getting along these days without Gabrielle. We still have mass said for her, every week."

Marcus' humor faded as the subject took a big turn, and not for the better. That wasn't something he wanted to discuss, but he had little choice. They couldn't go the entire conversation veering away from unhappy subjects.

And the subject of Marcus' wife was the unhappiest.

"I suppose the truth is that I do not know how I am getting along," he finally said. "I live in a world of lies."

"What do you mean?"

Marcus sighed faintly, averting his gaze as he thought on the wife he'd lost to a cancer two years earlier. Tall, kind, obedient, and beautiful, that was his Gabrielle.

He closed his eyes, seeing her in his mind.

"Because I pretend she's not gone," he said quietly. "I pretend she's only in the next chamber. Or mayhap she's out in the yard with the chickens. Or she's in the hall where I cannot see her. At night, when the darkness closes in around me and she is not there to stave it off, I pretend that she is up with one of the grandchildren and will return soon. If I pretend hard enough, then I believe it and I can sleep."

Christopher was watching him, sorrow glittering in his eyes. "And in the morning when you awake?"

Marcus shrugged. "She was always up before I was," he said. "It is not difficult to pretend that she has risen to see to the family."

Christopher didn't say anything for a moment, but Marcus felt a big, warm hand close around his left hand, which was braced on the bed. When he realized that Christopher had grasped it, meaning to give him comfort, he felt like weeping again. As if the touch of a dying man had shattered his composure like the most fragile glass. It was a grip that gave him strength but also weakness, all at the same time.

"Would you like for me to give her a message?" Christopher said softly.

Marcus looked at him, puzzled. "How do you mean to?"

Christopher squeezed his hand. "Marcus," he said, "you may pretend for your wife, but you will not pretend for me. I will not be here much longer and you must accept that. You must be strong because Dustin will need you to be. She will have enough on her mind without worrying over you, too."

Marcus stared at him as tears popped into his eyes. He could no longer stop them. But he shook his head firmly and looked away. "Nay," he said. "You are not going anywhere. You said it was temporary. I will hold you to it."

Christopher squeezed his hand weakly. "I lied," he said simply, watching Marcus flash a grin. "Listen to me. Will you?"

"I am listening."

There was a pause until Marcus looked up at him. Christopher wanted to make sure they had eye contact before continuing.

"I do not think I will see David again in this life," Christopher said hoarsely. "He is on his way here, but it may take weeks from Kent. I do not have weeks. I know that you and David have had your differences, but I am asking you to put those aside. I need you to tell David something for me. Please."

Marcus nodded. "Of course," he said, wiping away the tears on his face. "Anything you wish."

Christopher paused again, moving his gaze away from Marcus until he was staring up at the ceiling. He just seemed to stare, but the truth was that his mind was working. He had something to say to his brother that he had to entrust Marcus with. But the profound words wouldn't come.

Only memories.

"Chris?" Marcus prodded gently. "What is it?"

"I was just thinking," Christopher whispered. "About Ezz and his scimitar."

Marcus smiled faintly. "The man with the beautiful daughter in the Levant?"

"Aye."

"The same one who chased us around the marketplace for the better part of an hour?"

"The same."

"We were young and handsome and as wild as stallions, once."

"Those were good days."

"They were."

"Remember the women in the tavern at Tarkia?" Christopher said. "The ones who would crawl under the table and pleasure a man while he sat and drank his wine?"

Marcus closed his eyes and clapped a hand over his face. "God's Bones," he muttered. "You had to bring that up."

"Of course I did."

Marcus shook his head in disgust. "The same women who told David that if he allowed them to shove beads up his arse, it would magnify his pleasure?"

A low, rumbling sound began to fill the chamber and Marcus realized it was because Christopher was laughing. "He let them," he said. "My ridiculous brother let them."

"He was shitting them out for a week."

Both Christopher and Marcus lost themselves in the ridiculous memory of David, young and eager to seek sexual pleasure where he could find it, having to deal with pleasure beads in his rectum. A few moments of pleasure had turned into weeks of discomfort and even a visit to a physic to make sure there was no lasting damage. The more they thought about it, the more they laughed.

"He thought they were all out and then another would come along," Christopher said through his laughter. "He would make his squire pick out the beads and wash them."

"Awful," Marcus said, shuddering at the mere thought. "No wonder the lad ran off."

"I do not blame him," Christopher said, his laughter fading. The mood, once so jovial, suddenly turned somber again. "Marcus?"

"What is it?"

"I suppose if there was one thing I could say to my brother, it would be to thank him."

"Thank him? Why?"

"For being my brother," Christopher said, his gaze turning distant as he thought on the younger brother he loved so dearly. "For giving me joy. For never leaving my side. Even when he did leave me for a time, he was still with me. And I hope that I will always be with him, too. Brotherly love like ours doesn't die out, Marcus. No matter where David is, or even where you are, I carry you both with me, always. Other than my family, I have never been prouder of any achievement in my life than I am of my bond with David and with you. No man has ever had a better brother. Will you tell him that?"

Marcus wasn't laughing anymore. He felt as if he'd been stabbed in the gut. A knife that was plunging deeper and deeper as the moments ticked away and he found himself looking at Christopher's partially frozen face. Truth be told, he'd been avoiding the reality of the situation since he walked in the chamber, but he couldn't avoid it any longer.

There was only one answer he could give.

"I will tell him," he murmured.

"And... be kind to him. My passing will be difficult for him."

Marcus nodded, reluctant to admit that Christopher would, indeed, pass. They would all pass at some point, but he knew Christopher would pass before he did. That was why he was here, after all.

He'd come because it was the end.

Softly, he sighed.

"There is a belief among many that paradise is of our own making," he said. "God wants us to be happy, so he allows us to choose the heaven that will make us the happiest. The time in our lives where we were the most joyful and content. Do you know what I envision for that?"

Christopher grunted because he was unable to shake his head. "Nay," he mumbled. "Tell me."

Marcus squeezed the man's hand. "I envision that I will close my eyes for the last time on this earth, and when I awaken, I will be in a land of golden sands, beautiful women, and a sea that is bluer than the sky. I envision that I shall awaken in this land and find myself walking toward the encampment we had north of Acre, where you will be inside the tent we pitched and you will be sharpening your sword with a whetstone like you always did. When you see me, you will put the sword down and you will embrace me and tell me that you've missed me. You will be young and strong, the way I remember you, with skin the color of bronze and your hair made blonder by the sun. I too will be young and strong, with my hair back to the black color it used to be, and we will feast every night and be chased with scimitars every day. That is the heaven that awaits me, Chris. And I will see you there."

Tears were streaming from the corner of Christopher's eyes, down his temples and into his hair.

"What of Gabrielle?" he asked hoarsely.

Marcus had tears streaming down his face also. "She will be there," he said. "But she will be in my tent, not in your tent. If I find her in your tent, then you and I will have a problem."

Christopher made a noise that sounded suspiciously like a chuckle. "She will not be in my tent, I assure you," he said. "But I love your heaven. The time when we were the happiest, I think, before politics and kings and princes made a mess out of things."

"Then you will wait for me there?"

"I will."

"With Dustin?"

"It would not be heaven without her."

"Do you think she'll tolerate the wild streak we had back in those days?"

"She had a bit of a wild streak herself."

Marcus grinned. Then he leaned over, taking Christopher's hands in both of his big mitts. His gaze was intense.

"Thank you for this privilege," he whispered. "The first time you died, I was not with you and my turmoil, my confusion, nearly destroyed me. It nearly destroyed *us*. But this moment... this is the moment all people who love one another hope for when death is near. The privilege of seeing you out of this life and into the next. What an honor you have given me, Chris. I will be here until the end, I swear it. You'll not depart this earth alone."

More tears trickled down Christopher's temples as Marcus spoke of a time, long ago, when Christopher was mistakenly believed to have been killed in battle. It had been a horrible time and, indeed, one that nearly tore them all apart. Confusion and madness had been some of it. But the loss of a friendship had been most of it.

Something they both acknowledged.

Something that was binding them together at this moment.

"It is as I told you before," Christopher said. "I am never without you, Marcus. I carry you with me wherever I go. But it gives me comfort knowing you will be here when the time comes."

Marcus smiled bravely. "Good," he said, leaning over to kiss Christopher's hand. "Long ago, I was not always the friend you deserved, Chris. But I hope I have made amends over the years."

Christopher squeezed his hands. "You are the best friend a man could ask for," he said. "And I am going to ask you one more thing."

"Anything."

"When I am gone, I ask you to take care of my wife."

"You know I will always take care of Dustin."

Christopher tried to shake his head a little. "Nay," he said. "That is not what I am asking. Those years ago when all of England believed me to be dead, you came to claim my wife because you loved her. You had always loved her."

The warmth in Marcus' eyes faded. "And that is what I meant by not always being the friend you deserved."

"I was not looking for a confession, Marcus," Christopher said. "I know what Dustin meant to you. I know you fell in love with her when you first met her, just as I did. I also know you bedded her, once, though I do not believe that was planned. I think it was a mistake that simply happened. Would you agree with that?"

Marcus felt as if all of his past sins, the sins of that wild and reckless stallion he once was, were being rehashed by a dying man. Truthfully, there was nothing he could do but take it.

"I agree that I behaved abhorrently," he said. "But I swear to you that the incident you speak of was not deliberately planned. As you said, it simply happened and that is the truth. But I could have stopped it. I am guilty of that sin and I can only pray that even after all of these years, you forgive me."

"I forgave you long ago," Christopher said. "I am not trying to bring up your sins of the past, but I want to make a point."

"That point being?"

Christopher gave a tug on Marcus' hand. "The point is that, this time, I will not return from the dead," he muttered. "I asked you to take care of my wife when I am gone because you no longer have a wife. Dustin will no longer have a husband. Should you wish to marry her, for companionship and protection, and if she is agreeable, I have no objection. I do not want her to be alone the rest of her life, Marcus. That haunts me."

Marcus stared at him for a moment, realizing the man had just made a request of him that, years ago, would have made him happy. But at this moment, it didn't. For some reason, it only seemed to underscore the sense of loss he was feeling.

"I do not need to marry her to provide her with companionship and protection," he said. "Moreover, it would be an insult to your memory if I married your widow. The wife of the great Earl of Hereford and Worcester has already had the finest husband in England. I would not, and could not, compete with that. I will always be there for Dustin, but leave her with her memories of you. Let your lips be the last lips she kissed. You deserve that respect, Chris."

Christopher's right eye twinkled, suggesting he understood. And was, perhaps, even a little relieved that Marcus had no designs on his wife, though given what had happened those years ago, he had to make it clear that he wasn't opposed to history repeating itself if it meant Dustin wouldn't be alone.

But times had indeed changed from the events of sixty years ago.

"Will you do something for me, then?" Christopher asked.

"What is it?" Marcus asked.

"Bid me a final farewell and then send my wife to me," Christopher said softly. "I am feeling my fatigue and wish to spend my last waking moments with her."

Marcus nodded. Standing up, he moved to the other side of the big bed where Christopher was lying. Grasping the man's right hand again, he squeezed it tightly as he bent over and kissed Christopher on the forehead. It was a simple gesture that brought tears to his eyes again, but he struggled against them, unwilling to collapse at this moment. The last moment he would speak to the man who had been the most powerful influence in his life. His friend.

His brother.

His heart.

"I will see you on the sands," he whispered tightly. "I will expect good wine and good horses when I arrive."

Christopher smiled weakly, on the side of his face able to move. "You shall have them," he said. "I will look for you, every day."

Marcus nodded, trying to force a smile, but he couldn't

seem to manage it because grief was overwhelming him. Kissing Christopher's hand one last time, he gently released it.

"Godspeed, my friend," he murmured. "And thank you. For everything, thank you."

Christopher merely lifted his right hand, a gesture of farewell, as Marcus quit the chamber. He stood there, outside the shut door, and sobbed into his hand before composing himself enough to seek out Dustin. For Marcus Burton, this was the ending he'd always feared, yet a parting that had been gloriously made. He would always treasure that.

He would always treasure his friend.

Good night, Chris...

CB

THE FIRE WAS burning low in the hearth, but the room was quite warm and cozy. Dustin had been sitting next to her husband's bed for hours, watching him breathe heavily. The breathing was labored, but steady. As the hours ticked toward dawn, she got into bed beside him, gently stroking his forehead.

It was a moment of great peace.

The physic had come in a couple of hours earlier to check on him. After his examination, he told Dustin that Christopher wouldn't awaken again. He'd tried to rouse him, gently, but there had been no response. His pupils were fixed, indicative of the fact that he'd suffered another brain attack. He'd even stuck a pin in his foot, a pain test, and Christopher had remained still. That told the physic that the great Earl of Hereford and Worcester was on a steady decline. It was only a matter of time now.

And Dustin was going to be there until the end.

She didn't want anyone else there. She wanted this moment

to be between them, to be a tribute to the love they'd shared for so many years. It was an intensely private moment and, frankly, she wasn't sure her children could adequately handle it. The sons would brood; the daughters would weep. Soon, everyone would weep, and she didn't want that. Christopher had lived to his ninety-third year and she wanted him to leave this life in peace and warmth and love.

Her love.

Their relationship had started with her and it would end with her.

Scooting down on the bed, she gently laid her head on his left shoulder, her arm going about his chest as she held him to her. The night was still and quiet, with only the sounds of the gentle breeze beyond.

"Do you remember when we first met?" she whispered. "I fell out of that tree, right in front of you. Remember? Rebecca was with me. My dear friend. I have missed her so over the years."

Her chatter was met by the sounds of his deep breathing. Tenderly stroking her husband's chest, she continued.

"You picked me up when I fell," she said. "Then I asked you where my father was, and although you didn't tell me that he had died in the Holy Land, I knew. From the way you were answering my questions, or not answering them, I knew. And then I fainted. But we went back to Lioncross and Jeffrey was there to greet you. That was a difficult situation for him, you know. He'd been my father's knight for so long, and suddenly, in you came with your knights and your army, and he was shoved far down in the hierarchy of command. But you dealt with him well, Chris. You truly did. You made him want to stay."

The snapping of the fire in the hearth was the only response in the chamber. Not that Dustin expected him to answer, but she could see the faint streaks of morning splashed across the sky as the sun approached the horizon. A new day was coming. But looking at her enormous, powerful husband prone on the bed, felled by something in his head, she was suddenly struck by the travesty of it all. When the strongest of men was reduced in dignity at the end. Did Christopher deserve to die in battle, swinging a sword and bellowing in victory? Probably. But she was glad that he hadn't. Instead, he was a sick old man, lying in his bed with his wife by his side, phasing into eternity breath by breath.

Inch by inch.

This isn't how he wanted to live anymore. Even she knew that.

It was time to say her goodbyes.

"There is an old legend that says the door to heaven opens every morning when the sun peeks over the horizon," she said. "The colors we see across the sky are heavenly messengers, announcing the arrival of the veil between heaven and earth. It is there in an instant and equally gone in an instant. I believe that veil is approaching now, my love. It is coming for you."

Tears welled in her eyes as she sat up and grasped his hand, holding it against her lips as she gazed down at the man she had loved for over sixty years. She kissed his hand, smelling the familiar smell of his flesh, and even at this very moment, it made her heart race with excitement. She wanted to hold on to that hand forever.

But she knew she couldn't.

"Thank you, Christopher," she murmured as tears streamed down her face. "Thank you for tolerating me when we first met.

Thank you for loving me. Thank you for the children you gave me and the life we had together. We will always be part of one another, in the very fabric of our souls, and not even death can separate us, for I will take you with me everywhere I go. Every grandchild I hug will feel you in that embrace. Every kiss I give will have part of you in it. In that, you will always be part of me. But right now, you are weary. Your body has broken down. It is time for you to rise in glory, my dearest darling. The veil of heaven is just over the horizon. It is time to cross over. You have my permission."

Weeping softly, she kissed his hand again, holding it against her cheek. It was warm and rough, a hand she was very familiar with. Kissing it one last time, she put it on his chest and lay back down next to him, her head on his shoulder and her arm thrown protectively across him.

And she waited.

It wasn't long before Christopher's breathing became unsteady. It wasn't a sudden thing, but rather something that developed over the course of several minutes. As Dustin lay there, her right ear against his clavicle, she closed her eyes and held him tightly, listening to his increasingly erratic breathing.

"You see it, don't you?" she whispered through her tears. "You see the veil. Is it opening for you, my love? If it is, go through. Be young and strong and well again. Walk through the green grass of England again or through the sands of the Holy Land. You once told me about walking on those golden sands, how silky and hot they could be. I know that your friends are waiting just beyond the veil to guide you to heaven. Rhys and Gart and even Maxton. They are waiting for you, my love. Be free."

Christopher took several more unsteady breaths, some long,

some short. In her ear, Dustin could hear his heartbeat, but that, too, was erratic and faint.

And then it just faded away.

The breathing stopped.

Christopher had stepped through the veil.

It took her a few moments to realize that. When she did, Dustin burst into tears, holding him as tightly as she could. It would be the last time she ever lay with him, the last time it would ever be just the two of them. She was so devastated, yet also relieved. She couldn't stand seeing him crippled by apoplexy, the most powerful and wonderful man she had ever known. And she knew, without a doubt, that he didn't want to live like that.

Now, he was free.

She lay there with him as the sun rose, soaking up the last few moments. An hour passed before she was finally ready to release him and climb out of the bed, taking a long look at her husband one last time. He looked as if he were sleeping. Gently, she pulled the coverlet up to his shoulders because she knew her children would want to see him and say their farewells. Smoothing down his hair, she kissed him on the forehead.

"I love you," she whispered.

Taking a deep breath, Dustin went to the chamber door and opened it. As she knew, all of her children were waiting there with their spouses. The grandchildren had been kept down in the small hall of Lioncross's enormous keep because it was too crowded on the landing outside of the chamber. Dustin could see Marcus standing back behind the crowd, looking at her with great sorrow.

Taking another deep breath, Dustin faced her children.

"Papa went to sleep on this earth," she said softly. "But he has risen in glory and we give thanks for the years we had with him. He loved you all very much. Please come in and bid him farewell."

As she knew, the tears came. Christin, Brielle, Rebecca, and Olivia Charlotte were already overflowing. Westley and Curtis were overflowing. Peter, Christopher's eldest son, had his father's fair face and his eyes were red, an indication that he'd been overflowing all day. But Dustin's announcement had him going again.

Dustin extended a hand to him.

"Come, Peter," she said. "Come, all of you. Come say fare-well to Papa."

Peter had to steel himself before entering the room. He was followed by Curtis and Roi and the rest of them, all of them gathering around the bed as their father lay there in repose. The spouses, all of them, had purposely remained on the landing, letting the children reconcile themselves to Christopher's death first.

It was only right that they should.

Dustin stood in the doorway, watching her children kiss their father, watching them wipe away tears and comfort one another. Soon enough, the spouses entered and they, too, bade a fond farewell to the man who had been so kind to them. All of them. The chamber grew crowded and Dustin went out onto the landing, which was actually a gallery overlooking the two-storied entry of Lioncross's keep. Dustin had a perfect view of the entry below and a perfect view of a young, strong Christopher, just as he had been the moment she met him. He was looking up at her and then he turned for the door and was gone. It had been brief, but unmistakable. As startled as Dustin was by the glimpse of him, she was also comforted more than she could express.

Greatly comforted.

The man who had given her everything. Who had been her everything. A new day had dawned just as Christopher had taken his first step into heaven and Dustin couldn't be sad for him. He was whole again and that was all she could wish for. She would see him again, someday.

That was a promise.

Returning to the chamber where her family was gathered, Dustin found comfort in their love and in their sorrow. It was the beginning of a new chapter for the de Lohr family, with a bright future ahead for all of them.

A future built by a man they used to call Defender of the Realm.

And a legend that would never die.

IN ALTERA VITA

T HERE WERE VOICES all around him.

Opening his eyes, he could see a golden mist and the voices seemed to be in the mist itself. In fact, everything was golden, as if he were in the midst of a golden dream. But he could smell the sea upon the warm wind, blowing gently through his blond hair, and the sun, which had been all around him, gradually retreated until it was simply a bright globe in the sky. A sky of blue that was so pure, so deep, that it had a life all its own. Everything around him had a life all its own.

The golden mist was fading.

He was walking.

Walking in this golden mist that retreated until it was only at his feet, and that was when he realized that the golden mist had turned to sand. Golden sand all around him, with the brilliant blue sky above, and in front of him, on the horizon, he could see darkened shapes trying to take form. They were undulating and moving, and as he drew closer, the shapes finally became something he recognized.

An encampment.

He'd seen this encampment before. He'd spent three years

of his life here. He could see tents he recognized—the blue and white of de Royans was one. The black and red of de Russe was another. Tents of all sizes and shapes and colors sprouted up from that golden sand, and as the wind blew off the sea, it rippled the canvas sides and lashed the banners that were protruding from the poles.

It was Richard the Lionheart's encampment.

Instead of feeling shock or confusion, he felt… joy. Joy and delight. Joy and curiosity at what he was going to find at the center of that encampment, though he already knew. Excitement filled him.

He began to run.

It didn't occur to him that he hadn't been able to run in years. It didn't even occur to him that he wasn't wearing a tunic, but breeches and boots. His broadsword hung at his side. It was his usual attire when he'd haunted the sands of the Levant during King Richard's crusade. He stopped running as he neared the encampment, looking down at himself to note his state of dress, looking at his bare arms and chest and seeing them as they had been when he was young and in his prime. His skin was a golden brown, baked by the sun.

Aye, he knew where he was.

He knew it so very well.

He looked up at the encampment again only to see misty figures moving among the tents. They were clearer now than they had been before. He started walking again, heading toward those figures as they were moving toward him. As he watched, they took form. But then a very big wraith suddenly burst out from between a couple of the tents, and as it came close, it took on the form of something he hadn't seen in a very long time.

Boron.

The warhorse he'd had for seventeen years, the one who had been with him to hell and back, whether upon the sands of the Levant or the green fields of England. Boron had been killed in a tournament when a knight named Dennis la Londe had deliberately speared him in the chest in an attempt to kill the animal's rider.

Joy and awe filled Christopher as he realized it was his beloved steed.

"Boron," he murmured, running his hands over the silver coat. "My God… it *is* you."

The horse wanted ear scratches, and he happily complied. He even hugged the big animal's neck, so very happy to see him. But then he began to hear voices. People were calling his name.

Christopher!

Chris!

Still scratching his horse, he turned to see a group gathering right at the edge of the encampment. It took him a moment to realize he was looking at people he hadn't seen in many years, and two in particular were coming out to greet him. He fixed on them and memories from the deep came forth as he recognized them. But they looked much younger and much healthier than they did the last time he saw them. In fact, they looked to be about his age, young and beautiful and strong. The man had sky-blue eyes and neat, shoulder-length blond hair, while the woman had pale red hair and luminous dark eyes, something none of her children had inherited.

Christopher looked like his father.

Myles de Lohr reached out to greet his son.

"Boron has missed you," he said, his eyes glimmering with delight. "He knew you were coming before any of us did. Welcome home, lad. We are so very happy to see you."

That voice.

It was a voice Christopher had only heard in his dreams and it was just as he remembered it. Overwhelmed, he threw his arms around his father, a man he'd not held for more than eighty years. Christopher had been very young when his parents passed away of an infectious disease, both of them within in a short time. At seven years of age, he'd been orphaned along with his brother and infant sister. His parents had been older when he and his siblings had been born, so he'd only known them as older people. Not the two gorgeous, healthy-looking people before him. Releasing his father, Christopher took his mother in his arms and hugged her tightly.

"I have missed you so much," he whispered, releasing her even as she held on to him. "I can hardly believe it. It is so good to see you both."

"And you," his mother said, her eyes twinkling warmly. "Look how strong and handsome you are. This is such a proud moment for us, Chris."

Christopher grinned. "I am glad," he said. "But where do I begin? There's so much to tell you… so much to talk about."

Myles put his hand on Christopher's shoulder. "There will be plenty of time for that," he said. "When we heard you were approaching, we came here to pitch a tent and wait. We assumed you would want to remain here until David arrived. And your wife."

Christopher looked at both of his parents, so delighted he couldn't express it. He was shocked and awed and thrilled all at once. Then he looked beyond them at the people who were standing at the edge of the encampment, waiting for him. He was astonished to see so many wonderful friends from long ago, people who had passed on. People he had missed so terribly. He could see Erik de Russe and Gart Forbes, old and dear friends, who waved to him when they saw he was looking at him. Christopher chuckled and waved back. Next to them stood Rhys du Bois, one of his closest and dearest friends, alongside his old mentor, Juston de Royans. All men who had passed away over the years, people he sorely missed, but people who looked just the way he remembered them. Young and strong and healthy.

But there was someone else he saw.

Arthur Barringdon.

It was Dustin's father. The last time he saw Arthur, the man was dying of a sucking chest wound and, to make the old man happy, Christopher had agreed to marry his daughter. He'd been so angry about it. Furious was more like it. How he'd hated Arthur for forcing him to make that pledge. That was how he'd left Arthur—in anger.

He had to speak to him.

With his parents trailing behind him, and his mother still holding his hand, Christopher made his way over to Arthur, who was smiling at him as he approached. Even Arthur looked different from the last time Christopher had seen him, now a younger, healthier, and far more robust man who looked very much like Christopher's son, Westley. Christopher thought that was rather humorous—he never realized how much his youngest son looked like his wife's father. They both had the same big blue eyes and arched eyebrows. When Arthur grinned, Christopher could see Westley in that grin.

It was truly astonishing.

"I married your daughter," Christopher said as he approached the man. "Remember? You forced me into a marriage on your deathbed. Honestly, Arthur, I wanted to strangle you for it. Don't tell me that you do not remember."

Arthur laughed in a gesture that looked like Westley, too. "Of course I remember that," he said. Then he put his hands on Christopher's shoulders, his eyes full of warmth. "I also know that your marriage was blessed by the angels. I know that you love my daughter very much and she loves you."

Christopher's expression softened at the mention of Dustin. "Aye," he said. Then he glanced around. "This is heaven, is it not?"

"It is *your* heaven, lad."

Christopher looked at him curiously. "What does that mean?"

Arthur shrugged. "We all have our own personal heavens, Chris," he said. "There is not one heaven for everyone. We are allowed to choose our own. Whatever makes us the happiest is where we stay. Much like your parents, I knew you were going to be here today, so I came to greet you. You can see that many people have come to greet you, but I wanted to make sure you knew of my gratitude for marrying Dustin Mary Catherine. I know it was not always easy with her, but it was always good. Wasn't it?"

Christopher's lips twitched with a smile. "Aye, Arthur," he said softly. "It was always good. It is still good. It will be even better when she arrives and we can be together again."

Arthur smiled. "Of course it will," he said. "Her mother is here, too. She will be here soon, but she is trying to coerce the baby to sleep."

Christopher looked at him curiously. "Baby?" he said. "What baby?"

"The baby you and Dustin lost so long ago," Arthur said. "When she fell down the stairs in London. Remember? The one

Burwell delivered?"

Christopher did. "*That* baby is here?" he said, surprised.

Arthur nodded. "He came to us a baby," he said. "He is still a baby, but once Dustin arrives, he will start to grow. That is the way it works around here. For now, your son is with Mary. She is very happy to have him because it is a piece of Dustin, something she can tend and love. He is a delightful boy."

It was all quite astonishing to Christopher, who shook his head in wonder. "I cannot wait to meet him," he said. "But this… What an amazing place it is. Truly incredible."

Arthur laughed softly. "It is a little overwhelming, at first," he said. "But you will quickly get used to it. You've earned this paradise, Chris. Enjoy all it has to offer."

Christopher was still struggling a little to overcome his astonishment, but the more he looked at Arthur, the more he thought of Dustin. His heart, his mind, was lingering heavily on her.

"Arthur," he said, "I must say something to you. The last time we saw one another, I was not very happy. You were forcing me to marry your daughter and, as you know, I did not wish to marry."

Arthur smirked. "I know."

Christopher could see the humor in it. "What you do not know is that I have always wanted to thank you for forcing me to marry Dustin," he said quietly. "It was the best thing you could have ever done for me."

Arthur was still grinning. "Mayhap I knew something that you didn't," he said. "Mayhap I knew that you needed one another."

"We did. We still do."

Arthur's smile faded. "Do not fear," he said. "Dustin will be strong without you. She'll be here before you know it."

"I do not wish for her to die soon if that is what you mean," Christopher said. "We have children and grandchildren that need her. My loss will be difficult for them to take, but hers... it will be worse."

"That is not what I mean," Arthur said. "I simply meant that time here has no meaning. Nor does night or day. The days are always beautiful and balmy and the nights are always spectacular, with more stars in the sky than you can imagine. Mayhap only a day and night will pass here and Dustin will arrive. To you, it is a very short amount of time, but for her, it could be years. And you will know when she is coming."

"How?"

"You will be told."

"By God?"

"By his messengers," Arthur said. "Meanwhile, enjoy the people you've not seen in many years. Enjoy your parents. I like them, Chris. They are good people."

With that, Arthur patted him on the cheek and headed off again, losing himself in the encampment that seemed to have a golden sheen on it. Christopher was just noticing that. Everything had a golden sheen on it, like a layer of gold dust that couldn't be swept away. As he watched Arthur head off, he realized his parents were still standing with him and turned to look at them. They were smiling at him and he couldn't help but smile in return. He took his mother's hand again, kissing it sweetly.

"I will assume I have a tent around here, somewhere," he said, looking around. "Mayhap we can go there and talk. You know, I never had the chance to talk to you as an adult. I had always deeply regretted that."

Val smiled. "As did we," she said. "We left you so suddenly, Chris. You and David and Deborah were so young. It has only been a few weeks to us here, but I know it has been many years where you were."

Christopher nodded. "It was," he said. "So many years. Could you... could you see me? Could you see what was happening in my life?"

Myles nodded. "A little," he said. "If you thought about us, we could, but if you did not, we were content to linger here until you thought of us again. Your thoughts of us gave us a window into your world. It made us come alive again, as it were. But memories fade and it became more difficult for us to see you."

Christopher sighed. "I do not know how often I thought of you," he admitted. "You died when I was so young. The more time passed, the more you became a distant memory."

"But here you are now," Val said. "We know you had several children. I think the last one we saw was Myles, because you named him for your father and were thinking of him, but we didn't see any others after that."

Christopher smiled at her. "You will be happy to know that I have six sons and four daughters," he said. "Because I lost you when I was young, I made a point of being close to them. All of them. And my grandchildren, too. I wanted to give them memories that would last them a lifetime. I wanted to be an influence on their lives. I hope... I think... I have accomplished that."

Behind him, out in the desert, he could hear voices. They were swirling on the golden wind, whispered, just like he'd heard them before. Like ghosts trying to speak and he couldn't quite understand them. He let go of his mother and took a few steps toward the vast sea of golden sand beyond, listening.

"What is it, Chris?" his mother asked.

Christopher shook his head. "I am not certain," he said. "But I can hear voices. Do you not hear them?"

Val and Myles glanced knowingly at one another. It was Myles who came to stand beside his son, gazing out over the golden desert alongside him.

"Those voices are meant for your ears only," he said. "They are your family, Chris. Mayhap they are praying for you, or mayhap they are talking to you. If you listen closely enough, sometimes you can hear what they are saying. If you follow the sound of the voice, you'll be able to peek into their world a little, just as I told you. Not much, but a little. Sometimes you can even speak to them if the bond between you is strong enough."

Christopher sighed faintly. "I would like to think it is with Dustin," he said. "I saw her right before I ended up on these sands, but I did not speak to her. I would so like to reassure her that I am well."

Myles put his hand on Christopher's shoulder. "Your bond with her is very strong, so if you hear her voice, follow it," he said. "Tell her you are well. Sometimes it will come to her like a breeze, or sometimes a bird will carry the message for you. Sometimes it will even come to her in a dream. Speak to her and she will hear you, I promise. There were times when you were very young that I spoke to you, though I doubt you remember."

Christopher smiled weakly. "Probably not," he said. "But it is good to know that you heard me."

"I did," Myles said. "I do not know if you remember this, but once, around the time you married your wife, you asked me a question. I sent you an answer in the cry of a falcon, but you may not have heard me. Therefore, I will tell you now—my answer to your question is deeply, madly, and with all my heart."

Christopher looked at him curiously. "What did I ask you?"

"If I was proud of you."

Christopher looked at the man, feeling his answer hit deep. Although there were no tears in heaven from what he'd heard, he could feel himself welling up.

"Truly, Papa?" he whispered.

Myles nodded firmly. "Truly," he said. "I have had others tell me what a great man you became. The greatest knight of your generation, some said. No man could be prouder of his son, Christopher."

Christopher smiled at his father as tears stung his eyes. "Thank you," he murmured. "That means everything to me."

Myles winked at him. "Good," he said. "Now, you must greet all of those people who have been waiting to embrace you. I fear the crowd is growing by the moment now that news of your arrival has spread."

Myles was right. Christopher was greeted into heaven by hordes of people who were very glad to see him. Men he hadn't seen in decades, men who had perished in battle, or due to disease. Whatever the reason, they had come to greet him and he could not have been happier. The celebration of his arrival went on for at least a day and a night until a man named Michael came to tell Christopher that Marcus was on the approach.

He greeted the man with fine wine and horses, as promised.

But more days passed and more nights, too, until finally, the moment came that he had been waiting for. Michael returned to tell him that Dustin was on the approach, so he stood at the edge of the encampment and waited for her.

His father had been right.

It had all happened in the blink of an eye.

When Dustin walked across those golden sands, looking young and beautiful, with her long blonde hair waving in the wind and her youthful figure restored, Christopher was the first person to greet her with open arms. Proof, once and for all, that true love never died.

For Christopher and Dustin, it was the beginning all over again. Christopher had once told her when they were first married of his feelings for her, and they were something that carried through, as true as love itself, to the very moment they met in eternity.

You are my reason for living, lady, and I love you with all my heart.

He meant it.

Forever.

AUTHOR AFTERWORD

I hope you enjoyed this saga. And what a saga it was! It was very difficult to write in some places, as you can imagine, but I felt that it was such an important tale. I hope you do, too.

Usually, the epilogue contains what happened to the couple and gives the reader a view into their life a few years down the road, but this book was structured a little differently, as I mentioned, so the epilogue for Westley and Elysande was actually the beginning. It made more sense there to set up the rest of the story. Therefore, here is their brood:

Children of Westley and Elysande du Nor-de Lohr (shortened to du Lohr in later years)

Arius Christopher

Gaius

Sebastian

Augustus

Titus

Marius

Justina

Viviana

Emory

Vive la Maison de Lohr!

HOUSE OF DE LOHR—A FAMILY TREE

Note: These are my notes from the House of de Lohr on ages, etc. This is showing you, the reader, what I see, what I work off. These are the approximate ages/dates/etc., so enjoy this insight into my personal guidelines. The ages listed below is the age of the character in Lion of Thunder. *There's a lot of information here, but you'll see the tie-ins and recognize some of the names. You haven't met some of them yet, so keep that in mind.*

Christopher was 35 in 1192 when *Rise of the Defender* is set—
David was 32

Chris was born in 1157

David was born in 1160

Christopher died in 1249 (he was 92)

David died in 1260 (he was 100) According to *Shadowmoor*, he
    wasn't well in 1238, but Chad said he hadn't been well the
    last 20 years of his life.

Christopher and Dustin's children and their offspring: (there is some discrepancy here and the timeline of *Rise of the Defender*, so these dates are approximate)

Christin b. 1193

Brielle b. 1194

Curtis b.1200

Richard (Roi) b. 1202

Myles b. 1205

Rebecca b. 1208

Douglas b. 1211

Westley Henry b. 1214

Olivia Charlotte (the future Honey de Shera) 1216

Year the Sons of de Lohr books are set:

Lion of War 1228

Lion of Twilight 1245

Lion of Hearts 1236

Lion of Steel 1247

Lion of Thunder 1249

- Peter (The Splendid Hour) Lord Pembridge, eventually Earl of Farringdon
- Christin (A Time of End) Sherry is Lord Barrington, a courtesy title. Christin is Lady Barrington.
- Brielle (The Dark Conqueror). Husband is Lord Blackadder.
- Curtis (Lion of War) Earl of Leominster (heir apparent to the larger Earldom of Hereford and Worcester), Baron Ivington
- Richard (Lion of Twilight) Earl of Cheltenham
- Myles (Lion of Hearts)Lordship of Dore—Baron Monnington
- Rebecca
- Douglas (Lion of Steel)
- Westley (whose middle name is Henry and he was

sometimes referred to as "Henry" when he was young) (Lion of Thunder) Lord Ledbury, Duc de Nevele
- Olivia Charlotte (the future Honey de Shera from the Lords of Thunder series) Countess of Coventry

Peter (mother is Lady Amanda) b.1185
Peter and Liora's children

- Matthew
- Annalise
- Madelaine
- Aaron
- Ethan
- Gabriel
- Jared
- Nathan
- Elisabeth

Curtis—(he has 10 children total, 8 boys and 2 girls according to *Silversword*) Married Avrielle "Elle." Three generations of Curtis' descendants are listed here, for reference.

- Christopher "Chris" (had daughter Lily (married to William "Will" de Wolfe from WolfeLord) b. 1229
- Arthur b. 1231
- William b. 1233
- Mary
- Valeria
- August "Auggie"
- Adam

- Jasper
- Callum
- Powell

Chris married Alys Kaedia (daughter of Welsh chieftain) Only four sons are mentioned in *A Wolfe Among Dragons*.

- Lily (married Will de Wolfe and had a daughter, Athena)
- Morgen (more English than Welsh) b. 1257
- Rees (the Welsh Rebel)
- Dru
- Cade
- Rhianne
- Rhori
- David

Morgen de Lohr, son of Chris—wife is Kirra St. Hever, eldest sister of Keir and Kurtis from "Fragments of Grace." Aunt to Kenneth St. Hever. B. 1262 (ages as of 1312)

- Christopher "Christie" b. 1280 32
- Kurtis b. 1282 30
- Bingham "Bing" Twin of Blakeney b. 1285 27
- Blakeney "Blake" Twin of Bingham b. 1285 27
- Myles b. 1288 24
- Tevin b. 1290 22
- Abigail "Abbie" b. 1293 19
- Andrina b. 1296 16
- Camberley b. 1297 15
- Jeneth b. 1299 13

Roi and Diara's children

- Adalia (Odette)
- Dorian (Odette)
- Rex
- Beau
- Evan
- Daphne
- Rose
- Lucan
- Alex
- Willow

Myles and Veronica's children

- Sebastian b. 1237
- Evander b. 1240
- Cleo (stillborn) b.1241
- Demetrius b. 1243 (twin to Dustine)
- Dustine b. 1243
- Anne Sophia b. 1247
- Lenora b. 1249
- Barrett b. 1252
- Gifford "Giff" b. 1253

Douglas and Mera's children (Christopher lived to see the first two born):

- Isabel
- Aurelia

- Matilda
- Beatrice
- Nicholas
- Alessia
- Madeleine
- Dallas
- Rosamund
- Atlas

Christin (19 in 1211 when her story starts—Sherry is about 20 years older) in Westley's book in 1249, the children's ages are:

- Andrew b 1212 37
- Adam b 1215 34
- Gabriel b 1218 31
- Nicholas b 1220 29
- Liam b 1224 27
- Maxim b 1227 24
- Sophia b 1231 20

Brielle

- Maxim "Max" b. 1216 33
- Celestine—b. 1224 25
- Luciana b 1226 23
- Rhodes b 1227 22
- Laurent b 1229 20
- Portia b 1231 17
- Armand b 1233 15
- Evanthe b 1234 (mother of the heroine in "The Questing") 14

- Raphael "Rafe"—1238 10
- Tenner b. 1242 (hero in Bay of Fear—though there is some timeline discrepancy) 7

Rebecca's sons (boys mentioned in *Lion of Twilight*, only three that we know of)

- Vaughn
- James
- Westley

Children of Westley and Elysande du Nor-de Lohr (shortened to du Lohr in later years)

- Arius
- Gaius
- Sebastian
- Augustus
- Titus (named for Christopher's maternal grandfather, Titus du Reims)
- Marius
- Justina
- Viviana
- Emory

Olivia Charlotte "Honey" married Antoninus de Shera (her sons are the Lords of Thunder series)

- Gallus
- Maximus
- Tiberius

KATHRYN LE VEQUE NOVELS

Medieval Romance:

De Wolfe Pack Series:
Warwolfe
The Wolfe
Nighthawk
ShadowWolfe
DarkWolfe
A Joyous de Wolfe Christmas
BlackWolfe
Serpent
A Wolfe Among Dragons
Scorpion
StormWolfe
Dark Destroyer
The Lion of the North
Walls of Babylon
The Best Is Yet To Be
BattleWolfe
Castle of Bones

De Wolfe Pack Generations:
WolfeHeart
WolfeStrike
WolfeSword
WolfeBlade
WolfeLord
WolfeShield
Nevermore
WolfeAx
WolfeBorn
WolfeBite

The Executioner Knights:
By the Unholy Hand
The Mountain Dark
Starless
A Time of End
Winter of Solace
Lord of the Sky
The Splendid Hour
The Whispering Night
Netherworld
Lord of the Shadows
Of Mortal Fury
'Twas the Executioner Knight
Before Christmas
Crimson Shield
The Black Dragon

The de Russe Legacy:
The Falls of Erith
Lord of War: Black Angel
The Iron Knight
Beast
The Dark One: Dark Knight
The White Lord of Wellesbourne
Dark Moon
Dark Steel
A de Russe Christmas Miracle
Dark Warrior

The de Lohr Dynasty:
While Angels Slept
Rise of the Defender
Steelheart

Shadowmoor
Silversword
Spectre of the Sword
Unending Love
Archangel
A Blessed de Lohr Christmas
Lion of Twilight
Lion of War
Lion of Hearts
Lion of Steel
Lion of Thunder

The Brothers de Lohr:
The Earl in Winter

Lords of East Anglia:
While Angels Slept
Godspeed
Age of Gods and Mortals

Great Lords of le Bec:
Great Protector

House of de Royans:
Lord of Winter
To the Lady Born
The Centurion

Lords of Eire:
Echoes of Ancient Dreams
Lord of Black Castle
The Darkland

Ancient Kings of Anglecynn:
The Whispering Night
Netherworld

Battle Lords of de Velt:
The Dark Lord
Devil's Dominion
Bay of Fear

The Dark Lord's First Christmas
The Dark Spawn
The Dark Conqueror
The Dark Angel

Reign of the House of de Winter:
Lespada
Swords and Shields

De Reyne Domination:
Guardian of Darkness
The Black Storm
A Cold Wynter's Knight
With Dreams
Master of the Dawn
One Wylde Knight

House of d'Vant:
Tender is the Knight (House of d'Vant)
The Red Fury (House of d'Vant)

The Dragonblade Series:
Fragments of Grace
Dragonblade
Island of Glass
The Savage Curtain
The Fallen One
The Phantom Bride

Great Marcher Lords of de Lara
Lord of the Shadows
Dragonblade

House of St. Hever
Fragments of Grace
Island of Glass
Queen of Lost Stars

Lords of Pembury:
The Savage Curtain

422

Lords of Thunder: The de Shera Brotherhood Trilogy
The Thunder Lord
The Thunder Warrior
The Thunder Knight

The Great Knights of de Moray:
Shield of Kronos
The Gorgon

The House of De Nerra:
The Promise
The Falls of Erith
Vestiges of Valor
Realm of Angels

Highland Legion:
Highland Born
Highland Destroyer

Highland Warriors of Munro:
The Red Lion
Deep Into Darkness

The House of de Garr:
Lord of Light
Realm of Angels

Saxon Lords of Hage:
The Crusader
Kingdom Come

High Warriors of Rohan:
High Warrior
High King

The House of Ashbourne:
Upon a Midnight Dream

The House of D'Aurilliac:
Valiant Chaos

The House of De Dere:
Of Love and Legend

St. John and de Gare Clans:
The Warrior Poet

The House of de Bretagne:
The Questing

The House of Summerlin:
The Legend

The Kingdom of Hendocia:
Kingdom by the Sea

The BlackChurch Guild: Shadow Knights:
The Leviathan
The Protector
The Swordsman

Guard of Six:
Absolution

Regency Historical Romance:
Sin Like Flynn: A Regency
Historical Romance Duet
The Sin Commandments
Georgina and the Red Charger

Gothic Regency Romance:
Emma

Historical Fiction:
The Girl Made Of Stars

Contemporary Romance:

Kathlyn Trent/Marcus Burton Series:
Valley of the Shadow
The Eden Factor

Canyon of the Sphinx

Sons of Poseidon:
The Immortal Sea

The Eagle Brotherhood (under the pen name Kat Le Veque):
The Sunset Hour
The Killing Hour
The Secret Hour
The Unholy Hour
The Burning Hour
The Ancient Hour
The Devil's Hour

Pirates of Britannia Series (with Eliza Knight):
Savage of the Sea by Eliza Knight
Leader of Titans by Kathryn Le Veque
The Sea Devil by Eliza Knight
Sea Wolfe by Kathryn Le Veque

Note: All Kathryn's novels are designed to be read as stand-alones, although many have cross-over characters or cross-over family groups. Novels that are grouped together have related characters or family groups. You will notice that some series have the same books; that is because they are cross-overs. A hero in one book may be the secondary character in another.

There is NO reading order except by chronology, but even in that case, you can still read the books as stand-alones. No novel is connected to another by a cliff hanger, and every book has an HEA.

Series are clearly marked. All series contain the same characters or family groups except the American Heroes Series, which is an anthology with unrelated characters.

For more information, find it in **A Reader's Guide to the Medieval World of Le Veque**.

ABOUT KATHRYN LE VEQUE

Bringing the Medieval to Romance

KATHRYN LE VEQUE is a critically acclaimed, multiple USA TODAY Bestselling author, an Indie Reader bestseller, a charter Amazon All-Star author, and a #1 bestselling, award-winning, multi-published author in Medieval Historical Romance with over 100 published novels.

Kathryn is a multiple award nominee and winner, including the winner of Uncaged Book Reviews Magazine 2017 and 2018 "Raven Award" for Favorite Medieval Romance. Kathryn is also a multiple RONE nominee (InD'Tale Magazine), holding a record for the number of nominations. In 2018, her novel WARWOLFE was the winner in the Romance category of the Book Excellence Award and in 2019, her novel A WOLFE AMONG DRAGONS won the prestigious RONE award for best pre-16th century romance.

Kathryn is considered one of the top Indie authors in the world with over 2M copies in circulation, and her novels have been translated into several languages. Kathryn recently signed with Sourcebooks Casablanca for a Medieval Fight Club series, first published in 2020.

In addition to her own published works, Kathryn is also the President/CEO of Dragonblade Publishing, a boutique publishing house specializing in Historical Romance. Dragonblade's success has seen it rise in the ranks to become Amazon's #1 e-book publisher of Historical Romance (K-Lytics report July 2020).

Kathryn loves to hear from her readers. Please find Kathryn on Facebook at Kathryn Le Veque, Author, or join her on Twitter @kathrynleveque. Sign up for Kathryn's blog at www.kathrynleveque.com for the latest news and sales.